PEOPLE AND STORIES THAT SHOULD NOT BE FORGOTTEN

ADVENTURES

ADVENTURES

PEOPLE AND STORIES THAT SHOULD NOT BE FORGOTTEN

Winter 2025

ISBN: (PAPERBACK) 978-1-950464-60-9
ISBN: (EBOOK) 978-1-950464-61-6

WWW.OFFBEATREADS.COM

ADVENTURES

PEOPLE AND STORIES THAT SHOULD NOT BE FORGOTTEN

WINTER, 2023   **ISSUE #10**

WHAT

WHERE

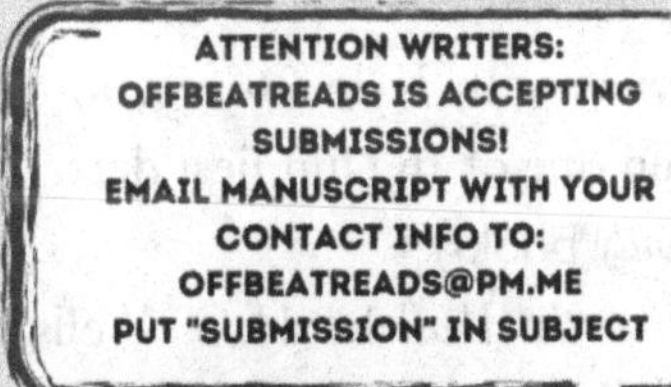

Editor's Note

Hello, *Adventures* fans! Starting with this issue, you'll see a new name on these intro pages. My name is Michael Brian, and I'm taking over for Robert - who did an amazing job here - so he can focus on some exciting new projects. To briefly introduce myself, I am a writer/editor/reviewer who loves books and stories of virtually all genres, and I myself had a story appear on these wonderful pages two years ago (*Detective Wolfram Gets A Case*). I love what Robert has created with this series, and I am incredibly excited to helm this project.

Now, without further ado, let's get to the stars of this edition - the stories!

In this issue you'll find:

- An interview with Kyle Owens, an OffBeat Reads authaor who has written one of the funniest detective series I've ever read (The *Vegas Chantly* books).
- *The Door in the Wall* by H.G. Wells, which is one of the most acclaimed things the literary giant ever wrote.
- One of my personal favorites, *The Call of the Wild* by Jack London. If you haven't read this story in a while, you might remember it simply as a story for children, but it's so much more than that.
- And rounding out the issue are stories by Joseph Hergesheimer, Lawrence L. Lynch, Jane Margaret Hooper, and K.R. Moore.

If you ever have any suggestions for stories to include in *Adventures*, leave a comment on our Facebook page or email us through our website.

Happy reading!

Michael Brian

THE DOOR IN THE WALL

H.G. WELLS

I

One confidential evening, not three months ago, Lionel Wallace told me this story of the Door in the Wall. And at the time I thought that so far as he was concerned it was a true story.

He told it me with such a direct simplicity of conviction that I could not do otherwise than believe in him. But in the morning, in my own flat, I woke to a different atmosphere, and as I lay in bed and recalled the things he had told me, stripped of the glamour of his earnest slow voice, denuded of the focussed shaded table light, the shadowy atmosphere that wrapped about him and the pleasant bright things, the dessert and glasses and napery of the dinner we had shared, making them for the time a bright little world quite cut off from every-day realities, I saw it all as frankly incredible. "He was mystifying!" I said, and then: "How well he did it!. . . . . It isn't quite the thing I should have expected him, of all people, to do well."

Afterwards, as I sat up in bed and sipped my morning tea, I found myself trying to account for the flavour of reality that perplexed me in his impossible reminiscences, by supposing they did in some way suggest, present, convey—I hardly know which word to use—experiences it was otherwise impossible to tell.

Well, I don't resort to that explanation now. I have got over my intervening doubts. I believe now, as I believed at the moment of telling, that Wallace did to the very best of his ability strip the truth of his secret for me. But whether he himself saw, or only thought he saw, whether he himself was the possessor of an inestimable privilege, or the victim of a fantastic dream, I cannot pretend to guess. Even the facts of his death, which ended my doubts forever, throw no light on that. That much the reader must judge for himself.

I forget now what chance comment or criticism of mine moved so reticent a man to confide in me. He was, I think, defending himself against an imputation of slackness and unreliability I had made in relation to a great public movement in which he had disappointed me. But he plunged suddenly. "I have" he said, "a preoccupation—"

"I know," he went on, after a pause that he devoted to the study of his cigar ash, "I have been negligent. The fact is—it isn't a case of ghosts or apparitions—but—it's an odd thing to tell of, Redmond—I am haunted. I am haunted by something—that rather takes the light out of things, that fills me with longings . . . . ."

He paused, checked by that English shyness that so often overcomes us when we would speak of moving or grave or beautiful things. "You were at Saint Athelstan's all through," he said, and for a moment that seemed to me quite irrelevant. "Well"—and he paused. Then very haltingly at first, but afterwards more easily, he began to tell of the thing that was hidden in his life, the haunting memory of a beauty and a happiness that filled his heart with insatiable longings that made all the interests and spectacle of worldly life seem dull and tedious and vain to him.

Now that I have the clue to it, the thing seems written visibly in his face. I have a photograph in which that look of detachment has been caught and intensified. It reminds me of what a woman once said of him—a woman who had loved him greatly. "Suddenly," she said, "the interest goes out of him. He forgets you. He doesn't care a rap for you—under his very nose . . . . ."

Yet the interest was not always out of him, and when he was holding his attention to a thing Wallace could contrive to be an extremely successful man. His career, indeed, is set with successes. He left me behind him long ago; he soared up over my head, and cut a figure in the world that I couldn't cut—anyhow. He was still a year short of forty, and they say now that he would have been in office and very probably in the new Cabinet if he had lived. At school he always beat me without effort—as it were by nature. We were at school together at Saint Athelstan's College in West Kensington for almost all our school time. He came into the school as my co-equal, but he left far above me, in a blaze of scholarships and brilliant performance. Yet I think I made a fair average running. And it was at school I heard first of the Door in the Wall—that I was to hear of a second time only a month before his death.

To him at least the Door in the Wall was a real door leading through a real wall to immortal realities. Of that I am now quite assured. And it came into his life early, when he was a little fellow between five and six. I remember how, as he sat making his confession to me with a slow gravity, he reasoned and reckoned the date of it. "There was," he said, "a crimson Virginia creeper in it—all one bright uniform crimson in a clear amber sunshine against a white wall. That came into the impression somehow, though I don't clearly remember how, and there were horse-chestnut leaves upon the clean pavement outside the green door. They were blotched yellow and green, you know, not brown nor dirty, so that they must have been new fallen. I take it that means October. I look out for horse-chestnut leaves every year, and I ought to know.

"If I'm right in that, I was about five years and four months old." He was, he said, rather a precocious little boy—he learned to talk at an abnormally early age, and he was so sane and "old-fashioned," as people say, that he was permitted an amount of initiative that most children scarcely attain by seven or eight. His mother died when he was born, and he was under the less vigilant and authoritative care of a nursery governess. His father was a stern, preoccupied lawyer, who gave him little attention, and expected great things of him. For all his brightness he found life a little grey and dull I think. And one day he wandered.

He could not recall the particular neglect that enabled him to get away, nor the course he took among the West Kensington roads. All that had faded among the incurable blurs of memory. But the white wall and the green door stood out quite distinctly. As his memory of that remote childish experience ran, he did at the very first sight of that door experience a peculiar emotion, an attraction, a desire to get to the door and open it and walk in. And at the same time he had the clearest conviction that either it was unwise or it was wrong of him—he could not tell which—to yield to this attraction. He insisted upon it as a curious thing that he knew from the very beginning—unless memory has played him the queerest trick—that the door was unfastened, and that he could go in as he chose.

I seem to see the figure of that little boy, drawn and repelled. And it was very clear in his mind, too, though why it should be so was never explained, that his father would be very angry if he went through that door.

Wallace described all these moments of hesitation to me with the utmost particularity. He went right past the door, and then, with his hands in his pockets, and making an infantile attempt to whistle, strolled right along beyond the end of the wall. There he recalls a number of mean, dirty shops, and particularly that of a plumber and decorator, with a dusty disorder of earthenware pipes, sheet lead ball taps, pattern books of wall paper, and tins of enamel. He stood pretending to examine these things, and coveting, passionately desiring the green door.

Then, he said, he had a gust of emotion. He made a run for it, lest hesitation should grip him again, he went plump with outstretched hand through the green door and let it slam behind him. And so, in a trice, he came into the garden that has haunted all his life. It was very difficult for Wallace to give me his full sense of that garden into which he came.

There was something in the very air of it that exhilarated, that gave one a sense of lightness and good happening and well being; there was something in the sight of it that made all its colour clean and perfect and subtly luminous. In the instant of coming into it one was exquisitely glad— as only in rare moments and when one is young and joyful one can be glad in this world. And everything was beautiful there . . . . .

Wallace mused before he went on telling me. "You see," he said, with the doubtful inflection of a man who pauses at incredible things, "there were two great panthers there . . . Yes, spotted panthers. And I was not afraid. There was a long wide path with marble-edged flower borders on either side, and these two huge velvety beasts were playing there with a ball. One looked up and came towards me, a little curious as it seemed. It came right up to me, rubbed its soft round ear very gently against the small hand I held out and purred. It was, I tell you, an enchanted garden. I know. And the size? Oh! it stretched far and wide, this way and that. I believe there were hills far away. Heaven knows where West Kensington had suddenly got to. And somehow it was just like coming home.

"You know, in the very moment the door swung to behind me, I forgot the road with its fallen chestnut leaves, its cabs and tradesmen's carts, I forgot the sort of gravitational pull back to the discipline and obedience of home, I forgot all hesitations and fear, forgot discretion, forgot all the intimate realities of this life. I became in a moment a very glad and wonder-happy little boy—in another world. It was a world with a different quality, a warmer, more penetrating and mellower light, with a faint clear gladness in its air, and wisps of sun-touched cloud in the blueness of its sky. And before me ran this long wide path, invitingly, with weedless beds on either side, rich with untended flowers, and these two great panthers. I put my little hands fearlessly on their soft fur, and caressed their round ears and the sensitive corners under their ears, and played with them, and it was as though they welcomed me home. There was a keen sense of home-coming in my mind, and when presently a tall, fair girl appeared in the pathway and came to meet me, smiling, and said Well?' to me, and lifted me, and kissed me, and put me down, and led me by the hand, there was no amazement, but only an impression of delightful rightness, of being reminded of happy things that had in some strange way been overlooked. There were broad steps, I remember, that came into view between spikes of delphinium, and up these we went to a great avenue between very old and shady dark trees. All down this avenue, you know, between the red chapped stems, were marble seats of honour and statuary, and very tame and friendly white doves . . . . .

"And along this avenue my girl-friend led me, looking down—I recall the pleasant lines, the finely-modelled chin of her sweet kind face—asking me questions in a soft, agreeable voice, and telling me things, pleasant things I know, though what they were I was never able to recall . . . And presently a little Capuchin monkey, very clean, with a fur of ruddy brown and kindly hazel eyes, came down a tree to us and ran beside me, looking up at me and grinning, and presently leapt to my shoulder. So we went on our way in great happiness . . . ."

He paused.

"Go on," I said.

"I remember little things. We passed an old man musing among laurels, I remember, and a place gay with paroquets, and came through a broad shaded colonnade to a spacious cool palace, full of pleasant fountains, full of beautiful things, full of the quality and promise of heart's desire. And there were many things and many people, some that still seem to stand out clearly and some that are a little vague, but all these people were beautiful and kind. In some way—I don't know how—it was conveyed to me that they all were kind to me, glad to have me there, and filling me with gladness by their gestures, by the touch of their hands, by the welcome and love in their eyes. Yes—"

He mused for awhile. "Playmates I found there. That was very much to me, because I was a lonely little boy. They played delightful games in a grass-covered court where there was a sun-dial set about with flowers. And as one played one loved . . . .

"But—it's odd—there's a gap in my memory. I don't remember the games we played. I never remembered. Afterwards, as a child, I spent long hours trying, even with tears, to recall the form of that happiness. I wanted to play it all over again—in my nursery—by myself. No! All I remember is the happiness and two dear playfellows who were most with me . . . . Then presently came a sombre dark woman, with a grave, pale face and dreamy eyes, a sombre woman wearing a soft long robe of pale purple, who carried a book and beckoned and took me aside with her into a gallery above a hall—though my playmates were loth to have me go, and ceased their game and stood watching as I was carried away. 'Come back to us!' they cried. 'Come back to us soon!' I looked up at her face, but she heeded them not at all. Her face was very gentle and grave. She took me to a seat in the gallery, and I stood beside her, ready to look at her book as she opened it upon her knee. The pages fell open. She pointed, and I looked, marvelling, for in the living pages of that book I saw myself; it was a story about myself, and in it were all the things that had happened to me since ever I was born . . . .

"It was wonderful to me, because the pages of that book were not pictures, you understand, but realities." Wallace paused gravely—looked at me doubtfully.

"Go on," I said. "I understand."

"They were realities—yes, they must have been; people moved and things came and went in them; my dear mother, whom I had near forgotten; then my father, stern and upright, the servants, the nursery, all the familiar things of home. Then the front door and the busy streets, with traffic to and fro: I looked and marvelled, and looked half doubtfully again into the woman's face and turned the pages over, skipping this and that, to see more of this book, and more, and so at last I came to myself hovering and hesitating outside the green door in the long white wall, and felt again the conflict and the fear.

"'And next?' I cried, and would have turned on, but the cool hand of the grave woman delayed me.

"'Next?' I insisted, and struggled gently with her hand, pulling up her fingers with all my childish strength, and as she yielded and the page came over she bent down upon me like a shadow and kissed my brow.

"But the page did not show the enchanted garden, nor the panthers, nor the girl who had led me by the hand, nor the playfellows who had been so loth to let me go. It showed a long grey street in West Kensington, on that chill hour of afternoon before the lamps are lit, and I was there, a wretched little figure, weeping aloud, for all that I could do to restrain myself, and I was weeping because I could not return to my dear playfellows who had called after me, 'Come back to us! Come back to us soon!' I was there. This was no page in a book, but harsh reality; that enchanted place and the restraining hand of the grave mother at whose knee I stood had gone—whither have they gone?"

He halted again, and remained for a time, staring into the fire.

"Oh! the wretchedness of that return!" he murmured.

"Well?" I said after a minute or so.

"Poor little wretch I was—brought back to this grey world again! As I realised the fulness of what had happened to me, I gave way to quite ungovernable grief. And the shame and humiliation of that public weeping and my disgraceful homecoming remain with me still. I see again the benevolent-looking old gentleman in gold spectacles who stopped and spoke to me—prodding me first with his umbrella. 'Poor little chap,' said he; 'and are you lost then?'—and me a London boy of five and more! And he must needs bring in a kindly young policeman and make a crowd of me, and so march me home. Sobbing, conspicuous and frightened, I came from the enchanted garden to the steps of my father's house.

"That is as well as I can remember my vision of that garden—the garden that haunts me still. Of course, I can convey nothing of that indescribable quality of translucent unreality, that difference from the

common things of experience that hung about it all; but that—that is what happened. If it was a dream, I am sure it was a day-time and altogether extraordinary dream . . . . . . H'm!—naturally there followed a terrible questioning, by my aunt, my father, the nurse, the governess—everyone .
. . . . .

"I tried to tell them, and my father gave me my first thrashing for telling lies. When afterwards I tried to tell my aunt, she punished me again for my wicked persistence. Then, as I said, everyone was forbidden to listen to me, to hear a word about it. Even my fairy tale books were taken away from me for a time—because I was 'too imaginative.' Eh? Yes, they did that! My father belonged to the old school . . . . . And my story was driven back upon myself. I whispered it to my pillow—my pillow that was often damp and salt to my whispering lips with childish tears. And I added always to my official and less fervent prayers this one heartfelt request: 'Please God I may dream of the garden. Oh! take me back to my garden! Take me back to my garden!'

"I dreamt often of the garden. I may have added to it, I may have changed it; I do not know . . . . . All this you understand is an attempt to reconstruct from fragmentary memories a very early experience. Between that and the other consecutive memories of my boyhood there is a gulf. A time came when it seemed impossible I should ever speak of that wonder glimpse again."

I asked an obvious question.

"No," he said. "I don't remember that I ever attempted to find my way back to the garden in those early years. This seems odd to me now, but I think that very probably a closer watch was kept on my movements after this misadventure to prevent my going astray. No, it wasn't until you knew me that I tried for the garden again. And I believe there was a period— incredible as it seems now—when I forgot the garden altogether—when I was about eight or nine it may have been. Do you remember me as a kid at Saint Athelstan's?"

"Rather!"

"I didn't show any signs did I in those days of having a secret dream?"

II

He looked up with a sudden smile.

"Did you ever play North-West Passage with me? . . . . . No, of course you didn't come my way!"

"It was the sort of game," he went on, "that every imaginative child plays all day. The idea was the discovery of a North-West Passage to school. The way to school was plain enough; the game consisted in finding some way that wasn't plain, starting off ten minutes early in some almost hopeless direction, and working one's way round through unaccustomed streets to my goal. And one day I got entangled among some rather low-class streets on the other side of Campden Hill, and I began to think that for once the game would be against me and that I should get to school late. I tried rather desperately a street that seemed a _cul de sac_, and found a passage at the end. I hurried through that with renewed hope. 'I shall do it yet,' I said, and passed a row of frowsy little shops that were inexplicably familiar to me, and behold! there was my long white wall and the green door that led to the enchanted garden!

"The thing whacked upon me suddenly. Then, after all, that garden, that wonderful garden, wasn't a dream!" . . . .

He paused.

"I suppose my second experience with the green door marks the world of difference there is between the busy life of a schoolboy and the infinite leisure of a child. Anyhow, this second time I didn't for a moment think of going in straight away. You see . . . For one thing my mind was full of the idea of getting to school in time—set on not breaking my record for punctuality. I must surely have felt _some_ little desire at least to try the door—yes, I must have felt that . . . . . But I seem to remember the attraction of the door mainly as another obstacle to my overmastering determination to get to school. I was immediately interested by this discovery I had made, of course—I went on with my mind full of it—but I went on. It didn't check me. I ran past tugging out my watch, found I had ten minutes still to spare, and then I was going downhill into familiar surroundings. I got to school, breathless, it is true, and wet with perspiration, but in time. I can remember hanging up my coat and hat . . . Went right by it and left it behind me. Odd, eh?"

He looked at me thoughtfully. "Of course, I didn't know then that it wouldn't always be there. School boys have limited imaginations. I suppose I thought it was an awfully jolly thing to have it there, to know my way back to it, but there was the school tugging at me. I expect I was a good deal distraught and inattentive that morning, recalling what I could of the beautiful strange people I should presently see again. Oddly enough I had no doubt in my mind that they would be glad to see me . . . Yes, I must have thought of the garden that morning just as a jolly sort of place to which one might resort in the interludes of a strenuous scholastic career.

"I didn't go that day at all. The next day was a half holiday, and that may have weighed with me. Perhaps, too, my state of inattention brought down impositions upon me and docked the margin of time necessary for the detour. I don't know. What I do know is that in the meantime the enchanted garden was so much upon my mind that I could not keep it to myself.

"I told—What was his name?—a ferrety-looking youngster we used to call Squiff."

"Young Hopkins," said I.

"Hopkins it was. I did not like telling him, I had a feeling that in some way it was against the rules to tell him, but I did. He was walking part of the way home with me; he was talkative, and if we had not talked about the enchanted garden we should have talked of something else, and it was intolerable to me to think about any other subject. So I blabbed.

"Well, he told my secret. The next day in the play interval I found myself surrounded by half a dozen bigger boys, half teasing and wholly curious to hear more of the enchanted garden. There was that big Fawcett—you remember him?—and Carnaby and Morley Reynolds. You weren't there by any chance? No, I think I should have remembered if you were . . . . .

"A boy is a creature of odd feelings. I was, I really believe, in spite of my secret self-disgust, a little flattered to have the attention of these big fellows. I remember particularly a moment of pleasure caused by the praise of Crawshaw—you remember Crawshaw major, the son of Crawshaw the composer?—who said it was the best lie he had ever heard. But at the same time there was a really painful undertow of shame at telling what I felt was indeed a sacred secret. That beast Fawcett made a joke about the girl in green—."

Wallace's voice sank with the keen memory of that shame. "I pretended not to hear," he said. "Well, then Carnaby suddenly called me a young liar and disputed with me when I said the thing was true. I said I knew where to find the green door, could lead them all there in ten minutes. Carnaby became outrageously virtuous, and said I'd have to—and bear out my words or suffer. Did you ever have Carnaby twist your arm? Then perhaps you'll understand how it went with me. I swore my story was true. There was nobody in the school then to save a chap from Carnaby though Crawshaw put in a word or so. Carnaby had got his game. I grew excited and red-eared, and a little frightened, I behaved altogether like a silly little chap, and the outcome of it all was that instead of starting alone for my enchanted garden, I led the way presently—cheeks flushed, ears hot, eyes smarting, and my soul one burning misery and shame—for a party of six mocking, curious and threatening school-fellows.

"We never found the white wall and the green door . . ."

"You mean?—"

"I mean I couldn't find it. I would have found it if I could.

"And afterwards when I could go alone I couldn't find it. I never found it. I seem now to have been always looking for it through my school-boy days, but I've never come upon it again."

"Did the fellows—make it disagreeable?"

"Beastly . . . . . Carnaby held a council over me for wanton lying. I remember how I sneaked home and upstairs to hide the marks of my blubbering. But when I cried myself to sleep at last it wasn't for Carnaby, but for the garden, for the beautiful afternoon I had hoped for, for the sweet friendly women and the waiting playfellows and the game I had hoped to learn again, that beautiful forgotten game . . . . .

"I believed firmly that if I had not told— . . . . . I had bad times after that—crying at night and wool-gathering by day. For two terms I slackened and had bad reports. Do you remember? Of course you would! It was _you_—your beating me in mathematics that brought me back to the grind again."

III

For a time my friend stared silently into the red heart of the fire. Then he said: "I never saw it again until I was seventeen.

"It leapt upon me for the third time—as I was driving to Paddington on my way to Oxford and a scholarship. I had just one momentary glimpse. I was leaning over the apron of my hansom smoking a cigarette, and no doubt thinking myself no end of a man of the world, and suddenly there was the door, the wall, the dear sense of unforgettable and still attainable things.

"We clattered by—I too taken by surprise to stop my cab until we were well past and round a corner. Then I had a queer moment, a double and divergent movement of my will: I tapped the little door in the roof of the cab, and brought my arm down to pull out my watch. 'Yes, sir!' said the cabman, smartly. 'Er—well—it's nothing,' I cried. '_My_ mistake! We haven't much time! Go on!' and he went on . . .

"I got my scholarship. And the night after I was told of that I sat over my fire in my little upper room, my study, in my father's house, with his praise—his rare praise—and his sound counsels ringing in my ears, and I smoked my favourite pipe—the formidable bulldog of adolescence—and thought of that door in the long white wall. 'If I had stopped,' I thought, 'I should have missed my scholarship, I should have missed Oxford—

muddled all the fine career before me! I begin to see things better!' I fell musing deeply, but I did not doubt then this career of mine was a thing that merited sacrifice.

"Those dear friends and that clear atmosphere seemed very sweet to me, very fine, but remote. My grip was fixing now upon the world. I saw another door opening—the door of my career."

He stared again into the fire. Its red lights picked out a stubborn strength in his face for just one flickering moment, and then it vanished again.

"Well", he said and sighed, "I have served that career. I have done—much work, much hard work. But I have dreamt of the enchanted garden a thousand dreams, and seen its door, or at least glimpsed its door, four times since then. Yes—four times. For a while this world was so bright and interesting, seemed so full of meaning and opportunity that the half-effaced charm of the garden was by comparison gentle and remote. Who wants to pat panthers on the way to dinner with pretty women and distinguished men? I came down to London from Oxford, a man of bold promise that I have done something to redeem. Something—and yet there have been disappointments . . . . .

"Twice I have been in love—I will not dwell on that—but once, as I went to someone who, I know, doubted whether I dared to come, I took a short cut at a venture through an unfrequented road near Earl's Court, and so happened on a white wall and a familiar green door. 'Odd!' said I to myself, 'but I thought this place was on Campden Hill. It's the place I never could find somehow—like counting Stonehenge—the place of that queer day dream of mine.' And I went by it intent upon my purpose. It had no appeal to me that afternoon.

"I had just a moment's impulse to try the door, three steps aside were needed at the most—though I was sure enough in my heart that it would open to me—and then I thought that doing so might delay me on the way to that appointment in which I thought my honour was involved. Afterwards I was sorry for my punctuality—I might at least have peeped in I thought, and waved a hand to those panthers, but I knew enough by this time not to seek again belatedly that which is not found by seeking. Yes, that time made me very sorry . . . . .

"Years of hard work after that and never a sight of the door. It's only recently it has come back to me. With it there has come a sense as though some thin tarnish had spread itself over my world. I began to think of it as a sorrowful and bitter thing that I should never see that door again. Perhaps I was suffering a little from overwork—perhaps it was what I've heard spoken of as the feeling of forty. I don't know. But certainly the keen brightness that makes effort easy has gone out of things recently, and that just at a time with all these new political developments—when I ought to be working. Odd, isn't it? But I do begin to find life toilsome, its rewards, as I come near them, cheap. I began a little while ago to want the garden quite badly. Yes—and I've seen it three times."

"The garden?"

"No—the door! And I haven't gone in!"

He leaned over the table to me, with an enormous sorrow in his voice as he spoke. "Thrice I have had my chance—_thrice!_ If ever that door offers itself to me again, I swore, I will go in out of this dust and heat, out of this dry glitter of vanity, out of these toilsome futilities. I will go and never return. This time I will stay . . . . . I swore it and when the time came—_I didn't go_.

"Three times in one year have I passed that door and failed to enter. Three times in the last year.

"The first time was on the night of the snatch division on the Tenants' Redemption Bill, on which the Government was saved by a majority of three. You remember? No one on our side—perhaps very few on the opposite side—expected the end that night. Then the debate collapsed like eggshells. I and Hotchkiss were dining with his cousin at Brentford, we were both unpaired, and we were called up by telephone, and set off at once in his cousin's motor. We got in barely in time, and on the way we passed my wall and door—livid in the moonlight, blotched with hot yellow as the glare of our lamps lit it, but unmistakable. 'My God!' cried I. 'What?' said Hotchkiss. 'Nothing!' I answered, and the moment passed.

"'I've made a great sacrifice,' I told the whip as I got in. They all have,' he said, and hurried by.

"I do not see how I could have done otherwise then. And the next occasion was as I rushed to my father's bedside to bid that stern old man farewell. Then, too, the claims of life were imperative. But the third time was different; it happened a week ago. It fills me with hot remorse to recall it. I was with Gurker and Ralphs—it's no secret now you know that I've had my talk with Gurker. We had been dining at Frobisher's, and the talk had become intimate between us. The question of my place in the reconstructed ministry lay always just over the boundary of the discussion. Yes—yes. That's all settled. It needn't be talked about yet, but there's no reason to keep a secret from you . . . . . Yes—thanks! thanks! But let me tell you my story.

"Then, on that night things were very much in the air. My position was a very delicate one. I was keenly anxious to get some definite word from Gurker, but was hampered by Ralphs' presence. I was using the best power of my brain to keep that light and careless talk not too obviously directed to the point that concerns me. I had to. Ralphs' behaviour since has more than justified my caution . . . . . Ralphs, I knew, would leave us beyond the Kensington High Street, and then I could surprise Gurker by a sudden frankness. One has sometimes to resort to these little devices. . . . . And then it was that in the margin of my field of vision I became aware once more of the white wall, the green door before us down the road.

"We passed it talking. I passed it. I can still see the shadow of Gurker's marked profile, his opera hat tilted forward over his prominent nose, the many folds of his neck wrap going before my shadow and Ralphs' as we sauntered past.

"I passed within twenty inches of the door. 'If I say good-night to them, and go in,' I asked myself, 'what will happen?' And I was all a-tingle for that word with Gurker.

"I could not answer that question in the tangle of my other problems. 'They will think me mad,' I thought. 'And suppose I vanish now!—Amazing disappearance of a prominent politician!' That weighed with me. A thousand inconceivably petty worldlinesses weighed with me in that crisis."

Then he turned on me with a sorrowful smile, and, speaking slowly; "Here I am!" he said.

"Here I am!" he repeated, "and my chance has gone from me. Three times in one year the door has been offered me—the door that goes into peace, into delight, into a beauty beyond dreaming, a kindness no man on earth can know. And I have rejected it, Redmond, and it has gone—"

"How do you know?"

"I know. I know. I am left now to work it out, to stick to the tasks that held me so strongly when my moments came. You say, I have success—this vulgar, tawdry, irksome, envied thing. I have it." He had a walnut in his big hand. "If that was my success," he said, and crushed it, and held it out for me to see.

"Let me tell you something, Redmond. This loss is destroying me. For two months, for ten weeks nearly now, I have done no work at all, except the most necessary and urgent duties. My soul is full of inappeasable regrets. At nights—when it is less likely I shall be recognised—I go out. I wander. Yes. I wonder what people would think of that if they knew. A Cabinet Minister, the responsible head of that most vital of all departments, wandering alone—grieving—sometimes near audibly lamenting—for a door, for a garden!"

IV

I can see now his rather pallid face, and the unfamiliar sombre fire that had come into his eyes. I see him very vividly to-night. I sit recalling his words, his tones, and last evening's _Westminster Gazette_ still lies on my sofa, containing the notice of his death. At lunch to-day the club was busy with him and the strange riddle of his fate.

They found his body very early yesterday morning in a deep excavation near East Kensington Station. It is one of two shafts that have been made in connection with an extension of the railway southward. It is protected from the intrusion of the public by a hoarding upon the high road, in which a small doorway has been cut for the convenience of some of the workmen who live in that direction. The doorway was left unfastened through a misunderstanding between two gangers, and through it he made his way . . . . .

My mind is darkened with questions and riddles.

It would seem he walked all the way from the House that night—he has frequently walked home during the past Session—and so it is I figure his dark form coming along the late and empty streets, wrapped up, intent. And then did the pale electric lights near the station cheat the rough planking into a semblance of white? Did that fatal unfastened door awaken some memory?

Was there, after all, ever any green door in the wall at all?

I do not know. I have told his story as he told it to me. There are times when I believe that Wallace was no more than the victim of the coincidence between a rare but not unprecedented type of hallucination and a careless trap, but that indeed is not my profoundest belief. You may think me superstitious if you will, and foolish; but, indeed, I am more than half convinced that he had in truth, an abnormal gift, and a sense, something—I know not what—that in the guise of wall and door offered him an outlet, a secret and peculiar passage of escape into another and altogether more beautiful world. At any rate, you will say, it betrayed him in the end. But did it betray him? There you touch the inmost mystery of these dreamers, these men of vision and the imagination. We see our world fair and common, the hoarding and the pit. By our daylight standard he walked out of security into darkness, danger and death. But did he see like that?

End

ACTRESS LOLA ALBRIGHT

TOL'ABLE DAVID

JOSEPH HERGESHEIMERA

I

He was the younger of two brothers, in his sixteenth year; and he had his father's eyes--a tender and idyllic blue. There, however, the obvious resemblance ended. The elder's azure gaze was set in a face scarred and riven by hardship, debauch and disease; he had been--before he had inevitably returned to the mountains where he was born--a brakeman in the lowest stratum of the corruption of small cities on big railroads; and his thin stooped body, his gaunt head and uncertain hands, all bore the stamp of ruinous years. But in the midst of this his eyes, like David's, retained their singularly tranquil color of sweetness and innocence.

David was the youngest, the freshest thing imaginable; he was overtall and gawky, his cheeks were as delicately rosy as apple blossoms, and his smile was an epitome of ingenuous interest and frank wonder. It was as if some quality of especial fineness, lingering unspotted in Hunter Kinemon, had found complete expression in his son David. A great deal of this certainly was due to his mother, a thick solid woman, who retained more than a trace of girlish beauty when she stood back, flushed from the heat of cooking, or, her bright eyes snapping, tramped with heavy pails from the milking shed on a winter morning.

Both the Kinemon boys were engaging. Allen, almost twenty-one, was, of course, the more conspicuous; he was called the strongest youth in Greenstream County. He had his mother's brown eyes; a deep bony box of a chest; rippling shoulders; and a broad peaceful countenance. He drove the Crabapple stage, between Crabapple, the village just over the back mountain, and Beaulings, in West Virginia. It was twenty-six miles from point to point, a way that crossed a towering range, hung above a far veil of unbroken spruce, forded swift glittering streams, and followed a road that passed rare isolated dwellings, dominating rocky and precarious patches and hills of cultivation. One night Allen slept in Beaulings; the next he was home, rising at four o'clock in order to take his stage out of Crabapple at seven sharp.

It was a splendid job, and brought them thirty-five dollars a month; not in mere trade at the store, but actual money. This, together with Hunter Kinemon's position, tending the rich bottom farm of State Senator Gait, gave them a position of ease and comfort in Greenstream. They were a very highly esteemed family.

Gait's farm was in grazing; it extended in deep green pastures and sparkling water between two high mountainous walls drawn across east and west. In the morning the rising sun cast long delicate shadows on one side; at evening the shadow troops lengthened across the emerald valley from the other. The farmhouse occupied a fenced clearing on the eastern rise, with a gray huddle of barn and sheds below, a garden patch of innumerable bean poles, and an incessant stir of snowy chickens. Beyond, the cattle moved in sleek chestnut-brown and orange herds; and farther out flocks of sheep shifted like gray-white clouds on a green-blue sky.

It was, Mrs. Kinemon occasionally complained, powerful lonely, with the store two miles up the road, Crabapple over a heft of a rise, and no personable neighbors; and she kept a loaded rifle in an angle of the kitchen when the men were all out in a distant pasturage. But David liked it extremely well; he liked riding an old horse after the steers, the all-night sap boilings in spring groves, the rough path across a rib of the mountain to school.

Nevertheless, he was glad when studying was over for the year. It finished early in May, on account of upland planting, and left David with a great many weeks filled only with work that seem to him unadulterated play. Even that didn't last all the time; there were hours when he could fish for trout, plentiful in cool rocky pools; or shoot gray squirrels in the towering maples. Then, of evenings, he could listen to Allen's thrilling tales of the road, of the gambling and fighting among the lumbermen in Beaulings, or of strange people that had taken passage in the Crabapple stage--drummers, for the most part, with impressive diamond rings and the doggonedest lies imaginable. But they couldn't fool Allen, however believing he might seem.... The Kinemons were listening to such a recital by their eldest son now.

They were gathered in a room of very general purpose. It had a rough board floor and crumbling plaster walls, and held a large scarred cherry bed with high posts and a gayly quilted cover; a long couch, covered with yellow untanned sheepskins; a primitive telephone; some painted wooden chairs; a wardrobe, lurching insecurely forward; and an empty iron stove with a pipe let into an original open hearth with a wide rugged stone. Beyond, a door opened into the kitchen, and back of the bed a raw unguarded flight of steps led up to the peaked space where Allen and David slept.

Hunter Kinemon was extended on the couch, his home-knitted socks comfortably free of shoes, smoking a sandstone pipe with a reed stem. Mrs. Kinemon was seated in a rocking-chair with a stained and torn red plush cushion, that moved with a thin complaint on a fixed base. Allen was over against the stove, his corduroy trousers thrust into greased laced boots, and a black cotton shirt open on a chest and throat like pink marble. And David supported his lanky length, in a careless and dust-colored garb, with a capacious hand on the oak beam of the mantel.

It was May, school had stopped, and a door was open on a warm still dusk. Allen's tale had come to an end; he was pinching the ear of a diminutive dog--like a fat white sausage with wire-thin legs and a rat tail--that never left him. The smoke from the elder Kinemon's pipe rose in a tranquil cloud. Mrs. Kinemon rocked vigorously, with a prolonged wail of the chair springs. "I got to put some tallow to that chair," Kinemon proclaimed.

"The house on Elbow Barren's took," Allen told him suddenly--"the one just off the road. I saw smoke in the chimney this evening." A revival of interest, a speculation, followed this announcement.

"Any women'll get to the church," Mr. Kinemon asserted. "I wonder? Did a person say who were they?"

"I asked; but they're strange to Crabapple. I heard this though: there weren't any women to them--just men--father and sons like. I drew up right slow going by; but nobody passed out a word. It's a middling bad farm place--rocks and berry bushes. I wouldn't reckon much would be content there."

David walked out through the open doorway and stood on the small covered portico, that with a bench on each side, hung to the face of the dwelling. The stars were brightening in the sky above the confining mountain walls; there was a tremendous shrilling of frogs; the faint clamor of a sheep bell. He was absolutely, irresponsibly happy. He wished the time would hurry when he'd be big and strong like Allen, and get out into the absorbing stir of the world.

II

He was dimly roused by Allen's departure in the beginning brightness of the following morning. The road over which the stage ran drew by the rim of the farm; and later David saw the rigid three-seated surrey, the leather mail bags strapped in the rear, trotted by under the swinging whip of his brother. He heard the faint sharp bark of Rocket, Allen's dog, braced at his side.

David spent the day with his father, repairing the fencing of the middle field, swinging a mall and digging post holes; and at evening his arms ached. But he assured himself he was not tired; any brother of Allen's couldn't give in before such insignificant effort. When Hunter Kinemon turned back toward house and supper David made a wide circle, ostensibly to see whether there was rock salt enough out for the cattle, but in reality to express his superabundant youth, staying qualities and unquenchable vivid interest in every foot of the valley.

He saw the meanest kind of old fox, and marked what he thought might be its hole; his flashing gaze caught the obscure distant retreat of ground hogs; he threw a contemptuous clod at the woolly-brained sheep; and with a bent willow shoot neatly looped a trout out upon the grassy bank. As a consequence of all this he was late for supper, and sat at the table with his mother, who never took her place until the men--yes, and boys of her family--had satisfied their appetites. The dark came on and she lighted a lamp swinging under a tin reflector from the ceiling. The kitchen was an addition, and had a sloping shed roof, board sides, a polished stove, and a long table with a red cloth.

His father, David learned, attacking a plateful of brown chicken swimming with greens and gravy, was having another bad spell. He had the familiar sharp pain through his back and his arms hurt him. "He can't be drove to a doctor," the woman told David, speaking, in her concern, as if to an equal in age and comprehension.

David had grown accustomed to the elder's periods of suffering; they came, twisted his father's face into deep lines, departed, and things were exactly as before--or very nearly the same. The boy saw that Hunter Kinemon couldn't support labor that only two or three years before he would have finished without conscious effort. David resolutely ignored this; he felt that it must be a cause of shame, unhappiness, to his father; and he never mentioned it to Allen. Kinemon lay very still on the couch; his pipe, beside him on the floor, had spilled its live core, burning into a length of rag carpet. His face, hung with shadows like the marks of a sooty finger, was glistening with fine sweat. Not a whisper of complaint passed his dry lips. When his wife approached he attempted to smooth out his corrugated countenance. His eyes, as tenderly blue as flowers, gazed at her with a faint masking of humor.

"This is worse'n usual," she said sharply. "And I ain't going to have you fill yourself with any more of that patent trash. You don't spare me by not letting on. I can tell as soon as you're miserable. David can fetch the doctor from Crabapple to-night if you don't look better."

"But I am," he assured her. "It's just a comeback of an old ache. There was a power of heavy work to that fence."

"You'll have to get more to help you," she continued. "That Galt'll let you kill yourself and not turn a hand. He can afford a dozen. I don't mind housing and cooking for them. David's only tol'able for lifting, too, while he's growing."

"Why," David protested, "it ain't just nothing what I do. I could do twice as much. I don't believe Allen could helt more'n me when he was sixteen. It ain't just nothing at all."

He was disturbed by this assault upon his manhood; if his muscles were still a little stringy it was surprising what he could accomplish with them. He would show her to-morrow.

"And," he added impetuously, "I can shoot better than Allen right now. You ask him if I can't. You ask him what I did with that cranky twenty-two last Sunday up on the mountain."

His clear gaze sought her, his lean face quivered with anxiety to impress, convince her of his virility, skill. His jaw was as sharp as the blade of a hatchet. She studied him with a new surprised concern.

"David!" she exclaimed. "For a minute you had the look of a man. A real steady look, like your father. Don't you grow up too fast, David," she directed him, in an irrepressible maternal solicitude. "I want a boy-- something young--round a while yet."

Hunter Kinemon sat erect and reached for his pipe. The visible strain of his countenance had been largely relaxed. When his wife had left the room for a moment he admitted to David:

"That was a hard one. I thought she had me that time."

The elder's voice was light, steady. The boy gazed at him with intense admiration. He felt instinctively that nothing mortal could shake the other's courage. And, on top of his mother's complimentary surprise, his father had confided in him, made an admission that, David realized, must be kept from fretting women. He couldn't have revealed more to Allen himself.

He pictured the latter swinging magnificently into Beaulings, cracking the whip over the horses' ears, putting on the grinding brake before the post-office. No one, even in that town of reckless drinking, ever tried to down Allen; he was as ready as he was strong. He had charge of Government mail and of passengers; he carried a burnished revolver in a holster under the seat at his hand. Allen would kill anybody who interfered with him. So would he--David--if a man edged up on him or on his family; if any one hurt even a dog of his, his own dog, he'd shoot him.

An inextinguishable hot pride, a deep sullen intolerance, rose in him at the thought of an assault on his personal liberty, his rights, or on his connections and belongings. A deeper red burned in his fresh young cheeks; his smiling lips were steady; his candid blue eyes, ineffably gentle, gazed widely against the candlelit gloom where he was making his simple preparations for bed. The last feeling of which he was conscious was a wave of sharp admiration, of love, for everything and everybody that constituted his home.

III

Allen, on his return the following evening, immediately opened an excited account of the new family, with no women, on the place by Elbow Barren.

"I heard they were from down hellwards on the Clinch," he repeated; "and then that they'd come from Kentucky. Anyway, they're bad. Ed Arbogast just stepped on their place for a pleasant howdy, and some one on the stoop hollered for him to move. Ed, he saw the shine on a rifle barrel, and went right along up to the store. Then they hired Simmons--the one that ain't good in his head--to cut out bush; and Simmons trailed home after a while with the side of his face all tore, where he'd been hit with a piece of board. Simmons' brother went and asked them what was it about; and one of the Hatburns--that's their name--said he'd busted the loony just because!"

"What did Simmons answer back?" Hunter Kinemon demanded, his coffee cup suspended.

"Nothing much; he'd law them, or something like that. The Simmonses are right spindling; they don't belong in Greenstream either." David commented: "I wouldn't have et a thing till I'd got them!" In the ruddy reflection of the lamp his pink-and-blue charm, his shy lips, resembled a pastoral divinity of boyhood. Allen laughed.

"That family, the Hatburns----" He paused. "Why, they'd just mow you down with the field daisies."

David flushed with annoyance. He saw his mother studying him with the attentive concern she had first shown the day before yesterday.

"You have no call to mix in with them," Kinemon told his elder son. "Drive stage and mind your business. I'd even step aside a little from folks like that."

A sense of surprised disappointment invaded David at his father's statement. It seemed to him out of keeping with the elder's courage and determination. It, too, appeared almost spindling. Perhaps he had said it because his wife, a mere woman, was there. He was certain that Allen would not agree with such mildness. The latter, lounging back from the table, narrowed his eyes; his fingers played with the ears of his dog, Rocket. Allen gave his father a cigar and lit one himself, a present from a passenger on the stage. David could see a third in Allen's shirt pocket, and he longed passionately for the day when he would be old enough to have a cigar offered him. He longed for the time when he, like Allen, would be swinging a whip over the horses of a stage, rambling down a steep mountain, or walking up at the team's head to take off some weight.

Where the stage line stopped in Beaulings the railroad began. Allen, he knew, intended in the fall to give up the stage for the infinitely wider world of freight cars; and David wondered whether Priest, the storekeeper in Crabapple who had charge of the awarding of the position, could be brought to see that he was as able a driver, almost, as Allen.

It was probable Priest would call him too young for the charge of the Government mail. But he wasn't; Allen had to admit that he, David, was the straighter shot. He wouldn't step aside for any Hatburn alive. And, he decided, he would smoke nothing but cigars. He considered whether he might light his small clay pipe, concealed under the stoop, before the family; but reluctantly concluded that that day had not yet arrived.

Allen passed driving the next morning as usual, leaving a gray wreath of dust to settle back into the tranquil yellow sunshine; the sun moved from the east barrier to the west; a cool purple dusk filled the valley, and the shrilling of the frogs rose to meet the night. The following day was almost identical--the shadows swept out, shortened under the groves of trees and drew out again over the sheep on the western slope. Before Allen reached home he had to feed and bed his horses, and walk back the two miles over the mountain from Crabapple; and a full hour before the time for his brother's arrival, David was surprised to see the stage itself making its way over the precarious turf road that led up to the Kinemons' dwelling. He was standing by the portico, and immediately his mother moved out to his side, as if subconsciously disturbed by the unusual occurrence. David saw, while the stage was still diminutive against the rolling pasture, that Allen was not driving; and there was an odd confusion of figures in a rear seat. Mrs. Kinemon said at once, in a shrill strange voice:

"Something has happened to Allen!" She pressed her hands against her laboring breast; David ran forward and met the surrey as it came through the fence opening by the stable shed. Ed Arbogast was driving; and a stranger--a drummer evidently--in a white-and-black check suit, was holding Allen, crumpled in a dreadful bloody faint.

"Where's Hunter?" Arbogast asked the boy.

"There he comes now," David replied, his heart pounding wildly and dread constricting his throat.

Hunter Kinemon and his wife reached the stage at the same moment. Both were plaster-white; but the woman was shaking with frightened concern, while her husband was deliberate and still.

"Help me carry him in to our bed," he addressed Ed Arbogast.

They lifted Allen out and bore him toward the house, his limp fingers, David saw, trailing through the grass. At first the latter involuntarily turned away; but, objurgating such cowardice, he forced himself to gaze at Allen. He recognized at once that his brother had not been shot; his hip was too smeared and muddy for that. It was, he decided, an accident, as Arbogast and the drummer lead Hunter Kinemon aside. David Kinemon walked resolutely up to the little group. His father gestured for him to go away, but he ignored the elder's command. He must know what had happened to Allen. The stranger in the checked suit was speaking excitedly, waving trembling hands--a sharp contrast to the grim immobility of the Greenstream men:

"He'd been talking about that family, driving out of Beaulings and saying how they had done this and that; and when we came to where they lived he pointed out the house. A couple of dark-favored men were working in a patch by the road, and he waved his whip at them, in a way of speaking; but they never made a sign. The horses were going slow then;

and, for some reason or other, his little dog jumped to the road and ran in on the patch. Sirs, one of those men spit, stepped up to the dog, and kicked it into Kingdom Come."

David's hands clenched; and he drew in a sharp sobbing breath.

"This Allen," the other continued, "pulled in the team and drawed a gun from under the seat before I could move a hand. You can hear me--I wouldn't have kicked any dog of his for all the gold there is! He got down from the stage and started forward, and his face was black; then he stopped, undecided. He stood studying, with the two men watching him, one leaning careless on a grub hoe. Then, by heaven, he turned and rested the gun on the seat, and walked up to where laid the last of his dog. He picked it up, and says he: "'Hatburn, I got Government mail on that stage to get in under contract, and there's a passenger too--paid to Crabapple; but when I get them two things done I'm coming back to kill you two dead to hear the last trumpet.'

"The one on the hoe laughed; but the other picked up a stone like my two fists and let Allen have it in the back. It surprised him like; he stumbled forward, and the other stepped out and laid the hoe over his head. It missed him mostly, but enough landed to knock Allen over. He rolled into the ditch, like, by the road; and then Hatburn jumped down on him, deliberate, with lumbermen's irons in his shoes."

David was conscious of an icy flood pouring through him; a revulsion of grief and fury that blinded him. Tears welled over his fresh cheeks in an audible crying. But he was silenced by the aspect of his father. Hunter Kinemon's tender blue eyes had changed apparently into bits of polished steel; his mouth was pinched until it was only a line among the other lines and seaming of his worn face.

"I'd thank you to drive the stage into Crabapple, Ed," he said; "and if you see the doctor coming over the mountain--he's been rung up for--ask him, please sir, will he hurry." He turned and walked abruptly away, followed by David.

Allen lay under the gay quilt in the Kinemons' big bed. His stained clothes drooped from a chair where Mrs. Kinemon had flung them. Allen's face was like white paper; suddenly it had grown as thin and sharp as an old man's. Only a slight quiver of his eyelids showed that he was not dead.

Hunter Kinemon sat on the couch, obviously waiting for the doctor. He, too, looked queer, David thought. He wished his father would break the dreadful silence gathering over them; but the only sound was the stirring of the woman in the kitchen, boiling a pot of water. Allen moved and cried out in a knifelike agony, and a flicker of suffering passed over his father's face.

An intolerable hour dragged out before the doctor arrived; and then David was driven from the room. He sat outside on the portico, listening to the passage of feet about Allen in a high shuddering protest. David's hands and feet were still cold, but he was conscious of an increasing stillness within, an attitude not unlike his father's. He held out an arm and saw that it was as steady as a beam of the stoop roof. He was without definite plan or knowledge of what must occur; but he told himself that any decision of Hunter Kinemon's must not exclude him.

There were four Hatburns; but two Kinemons were better; and he meant his father and himself, for he knew instinctively that Allen was badly hurt. Soon there would be no Hatburns at all. And then the law could do as it pleased. It seemed to David a long way from the valley, from Allen broken in bed, to the next term of court--September--in Crabapple. The Kinemons could protect, revenge, their own.

The doctor passed out, and David entered where his mother was bent above her elder son. Hunter Kinemon, with a blackened rag, was wiping the lock of an old but efficient repeating rifle. His motions were unhurried, careful. Mrs. Kinemon gazed at him with blanching lips, but she interposed no word. There was another rifle, David knew, in the long cupboard by the hearth; and he was moving to secure it when his father's voice halted him in the middle of the floor. "You David," he said, "I want you to stop along here with your mother. It ain't fit for her to be left alone with Allen, and there's a mess of little things for doing. I want those cows milked dry, and catch in those little Dominicker chickens before that old gander eats them up."

David was about to protest, to sob out a passionate refusal, when a glimpse of his father's expression silenced him. He realized that the slightest argument would be worse than futile. There wasn't a particle of familiar feeling in the elder's voice; suddenly David was afraid of him.

Hunter Kinemon slipped a number of heavily greased cartridges into the rifle's magazine. Then he rose and said:

"Well, Mattie?"

His wife laid her hand on his shoulder.

"Hunter," she told him, "you've been a mighty sweet and good husband." He drew his hand slowly and lovingly across her cheek.

"I'm sorry about this, Mattie," he replied; "I've been powerful happy along with you and all of us. David, be a likely boy." He walked out of the room, across the grass to the stable shed.

"He's going to drive to Elbow Barren," David muttered; "and he hadn't ought to have left me to tend the cows and chickens. That's for a woman to do. I ought to be right along with him facing down those Hatburns. I can shoot, and my hand is steady as his."

He stood in the doorway, waiting for the reappearance of his father with the roan horse to hitch to their old buggy. It didn't occur to David to wonder at the fact that the other was going alone to confront four men. The Kinemons had a mort of friends who would have gladly accompanied, assisted Hunter; but this, the boy told himself, was their own affair--their own pride.

From within came the sound of his mother, crying softly, and of Allen murmuring in his pain. David was appalled by the swift change that had fallen over them--the breaking up of his entire world, the shifting of every hope and plan. He was appalled and confused; the thoughtless unquestioning security of his boyhood had been utterly destroyed. He looked about dazed at the surrounding scene, callous in its total carelessness of Allen's injury, his haggard father with the rifle. The valley was serenely beautiful; doves were calling from the eaves of the barn; a hen clucked excitedly. The western sky was a single expanse of primrose on which the mountains were jagged and blue.

He had never known the elder to be so long getting the bridle on the roan; the buggy was drawn up outside. An uneasy tension increased within him--a pressing necessity to see his father leading out their horse. He didn't come, and finally David was forced to walk over to the shed.

The roan had been untied, and turned as the boy entered; but David, at first, failed to find Hunter Kinemon; then he almost stepped on his hand. His father lay across a corner of the earthen floor, with the bridle tangled in stiff fingers, and his blue eyes staring blankly up.

David stifled an exclamation of dread, and forced himself to bend forward and touch the gray face. Only then he realized that he was looking at death. The pain in his father's back had got him at last! The rifle had been carefully placed against the wall; and, without realizing the significance of his act, David picked it up and laid the cold barrel against his rigid young body.

IV

On the evening after Hunter Kinemon's burial in the rocky steep graveyard above Crabapple, David and his mother sat, one on the couch, the other in her creaking rocking-chair, lost in heavy silence. Allen moved in a perpetual uneasy pain on the bed, his face drawn and fretful, and shadowed by a soft young beard. The wardrobe doors stood open, revealing a stripped interior; wooden chairs were tied back to back; and two trunks--one of mottled paper, the other of ancient leather-- stood by the side of a willow basket filled with a miscellany of housekeeping objects.

What were left of the Kinemons were moving into a small house on the edge of Crabapple; Senator Galt had already secured another tenant for the care of his bottom acres and fat herds. The night swept into the room, fragrant and blue, powdered with stars; the sheep bells sounded in a faintly distant clashing; a whippoorwill beat its throat out against the piny dark.

An overpowering melancholy surged through David; though his youth responded to the dramatic, the tragic change that had enveloped them, at the same time he was reluctant to leave the farm, the valley with its trout and ground hogs, its fox holes and sap boilings. These feelings mingled in the back of his consciousness; his active thoughts were all directed toward the time when, with the rifle, the obligation that he had picked up practically from his dead father's hand, he would walk up to the Hatburn place and take full payment for Allen's injury and their paternal loss.

He felt uneasily that he should have gone before this--at once; but there had been a multitude of small duties connected with the funeral, intimate things that could not be turned over to the kindest neighbors; and the ceremony itself, it seemed to him, should be attended by dignity and repose.

Now, however, it was over; and only his great duty remained, filling the entire threshold of his existence. He had no plan; only a necessity to perform. It was possible that he would fail--there were four Hatburns; and that chance depressed him. If he were killed there was no one else, for Allen could never take another step. That had been disclosed by the most casual examination of his injury. Only himself, David, remained to uphold the pride of the Kinemons.

He gazed covertly at his mother; she must not, certainly, be warned of his course; she was a woman, to be spared the responsibility borne by men. A feeling of her being under his protection, even advice, had grown within him since he had discovered the death in the stable shed. This had not changed his aspect of blossoming youth, the intense blue candor of his gaze; he sat with his knees bent boyishly, his immature hands locked behind his head.

An open wagon, piled with blankets, carried Allen to Crabapple, and Mrs. Kinemon and David followed in the buggy, a great bundle, folded in the bright quilt, roped behind. They soon crossed the range and dropped into a broader valley. Crabapple lay on a road leading from mountain wall to wall, the houses quickly thinning out into meadow at each end.

A cross-roads was occupied by three stores and the courthouse, a square red-brick edifice with a classic white portico and high lantern; and it was out from that, where the highway had degenerated into a sod-cut trail, that the future home of the Kinemons lay. It was a small somber frame dwelling, immediately on the road, with a rain-washed patch rising abruptly at the back. A dilapidated shed on the left provided a meager shelter for the roan; and there was an aged and twisted apple tree over the broken pump.

"You'll have to get at that shed, David," his mother told him; "the first rain would drown anything inside."

She was settling Allen on the couch with the ragged sheepskin. So he would; but there was something else to attend to first. He would walk over to Elbow Barren, to-morrow. He involuntarily laid his hand on the barrel of the rifle, temporarily leaned against a table, when his mother spoke sharply from an inner doorway.

"You David," she said; "come right out into the kitchen."

There he stood before her, with his gaze stubbornly fixed on the bare floor, his mouth tight shut.

"David," she continued, her voice now lowered, fluctuating with anxiety, "you weren't reckoning on paying off them Hatburns? You never?" She halted, gazing at him intently. "Why, they'd shoot you up in no time! You are nothing but a--"

"You can call me a boy if you've a mind to," he interrupted; "and maybe the Hatburns'll kill me--and maybe they won't. But there's no one can hurt Allen like that and go plumb, sniggering free; not while I can move and hold a gun."

"I saw a look to you that was right manlike a week or two back," she replied; "and I said to myself: 'There's David growing up overnight.' I favored it, too, though I didn't want to lose you that way so soon. And only last night I said again: 'Thank God, David's a man in his heart, for all his pretty cheeks!' I thought I could build on you, with me getting old and Allen never taking a mortal step. Priest would give you a place, and glad, in the store--the Kinemons are mighty good people. I had it all fixed up like that, how we'd live here and pay regular.

"Oh, I didn't say nothing to your father when he started out--he was too old to change; but I hoped you would be different. I hoped you would forget your own feeling, and see Allen there on his back, and me ... getting along. You're all we got, David. It's no use, I reckon; you'll go like Allen and Hunter, full up with your own pride and never----" She broke off, gazing bitterly at her hands folded in her calico lap.

A new trouble filled David's heart. Through the open doorway he could see Allen, twisting on the couch; his mother was older, more worn, than he had realized. She had failed a great deal in the past few days. She was suddenly stripped of her aspect of authority, force; suddenly she appeared negative, dependent. A sharp pity for her arose through his other contending emotions.

"I don't know how you figure you will be helping Allen by stepping off to be shot instead of putting food in his mouth," she spoke again. "He's got nobody at all but you, David."

That was so; and yet--

"How can I let those skunks set their hell on us?" he demanded passionately. "Why, all Greenstream will think I'm afraid, that I let the Hatburns bust Allen and kill my father. I couldn't stand up in Priest's store; I couldn't bear to look at anybody. Don't you understand how men are about those things?"

She nodded.

"I can see, right enough--with Hunter in the graveyard and Allen with both hips broke. What I can't see is what we'll do next winter; how we'll keep Allen warm and fed. I suppose we can go to the County Home."

But that, David knew, was as disgraceful as the other--his own mother, Allen, objects of public charity! His face was clouded, his hands clenched. It was only a chance that he would be killed; there were four Hatburns though. His heart, he thought, would burst with misery; every instinct fought for the expression, the upholding of the family prestige, honor. A hatred for the Hatburns was like a strangling hand at his throat.

"I got to!" he said; but his voice was wavering; the dull conviction seized him that his mother was right.

All the mountains would think of him as a coward--that Kinemon who wouldn't stand up to the men who had destroyed Allen and his father!

A sob heaved in his chest; rebellious tears streamed over his thin cheeks. He was crying like a baby. He threw an arm up across his eyes and stumbled from the room.

V

However, he had no intention of clerking back of a counter, of getting down rolls of muslin, papers of buttons, for women, if it could be avoided. Priest's store was a long wooden structure with a painted façade and a high platform before it where the mountain wagons unloaded their various merchandise teamed from the railroad, fifty miles distant. The owner had a small glass-enclosed office on the left as you entered the store; and there David found him. He turned, gazing over his glasses, as the other entered.

"How's Allen?" he asked pleasantly. "I heard he was bad; but we certainly look to have him back driving stage."

"I came to see you about that," David replied. "Allen can't never drive again; but, Mr. Priest, sir, I can. Will you give me a try?"

The elder ignored the question in the concern he exhibited for Allen's injury.

"It is a cursed outrage!" he declared. "Those Hatburns will be got up, or my name's not Priest! We'd have them now, but the jail wouldn't keep them overnight, and court three months off."

David preserved a stony silence--the only attitude possible, he had decided, in the face of his patent dereliction.

"Will you try me on the Beaulings stage?" he repeated. "I've been round horses all my life; and I can hold a gun straighter than Allen."

Priest shook his head negatively.

"You are too light--too young," he explained; "you have to be above a certain age for the responsibility of the mail. There are some rough customers to handle. If you only had five years more now--We are having a hard time finding a suitable man. A damned shame about Allen! Splendid man!"

"Can't you give it to me for a week," David persisted, "and see how I do?"

They would have awarded him the position immediately, he felt, if he had properly attended to the Hatburns. He wanted desperately to explain his failure to Priest, but a dogged pride prevented. The storekeeper was tapping on an open ledger with a pen, gazing doubtfully at David.

"You couldn't be worse than the drunken object we have now," he admitted. "You couldn't hold the job permanent yet, but I might let you drive extra--a day or so--till we find a man. I'd like to do what I could for Mrs. Kinemon. Your father was a good man, a good customer.... Come and see me again--say, day after to-morrow."

This half promise partly rehabilitated his fallen pride. There was no sign in the men he passed that they held him in contempt for neglecting to kill the Hatburns; and his mother wisely avoided the subject. She wondered a little at Priest's considering him, even temporarily, for the stage; but confined her wonder to a species of compliment. David sat beside Allen, while the latter, between silent spaces of suffering, advised him of the individual characters and attributes of the horses that might come under his guiding reins.

It seemed incredible that he should actually be seated in the driver's place on the stage, swinging the heavy whip out over a team trotting briskly into the early morning; but there he was. There were no passengers, and the stage rode roughly over a small bridge of loose boards beyond the village. He pulled the horses into a walk on the mountain beyond, and was soon skirting the Gait farm, with its broad fields, where he had lived as a mere boy.

David slipped his hand under the leather seat and felt the smooth handle of the revolver. Then, on an even reach, he wrapped the reins about the whipstock and publicly filled and lighted his clay pipe. The smoke drifted back in a fragrant cloud; the stage moved forward steadily and easily; folded in momentary forgetfulness, lifted by a feeling of mature responsibility, he was almost happy. But he swung down the mountain beyond his familiar valley, crossed a smaller ridge, and turned into a stony sweep rising on the left.

It was Elbow Barren. In an instant a tide of bitterness, of passionate regret, swept over him. He saw the Hatburns' house, a rectangular bleak structure crowning a gray prominence, with the tender green of young pole beans on one hand and a disorderly barn on the other, and a blue plume of smoke rising from an unsteady stone chimney against an end of the dwelling. No one was visible.

Hot tears filled his eyes as the stage rolled along past the moldy ditch into which Allen had fallen. The mangy curs! His grip tightened on the reins and the team broke into a clattering trot, speedily leaving the Barren behind. But the day had been robbed of its sparkle, his position of its pleasurable pride. He saw again his father's body on the earthen floor of the stable, the bridle in his stiff fingers; Allen carried into the house. And he, David Kinemon, had had to step back, like a coward or a woman, and let the Hatburns triumph.

The stage drew up before the Beaulings post-office in the middle of the afternoon. David delivered the mail bags, and then led the team back to a stable on the grassy verge of the houses clustered at the end of tracks laid precariously over a green plain to a boxlike station. Beaulings had a short row of unpainted two-story structures, the single street cut into deep muddy scars; stores with small dusty windows; eating houses elevated on piles; an insignificant mission chapel with a tar-papered roof; and a number of obviously masked depots for the illicit sale of liquor.

A hotel, neatly painted white and green, stood detached from the main activity. There, washing his face in a tin basin on a back porch, David had his fried supper, sat for a while outside in the gathering dusk, gazing at the crude-oil flares, the passing dark figures beyond, the still obscured immensity of mountain and forest. And then he went up to a pine sealed room, like the heated interior of a packing box, where he partly undressed for bed.

VI

The next mid-morning, descending the sharp grade toward Elbow Barren, there was no lessening of David's bitterness against the Hatburns. The flavor of tobacco died in his mouth, he grew unconscious of the lurching heavy stage, the responsibility of the mail, all committed to his care. A man was standing by the ditch on the reach of scrubby grass that fell to the road; and David pulled his team into the slowest walk possible. It was his first actual sight of a Hatburn. He saw a man middling tall, with narrow high shoulders, and a clay-yellow countenance, extraordinarily pinched through the temples, with minute restless black eyes. The latter were the only mobile feature of his slouching indolent pose, his sullen regard. He might have been a scarecrow, David thought, but for that glittering gaze.

The latter leaned forward, the stage barely moving, and looked unwaveringly at the Hatburn beyond. He wondered whether the man knew him--David Kinemon? But of course he did; all the small details of mountain living circulated with the utmost rapidity from clearing to clearing. He was now directly opposite the other; he could take out the revolver and kill that Hatburn, where he stood, with one precise shot. His hand instinctively reached under the seat. Then he remembered Allen, forever dependent on the couch; his mother, who had lately seemed so old.

The stage was passing the motionless figure. David drew a deep painful breath, and swung out his whip with a vicious sweep.

His pride, however, returned when he drove into Crabapple, down the familiar street, past the familiar men and women turning to watch him, with a new automatic measure of attention, in his elevated position. He walked back to his dwelling with a slight swagger of hips and shoulders, and, with something of a flourish, laid down the two dollars he had been paid for the trip to Beaulings.

"I'm to drive again to-morrow," he stated to his mother and Allen; "after that Priest has a regular man. I suppose, then, I'll have to go into the store."

The last seemed doubly difficult now, since he had driven stage. As he disposed of supper, eating half a pie with his cracklings and greens, his mother moved from the stove to the table, refilled his plate, waved the paper streamers of the fly brush above his head, exactly as she had for his father. Already, he assured himself, he had become a man.

The journey to Beaulings the following day was an unremarkable replica of the one before. He saw no Hatburns; the sun wheeled from east to west at apparently the same speed as the stage; and Beaulings held its inevitable surge of turbulent lumbermen, the oil flares made their lurid note on the vast unbroken starry canopy of night.

The morning of his return was heavy with a wet low vapor. The mail bags, as he strapped them to the rear rack, were slippery; the dawn was a slow monotonous widening of dull light. There were no passengers for Crabapple, and David, with his coat collar turned up about his throat, urged the horses to a faster gait through the watery cold.

The brake set up a shrill grinding, and then the stage passed Elbow Barren in a smart rattle and bumping.

After that David slowed down to light his pipe. The horses willingly lingered, almost stopping; and, the memory of the slippery bags at the back of his head, David dismounted, walked to the rear of the stage.

A chilling dread swept through him as he saw, realized, that one of the Government sacks was missing. The straps were loose about the remaining two; in a minute or more they would have gone. Panic seized him, utter misery, at the thought of what Priest, Crabapple, would say. He would be disgraced, contemptuously dismissed--a failure in the trust laid on him.

He collected his faculties by a violent effort; the bags, he was sure, had been safe coming down the last mountain; he had walked part of the way, and he was certain that he would have noticed anything wrong. The road was powerful bad through the Barren....

He got up into the stage, backed the team abruptly on its haunches, and slowly retraced his way to the foot of the descent. There was no mail lying on the empty road. David turned again, his heart pounding against his ribs, tears of mortification, of apprehension, blurring his vision. The bag must have fallen here in Elbow Barren. Subconsciously he stopped the stage. On the right the dwelling of the Hatburns showed vaguely through the mist. No one else could have been on the road. A troubled expression settled on his glowing countenance, a pondering doubt; then his mouth drew into a determined line.

"I'll have to go right up and ask," he said aloud.

He jumped down to the road, led the horses to a convenient sapling, where he hitched them. Then he drew his belt tighter about his slender waist and took a step forward. A swift frown scarred his brow, and he turned and transferred the revolver to a pocket in his trousers.

The approach to the house was rough with stones and muddy clumps of grass. A track, he saw, circled the dwelling to the back; but he walked steadily and directly up to the shallow portico between windows with hanging, partly slatted shutters. The house had been painted dark brown a long while before; the paint had weathered and blistered into a depressing harmony with the broken and mossy shingles of the roof, the rust-eaten and sagging gutters festooning the ragged eaves.

David proceeded up the steps, hesitated, and then, his mouth firm and hand steady, knocked. He waited for an apparently interminable space, and then knocked again, more sharply. Now he heard voices within. He waited rigidly for steps to approach, the door to open; but in vain. They had heard, but chose to ignore his summons; and a swift cold anger mounted in him. He could follow the path round to the back; but, he told himself, he--David Kinemon--wouldn't walk to the Hatburns' kitchen door. They should meet him at the front. He beat again on the scarred wood, waited; and then, in an irrepressible flare of temper, kicked the door open.

He was conscious of a slight gasping surprise at the dark moldy-smelling hall open before him. A narrow bare stairway mounted above, with a passage at one side, and on each hand entrances were shut on farther interiors. The scraping of a chair, talking came from the left; the door, he saw, was not latched. He pushed it open and entered. There was a movement in the room still beyond, and he walked evenly into what evidently was a kitchen.

The first thing he saw was the mail bag, lying intact on a table. Then he was meeting the concerted stare of four men. One of two, so similar that he could not have distinguished between them, he had seen before, at the edge of the road. Another was very much older, taller, more sallow. The fourth was strangely fat, with a great red hanging mouth. The latter laughed uproariously, a jangling mirthless sound followed by a mumble of words without connective sense. David moved toward the mail bag:

"I'm driving stage and lost those letters. I'll take them right along."

The oldest Hatburn, with a pail in his hand, was standing by an opening, obviously at the point of departure on a small errand. He looked toward the two similar men, nearer David.

"Boy," he demanded, "did you kick in my front door?"

"I'm the Government's agent," David replied. "I've got to have the mail. I'm David Kinemon too; and I wouldn't step round to your back door, Hatburn--not if there was a boiling of you!"

"You'll learn you this," one of the others broke in: "it will be the sweetest breath you ever draw'd when you get out that back door!"

The elder moved on to the pounded earth beyond. Here, in their presence, David felt the loathing for the Hatburns a snake inspires--dusty brown rattlers and silent cottonmouths. His hatred obliterated every other feeling but a dim consciousness of the necessity to recover the mail bag. He was filled with an overpowering longing to revenge Allen; to mark them with the payment of his father, dead in the stable shed.

His objective senses were abnormally clear, cold: he saw every detail of the Hatburns' garb--the soiled shirts with buttoned pockets on their left breasts; the stained baggy breeches in heavy boots--such boots as had stamped Allen into nothingness; dull yellow faces and beady eyes; the long black hair about their dark ears.

The idiot thrust his fingers into his loose mouth, his shirt open on a hairy pendulous chest. The Hatburn who had not yet spoken showed a row of tobacco-brown broken teeth.

"He mightn't get a heave on that breath," he asserted.

The latter lounged over against a set of open shelves where, David saw, lay a heavy rusted revolver. Hatburn picked up the weapon and turned it slowly in his thin grasp.

"I'm carrying the mail," David repeated, his hand on the bag. "You've got no call on this or on me."

He added the last with tremendous effort. It seemed unspeakable that he should be there, the Hatburns before him, and merely depart.

"What do you think of putting the stage under a soft little strawberry like that?" the other inquired.

For answer there was a stunning report, a stinging odor of saltpeter; and David felt a sharp burning on his shoulder, followed by a slow warmish wet, spreading.

"I didn't go to do just that there!" the Hatburn who had fired explained. "I wanted to clip his ear, but he twitched like."

David picked up the mail bag and took a step backward in the direction he had come. The other moved between him and the door.

"If you get out," he said, "it'll be through the hog-wash."

David placed the bag on the floor, stirred by a sudden realization-- he had charge of the stage, official responsibility for the mail. He was no longer a private individual; what his mother had commanded, entreated, had no force here and now. The Hatburns were unlawfully detaining him.

As this swept over him, a smile lighted his fresh young cheeks, his frank mouth, his eyes like innocent flowers. Hatburn shot again; this time the bullet flicked at David's old felt hat. With his smile lingering he smoothly leveled the revolver from his pocket and shot the mocking figure in the exact center of the pocket patched on his left breast.

David wheeled instantly, before the other Hatburn running for him, and stopped him with a bullet as remorselessly placed as the first. The two men on the floor stiffened grotesquely and the idiot crouched in a corner, whimpering.

David passed his hand across his brow; then he bent and grasped the mail bag. He was still pausing when the remaining Hatburn strode into the kitchen. The latter whispered a sharp oath. David shifted the bag; but the elder had him before he could bring the revolver up. A battering blow fell, knocked the pistol clattering over the floor, and David instinctively clutched the other's wrist.

The blows multiplied, beating David into a daze, through which a single realization persisted--he must not lose his grip upon the arm that was swinging him about the room, knocking over chairs, crashing against the table, even drawing him across the hot iron of the stove. He must hold on!

He saw the face above him dimly through the deepening mist; it seemed demoniacal, inhuman, reaching up to the ceiling--a yellow giant bent on his destruction....

His mother, years ago, lives away, had read to them--to his father and Allen and himself--about a giant, a giant and David; and in the end----

He lost all sense of the entity of the man striving to break him against the wooden angles of the room; he had been caught, was twisting, in a great storm; a storm with thunder and cruel flashes of lightning; a storm hammering and hammering at him.... Must not lose his hold on--on life! He must stay fast against everything! It wasn't his hand gripping the destructive force towering above him, but a strange quality within him, at once within him and aside, burning in his heart and directing him from without.

The storm subsided; out of it emerged the livid face of Hatburn; and then, quite easily, he pitched David back across the floor. He lay there a moment and then stirred, partly rose, beside the mail bag. His pistol was lying before him; he picked it up.

The other was deliberately moving the dull barrel of a revolver up over his body. A sharp sense of victory possessed David, and he whispered his brother's name. Hatburn fired--uselessly. The other's battered lips smiled.

Goliath, that was the giant's name. He shot easily, securely--once.

Outside, the mail bag seemed weighted with lead. He swayed and staggered over the rough declivity to the road. It required a superhuman effort to heave the pack into the stage. The strap with which he had hitched the horses had turned into iron. At last it was untied. He clambered up to the enormous height of the driver's seat, unwrapped the reins from the whipstock, and the team started forward.

He swung to the lurching of the stage like an inverted pendulum; darkness continually thickened before his vision; waves of sickness swept up to his head. He must keep the horses on the road, forward the Government mail!

A grim struggle began between his beaten flesh, a terrible weariness, and that spirit which seemed to be at once a part of him and a voice. He wiped the blood from his young brow; from his eyes miraculously blue like an ineffable May sky.

"Just a tol'able David," he muttered weakly--"only just tol'able!"

The End

PARAMOUNT presents
JAMES STEWART · DORIS DAY
ALFRED HITCHCOCK'S
THE MAN WHO KNEW TOO MUCH
COLOR BY TECHNICOLOR
DIRECTED BY ALFRED HITCHCOCK
SCREENPLAY BY JOHN MICHAEL HAYES
BASED ON A STORY BY CHARLES BENNETT AND D.B. WYNDHAM LEWIS
VISTAVISION

Dark Corners
Elmedina Hota

ELMEDINA HOTA IS AN ARTIST
BASED IN SARAJEVO, BOSNIA
AND HERZEGOVINA.
FOR MORE ABOUT HER
BREATHS OF LIFE VISIT
INSTAGRAM & TWITTER:
@HELLMEDINCIC

Cursed Were Her Crystal Blue Eyes

The pure soul disguised as a child has left
this gruesome land,
a tragic death was destined for that mite;
her mother surrendered to her mind's
obscure demands
as her daughter's body lacked the
strength to fight

The restless water awaited her blue eyes,
she entered, believing undoubtedly in her
mother's lies

Lost, she's searched for someone to
believe
to hear the truth and set her spirit free
to cross beyond this Earth to the land of
the dreams
to touch a divine
with all of her fantasy themes

Very soon she shall haunt these corners
she will let go of her mourners
bury the wish they could ever understand
for what her childly heart demands

On one winter eve she came
with her heart in a burning flame
her skin was as pale
as on the shore was the snow,
in the white dress she appeared to escape
her sorrow

For months I tried to escape her appearance
until I finally thought about her deliverance -
'Come to me child, share with me your sore'
I heard the story,
then she told me I'll see her no more

Her soul, at last, has found someone to believe
to hear the truth and set her spirit free,
she crossed beyond this Earth
to the land of the dreams;
touched the divine
enjoyed her fantasy themes

Once upon a time, her presence filled the evening air
through the glass before the crashing waves
felt as if I was kissed by the despair,
soon enough the vision faded, as did her cold kiss
for serenity my disturbed mind craves
as I finally return to my isolated bliss.

BRING ME A LIGHT!

A GHOST STORY

BY JANE MARGARET HOOPER

My name is Thomas Whinmore, and when I was a young man I went to spend a college vacation with a gentleman in Westmoreland. He had known my father's family, and had been appointed the trustee of a small estate left me by my great aunt, Lady Jane Whinmore. At the time I speak of I was one-and-twenty, and he was anxious to give up the property into my hands. I accepted his invitation to "come down to the old place and look about me." When I arrived at the nearest point to the said "old place," to which the Carlisle coach would carry me, I and my portmanteau were put into a little cart, which was the only wheeled thing I could get at the little way-side inn.

"How far is it to Whinmore?" I asked of a tall grave-looking lad, who had already informed me I could have "t'horse and cairt" for a shilling a mile.

"Twal mile to t'ould Hall gaet—a mile ayont that to Squire Erle's farm."

As I looked at the shaggy wild horse, just caught from the moor for the purpose of drawing "t'cairt," I felt doubtful as to which of us would be the master on the road. I had ascertained that the said road lay over moor and mountain—just the sort of ground on which such a steed would gambol away at his own sweet will. I had no desire to be run away with.

"Is there any one here who can drive me to Mr. Erle's?" I asked of the tall grave lad.

"Nobbut fayther."

I was puzzled; and was about to ask for an explanation, when a tall, strong old man, as like the young one as might be, came out from the door of the house with his hat on, and a whip in his hand. He got up into the cart, and looking at me, said,

"Ye munna stan here, sir. We shan't pass Whinmore Hall afore t'deevil brings a light."

"But I want something to eat before we start," I remonstrated. "I've had no dinner."

"Then ye maun keep your appetite till supper time," replied the old man. "I canna gae past Whinmore lights for na man—nor t'horse neither. Get up wi' ye! Joe, lend t'gentleman a hand."

Joe did as he was desired, and then said—

"Will ye be home the night, fayther?"

"May be yees, may be na, lad; take care of t'place."

In a moment the horse started, and we were rattling over the moor at the rate of eight miles an hour. Surprise, indignation, and hunger possessed me. Was it possible I had been whirled off dinnerless into this wilderness against my own desire?

"I say, my good man," I began.

"My name is Ralph Thirlston."

"Well! Mr. Thirlston, I want something to eat. Is there any inn between this desert and Mr. Erle's house!"

"Nobbut Whinmore Hall," said the old man, with a grin.

"I suppose I can get something to eat there, without being obliged to anybody. It is my own property."

Mr. Thirlston glanced at me sharply.

"Be ye t'maister, lad?"

"I am, Mr. Thirlston," said I. "My name is Whinmore."

"Maister Tom!"

"The same. Do you know anything about me and my old house?"

"'Deed do I. You're the heir of t'ould leddy. Mr. Erle is your guardian, and farms your lands."

"I know so much, myself," I replied. "I want you to tell me who lives in Whinmore Hall now, and whether I can get a dinner there, for I'm *clem*, as you say here."

"Weel, weel. It is a sore trial to a young stomach! You must e'en bear it till we get to Mr. Erle's."

"But surely there is somebody, some old woman or other, who lives in the old house and airs the rooms!"

"'Deed is there. But it's nobbut ghosts and deevil's spawn of that sort."

"I am surprised, Mr. Thirlston, to hear a man like you talk such nonsense."

"What like man do ye happen know that I am, Maister Whinmore? Tho' if I talk nonsense (and I'm no gainsaying what a learned colleger like you can tell about nonsense), yet it's just the things I have heard and seen mysell I am speaking of."

"What have you heard and seen at Whinmore Hall?"

"What a' body hears and sees to Whinmore, 'twixt sunset and moonlight;—and what I used to see times and oft, when I lived there farming-man to t'ould Leddy Jane,—what I'm not curious to see again, now. So get on, Timothy," he added to the horse, "or we may chance to come in for a fright."

I did not trouble myself about the delay, as he did, but watched him.

This man is no fool, I thought. I wonder what strange delusion has got possession of the people about this old house of mine. I remembered that Mr. Erle had told me in one of the very few letters I ever received from him, that it was difficult to find a tenant for Whinmore Hall. Curiosity took precedence of hunger, and I began to think how I could best soothe my irritated companion, and get him to tell me what he believed.

We were back on the road again, and going across the shoulder of a great fell;—the sun had just disappeared behind a distant range of similar fells; it left no rosy clouds, no orange streaks in the sky—black rain-clouds spread all over the great concave, and in a very few minutes they burst upon us. There was a cold, piercing wind in our teeth. I felt my spirits rise. The vast monotonous moor, the threatening sky, and the fierce rushing blast had something for me sublime and invigorating. I looked round at the new range of moorland which we were gradually commanding, as we rounded the hill.

"I like this wild place, Mr. Thirlston," I said.

"Wild enough!" he grumbled in reply. "'Tis college learning is a deal better than such house and land. Beggars won't live in th' house, and th' land is the poorest in all England."

"Is that the house, yonder, on the right?"

"There's na ither house, good or bad, to be seen from this," he replied: but I observed that he did not turn his head in the direction I had indicated. He kept a look-out straight between the horse's ears; I, on the contrary, never took my eyes off the grey building which we were approaching. Nearer and nearer we came, and I saw that there was a sort of large garden or pleasure-ground enclosed round the house, and that the road ran past a part of this enclosure, and also past a large open-worked iron gate, which was the chief entrance. Very desolate, cold, and inhospitable looked this old house of mine; wild and tangled looked the garden. The tall, smokeless chimneys were numerous, and stood up white against the blackness of the sky; the windows, more numerous still, looked black, in contrast with the whitish-grey stone of the walls. Just as we entered the shadow cast by the trees of the shrubbery, our horse snorted, and sprang several yards from the enclosure.

"Now for it! It is your own fault for running away, and bringing us late," muttered Ralph Thirlston, grasping the reins and standing up to get a better hold of the horse. Timothy now stood still; and to my surprise he was trembling in every limb, and shaking with terror.

"Something has frightened the beast," said I. "I shall just go and see what it was," and was about to jump down, when I felt Ralph Thirlston's great hand on my arm: it was a powerful grip.

"For the love of God, lad, stay where ye are!" he said, in a frightened whisper. "It's just here that my brother met his death, for doing what you want to do now."

"What! For walking up to that fence and seeing what trifle frightened a skittish horse?" And I looked at the fence intently. There was nothing to be seen but a straggling bough of an elder bush which had forced its way through a chink in the rotten wood and was waving in the wind.

Finding that the man was really frightened as well as the horse, I humoured him. He still held my arm.

"There is no need for any one to go closer to see the cause of poor Timothy's fear," I said, laughing. "If you will look, Mr. Thirlston, you will see what it was."

"Na! lad, na! I'm not going to turn my face towards the deevil and his works. 'Lord have mercy upon us! Christ have mercy upon us! Our Father which art in heaven—'" and he repeated the whole prayer with emphasis, slowness, and with his eyes closed. I sat still, an amazed witness of his state of mind. When he had said "Amen," he opened his eyes, and looking down at the horse, who seemed to have recovered, as I judged by his putting his head down to graze, he gave a low whistle, and tightening the reins once more, Timothy allowed himself to be driven forward. Thirlston kept his face away from the enclosure on his right hand, and looked steadily at Timothy. I gave another glance towards the innocent elder bough,—but what was my astonishment to see where it had been, or seemed to be, the figure of a man with a drawn sword in his hand.

"Stop, Thirlston! stop!" I cried. "There is somebody there. I see a man with a sword. Look! Turn back, and I'll soon see what he is doing there."

"Na! na! Never turn back to meet the deevil, when ye have once got past him!" And Thirlston drove on rapidly.

"But he may overtake you," I cried, laughing. But as I looked back I saw that a pursuit was not intended, for the figure I had seen was gone. "I'll pay a visit to that devil to-morrow," I added. "I shall not harbour such game in my preserves."

"Lord's sake, don't talk like that, Maister Whinmore!" whispered Thirlston. "We're just coming to the gaet! May be they may strike Timothy dead!"

"They?—who? Not the ghosts, surely?" I looked through the great gate as we passed, and saw the whole front of the house. "Why, Mr. Thirlston, you said no one lived in the old Hall! Look! There are lights in the windows."

"Ay! ay! I thought you would see them," he said, in a terrified whisper, without turning his head.

"Why, look at them yourself," cried I, pointing to the house.

"God forbid!" he exclaimed; and he gave Timothy a stroke with the whip, that sent him flying past the rest of the garden of the Hall. Our ground rose again, and in a few minutes a good view of the place was obtained. I looked back at it with vivid interest. No lights were to be seen now; no moving thing; the black windows contrasted with the grey walls, and the grey chimneys with the black clouds, as when the place first appeared to me. The moon now rose above a dark hill on our left. Thirlston allowed Timothy to slacken his speed, and, turning round his head, he also looked back at Whinmore Hall.

"We are safe enough now," he said. "The only dangerous time is betwixt sunset and moonrise, when people are passing close to the accursed ould place."

About a mile further, the barking of a housedog indicated that we were approaching Mr. Erle's. The driver stopped at a small wicket-gate leading into a shrubbery, got down, and invited me to do the same. He then fastened Timothy to the gatepost. The garden and the house have nothing to do with my present tale, and are far too dear to me to be flung in as an episodical adornment. They form the scenery of the romantic part of my own life; for Miss Erle became my wife a few years after this first visit to Whinmore. I saw her that evening, and forgot Ralph Thirlston, the old Hall, its ghosts and mysterious lights. However, the next morning I was forced back to this work-a-day world in her father's study. There I heard Mr. Erle's account of my property. All the land was farmed by himself, except the few acres round the Hall, which no one would take because it was not worth tillage, and because of the evil name of the house itself.

"I suppose you know why no tenant can be found for the Hall, since Ralph Thirlston drove you over?"

"Yes," I said, smiling. "But I could get no rational account from him. What is this nonsense about ghosts and lights? Who lives in the Hall?"

"No one, my good fellow. Why, you would not get the stoutest man in the parish, and that's Thirlston, to go into the house after sunset, much less live in it."

"But I have seen lights in some of the windows myself."

"So have I," he replied.

"Do you mean to say that no human beings make use of the house, in virtue of the superstition about it? Tricks of this kind are not uncommon."

"At the risk of seeming foolish in your eyes, I must reply, that I believe no human beings now living have any hand in the operations which go on in Whinmore Hall." Mr. Erle looked perfectly grave as he said this.

"I saw a man with a sword in his hand start from a part of the fence. I think he frightened our horse."

"I, too, have seen the figure you speak of. But I do not think it is a living man."

"What do you suppose it to be?" I asked, in amazement; for Mr. Erle was no ignorant or weak-minded person. He had already impressed me with real respect for his character and intellect.

He smiled at my impetuous tone.

"I live apart from what is called the world," said he. "Grace and I are not polite enough to think everything which we cannot account for either impossible or ridiculous. Ten years ago, I myself was a new resident in this county, and wishing to improve your property, I determined to occupy the old Hall myself. I had it prepared for my family. No mechanic would work about the place after sunset. However, I brought all my servants from a distance; and took care that they should have no intercourse with any neighbour for the first three days. On the third evening they all came to me and said that they must leave the next morning—all but Grace's nurse, who had been her mother's attendant, and was attached to the family. She told me that she did not think it safe for the child to remain another night, and that I must give her permission to take her away."

"What did you do?" said I.

"I asked for some account of the things that had frightened them. Of course, I heard some wild and exaggerated tales; but the main phenomena related were what I myself had seen and heard, and which I was as fully determined as they were not to see and hear again, or to let my child have a chance of encountering. I told them so, candidly; and at the same time declared that it was my belief God's Providence or punishment was at work in that old house, as everywhere else in creation, and not the devil's mischievous hand. Once more I made a rigorous search for secret devices and means for producing the sights and sounds which so many had heard and seen; but without any discovery: and before sunset that afternoon the Hall was cleared of all human occupants. And so it has remained until this day."

"Will you tell me the things you saw and heard?"

"Nay, you had better see and hear them for yourself. We have plenty of time before sunset. I can show you over the whole house, and if your courage holds good, I will leave you there to pass an hour or so between sunset and moonrise. You can come back here when you like; and if you are in a condition to hear, and care to hear, the story which peoples your old Hall with horrors, I will tell it you."

"Thank you," said I. "Will you lend me a gun and pistols to assist me in my investigations?"

"Surely." And taking down the weapons I had pointed out, he began to examine them.

"You want them loaded?"

"Certainly, and with bullets. I am not going to play."

Mr. Erle loaded both gun and pistols. I put the latter into my pocket, and we left the room by the window. Grace Erle met us on the moor, riding a shaggy pony.

"Where are you going, so near dinner time?" she asked.

"Mr. Whinmore is going to look at the old Hall."

"And his gun?" she asked, smiling.

"I want to shoot vermin there."

She looked as if she were about to say something eagerly, but checked herself, and rode slowly away. I looked after her, and wondered what she was going to say. Perhaps she wished to prevent me from going.

Presently we stood before the great iron gate of Whinmore. Mr. Erle took two keys from his pocket. With one he unlocked the gate, with the other the chief door. There were no other fastenings. These were very rusty, and were moved with difficulty.

"People don't get in this way," said I. "That is clear."

The garden was a sad wilderness, and grass grew on the broad steps which led up to the door.

As soon as we had crossed the threshold, I felt the influence of that desolate dwelling creep over my spirits. There was a cold stagnation in the air—a deathly stillness—a murky light in the old rooms that was indescribably depressing. All the lower windows had their pierced shutters fastened, and cobwebs and dust adorned them plentifully.

Yet I could have sworn I saw lights in two, at least, of these lower windows. I said so to my companion. He replied—

"Yes. It was in this very room you saw a light, I dare say. This is one in which I have seen lights myself. But I do not wish to spoil my dinner by seeing anything supernatural now. We will leave it, and I will hasten to the lady's bed-chamber and dressing-room, where the apparitions and noises are most numerous."

I followed him, but cast a glance round the room before I shut the door carefully. It was partly furnished like a library, but on one side was a bed, and beside it an easy-chair. "What name is given to this room? It looks ominous of some evil deed," I said.

"It is called 't'ould Squire's Murder Room,' by the people who know the story connected with it."

"Ah!" I said; "then I may look for a ghost there?"

"You will perhaps see one, or more, if you stay long enough," said Mr. Erle, with the utmost composure. "This way."

I followed him along a gallery on the first floor to the door of a room. He opened it, and we entered what had been apparently one of the principal bedrooms. It was a regular lady's chamber, of the seventeenth century, with dark plumes waving on the top of the bed-pillars of black oak. The massy toilette, with its oval looking-glass, set in silver and shrouded in old lace—the carved chairs and lofty mantelpiece—gave an air of quaint elegance to the dignity of the apartment. I had but little time to examine the objects here, for Mr. Erle had passed on to an inner room, which was reached by ascending a short flight of steps.

"Come up here," cried a voice which did not sound like Mr. Erle's. I ran up the stairs and found him alone in a small room which contained little else than an escritoire, a cabinet, and two great chairs. On one side, a large Parisian looking-glass, *à la Régence*, was fixed on the wall. The branches for lights still held some yellow bits of wax-candle covered with dust. I joined Mr. Erle, who was looking through the window over a vast expanse of mountainous moorland. "What a grand prospect!" I exclaimed. "I like these two rooms very much. I shall certainly come and live here."

"You shall tell me your opinion about that to-morrow," said Mr. Erle. "I must go now."

Concealing as much as possible the contempt I felt for his absurd superstition, I accompanied him down-stairs again. "Are these the only rooms worth looking at?" I asked.

"No; most of the rooms are good enough for a gentleman's household. The rooms I have shown you, and the passages and staircase which lead from one to the other, are the only portions of the house in which you are subjected to annoyance. I have slept in both the rooms, and advise no one else to do so."

"You had bad dreams?" I asked, with an involuntary smile, as I took my gun from the hall-table, where I had left it.

"As you please," said Mr. Erle, smiling also.

I stretched out my hand to him when we stood at the gate together.

"Good night!" said I. "I think I shall sleep in one of those rooms, and return to you in the morning."

Mr. Erle shook his head. "You will be back at my house within three hours, Tom Whinmore; so, *au revoir!*"

He strode away over the moor. His fine figure appeared almost gigantic as it moved between me and the setting sun.

"That does not look like a man who should be a prey to weak superstition, any more than good Ralph Thirlston, who drove home alone willingly enough past this same gate and fence at nine o'clock last night! The witching hour, it seems, is just after sunset. Well, it wants a quarter of an hour of that now," I continued, thinking silently. "There will be time enough for me to explore the garden a little, before I return to the house and wait for my evening's entertainment."

As I walked through the shrubbery, I recollected the figure I had seen outside the fence on the previous evening. I must find out how *that* trick is managed, thought I, and if I get a chance I will certainly wing that ghost, *pour encourager les autres.*

Ascertaining, as well as I was able, the part of the shrubbery near which I saw the man, I began to search for footsteps or marks of human ingenuity. I soon discovered the elder bush that had sent some of its branches through a hole in the fence. I crept round it, and examined the fence. No plank was loose, though some boughs had grown through the hole. I could see no footstep except my own on the moist, dank leafy mould. I got over the fence and saw no marks outside. Baffled, and yet suspicious, I went back and continued my walk, in the course of which I came upon sundry broken and decayed summer-houses and seats. In the tangled flower-garden, on the south-west side, were a few rich blossoms, growing amicably with the vilest weeds. I tore up a great root of hemlock to get at a branch of Provence rose, and then seeing that the sun had disappeared below the opposite fell, I pursued my course and arrived again at the broad gravel path leading from the gate to the hall-door.

Both stood open, as I had left them. I lingered on the grass-grown steps to look at the last rays of the sun, reddening the heather on the distant fell. As I leaned on my gun enjoying the profound stillness of this place, far from all sounds of village, or wood, or sea—a stillness that seemed to deepen and deepen into unearthly intensity—the charm was broken by a human voice speaking near me—the tone was hollow and full of agony—*"Bring me a light! Bring me a light!"* it cried. It was like a sick or dying man. The voice came, I thought, from the room next to me on the right hand of the Hall. I rushed into the house and to the door of that room; it was the first which Mr. Erle had shown me. I remembered shutting the door—it now stood wide open; and there was a sound of hurrying footsteps within.

"Who is there?" I shouted. No answer came. But there passed by me, as it were, in the very doorway, the figure of a young and, as I could see at a glance, very beautiful woman.

When she moved onwards I could not choose but follow, trembling with an indefinable fear, yet borne on by a mystic attraction. At the foot of the stairs she turned on me again, and smiled, and beckoned me with an upraised arm, whereon great jewels flashed in the gloom. I followed her quickly, but could not overtake her. My limbs—I am not ashamed to say it—shook with strange fear; yet I could not turn back from following that fair form. Onward she led me—up the stairs and through the gallery to the door of the lady's chamber. There she paused a moment, and again turned her bewitching face, radiant with smiles, upon me before she disappeared within the dark doorway. I followed into the room, and saw her stand before the antique toilette and arrange in her bosom a spray of roses—the very spray that I had so lately pulled in the garden, it seemed—then she kissed her hand to me and glided to the narrow stairs that led to the little room above. Then came a loud haughty voice—the voice of a woman accustomed to command. It sounded from the little room above, and it could not be the voice of that fair girl, I felt sure. It said:

"*Bring me a light! Bring me a light!*"

I shuddered at the sound; I knew not why, but I stood there still. I then saw the figure of an old female servant, rise from a chair by one of the windows. She approached the toilette, and there I saw her light two tapers, with her breath, it seemed.

"*Bring me a light!*" was repeated in an angry tone from the upper room.

The old woman passed rapidly to the stairs. Thither I followed in obedience to a sign from her; and, mounting to the top, saw into the room.

That beautiful girl stood in the centre, with her costly lace gown sweeping the floor, and her bright curls drooping to the waist. Her back was towards me, but I could see her innocent, sweet face in the great glass. What a lovely, happy face it was!

Behind her stood another lady, taller, and more majestic. She pretended to caress her, but her proud eyes, unseen by the young lady, brightened with triumphant malice. They danced gladly in the light of the taper which she took from the maid. "God of heaven! can a woman look so wicked?" I thought.

"*Watch her!*" whispered a voice in my ear—a voice that stirred my hair.

I did watch her. Would to God I could forget that vision! She—the woman, the fiend—bent carefully to the floor, as though to set right something amiss in the border of the fair bride's robe. I saw her lower the flame of the candle, and set fire to the dress of the smiling, trusting girl. Ere I could move she was enveloped in flames, and I heard her wild shrieks mingling with the low demoniac laughter of her murderess.

I remember suddenly raising the gun in my hand and firing at the horrid apparition. But still she laughed and pointed with mocking gestures to the flames and the writhing figure they enveloped. I ran forward to extinguish them;—my arms struck against the wall, and I fell down insensible.

WHEN I RECOVERED MY SENSES I FOUND MYSELF LYING ON THE FLOOR OF THAT little room, with the bright cold moon looking in on me. I waited without moving, listening for some more of those demon sounds. All was still. I rose—went to the window—the moon was high in heaven, and all the great moor seemed light as day. The air of that room was stifling. I turned and fled. Hastily I ran down those few steps—quicker yet through the great chamber and out into the gallery. As I began to go down the stairs, I saw a figure coming up.

I was now a very coward. Grasping the banister with one hand, and feeling for the unused pistol with the other, I called out—

"Who are you?" and with stupid terror I fired at the thing, without pausing.

There was a slight cry; a very human one. Then a little laugh.

"Don't fire any more pistols at me, Mr. Whinmore. I'm not a ghost."

Something in the voice sent the blood once more coursing through my veins.

"Is it ——?" I could not utter another word.

"It is I, Grace Erle."

"What brought you here?" I said, at length, after I had descended the stairs, and had seized her hand that I might feel sure it was of flesh and blood.

"My pony. We began to get uneasy about you. It is nearly midnight. So papa and I set off to see what you were doing."

"What the devil are you firing at, Whinmore?" asked Mr. Erle, coming hurriedly from a search in the lower rooms.

"Only at *me*, papa!" answered his daughter, archly, glancing up at my face. "But he is a bad shot, for he didn't hit me."

"Thank God!" I ejaculated—"Miss Erle, I was mad."

"No, only very frightened. Look at him, papa!"

Mr. Erle looked at me. He took my arm.

"Why! Whinmore, you don't look the better for seeing the spirits of your ancestors. However, I see it is no longer a joking matter with you. You do not wish to take up your abode here immediately."

I rallied under their kindly *badinage*.

"Let me get out of this horrible place," said I.

Mr. Erle led me beyond the gate. I leaned against it, in a state of exhaustion.

"Here. Try your hand at my other pocket-pistol!" said Mr. Erle, as he put a precious flask of that kind to my lips. After a second application of the remedy I was decidedly better.

Miss Erle mounted her pony, and we set off across the moor. I was very silent, and my companions talked a little with each other. My mind was too confused to recollect just then all that I had experienced during my stay in the house, and I wished to arrange my thoughts and compose my nerves before I conversed with Mr. Erle on the strange visions of that night.

I excused myself to my host and his daughter, in the best way I could, and after taking a slice of bread and a glass of water, I went to bed.

The next day I rose late; but in my right mind. I was much shocked to think of the cowardly fear which had led me to fire a pistol at Miss Erle. I began my interview with my host, by uttering some expressions of this feeling. But it was an awkward thing to declare myself a fool and a coward.

"The less we say about that the better," said her father, gravely. "Fear is the strongest human passion, my boy; and will lead us to commit the vilest acts, if we let it get the mastery."

"I acknowledge that I was beside myself with terror at the sights and sounds of that accursed house. I was not sane, at the moment, I saw your daughter! I shall never—"

"Whinmore, she hopes you will never mention it again! *We* certainly shall not. Now, if you are disposed to hear the story of your ancestor's evil deeds, I am ready to fulfil the promise I made you last night. I see you know too much, now, to think me a fool for believing my own senses, and keeping clear of disagreeable creatures that will not trouble themselves about me. I don't raise the question of *what* they are, or *how* they exist— nor even whether they exist at all. It is sufficient that they appear; and that by their appearance they put a stop to normal human life. You may be a philosopher; and may find some means of banishing these supernatural horrors. I shall like you none the less, if you can do what I cannot."

"I will try. Will you tell the story?"

"Yes, if you will take a cigar with me first."

After we had composed ourselves comfortably before the fire in his study, Mr. Erle began.

"How long ago, I can't exactly find out, but some time between the Reformation and the Great Rebellion, the Whinmores settled in this part of the county, and owned a large tract of land. They were of gentle blood, and most ungentle manners; for they quarrelled with every one, and carried themselves in an insolent fashion, to the simple below them, and to the noble above. The Whinmores were iron-handed and iron-hearted, staunch Catholics and staunch Jacobites, during the religious and political dissensions of the end of the seventeenth and beginning of the eighteenth centuries. After the establishment of Protestantism in the reigns of William III. and Anne, the position of the proud house of Whinmore was materially altered. The cadets went early into foreign service as soldiers and priests, and the first-born remained at home to keep up a blighted dignity. After the establishment of the Hanoverian dynasty, the Whinmores of Whinmore Hall ceased to take any part in public affairs. They were too proud to farm their own land; and putting trust in a nefarious steward, the Whinmore who reigned at the Hall when King George the Second reigned over England was compelled to keep up appearances by selling half the family estate.

"The Whinmore in question, '*t'ould squire,*' as the people call him, was a melancholy man, not much blest in the matrimonial lottery. His wife, Lady Henrietta Whinmore, was the daughter of a poor Catholic Earl. Tradition says she was equally beautiful and proud; and I believe it.

"To return. This couple had only one child, a son. When Lady Henrietta found that her husband was a gentleman of a moping and unenterprising turn of mind, that she could not persuade him to compromise his principles, and so find favour with the new government, she devoted herself to the education of her son, Graham. As he was a clever boy, with strong health and good looks, she determined that he should retrieve the fortunes of the family. She kept him under her own superintendence till he was ten years of age. She then sent him to Eton, with his cousin the little Earl of ———. He was brought up a Protestant, and thus the civil disabilities of the family would be removed. He was early accustomed to the society of all ranks, to be found in a first-class English public school; and his personal gifts as well as his mental excellence helped to win him the good opinion of others. Graham came home from Oxford in his twenty-third year, a first-class man."

"Indeed!" I exclaimed. "I hope I am descended from him, and that his good luck will be a part of my inheritance. Is there any portrait of this fine young English gentleman of the olden time?"

"A very good one. It is in my daughter's sitting-room. We are both struck by your likeness to your grandfather, Graham Whinmore."

"I shall never take a first-class," I sighed; "but go on."

"When Graham returned home after his success at college, he found his father a hopeless valetudinarian, who had had his bed brought down to his library, because he thought himself too feeble to go up and down stairs. He showed little emotion at sight of his son, and seemed to be fast sinking to idiotcy. His mother, on the contrary, was radiant with joy; and had made the old ruined house look its best to welcome the heir. For, at that time, the place was much dilapidated, and only a small portion was habitable, that is the part you saw yesterday, the south front.

"And Graham stayed at home for a month or two in repose, after the fatigues of study. One afternoon as he rode home from a distant town, he paused on the top of Whinmore Hill, which commands a good view of the Hall. The simple bareness of the great hills around, the antique beauty and retirement of the Hall—above all, the sweet impressive stillness of the place, had often charmed Graham, as a boy. Now he gazed with far stronger feeling at it all.

"'It shall *not* be lost to me and my children,' he vowed, inwardly. 'I will redeem the mortgage on the house, I will win back every acre of the old Whinmore land. Yes, I will work for wealth; but I must lose no time, or my opportunity will be gone.'

"He looked at the ruined part of the house, and began to calculate the cost of rebuilding as he hastened forward. As soon as he entered the house he went to see his father, whom he had not seen that day. He found him in his bed, with the nurse asleep in the easy chair beside it. His father did not recognise him, and to Graham's mind, looked very much changed since the previous day. He left the room in search of his mother; thinking, in spite of his love for her, that she neglected her duty as a wife. 'She should be beside him now,' he thought. Still, he framed the best excuse he could for her then, for he loved and reverenced her. She was so strong-minded, so beautiful. Above all, she loved him with such passionate devotion. He dreaded to tell her the resolution he had formed. She was an aristocrat and a woman. She did not understand the mutation of things in that day; she would not believe that the best way to wealth and power was not through the Court influence, but by commercial enterprise. He went to her bed-room, the Lady's Chamber, in which you were last night. She was not there, and he was about to retreat, when he heard her voice in anger speaking to some one, in the dressing-room or oratory above. Graham went towards the stairs, and was met by an old female servant who was in his mother's confidence, and acted as her maid and head-nurse to his father. She came down in tears, murmuring, 'I cannot bear it. It was you gave me the draught for him. I will send for a doctor.'

"'A doctor, indeed! He wants no doctor,' cried the angry mistress. 'And don't talk any more nonsense, my good woman, if you value your place.'

"In her agitation the woman did not see her young master, and hastily left the room.

"Astonished at the woman's words, he slowly ascended the steps to the dressing-room. He found his mother standing before the long looking-glass arrayed in a rich dress of old point lace, over a brocaded petticoat, with necklace, bracelets, and tiara of diamonds. She looked very handsome as her great eyes still flashed and her cheek was yet crimson with anger. She turned hastily as her son's foot was heard on the topmost stair. When she saw who it was her face softened with a smile.

"'You here, Graham! I have been wanting you. Read that.'

"He could scarcely take his admiring eyes from the brilliant figure before him as he received the letter.

"It was addressed to his mother, and came from his cousin, the Earl, informing her that he had obtained a certain post under government for Graham.

"She kissed him as he sat down after reading the letter.

"'There is your first step on fortune's ladder, my son. You are sure to rise.'

"'I hope so, mother. But where are you going decked out in the family diamonds and lace?'

"'Have you forgotten?—To the ball at the Lord-Lieutenant's. You must dress quickly, or we shall be late. Your cousin will be there, and we must thank him for that letter.'

"'Yes, mother,' he replied, 'but we must refuse the place—I have other views.'

"Lady Henrietta's brow darkened.

"'Mother! I have vowed to recover the estate of my ancestors. It will require a large fortune to do this. I cannot get a large fortune by dangling about the Court—I am going to turn merchant.'

"Lady Henrietta stared at him in amazement.

"'You?—My son become a merchant?'

"'Why not, mother? Sons of nobler houses have done so; and I have advantages that few have ever had. Listen, dear mother. I saved the life of a college friend, who was drowning. His father is one of the wealthiest merchants in London—in all England. He wrote to tell me that if it suited my views and those of my family, he was ready to receive me, at once, as a junior partner in his firm. He had learned from his son that I wished to become rich that I might buy back my ancestral estate. His offer puts it in my power to become rich in a comparatively short space of time.—I intend to accept his munificent offer.'

"Lady Henrietta's proud bosom swelled; but there was something in her son's tone which made her feel that anger and persuasion were alike vain. After some minutes' silence, she said bitterly:

"'The world is changed indeed, Graham, if men of gentle blood can become traders and not lose their gentility.'

"'They can, mother. And I do not think the world can be much changed in that particular. A man of gentle blood, who is, in very truth, a gentleman, cannot lose that distinction in any occupation. Come, good mother, give me a smile! I am about to go forth to win an inheritance. I shall fight with modern weapons—the pen and the ledger—instead of sword and shield.'

"At that moment hasty steps were heard in the chamber below, and a voice called:

"'My lady! my lady! come quick! The Squire is dying!'

"Mother and son went fast to Mr. Whinmore's room. They arrived in time to see the old man die. He pointed to her, and cried with his last breath,

"*She did it! She did it!*

"Lady Henrietta sat beside his bed and listened to these incoherent words without any outward emotion. She watched the breath leave the body, and then closed the eyes herself. But though she kept up so bravely then, she was dangerously ill for several months after her husband's death, and was lovingly tended by her son and the old servant.

"I MUST NOW PASS OVER TEN YEARS. BEFORE THE END OF THAT TIME GRAHAM Whinmore had become rich enough to buy back every acre of the land and to build a bran new house, twenty times finer than the old one, if he were so minded. But he was by no means so minded. He restored the old house—made it what it now is. He would not have accepted Chatsworth or Stowe in exchange.

"The Lady Henrietta lived there still; and superintended all the improvements. She had become reconciled to her son's occupation for the sake of the result in wealth. She entered eagerly into all his plans for the improvement of his property, and she had some of her own to propose.

"It was the autumn of the tenth year since her husband's death, and she was expecting Graham shortly for his yearly visit to the Hall. She sat looking over papers of importance in her dressing-room; the old servant (who seems to have grown no older) sat sewing in the bedroom below, when a housemaid brought in a letter which the old servant took immediately to her mistress.

"Lady Henrietta opened the letter quickly, for she saw that the handwriting was her son's. 'Perhaps he is coming this week,' she thought with a thrill of delight. 'Yes, he will come to take me to the Lord-Lieutenant's ball. He is proud of his mother yet, and I must look my best.' But she had not read a dozen words before the expression of her face changed. Surprise darkened into contempt and anger—anger deepened into rage and hatred. She uttered a sharp cry of pain. The old servant ran to her in alarm; but her mistress had composed herself, though her cheek was livid.

"'Did your ladyship call me?'

"'Yes. Bring me a light!'

"In this letter Graham announced his return home the following week—with a wife;—a beautiful girl—penniless and without connections of gentility. No words can describe the bitter rage and disappointment of this proud woman. He had a second time thwarted her plans for his welfare, and each time he had outraged her strongest feelings. He had turned merchant, and by his plebeian peddling had bought the land which his ancestors had won at the point of the sword. She had borne that, and had submitted to help him in his schemes. But receive a beggarly, low-born wench for her daughter-in-law?—No! She would never do that. She paced the room with soft, firm steps, like a panther. After a time thought became clearer, and she saw that there was no question of her willingness to receive her daughter-in-law, but of that daughter-in-law's willingness to allow her to remain in the house. Ah! but it was an awful thing to see the proud woman when she looked that fact fully in the face. She hated her unseen daughter with a keen cold hate—a remorseless hate born of that terrible sin, Pride. But she was not a woman to hate passively. She paced to and fro, turning and returning with savage, stealthy quickness. The day waned, and night began. Her servant came to see if she were wanted, and was sent away with a haughty negative. 'She is busy with some wicked thought,' murmured the old woman.

"Graham Whinmore's bride was, as he had said, 'so good and so lovely,' that no one ever thought of asking who were her parents.' She was also accomplished and elegant in manner. She was in all respects but birth superior to the Duke's daughter whom Lady Henrietta had selected for her son's wife. The beautiful Lilian's father was a music master, and she had given lessons in singing herself. Lady Henrietta learned this and everything else concerning her young daughter-in-law that could be considered disgraceful in her present station. But she put restraint on her contempt, and received her with an outward show of courtesy and stately kindness. Graham believed that for his sake his mother was determined to forget his wife's low origin, and he became easy about the result of their connection after he had seen his mother caress his wife once or twice. He felt sure that no one could know Lilian and not love her. He was proud and happy to think that two such beautiful women belonged to him.

"The Lord-Lieutenant's ball was expected to be unusually brilliant that year, and Graham was anxious that his wife should be the queen of the assembly.

"'I should like her to wear the old lace and the jewels, mother,' said Graham.

"The Lady Henrietta's eyebrows were contracted for a moment, and she shot forth a furtive glance at Lilian, who sat near, playing with a greyhound.

"If Graham had seen that glance! But her words he believed.

"'Certainly, my son. It is quite proper that your wife should wear such magnificent heirlooms. There is no woman of quality in this county that can match them. I am proud to abdicate my right in her favour.'

"'There, Lilian! Do you hear, you are to eclipse the Duchess herself!'

"'I will do so, if you wish it,' said Lilian. 'But I do not think that will amuse me so much as dancing.'

"BALLS, IN THOSE TIMES, BEGAN AT A REASONABLE HOUR. LADIES WHO WENT to a ball early in November, began to dress by daylight.

"Lilian had been dressed by her maid. Owing to a certain sentimental secret between her and her husband, she wore her wedding-dress of white Indian muslin, instead of a rich brocaded silk petticoat, underneath the grand lace robe. The diamonds glittered gaily round her head and her softly-rounded throat and arms. She went to the old library, where Graham sat awaiting the ladies. She wanted his opinion concerning her appearance. The legend does not tell how he behaved on this occasion, but leaves it to young husbands to imagine.

"'You must go to my mother, and let her see how lovely you look. Walk first, that I may see how you look behind.' So she took from his hand a spray of roses he had gathered, and preceded him from the room, and up the staircase to his mother's chamber. She was in the dressing-room above.

"'Go up by yourself,' said Graham; 'I will remain on the stairs, and watch you both. I should like to hear what she says, when she does not think I hear; for she never praises you much to me, for fear of increasing my blind adoration, I suppose.'

"Lilian smiled at him, and disappeared up the stairs. It was now becoming dark, and as he approached the stairs, a few minutes afterwards, to hear what was said, his mother's voice, in a strange, eager tone, called from above,

"'*Bring me a light! Bring me a light!*'

"Then Graham saw his mother's old servant run quickly from her seat by the window, and light a tall taper on the toilette. She carried this up to her mistress, and found Graham on the stair on her return. She grasped his arm, and whispered fearfully,

"'Watch her! Watch her!'

"He did watch, and saw—"

"For God's sake, Mr. Erle," I interrupted, "don't tell me what he saw—for I saw the same dreadful sight!"

"I have no doubt you did, since you say so; and because I have seen it myself."

We were silent for some moments, and then I asked if he knew anything more of these people.

"Yes—the rest is well known to every one who lives within twenty miles. Graham Whinmore vowed not to remain under the same roof with his mother, after he had seen his wife's blackened corpse. His grief and resentment were quiet and enduring. He would not leave the corpse in the house; but before midnight had it carried to a summer-house in the shrubbery, where he watched beside it, and allowed no one to approach, except the old servant who figures in this story. She brought him food, and carried his commands to the household. From the day of Lilian's death till the day of her burial in the family vault at Whinmore Church, Graham guarded the summer-house where his wife lay, with his drawn sword as he walked by night round about. It was known that he would not allow the family jewels to be taken from the body, and that they were to be buried with it. Some say that he finally took them from the body himself, and buried them in the shrubbery, lest the undertakers, tempted by the sight of the jewels on the corpse, might desecrate her tomb afterwards for the sake of stealing them. This opinion is supported by the fact that a portion of the shrubbery is haunted by the apparition of Graham Whinmore, in mourning garments, and with a drawn sword in his hand.

"Would you advise me to institute a search for those old jewels?" I asked smiling.

"I would," said he. "But take no one into your confidence, Tom Whinmore. You may raise a laugh against you, if you are unsuccessful. And if you find them, and take them away—"

"Which I certainly should do," I interrupted.

"You will raise a popular outcry against you. The superstitious people will believe that you have outraged the ghost of your great-grandfather, who will become mischievous, in consequence."

I saw the prudence of this remark; and it was agreed between us, that we should do all the digging ourselves, unknown to any one. I then asked how it was that I was descended from this unfortunate gentleman.

Mr. Erle's story continued thus:—

"After his wife's funeral, Graham Whinmore did not return to the Hall, but went away to the south, and never came here again, not even to visit his mother on her death-bed, a year after. In a few years he married again, and had sons and daughters. To an unmarried daughter, Jane Whinmore,—always called 'Leddy Jane' by our neighbours,—he left the house and lands. He did not care to keep it in the family, and she might leave it to a stranger, or sell it, if she pleased. It was but a small portion of Graham Whinmore's property, as you must know. She, however—this 'Leddy Jane'—took a great fancy to the old place. She is said to have lived on terms of familiarity with the ghost of her grandmother, and still more affectionately with her father's first wife. She heard nothing of the buried jewels, and saw nothing of her own father's ghost during his lifetime. That part of the story did not come to light until after the death of Graham Whinmore; when the 'Leddy Jane' herself was startled one evening in the shrubbery, by meeting the apparition of her father. It is said that she left her property to her youngest nephew's youngest son, in obedience to his injunctions during that interview."

"So that though unborn at the time, I may consider myself lord of Whinmore Hall, by the will of my great-grandfather!" I said.

"Precisely so. I think it an indication that the ghostly power is to die out in your time. The last year of the wicked Lady Henrietta's life was very wretched, as you may suppose. Her besetting and cherished sins brought their own reward—and her crowning crime was avenged without the terror of the law. For it is said that every evening at sunset the apparition of her murdered daughter-in-law came before her, wearing the rich dress which was so dear to the proud woman; and that she was compelled to repeat the cruel act, and to hear her screams and the farewell curses of her adored son. The servants all left the Hall in affright; and no one lived with the wicked Lady except the faithful old servant, Margaret Thirlston, who stayed with her to the last, followed her to the grave, and died soon after.

"Her son and his wife were sought for by Jane Whinmore on her arrival here. She gave them a home and everything they wanted as housekeeper and farm-manager at the Hall. And at the death of Giles Thirlston, his son Ralph became farm-manager in his place. He continued there till 't' Leddy's' death, when he settled at the little wayside inn which you have seen, and which he calls 'Leddy Jane's Gift.'"

I HAVE BUT LITTLE MORE TO SAY. MR. ERLE AND I SOUGHT LONG FOR THE hidden treasure. We found it, after reading a letter secreted in the escritoire, addressed to 'My youngest nephew's youngest son.' In that letter directions were given for recovering the hidden jewels of the family. They were buried outside the garden fence, on the open moor, on the very spot where I can swear I saw the figure of a man with a sword—my great-grandfather, Graham Whinmore.

After I married, we came to live in the south; and I took every means to let my little estate of Whinmore. To my regret the Hall has never found a tenant, and it is still without a tenant after these twenty-five years.

The End

TAKE A BREAK!!!

Helvetica and Times New Roman walk into a bar.

"Get out of here!" shouts the bartender. "We don't serve your type."

Yesterday I saw a guy spill all his Scrabble letters on the road. I asked him, "What's the word on the street?"

quick

2 out of 3 with someone near.

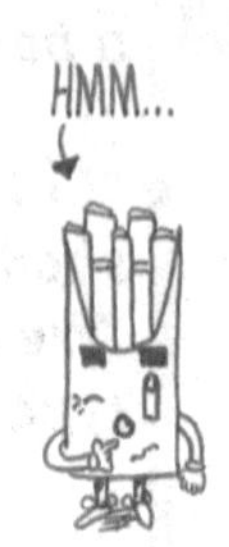

SUDOKU

			9	4				
4					2	5		
						2	4	
3		4		5		6		
	7	2		6	9			
5	1				4	3		
				2		1		
		7				8		3
			5		1	9		6

(MEDIUM DIFFICULTY; ANSWERS IN BACK OF BOOK)

> The only thing that happens overnight is recognition. Not talent.
> -Actress Carol Haney

THE LAST STROKE: A DETECTIVE STORY

BY LAWRENCE L. LYNCH

CHAPTER I
SOMETHING WRONG

It was a May morning in Glenville. Pretty, picturesque Glenville, low lying by the lake shore, with the waters of the lake surging to meet it, or coyly receding from it, on the one side, and the green-clad hills rising gradually and gently on the other, ending in a belt of trees at the very horizon's edge.

There is little movement in the quiet streets of the town at half-past eight o'clock in the morning, save for the youngsters who, walking, running, leaping, sauntering or waiting idly, one for another, are, or should be, on their way to the school-house which stands upon the very southernmost outskirts of the town, and a little way up the hilly slope, at a reasonably safe remove from the will ow-fringed lake shore.

The Glenville school-house was one of the earliest public buildings erected in the village, and it had been "located" in what was confidently expected to be the centre of the place. But the new and late-coming impetus, which had changed the hamlet of half a hundred dwellings to one of twenty times that number, and made of it a quiet and not too fashionable little summer resort, had carried the business of the place northward, and its residences still farther north, thus leaving this seat of learning aloof from, and quite above the newer town, in isolated and lofty dignity, surrounded by trees; in the outskirts, in fact, of a second belt of wood, which girdled the lake shore, even as the further and loftier fringe of timber outlined the hilltops at the edge of the eastern horizon and far away.

"Les call 'er the 'cademy?" suggested Elias Robbins, one of the builders of the school-house, and an early settler of Glenville. "What's to hinder?"

"Nothin'," declared John Rote, the village oracle. "'Twill sound first-rate."

They were standing outside the building, just completed and resplendent in two coats of yellow paint, and they were just from the labour of putting in, "hangin'" the new bell.

All of masculine Glenville was present, and the other sex was not without representation.

"Suits me down ter the ground!" commented a third citizen; and no doubt it would have suited the majority, but when Parson Ryder was consulted, he smiled genially and shook his head.

"It won't do, I'm afraid, Elias," he said. "We're only a village as yet, you see, and we can't even dub it the High School, except from a geographical point of view. However, we are bound to grow, and our titles will come with the growth."

The growth, after a time, began; but it was only a summer growth; and the school-house was still a village school-house with its master and one under, or primary, teacher; and to-day there was a frisking group of the smaller youngsters rushing about the school-yard, while the first bell rang out, and half a dozen of the older pupils clustered about the girlish under-teacher full of questions and wonder; for Johnny Robbins, whose turn it was to ring the bell this week, after watching the clock, and the path up the hill, alternately, until the time for the first bell had come, and was actually twenty seconds past, had reluctantly but firmly seized the rope and began to pull.

"'Taint no use, Miss Grant; I'll have to do it. He told me not to wait for nothin', never, when 'twas half-past eight, and so"—cling, clang, cling—"I'm bound"—cling—"ter do it!" Clang. "You see"—cling—"even if he aint here——" Clang, clang, clang.

The boy pulled lustily at the rope for about half as long as usual, and then he stopped.

"You don't s'pose that clock c'ud be wrong, do yo', Miss Grant? Mr. Brierly's never been later'n quarter past before."

Miss Grant turned her wistful and somewhat anxious eyes toward the eastern horizon, and rested a hand upon the shoulder of a tall girl at her side.

"He may be ill, Johnny," she said, reluctantly, "or his watch may be wrong. He's sure to come in time for morning song service. Come, Meta, let us go in and look at those fractions."

Five—ten—fifteen minutes passed and the two heads bent still over book and slate. Twenty minutes, and Johnny's head appeared at the door, half a dozen others behind it.

"Has he come, Johnny?"

"No'm; sha'n't I go an' see——"

But Miss Grant arose, stopping him with a gesture. "He would laugh at us, Johnny." Then, with another look at the anxious faces, "wait until nine o'clock, at least."

Johnny and his followers went sullenly back to the porch, and Meta's lip began to quiver.

"Somethin's happened to him, Miss Grant," she whimpered; "I know somethin' has happened!"

"Nonsense," said Miss Grant. But she went to the window and called to a little girl at play upon the green.

"Nellie Fry! Come here, dear."

Nellie Fry, an a, b, c student, came running in, her yellow locks flying straight out behind her.

"What is it, Miss Grant?"

"Nellie, did you see Mr. Brierly at breakfast?"

"Yes'm!"

"And—quite well?"

"Why—I guess so. He talked just like he does always, and asked the blessin'. He—he ate a lot, too—for him. I 'member ma speakin' of it."

"You remember, Nellie."

Miss Grant kissed the child and walked to her desk, bending over her roll call, and seeming busy over it until the clock upon the opposite wall struck the hour of nine, and Johnny's face appeared at the door, simultaneously with the last stroke.

"Sh'll I ring, Miss Grant?"

"Yes." The girl spoke with sudden decision. "Ring the bell, and then go at once to Mrs. Fry's house, and ask if anything has happened to detain Mr. Brierly. Don't loiter, Johnny."

There was an unwonted flush now upon the girl's usually pale cheeks, and sudden energy in her step and voice.

The school building contained but two rooms, beside the large hall, and the cloak rooms upon either side; and as the scholars trooped in, taking their respective places with more than their usual readiness, but with unusual bustle and exchange of whispers and inquiring looks, the slender girl went once more to the entrance and looked up and down the path from the village.

There was no one in sight, and she turned and put her hand upon the swaying bell-rope.

"Stop it, Johnny! There's surely something wrong! Go, now, and ask after Mr. Brierly. He must be ill!"

"He'd 'a sent word, sure," said the boy, with conviction, as he snatched his hat from its nail. But Miss Grant only waved him away and entered the south room, where the elder pupils were now, for the most part, assembled.

"Girls and boys," she said, the colour still burning in her cheeks, "something has delayed Mr. Brierly. I hope it will be for a short time only. In the meantime, until we know—know what to expect, you will, of course, keep your places and take up your studies. I am sure I can trust you to be as quiet and studious as if your teacher was here; and while we wait, and I begin my lessons, I shall set no monitor over you. I am sure you will not need one."

The pupils of Charles Brierly were ruled by gentleness and love, and they were loyal to so mild a ruler. With low whispers and words of acquiescence, they took up their books, and Miss Grant went back to her more restless small people, leaving the connecting door between the north and south rooms open.

Mrs. Fry's cottage was in the heart of the village, and upon the hillside, but Johnny stayed for nothing, running hither, hat in hand, and returning panting, and with a troubled face.

"Miss Grant," he panted, bursting into her presence with scant ceremony, "he aint there! Mrs. Fry says he came to school before eight o'clock. He went out while she was combin' Nellie's hair, an' she aint seen him since!"

Hilda Grant walked slowly down from her little platform, and advanced, with a waving movement, until she stood in the doorway between the two rooms. The colour had all faded from her face, and she put a hand against the door-pane as if to steady herself, and seemed to control or compose herself with an effort.

"Boys—children—have any of you seen Mr. Brierly this morning?"

For a moment there was an utter silence in the school-room. Then, slowly, and with a sheepish shuffling movement, a stolid-faced boy made his way out from one of the side seats in Miss Grant's room, and came toward her without speaking. He was meanly dressed in garments ill-matched and worse fitting; his arms were abnormally long, his shoulders rounded and stooping, and his eyes were at once dull and furtive. He was the largest pupil, and the dullest, in Miss Grant's charge, and as he came toward her, still silent, but with his mouth half open, some of the little ones tittered audibly.

"Silence!" said the teacher, sternly. "Peter, come here." Her tone grew suddenly gentle. "Have you seen Mr. Brierly this morning?"

"Uh hum!" The boy stopped short and hung his head.

"That's good news, Peter. Tell me where you saw him."

"Down there," nodding toward the lake.

"At the—lake?"

"Yep!"

"How long ago, Peter?"

"'Fore school—hour, maybe."

"How far away, Peter?"

"Big ways. Most by Injun Hill."

"Ah! and what was he doing?"

"Set on ground—lookin'."

"Miss Grant!" broke in the boy Johnny. "He was goin' to shoot at a mark; I guess he's got a new target down there, an' him an' some of the boys shoots there, you know. Gracious!" his eyes suddenly widening, "Dy'u s'pose he's got hurt, anyway?"

Miss Grant turned quickly toward the simpleton.

"Peter, you are sure it was this morning that you saw Mr. Brierly?"

"Uh hum."

"And, was he alone?"

"Uh hum."

"Who else did you see down there, Peter?"

The boy lifted his arm, shielding his eyes with it as if expecting a blow.

"I bet some one's tried ter hit him!" commented Johnny.

"Hush, Johnny! Peter, what is it? Did some one frighten you?"

The boy wagged his head.

"Who was it?"

"N—Nothin'—" Peter began to whimper.

"You must answer me, Peter; was any one else by the lake? Whom else did you see?"

"A—a—ghost!" blubbered the boy, and this was all she could gain from him.

And now the children began to whisper, and some of the elder to suggest possibilities.

"Maybe he's met a tramp."

"P'r'aps he's sprained his ankle!"

"P'r'aps he's falled into the lake, teacher," piped a six-year-old.

"Poh!" retorted a small boy. "He kin swim like—anything."

"Children, be silent!" A look of annoyance had suddenly relaxed the strained, set look of the under teacher's white face as she recalled, at the moment, how she had heard Mr. Samuel Doran—president of the board of school directors—ask Mr. Brierly to drop in at his office that morning to look at some specimen school books. That was the evening before, and, doubtless, he was there now.

Miss Grant bit her lip, vexed at her folly and fright. But after a moment's reflection she turned again to Johnny Robbins, saying:

"Johnny, will you go back as far as Mr. Doran's house? Go to the office door, and if Mr. Brierly is there, as I think he will be, ask him if he would like me to hear his classes until he is at liberty."

Again the ready messenger caught up his flapping straw hat, while a little flutter of relief ran through the school, and Miss Grant went back to her desk, the look of vexation still upon her face.

Five minutes' brisk trotting brought the boy to Mr. Doran's door, which was much nearer than the Fry homestead, and less than five minutes found him again at the school-house door.

"Miss Grant," he cried, excitedly, "he wa'n't there, nor haint been; an' Mr. Doran's startin' right out, with two or three other men, to hunt him. He says there's somethin' wrong about it."

CHAPTER II
FOUND

"I suppose it's all right," said Samuel Doran, as he walked toward the school-house, followed by three or four of the villagers, "called" because of their nearness, rather than "chosen"; "but Brierly's certainly the last man to let any ordinary matter keep him from his post. We'll hear what Miss Grant has to say."

Miss Grant met the group at the gate, and when she had told them all she had to tell, ending with the testimony of the boy Peter, and the suggestion concerning the target-shooting.

"Sho!" broke in one of the men, as she was about to express her personal opinion and her fears, "that's the top an' bottom of the hull business! Brierly's regularly took with ashootin' at a mark. I've been out with him two or three evenin's of late. He's just got int'rusted, and forgot ter look at his watch. We'll find him safe enough som'e'res along the bank; let's cut across the woods."

"He must have heard the bell," objected Mr. Doran, "but, of course, if Peter Kramer saw him down there, that's our way. Don't be anxious, Miss Grant; probably Hopkins is right."

The road which they followed for some distance ran a somewhat devious course through the wood, which one entered very soon after leaving the school-house. It ran along the hillside, near its base, but still somewhat above the stretch of ground, fully a hundred yards in width, between it and the lake shore.

Above the road, to eastward, the wooded growth climbed the gentle upward slope, growing, as it seemed, more and more dense and shadowy as it mounted. But between the road and the river the trees grew less densely, with numerous sunny openings, but with much undergrowth, here and there, of hazel and sumach, wild vines, and along the border of the lake the low overhanging scrub willow.

For more than a fourth of a mile the four men followed the road, walking in couples, and not far apart, and contenting themselves with an occasional "hallo, Brierly," and with peering into the openings through which they could see the lake shore as they passed along.

A little further on, however, a bit of rising ground cut off all sight of the lake for a short distance. It was an oblong mound, so shapely, so evenly proportioned that it had became known as the Indian Mound, and was believed to have been the work of the aborigines, a prehistoric fortification, or burial place.

As they came opposite this mound, the man Hopkins stopped, saying:

"Hadn't a couple of us fellers better go round the mound on t'other side? Course, if he's on the bank, an' all right, he'd ort to hear us—but——"

"Yes," broke in the leader, who had been silent and very grave for some moments. "Go that way, Hopkins, and we'll keep to the road and meet you at the further end of the mound."

They separated silently, and for some moments Mr. Doran and his companions walked on, still silent, then—

"We ought to have brought that simpleton along," Doran said, as if meditating. "The Kramers live only a quarter of a mile beyond the mound, and it must have been near here—Stop!"

He drew his companions back from the track, as a pony's head appeared around a curve of the road; and then, as a black shetland and low phaeton came in sight, he stepped forward again, and took off his hat.

He was squarely in the middle of the road, and the lady in the little phaeton pulled up her pony and met his gaze with a look of mute inquiry. She was a small, fair woman, with pale, regular features and large blue eyes. She was dressed in mourning, and, beyond a doubt, was not a native of Glenville.

"Excuse my haste, ma'am," said Doran, coming to the side of the phaeton. "I'm James Doran, owner of the stable where this horse belongs, and we are out in search of our schoolmaster. Have you seen a tall young man along this road anywhere?"

The lady was silent a moment, then—"Was he a fair young man?" she asked, slowly.

"Yes, tall and fair."

The lady gathered up her reins.

"I passed such a person," she said, "when I drove out of town shortly after breakfast. He was going south, as I was. It must have been somewhere not far from this place."

"And—did you see his face?"

"No; the pony was fresh then, and I was intent upon him."

She lifted the reins, and then turned as if to speak again when the man who had been a silent witness of the little dialogue came a step nearer.

"I s'pose you hav'n't heard any noise—a pistol shot—nor anythin' like that, have ye, ma'am?"

"Mercy! No, indeed! Why, what has happened?"

Before either could answer, there came a shout from the direction of the lake shore.

"Doran, come—quick!"

They were directly opposite the mound, at its central or highest point, and, turning swiftly, James Doran saw the man Hopkins at the top of it, waving his arms frantically.

"Is he found?" called Doran, moving toward him.

"Yes. He's hurt!"

With the words Hopkins disappeared behind the knoll, but Doran was near enough to see that the man's face was scared and pale. He turned and called sharply to the lady, who had taken up her whip and was driving on.

"Madam, stop! There's a man hurt. Wait there a moment; we may need your horse." The last words were uttered as he ran up the mound, his companions close at his heels. And the lady checked the willing pony once more with a look half reluctant, wholly troubled.

"What a position," she said to herself, impatiently. "These villagers are not diffident, upon my word."

A few moments only had passed when approaching footsteps and the sound of quick panting breaths caused her to turn her head, and she saw James Doran running swiftly toward her, pale faced, and too full of anxiety to be observant of the courtesies.

"You must let me drive back to town with you, madam," he panted, springing into the little vehicle with a force that tried its springs and wrought havoc with the voluminous folds of the lady's gown. "We must have the doctor, and—the coroner, too, I fear—at once!"

He put out his hand for the reins, but she anticipated the movement and struck the pony a sharp and sudden blow that sent him galloping townward at the top of his speed, the reins still in her two small, perfectly-gloved hands.

For a few moments no word was spoken; then, without turning her eyes from the road, she asked:

"What is it?"

"Death, I'm afraid!"

"What! Not suicide?"

"Never. An accident, of course."

"How horrible!" The small hands tightened their grasp upon the reins, and no other word was spoken until they were passing the school-house, when she asked—

"Who was it?"

"Charles Brierly, our head teacher, and a good man."

Miss Grant was standing at one of the front windows and she leaned anxiously out as the little trap darted past.

"We can't stop," said Doran, as much to himself as to his companion. "I must have the pony, ma'am. Where can I leave you?"

"Anywhere here. Is there anything—any message I can deliver? I am a stranger, but I understand the need of haste. Ought not those pupils to be sent home?"

He put his hand upon the reins. "Stop him," he said. "You are quick to think, madam. Will you take a message to the school-house—to Miss Grant?"

"Surely."

They had passed the school-house and as the pony stopped, Doran sprang out and offered his hand, which she scarcely touched in alighting.

"What shall I say?" she asked as she sprang down.

"See Miss Grant. Tell her privately that Mr. Brierly has met with an accident, and that the children must be sent home quietly and at once. At once, mind."

"I understand." She turned away with a quick, nervous movement, but he stopped her.

"One moment. Your name, please? Your evidence may be wanted."

"By whom?"

"By the coroner; to corroborate our story."

"I see. I am Mrs. Jamieson; at the Glenville House."

She turned from him with the last word, and walked swiftly back toward the school-house.

Hilda Grant was still at the window. She had made no attempt to listen to recitations, or even to call the roll; and she hastened out, at sight of the slight black robed figure entering the school yard, her big grey eyes full of the question her lips refused to frame.

They met at the foot of the steps, and Mrs. Jamieson spoke at once, as if in reply, to the wordless inquiry in the other's face.

"I am Mrs. Jamieson," she said, speaking low, mindful of the curious faces peering out from two windows, on either side of the open door. "I was stopped by Mr.—"

"Mr. Doran?"

"Yes. He wished me to tell you that the teacher, Mr. ——"

"Brierly?"

"Yes; that he has met with an accident; and that you had better close the school, and send the children home quietly, and at once."

"Oh!" Suddenly the woman's small figure swayed; she threw out a hand as if for support and, before the half-dazed girl before her could reach her, she sank weakly upon the lowest step. "Oh!" she sighed again. "I did not realise—I—I believe I am frightened!" And then, as Miss Grant bent over her, she added weakly: "Don't mind me. I—I'll rest here a moment. Send away your pupils; I only need rest."

When the wondering children had passed out from the school-rooms, and were scattering, in slow-moving, eagerly-talking groups, Hilda Grant stood for a moment beside her desk, rigid and with all the anguish of her soul revealed, in this instant of solitude, upon her face.

"He is dead!" she murmured. "I know it, I feel it! He is dead." Her voice, even to herself, sounded hard and strange. She lifted a cold hand to her eyes, but there were no tears there; and then suddenly she remembered her guest.

A moment later, Mrs. Jamieson, walking weakly up the steps, met her coming from the school-room with a glass of water in her hand, which she proffered silently.

The stranger drank it eagerly. "Thank you," she said. "It is what I need. May I come inside for a little?"

Hilda led the way in silence, and, when her visitor was seated, came and sat down opposite her. "Will you tell me what you can?" she asked hesitatingly.

"Willingly. Only it is so little. I have been for some time a guest at the Glenville House, seeking to recover here in your pure air and country quiet, from the effects of sorrow and a long illness. I have driven about these hills and along the lake shore almost daily."

"I have seen you," said Hilda, "as you drove past more than once."

"And did you see me this morning?"

"No."

"Still, I passed this spot at eight o'clock; I think, perhaps, earlier. My physician has cautioned me against long drives, and this morning I did not go quite so far as usual, because yesterday I went too far. I had turned my pony toward home just beyond that pretty mill where the little streams join the lake, and was driving slowly homeward when this Mr. Doran—is not that right?—this Mr. Doran stopped me to ask if I had seen a man, a tall, fair man——"

"And had you?"

"I told him yes; and in a moment some one appeared at the top of the Indian Mound, and called out that the man was found."

"How—tell me how?"

Mrs. Jamieson drew back a little and looked into the girl's face with strange intentness.

"I—I fear he was a friend of yours," she said in a strangely hesitating manner, her eyes swiftly scanning the pale face.

"You fear! Why do you fear? Tell me. You say he is injured. Tell me all—the worst!"

Still the small, erect, black-clad figure drew back, a look of sudden understanding and apprehension dawning in her face. She moved her lips, but no sound came from them.

"Tell me!" cried the girl again. "In mercy—oh, don't you understand?"

"Yes, I understand now." The lady drew weakly back in the seat and seemed to be compelling her own eyes and lips to steadiness.

"Listen! We must be calm—both of us. I—I am not strong; I dare not give way. Yes, yes; this is all I can tell you. The man, Mr. Doran, asked me to wait in the road with the pony. He came back soon, and said that we must find the doctor and the coroner at once; there had been an accident, and the man—the one for whom they searched—was dead, he feared."

She sprang suddenly to her feet.

"You must not faint. If you do, I—I cannot help you; I am not strong enough."

"I shall not faint," replied Hilda Grant, in a hard strange voice, and she, too, arose quickly, and went with straight swift steps through the open door between the two rooms and out of sight.

Mrs. Jamieson stood looking after her for a moment, as if in doubt and wonder; then she put up an unsteady hand and drew down the gauze veil folded back from her close-fitting mourning bonnet.

"How strange!" she whispered. "She turns from me as if—and yet I had to tell her! Ugh! I cannot stay here alone. I shall break down, too, and I must not. I must not. Here, and alone!"

A moment she stood irresolute, then walking slowly she went out of the school-room, down the stone steps, and through the gate, townward, slowly at first, and then her pace increasing, and a look of apprehension growing in her eyes.

"Oh," she murmured as she hurried on, "what a horrible morning!" And then she started hysterically as the shriek of the incoming fast mail train struck her ears. "Oh, how nervous this has made me," she murmured, and drew a sigh of relief as she paused unsteadily at the door of her hotel.

For fully fifteen minutes after Hilda Grant had reached the empty solitude of her own school-room she stood crouched against the near wall, her hands clenched and hanging straight at her side, her eyes fixed on space. Then, with eyes still tearless, but with dry sobs breaking from her throat, she tottered to her seat before the desk, and let her face fall forward upon her arms, moaning from time to time like some hurt animal, and so heedless of all about her that she did not hear a light step in the hall without, nor the approach of the man who paused in the doorway to gaze at her in troubled surprise.

He was a tall and slender young fellow, with a handsome face, an eye clear, frank, and keen, and a mouth which, but for the moustache which shadowed it, might have been pronounced too strong for beauty.

A moment he stood looking with growing pity upon the grieving woman, and then he turned and silently tip-toed across the room and to the outer door. Standing there he seemed to ponder, and then, softly stepping back to the vacant platform, he seated himself in the teacher's chair and idly opened the first of the volumes scattered over the desk, smiling as he read the name, Charles Brierly, written across the fly-leaf.

"Poor old Charley," he said to himself, as he closed the book. "I wonder how he enjoys his pedagogic venture, the absurd fellow," and then by some strange instinct he lifted his eyes to the clock on the opposite wall, and the strangeness of the situation seemed to strike him with sudden force and brought him to his feet.

What did it mean! This silent school-room! These empty desks and scattered books! Where were the pupils? the teacher? And why was that brown-tressed head with its hidden face bowed down in that other room, in an agony of sorrow?

Half a dozen quick strides brought him again to the door of communication, and this time his strong, firm footsteps were heard, and the bowed head lifted itself wearily, and the eyes of the two met, each questioning the other.

"I beg your pardon," spoke a rich, strong voice. "May I ask where I shall find Mr. Brierly?"

Slowly, as if fascinated, the girl came toward him, a look almost of terror in her face.

"Who are you?" she faltered.

"I am Robert Brierly. I had hoped to find my brother here at his post. Will you tell me——"

But the sudden cry from her lips checked him, and the pent-up tears burst forth as Hilda Grant, her heart wrung with pity, flung herself down upon the low platform, and sitting there with her face bent upon her sleeves, sobbed out her own sorrow in her heartbreak of sympathy for the grief that must soon overwhelm him and strike the happy light from his face.

Sobs choked her utterance, and the young man stood near her, uncertain, anxious, and troubled, until from the direction of the town the sound of flying wheels smote their ears, and Hilda sprang to her feet with a sharp cry.

"I must tell you; you must bear it as well as I. Hark! they are going to him; you must go too!" She turned toward the window, swayed heavily, and was caught in his arms.

It was a brief swoon, but when she opened her eyes and looked about her, the sound of the flying wheels was dying away in the distance, southward.

He had found the pail of pure spring water, and applied some of it to her hands and temples with the quickness and ease of a woman, and he now held a glass to her lips.

She drank feverishly, put a hand before her eyes, raised herself with an effort, and seemed to struggle mutely for self-control. Then she turned toward him.

"I am Hilda Grant," she said, brokenly.

"My brother's friend! My sister that is to be!"

"No, no; not now. Something has happened. You should have gone with those men—with the doctor. They are going to bring him back."

"Miss Grant, sister!" His hands had closed firmly upon her wrists, and his voice was firm. "You must tell me the worst, quick. Don't seek to spare me; think of him! What is it?"

"He—he went from home early, with his pistol, they say, to shoot at a target. He is dead!"

"Dead! Charley dead! Quick! Where is he? I must see, I must. Oh! there must be some horrible mistake."

He sprang toward the door, but she was before him.

"Go this way. Here is his wheel. Take it. Go south—the lake shore— the Indian Mound."

A moment later a young man with pallid face, set mouth and tragic eyes was flying toward the Indian Mound upon a swift wheel, and in the school-room, prone upon the floor, a girl lay in a death-like swoon.

CHAPTER III

NEMESIS

"**M**r. Brierly, are you strong enough to bear a second shock? I must confer with you before—before we remove the body."

It was Doctor Barnes who thus addressed Robert Brierly, who, after the first sight of the outstretched figure upon the lake shore, and the first shock of horror and anguish, had turned away from the group hovering about the doctor, as he knelt beside the dead, to face his grief alone.

Doctor Barnes, besides being a skilled physician, possessed three other qualities necessary to a successful career in medicine—he was prompt to act, practical and humane.

Robert Brierly was leaning against a tall tree, his back toward that group by the water's edge, and his face pressed against the tree's rugged trunk. He lifted his head as the doctor spoke, and turned a white, set face toward him. The look in his dark eyes was assurance sufficient that he was ready to listen and still able to manfully endure another blow.

The two men moved a few steps away, and then the doctor said: "I must be brief. You know, do you not, the theory, that of these men, as to the cause of this calamity?"

"It was an accident, of course."

"They make it that, or suicide."

"Never! Impossible! My brother was a God-fearing man, a happy man."

"Still, there is a bullet-hole just where self-inflicted wounds are oftenest made."

Brierly groaned aloud. "Still," he persisted, "I will never believe it."

"You need not." Doctor Barnes sank his voice to a yet lower pitch. "Mr. Brierly, there is a second bullet-wound in the back!"

"The back! And that means——"

"It means murder, without a doubt. No huntsman could so mistake his mark in this open woodland, along the lake. Besides, hunting is not allowed so near the village. Wait," as the young man was about to speak, "we have no time to discuss motives now, or the possible assassin. What I wish to know is, do you want this fact known now—at once?"

"I—I fear I don't understand. Would you have my brother's name——"

"Stop, man! Knowing that these men have already jumped at a theory, the thought occurred to me that the work of the officers might be made easier if we let the theory of accident stand."

He broke off, looking keenly at the other. He was a good judge of faces, and in that of Robert Brierly he had not been deceived.

The young man's form grew suddenly erect and tense, his eye keen and resolute.

"You are right!" he said, with sudden energy, as he caught at the other's hand. "They must not be enlightened yet."

"Then, the sooner we are back where we can guard this secret, the safer it will be. Come. This is hard for you, Mr. Brierly, I know, and I could say much. But words, no matter how sincerely sympathetic, cannot lighten such a blow as this. I admire your strength, your fortitude, under such a shock. Will you let me add that any service I can render as physician, as man, or as friend, is yours for the asking?"

The doctor hesitated a moment, then held out his hand, and the four watchers beside the body exchanged quick glances of surprise upon seeing the two men grasp hands, silently and with solemn faces, and then turn, still silently, back to the place where the body lay.

"Don't touch that pistol, Doran," the doctor spoke, in his capacity of coroner.

"Certainly not, Doc. I wanted to feel, if I could, whether those side chambers had been discharged or not. You see," he added, rising to his feet, "when we saw this, we knew what we had to do, and it has been 'hands off.' We've only used our eyes so far forth."

"And that I wish to do now with more calmness," said Robert Brierly, coming close to the body and kneeling beside it.

It lay less than six feet from the very water's edge, the body of a tall, slender young man, with a delicate, high-bred face that had been fair when living, and was now marble-white, save for the blood-stains upon the right temple, where the bullet had entered. The hair, of that soft blonde colour, seen oftenest upon the heads of children, and rarely upon adults, was thick and fine, and long enough to frame the handsome face in close half rings that no barber's skill could ever subdue or make straight. The hands were long, slender, and soft as a woman's; the feet small and arched, and the form beneath the loose outlines of the blue flannel fatigue suit in which it was clad, while slender and full of grace, was well built and not lacking in muscle.

It lay as it had fallen, upon its side, and with one arm thrown out and one limb, the left, drawn up. Not far from the outstretched right arm and hand lay the pistol, a six-shooter, which the brother at once recognised, with two of the six chambers empty, a fact which Mr. Doran had just discovered, and was now holding in reserve.

The doctor, upon his discovery of the second bullet-wound, had at once flung his own handkerchief over the prostrate head, and called for the carriage robe from his own phaeton, which, fortunately for the wind and legs of the black pony, had stood ready at his office door, and was now in waiting, the horse tethered to a tree at the edge of the wood not far away.

This lap robe Robert Brierly reverently drew away as he knelt beside the still form, and thus, for some moments remained, turning his gaze from right to left, from the great tree which grew close at the motionless feet, and between the group and the water's edge, its branches spreading out above them and forming a canopy over the body to a dead stump some distance away, where a small target leaned, its rings of white and black and red showing how often a steady hand had sent the ball, close and closer, until the bull's eye was pierced at last.

No word was uttered as he knelt there, and before he arose he placed a hand upon the dead man's shoulder with an impulsive caressing motion, and bending down, kissed the cold temple just above the crimson death-mark. Then, slowly, reverently, he drew the covering once more over the body and arose.

"That was a vow," he said to the doctor, who stood close beside him. "Where is—ah!" He turned toward the group of men who, when he knelt, had withdrawn to a respectful distance.

"Which of you suggested that he had fallen—tripped?"

Doran came forward and silently pointed to the foot of the tree, where, trailing across the grass, and past the dead man's feet, was a tendril of wild ivy entangled and broken.

"Oh!" exclaimed Brierly. "You saw that too?"

"It was the first thing I did see," said the other, coming to his side, "when I looked about me. It's a very clear case, Mr. Brierly. Target-shooting has been quite a pastime here lately. And see! There couldn't be a better place to stand and shoot at that target, than right against that tree, braced against it. It's the right distance and all. He must have stood there, and when he hit the bull's eye, he made a quick forward step, caught his foot in that vine and tripped. A man will naturally throw out his arm in falling so, especially the right one, and in doing that, somehow as he lunged forward it happened."

"Yes," murmured Brierly, "it is a very simple theory. It—it might have happened so."

"There wasn't any other way it could happen," muttered one of Doran's companions. And at that moment the wheels of an approaching vehicle were heard, and all turned to look toward the long black hearse, divested of its plumes, and with two or three thick blankets upon its velvet floor.

It was the doctor who superintended the lifting of the body, keeping the head covered, and when the hearse drove slowly away with its pathetic burden, he turned to Doran.

"I'll drive Mr. Brierly back to town, Doran," he said, "if you don't mind taking his wheel in charge;" and scarcely waiting for Doran's willing assent, he took Richard Brierly's arm and led him toward his phaeton.

The young man had picked up his brother's hat, as they lifted the body from the ground, and he now carried it in his hand, laying it gently upon his knees as he took his seat.

When the doctor had taken his place and picked up the reins he leaned out and looked about him. Two or three horsemen were riding into the wood toward them, and a carriage had halted at the side of the road, while a group of schoolboys, headed by Johnny, the bell ringer, were hurrying down the slope toward the water's edge.

"They're beginning to gather," the physician said, grimly. "Well, it's human nature, and your brother had a host of friends, Mr. Brierly."

Robert Brierly set his lips and averted his face for a moment.

"Doran," called the doctor. "Come here, will you."

Doran, who had begun to push the shining wheel up the slope, placed it carefully against a tree and came toward them, the doctor meanwhile turning to Brierly.

"Mr. Brierly, you are a stranger here. Will you let me arrange for you?"

The other nodded, and then said huskily: "But it hurts to take him to an undertaker's!"

"He shall not be taken there," and the doctor turned to Doran, now standing at the wheel.

"Mr. Doran, will you take my keys and ride ahead as fast as possible? Tell the undertaker, as you pass, to drive to my house. Then go on and open it. We will put the body in the private office. Do not remonstrate, Mr. Brierly. It is only what I would wish another to do for me and mine in a like affliction." And this was the rule by which this man lived his life, and because of which death had no terrors.

"I am a bachelor, you must know," the doctor said, as they drove slowly in the wake of the hearse. "And I have made my home and established my office in a cosy cottage near the village proper. It will save you the ordeal of strange eyes, and many questions, perhaps, if you will be my guest for a day or two, at least."

Robert Brierly turned and looked this friend in need full in the face for a moment; then he lifted his hand to brush a sudden moisture from his eye.

"I accept all your kindness," he said, huskily, "for I see that you are as sincere as you are kind."

When the body of Charles Brierly had been carried in and placed as it must remain until the inquest was at an end, and when the crowd of sorrowing, anxious and curious people had dispersed, the doctor, who was masterful at need, making Doran his lieutenant, arranged for the securing of a jury; and, after giving some quiet instructions, sent him away, saying:

"Tell the people it is not yet determined how or when we shall hold the inquiry. Miss Grant, who must be a witness, will hardly be able to appear at once, I fear," for, after looking to his guest's bodily comfort, the doctor had left him to be alone with his grief for a little while, and had paid a flying visit to Hilda Grant, who lived nearly three blocks away.

When at length the little house was quiet, and when the doctor and his heavy-hearted companion had made a pretence of partaking of luncheon, the former, having shut and locked the door upon the elderly African who served him, drew his chair close to that of his guest, and said:

"Are you willing to take counsel with me, Mr. Brierly? And are you quite fit and ready to talk about what is most important?"

"I am most anxious for your advice, and for information."

"Then, let us lose no time; there is much to be done."

"Doctor," Robert Brierly bent toward the other and placed a hand upon his knee. "There are emergencies which bring men together and reveal them, each to each, in a flash, as it were. I cannot feel that you know me really; but I know you, and would trust you with my dearest possession, or my most dangerous secret. You will be frank with me, I know, if you speak at all; and I want you to tell me something."

"What is it?"

"You have told me how, in your opinion, my poor brother really met his death. Will you put yourself in my place, and tell me how you would act in this horrible emergency? What is the first thing you would do?"

The doctor's answer came after a moment's grave thought.

"I am, I think, a Christian," he said, gravely, "but I think—bah! I know that I would make my life's work to find out the truth about that murder, for that it was a murder, I solemnly believe."

CHAPTER IV
FERRARS

Robert Brierly caught his breath.

"And your reason?" he gasped, "for you have a reason other than the mere fact of the bullet-wound in the neck."

"I have seen just such deeds in the wild west and I know how they are done. But this is also professional knowledge. Besides, man, call reason to your aid! Oh, I expect too much. The hurt is too fresh, you can only feel now, but the man shot by accident, be it by his own hand or that of another, is not shot twice."

"Good heavens, no!"

"But when one who creeps upon his victim unawares, shoots him from behind, and, as he falls, fearing the work is not completed, shoots again, the victim, as you must see, receives the wound further to the front as the body falls forward and partially turns in falling. Do you see? Do you comprehend?"

"Yes." Brierly shuddered.

"Brierly, this talk is hurting you cruelly. Let us drop details, or postpone them."

"Not the essential ones. I must bear what I must. Go on, doctor. I quite agree with you. It looks like a murder, and we must—I must know the truth—must find the one who did the deed. Doctor, advise me."

"About——"

"How to begin, no time should be lost."

"That means a good detective, as soon as possible. Do you chance to know any of these gentry?"

"I——No, indeed! I suppose a telegram to the chief of police——"

"Allow me," broke in Doctor Barnes. "May I make a suggestion?"

"Anything. I seem unable to think."

"And no wonder! I know the right man for you if he is in Chicago. You see, I was in hospital practice for several years, and have also had my share of prison experience. While thus employed I met a man named Ferrars, an Englishman, who for some years has spent the greater part of his time in this country, in Chicago, in fact. There's a mystery and a romance attached to the man, or his history. He's not connected with any of the city offices, but he is one of three retired detectives—retired, that is, from regular work—who work together at need when they feel a case to be worth their efforts. I think a case like this will be certain to attract Ferrars."

"And he is your choice of the three?"

The doctor smiled. "The others are married," he said, "and not so ready to go far afield as is Ferrars."

"You think him skilful?"

"None better."

"Then, do you know his address?"

Brierly got up and began to walk about, his eyes beginning to glow with the excitement so long suppressed. "Because we can't get him here too soon."

"I agree with you. And now one thing more. To give him every advantage he should not be known, and the inquest should not begin until he is here."

"Can that be managed?"

"I think so."

Brierly was now nervously eager. He seemed to have shaken off the stupor which at first had seemed to seize upon and hold him, and his questions and suggestions came thick and fast. It ended, of course, in his putting himself into the doctor's hands, and accepting his plans and suggestions entirely. And very soon, Dr. Barnes, having given his factotum distinct instructions as regarded visitors, and inquiries, had set off, his medicine case carried ostentatiously in his hand, not for the telegraph office, but for the cottage, close by, where Hilda Grant found a home.

It was a small, neatly-kept cottage, and Mrs. Marcy, a gentle, kindly widow, and the young teacher were its only occupants.

The widow met him at the door, her face anxious, her voice the merest whisper.

"Doctor, tell me; do you think she will really be ill?"

"Why no, Mrs. Marcy; at least not for long. It has been a shock, of course; a great shock. But she——"

"Ah, doctor, she is heart-broken. I—I think I surely may tell you. It will help you to understand. They were engaged, and for a little while, such a pitiful little while it seems now, they have been so happy."

The doctor was silent a moment, his eyes turned away.

"And now," went on the good woman, "she will be lonelier than ever. You know she was very lonely here at first. She has no relatives nearer than a cousin anywhere in the world, to her knowledge. And he has never been to see her. He lives in Chicago, too, not so far away."

"Yes, surely he ought to visit her now, really. Just ask her if I may come up, Mrs. Marcy. I—I'm glad you told me of this. Thank you. It will help me."

Ten minutes later Doctor Barnes was hastening toward the telegraph office, where he sent away this singular and wordy message:

> "Frank Ferrars, No. ... Street, Chicago—
>
> "Your cousin, Miss Hilda Grant, is ill, and in trouble. It is a case in which you are needed as much as I. Come, if possible, by first evening train.
>
> "WALTER BARNES."

"That will fetch him," he mused, as he hastened homeward. "Ferrars never breaks a promise, though I little expected to have to remind him of it within the year."

"Well," began Brierly, when he entered his own door. "Have you seen her? Was she willing?"

"Willing and anxious. She is a brave and sensible little woman. She will do her part, and she has never for one moment believed in the theory of an accident."

"And she will receive me?"

"This evening. She insists that we hold our council there, in her presence. At first I objected, on account of her weakness, but she is right in her belief that we should be most secure there, and Ferrars should not be seen abroad to-night. We will have to take Mrs. Marcy into our confidence, in part at least, but she can be trusted. We will all be observed, more or less, for a few days. But, of course, I shall put Ferrars up for the night. That will be the thing to do after he has spent a short evening with his cousin."

Brierly once more began his restless pacing to and fro, turning presently to compare his watch with the doctor's Dutch clock.

"It will be the longest three hours I ever passed," he said, and a great sigh broke from his lips.

But, before the first hour had passed, a boy from the telegraph office handed in a blue envelope, and the doctor hastily broke the seal and read—

"Be with you at 6.20.

"FERRARS."

When the first suburban train for the evening halted, puffing, at the village station, Doctor Barnes waiting upon the platform, saw a man of medium height and square English build step down from the smoking car and look indifferently about him.

There was the usual throng of gaping and curious villagers, and some of them heard the stranger say, as he advanced toward the doctor, who waited with his small medicine case in his hand—

"Pardon me; is this doctor—doctor Barnes?" And when the doctor nodded he asked quickly, "How is she?"

"Still unnerved and weak. We have had a terrible shock, for all of us."

When the two men had left the crowd of curious loungers behind them the doctor said—

"It is awfully good of you, Ferrars, to come so promptly at my call. Of course, I could not explain over the wires. But, you understand."

"I understand that you needed me, and as I'm good for very little, save in one capacity, I, of course, supposed there was a case for me. The evening paper, however, gave me—or so I fancy—a hint of the business. Is it the young schoolmaster?"

The doctor started. It seemed impossible that the news had already found its way into print.

"Some one has made haste," he said, scornfully.

"Some one always does in these cases, and the _Journal_ has a 'special correspondent' in every town and village in the country almost. It was only a few lines." He glanced askance at his companion as he spoke. "And it was reported an accident or suicide."

"It was a murder!"

"I thought so."

"You—why?"

"'The victim was found,' so says the paper, 'face downward, or nearly so.' 'Fallen forward,' those were the words. Was that the case?"

"Yes."

"Well, did you ever see or hear of a suicide who had fallen directly forward and face downward, supposing him to have shot himself?"

"No, no."

"On the other hand, have you ever noted that a man taken unawares, shot from the side, or rear, falls forward? If shot standing, that is. It is only when he receives a face charge that he falls backward."

"I had not thought of that, and yet it looks simple and rational enough," and then, while they walked down the quiet street running parallel with Main, and upon which Mrs. Marcy's cottage stood, the doctor told the story of the morning, briefly but clearly, adding, at the end, "In telling this much, I am telling you actually all that I know."

"All—concerning Miss Grant, too?"

"Everything."

The doctor did not lift his eyes from the path before them, and again the detective shot a side glance from the corner of his eye, and the shadow of a smile crossed his face.

"How does it happen that this brother is here so—I was about to say—opportunely?"

"He told me that he came by appointment, but on an earlier train than he had at first intended to take, to pass Sunday with his brother."

"Now see," mused Ferrars, "what little things, done or left undone, shape or shorten our lives! If he had telegraphed to his brother announcing his earlier arrival, there would have been no target practice, but a walk to the station instead."

The doctor sighed, and for a few moments walked on in silence. Then, as they neared the cottage he almost stopped short and turned toward the detective.

"I'm afraid you will think me a sad bungler, Ferrars. I should have told you at once that Robert Brierly awaits us at Mrs. Marcy's cottage."

"Robert Brierly? Is that his name? I wonder if he can be the Robert Brierly who has helped to make one of our morning papers so bright and breezy. A rising young journalist, in fact. But it's probably another of the name."

"I don't know. He has not spoken of himself. Will it suit you to meet him at once?"

"We don't often get the chance to begin as would best suit us, we hunters of our kind. I would have preferred to go first to the scene of the death, but I suppose the ground has been trampled over and over, and, besides, I don't want to advertise myself until I am better informed at least. Go on, we will let our meeting come as it will."

But things seldom went on as they would for long, when Frank Ferrars was seeking his way toward a truth or fact. They found Mrs. Marcy at the door, and she at once led them to the upper room which looked out upon the side and rear of the little lawn, and was screened from inlookers, as well as from the sun's rays, by tall cherry trees at the side, and thick and clinging morning glory vines at the back.

"You'll be quite safe from intrusion here," she murmured, and left them as she had received them at the door.

If Doctor Barnes had feared for his patient's strength, and dreaded the effect upon her of the coming interview, he was soon convinced that he had misjudged the courage and will power of this slight, soft-eyed, low-voiced and unassertive young woman. She was very pale, and her eyes looked out from their dark circles like wells of grief. But no tears fell from them, and the low pathetic voice did not falter when she said, after the formal presentation, and before either of the others had spoken:

"I have asked to be present at this interview, Mr. Ferrars, and am told that it rests with you whether I am admitted to your confidences. Charles Brierly is my betrothed, and I would to God I had yielded to his wish and married him a week ago. Then no one could have shut me out from ought that concerns him, living or dead. In the sight of heaven he is my husband, for we promised each other eternal faithfulness with our hands clasped above his mother's Bible."

Francis Ferrars was a singular mixture of sternness and gentleness, of quick decision at need and of patient considerateness, and he now took one of the cold little hands between his own, and gently but firmly led her to the cosy chair from which she had arisen.

"You have proved your right to be here, and no one will dispute it. We may need your active help soon, as much as we need and desire your counsel and your closer knowledge of the dead man now."

In moments of intense feeling conventionalities fall away from us and strong soul speaks to strong soul. While they awaited the coming of the doctor and Francis Ferrars, Hilda Grant and Robert Brierly had been unable to break through the constraint which seemed to each to be the mental attitude of the other, and then, too, both were engrossed with the same thought, the coming of the detective, and the possibilities this suggested, for underlying the grievous sorrow of both brother and sweetheart lay the thought, the silent appeal for justice as inherent in our poor human nature as is humanity itself.

But Hilda's sudden claim, her prayer for recognition struck down the barrier of strangeness and the selfishness of sorrow, than which sometimes nothing can be more exclusive, in the mind and heart of Robert Brierly, and he came swiftly to her side, as she sank back, pallid and panting, upon her cushions.

"Miss Grant, my sister; no other claim is so strong as yours. It was to meet you, to know you, that I set out for this place to-day. In my poor brother's last letter—you shall read it soon—he said, 'I am going to give you something precious, Rob; a sister. It is to meet her that I have asked you to come just now.' I claim that sister, and need her now if never before. Don't look upon me as a stranger, but as Charlie's brother, and yours." He placed his hand over hers as it rested weakly upon the arm of her chair, and as it turned and the chill little fingers closed upon his own, he held it for a moment and then, releasing it gently, drew a seat beside her and turned toward the detective.

"Mr. Ferrars, your friend has assured me that I may hope for your aid. Is that so?"

"When I have heard all that you can tell me, I will answer," replied Ferrars. "If I see a hope or chance of unravelling what now looks like a mystery—should it be proved a mystery—I will give you my promise, and my services."

He had seated himself almost opposite Hilda Grant, and while he quietly studied her face, he addressed the doctor.

"Tell me," he said, "all you know and have been told by others, and be sure you omit not the least detail."

Beginning with the appearance of Mr. Doran at his office door, with the panting and perspiring black pony, the doctor detailed their drive and his first sight of the victim, reviewing his examination of the body in detail, while the detective listened attentively and somewhat to the surprise of the others, without interruption, until the narrator had reached the point when, accompanied by Brierly, he had followed the hearse, with its pitiful burden, back to the village. Then Ferrars interposed.

"A moment, please," taking from an inner pocket a broad, flat letter-case and selecting from it a printed card, which, with a pencil, he held out to the doctor. "Be so good," he said, "as to sketch upon the blank back of this the spot where you found the dead man, the mound in full, with the road indicated, above and beyond it. I remember you used to be skilful at sketching things."

CHAPTER V
IN CONSULTATION

When the doctor had completed his hasty sketch, he returned the card upon which it was made, to the detective and silently awaited his comment.

"It is very helpful," said Ferrars. "It would seem, then, that just opposite the mound the lake makes an inward curve?"

"Yes."

"And that the centre of the mound corresponds to the central or nearest point of the curve?"

The doctor nodded assent.

"Now am I right in thinking that anything occurring at this central point would be unseen from the road?"

"Quite right. The mound rises higher than the road, and its length shuts off the view at either end, that and the line of the road, which curves away from the lake at the north end, and runs in an almost straight direction for some distance at the other."

"I see." And again for a moment Ferrars consulted the sketch. Then—

"Did you measure the distance between the target and the spot where the body was found?"

"No. It was the usual distance for practice, I should think."

"It was rather a long range," interposed Brierly. "I am something of a shot myself and I noticed that."

Again the detective pondered over the sketch.

"By this time I dare say," he said presently, "there will be any number of curious people in the wood and about that spot."

"I doubt it," replied Doctor Barnes. "I thought of that, and spoke to Doran. Mr. Brierly was so well liked by all that it only needed a word to keep the men and boys from doing anything that might hinder a thorough investigation. Two men are upon the road just below the school-house to turn back the thoughtless curious ones. It was Doran's foresight," added the honest physician. "I suppose you will wish to explore the wood near the mound?"

Ferrars laid aside the sketch. "As the coroner," he said, "you can help me. Of course, you can have no doubt as to the nature of the shooting. There could be no mistake."

"None. The shot at the back could not have been self-inflicted."

"Then if you can rely upon your constables and this man Doran, let them make a quiet inquiry up and down the wood road in search of any one who may have driven over it between the hours of——"

"Eight and ten o'clock," said Hilda Grant. "He," meaning her late friend, "left his boarding place at eight o'clock, or near it, and he was found shortly before ten."

Her speech was low and hesitating, but it did not falter.

"Thank you," said the detective, and turned again to the doctor.

"Next," said he, "if you can find a trusty man, who will find out for us if any boat or boats have been seen about the lake shore during those hours, it will be another step in the right direction. And now, you have told me that you suspect no one; that there is no clue whatever." He glanced from one to the other. "Still we are told that very often by those who should know best, but who were not trained to such searching. To begin, I must know something, Mr. Brierly, about your brother and his past. Is he your only brother?"

"Yes. We lost a sister ten years ago, a mere child. There were no other children."

"And—your parents?"

"Are both dead."

"Ah! Mr. Brierly, give me, if you please, a sketch of your life and of your brother's, dating, let us say, from the time of your father's death."

If the request was unexpected or unwelcome to Robert Brierly he made no sign, but began at once.

"If I do not go into details sufficiently, Mr. Ferrars," he said, by way of preamble, "you will, of course, interrogate me."

The detective nodded, and Brierly went on.

"My father was an Episcopalian clergyman, and, at the time of his death, we were living in one of the wealthy suburbs of Chicago, where he had held a charge for ten years, and where we remained for six years after he gave up the pulpit. Being in comfortable circumstances, we found it a most pleasant place of residence. My sister's death brought us our first sorrow, and it was soon followed by the loss of our mother. We continued to live, however, in the old home until my brother and I were ready to go to college, and then my father shut up the house and went abroad with a party of congenial friends. My father was not a business man, and the man to whom he had confided the management of his affairs misarranged them during his absence, to what extent we never fully knew until after my father's death, when we found ourselves, after all was settled, with something like fifteen thousand dollars each, and our educations. My brother had already begun to prepare for the ministry, and I had decided early to follow the career of a journalist."

"Are you the elder?" asked the detective.

"Yes." Brierly paused for further comment, but none came, and he resumed. "It had been the intention of my father that my brother and I should make the tour of the two continents when our studies were at an end; that is, our school days. He had made this same journey in his youth, and he had even mapped out routes for us, and told us of certain strange and little explored places which we must not miss, such as the rock temples of Kylas in Central India, and various wonders of Egypt. It was a favourite project of his. 'It will leave you less money, boys,' he used to say, 'but it will give what can never be taken from you. When a man knows his own world, he is better fitted for the next.' And so, after much discussion we determined to make the journey. Indeed, to Charley it began to seem a pilgrimage, in which love, duty, and pleasure intermingled."

He paused, and Hilda turned away her face as a long sighing breath escaped his lips.

"Shortly after our return I took up journalistic work in serious earnest, and my brother, having been ordained, was about to accept a charge when he met with an accident which was followed by a long illness. When he arose from this, his physicians would not hear of his assuming the labours of a pastor over a large and active suburban church, and, as my brother could not bear to be altogether idle, and the country was thought to be the place for him, it ended in his coming here, to take charge of the little school. He was inordinately fond of children, and a born instructor, so it seemed to me. He was pleased with the beauty of the place and the quiet of it, from the first, and he was not long in finding his greatest happiness here."

His voice sank, and he turned a face in which gratitude and sorrow blended, upon the girl who suddenly covered her own with her trembling hands.

But the detective, with a new look of intentness upon his face, and without a moment's pause, asked quickly.

"Then you have been in this place before, of course?"

"No, I have not. For the first three months Charley was very willing to come to me, in the city. Then came a very busy time for me and he came twice, somewhat reluctantly, I thought. Six months ago I was sent to New Mexico to do some special work, and returned to the city on Tuesday last." His voice broke, and he got up and walked to the window farthest from the group.

While he had been speaking, Ferrars had scribbled aimlessly and a stroke at a time, as it seemed, upon the margin of the printed side of the card which bore the sketch made by Doctor Barnes; and now, while Hilda's face was again turned away, the young man at the window still stood with his back towards all in the room, he pushed the card from the edge of the table, and shot a significant glance toward the doctor.

Picking up the card, Doctor Barnes glanced at it carelessly, and then replaced it upon the table, having read these words—

"I wish to speak with her alone. Make it a professional necessity."

As Brierly turned toward them once more the detective turned to the young girl. "I would like to hear something from you, Miss Grant, if you find yourself equal to it."

Hilda set her lips in firm lines, and after a moment said steadily—

"I am quite at your service."

"One minute." The doctor arose and addressed himself to the detective.

"I feel sure that it will be best for Miss Grant that she talk with you alone. As her physician, I will caution her against putting too great a restraint upon herself, upon her feelings. While you talk with her, Ferrars, Mr. Brierly and I will go back to my quarters, unless you bid us come back."

"I do not," interposed the detective. "I will join you soon, and if need be, you can then return, doctor."

At first it seemed as if Hilda were about to remonstrate. But she caught the look of intelligence that flashed from his eyes to hers, and she sat in silence while Doctor Barnes explained the route to his cottage and murmured a low good-bye, while Brierly took her hand and bent over her with a kind adieu.

"I may see you to-morrow," he whispered. "You will let me come, sister?" The last word breathed close to her ear.

Her lips moved soundlessly, but he read her eager consent in her timid return of his hand clasp and the look in her sad, grey eyes, and followed the doctor from the room.

When Frank Ferrars had closed the door behind the two men, he wasted no time in useless words, but, seating himself opposite the girl, and so close that he could catch, if need be, her faintest whisper, he began, his own tones low and touched with sympathy—

"Miss Grant," he said, "I already feel assured that you know how many things must be considered before we can ever begin such a search as I foresee before me. Of course it may happen that before the end of the coroner's inquest some clue or key to the situation may have developed. But, if I have heard all, or, rather, if there has not been some important fact or feature overlooked, we must go behind the scenes for our data, our hints and possible clues. Do you comprehend me?"

Hilda Grant had drawn herself erect, and was listening intently with her clear eyes fixed upon his face, and she seemed with her whole soul to be studying this man, while, with her ears she took in and comprehended his every word.

"You mean," she answered slowly, "that there may be something in himself or some event or fact in his past, or that of his family, which has brought about this?" She turned away her face. She could not put the awful fact into words.

"I knew you would understand me, and it is not to his past alone that I must look for help, but to others."

"Do you mean mine?"

"Yes. You do understand!"

There was a look of relief in his eyes. His lips took on a gentler curve. "I see that you are going to help me."

"If it is in my power, I surely am. Where shall we begin?"

"Tell me all that you can about Charles Brierly, all that he has told you about himself. Will it be too hard?"

"No matter." She drew herself more erect. "I think if you will let me tell my own story briefly, and then fill it out at need, by interrogation, it will be easiest for me."

"And best for me. Thank you." He leaned back and rested his hands upon the arms of his chair.

"I am ready to hear you," he said, and withdrew his full gaze from her face, letting his eyelids fall and sitting thus with half-closed eyes.

"Of course," she began, "it was only natural, or so it appeared to me, that we should become friends soon, meeting, as we must, daily, and being so constantly brought together, as upper and under teachers in this little village school. He never seemed really strange to me, and we seemed thrown upon each other for society, for the young people of the village held aloof, because of our newness, and our position, I suppose, and the people of the hotels and boarding-houses found, naturally, a set, or sets, by themselves. I grew up in what you might call a religious atmosphere, and when I knew that he was a minister of the gospel, I felt at once full confidence in him and met his friendly advances quite frankly. I think we understood each other very soon. You perhaps have not been told that he filled a vacancy, taking the place of a young man who was called away because of his mother's illness, and who did not return, giving up the school at her request. It was in April, a year ago, that he—Charlie—took up the work, coming back, as I did, after the summer vacation. It was after that that he began telling me about himself a little; to speak often of his brother, who was, to his eyes, a model of young manhood and greatly his intellectual superior."

She paused a moment, and then with a little proud lifting of her rounded chin, resumed—

"I was not quite willing to agree as to the superiority; for Charles Brierly was as bright, as talented and promising a young man, as good and as modest as any I ever knew or hope to know, and I have met some who rank high as pastors and orators."

"I can well believe you," he said, with his eyes upon her face, and his voice was sincere and full of sympathy.

"We were not engaged until quite recently. Although we both, I think, understood ourselves and each other long before. And now, what more can I say? He has told me much of his school days, of his student life, and, of course, of his brother's also. In fact, without meaning it, he has taught me to stand somewhat in awe of this highly fastidious, faultless and much-beloved brother, but I have heard of no family quarrel, no enemy, no unpleasant episode of any sort. For himself, he told me, and I believe his lightest word, that he never cared for any other woman; had never been much in women's society, in fact, owing to his almost constant study and travel. Here in the village all was his friends; his pupils were all his adorers, young and old alike were his admirers, and he had room in his heart for all. No hand in Glenville was ever raised against him, I am sure."

"You think then that it was perhaps an accident, a mistake?" He was eyeing her keenly from beneath his drooping lashes.

"No!" She sprang suddenly to her feet and stood erect before him. "No, Mr. Ferrars, I do not! I cannot. I was never in my life superstitious. I do not believe it is superstition that compels me to feel that Charles Brierly was murdered of intent, and by an enemy, an enemy who has stalked him unawares, for money perhaps, and who has planned cunningly, and hid his traces well."

CHAPTER VI
WHICH?

"Give me a few moments of your time, doctor, after your guest has retired for the night."

For more than two hours after his parting with Hilda Grant, Ferrars had talked, first with Robert Brierly alone, and then with the doctor as a third party. At the end, the three had gone together to look upon the face of the dead, and now, as the doctor nodded over his shoulders and silently followed, or, rather, guided Brierly from the room and toward his sleeping apartment, the detective turned back, and when they were out of hearing, removed the covering from the still face, and taking a lamp from the table near, stood looking down upon the dead.

"No," he murmured at last, as he replaced the lamp and turned back to the side of the bier. "You never earned such a fate. You must have lived and died a good man; an honest man, and yet——" He turned quickly at the sound of the opening door. "Doctor, come here and tell me how your keen eyes and worldly intelligence weighed, measured and gauged this man who lies here with that look, that inscrutable look they all wear once they have seen the mystery unveiled. What manner of man did you find him?"

Doctor Barnes came closer and gazed reverently down upon the dead face.

"There lies a man who could better afford to face the mystery suddenly, without warning, than you or I or any other living man I know. A good man, a true Christian gentleman I honestly believe, too modest perhaps to ever claim and hold his true place in this grasping world. That he should be struck down by the hand of an assassin is past belief, and yet——" He paused abruptly and bent down to replace the covering over the still, handsome face.

"And yet," repeated the detective, "do you really think that this man was murdered?"

"Ferrars!" Both men were moving away from the side of the bier, one on either hand, and, as they came together at its foot, the speaker put a hand upon the shoulder of the detective. "To-morrow I hope you will thoroughly overlook the wood road beyond the school house, the lake shore, from the village to the knoll or mound; and the thin strip of wood between, and then tell me if you think it possible for any one, however stupid or erratic of aim, to shoot by accident a man standing in that place. There is no spot from which a bullet could have been fired whence a man could not have been seen perfectly by that figure by the lake side. The trees are so scattered, the bushes so low, the view up and down so open. It's impossible!"

"That is your fixed opinion?"

"It is. Nothing but actual proof to the contrary would change it."

When they had passed from the room and the doctor had softly closed the door, leaving the dead alone in the silence and the shaded lamp-light, they paused again, face to face, in the outer office.

"Have you any suggestions as regards the inquest, Ferrars?" asked the one.

"I have been thinking about that foolish lad, the one who saw poor Brierly in the wood. Could you get him here before the inquiry? We might be able to learn more in this way. You know the lad, of course?"

"Of course. There will be very little to be got from him. But I'll have him here for you."

"Do so. And the lady, the one who drove the pony; you will call her, I suppose?"

"Certainly."

"That is all, I think. If you can drive me to the spot very early, before we breakfast even, I would like it. You need not stop for me. I can find my way back, prefer to, in fact. You say it is not far?"

"Little more than half a mile from the school-house."

"Then—good night, doctor."

Doctor Barnes occupied a six-room cottage with a mansard, and he had fitted up the room originally meant to be a sitting-room, for his own sleeping apartment. It was at the front of the main cottage, and back of it was the inner office where the body lay, the outer office being in a wing built out from this rear room and opening conveniently outward, in view of the front entrance, and very close to a little side gate. A porch fitted snugly into the angle made by the former sitting-room and this outer office, and both of these rooms could be entered from this convenient porch. Robert Brierly occupied the room opposite that assigned the detective with the width of the hall between them, and the doctor, although Ferrars did not know this, had camped down in his outer office.

Half an hour after he had parted from the doctor, Frank Ferrars, as he was called by his nearest and most familiar friends, opened the door upon the corner porch and stepped noiselessly out. When he believed that he had found an unusual case—and he cared for no others—he seldom slept until he had thought out some plan of work, adopted some theory, or evolved a possibility, or, as he whimsically termed it, a "stepping stone" toward clearer knowledge.

He had answered the doctor's summons with little thought of what it might mean, or lead to, and simply because it was from "Walt." Barnes. Then he had heard the doctor's brief story with some surprise, and an inclination to think it might end, after all, in a case of accidental shooting, or self-inflicted death. But when he looked into the woeful eyes of lovely Hilda Grant, and clasped the hand of the dead man's brother, the case took on a new interest. Here was no commonplace village maiden hysterical and forlorn, no youth breathing out dramatic vows of vengeance upon an unknown foe. At once his heart went out to them, his sympathy was theirs, and the sympathy of Francis Ferrars was of a very select nature indeed.

And thus he had looked at the beautiful refined face of the dead man, a face that told of gentleness, sweetness, loyalty, all manifest in the calm dignity of death. Not a strong face, as his brother's face was strong, but manly with the true Christian manliness, and strong with the strength of truth. Looking upon this face, all thought of self-destruction forsook the detective, and he stood, after that first long gaze, vowed to right this deadly wrong in the only way left to a mortal.

But how strange that such a man, in such a place, should be snatched out of life by the hand of an assassin! He must think over it, and he could think best when passing slowly along some quiet by-way or street. So he closed his door softly, and all unconscious that he was observed from the window of the outer office, he vaulted across the low fence, striking noiselessly upon the soft turf on the further side; and, after a moment of hesitation, turned the corner and went down Main Street.

Past the shops, the fine new church, the two hotels, one new and one old. Past the little park and around it to the street, terraced and tree planted, where the more pretentious dwellings and several modish new houses, built for the summer boarder, stood. It was a balmy night. Every star seemed out, and there was a moon, bright, but on the wane.

Ferrars walked slowly upon the soft turf, avoiding the boards and stones of the walks and street crossings. Now and then he paused to look at some fair garden, lovely in the moonlight, or up at the stars, and once, at least, at a window, open to the breezes of night and revealing that which sent Ferrars homeward presently with a question on his lips. He paced the length of the terraced street, and passed by the cottage where Hilda Grant waked and wept perchance, and as he re-entered his room silently and shadow-like, he said to himself—

"Is it fate or Providence that prompts us to these reasonless acts? I may be wrong, I may be mistaken, but I could almost believe that I have found my first clue."

And yet he had heard nothing, and yet all he had seen was a woman's shadow, reflected fitfully by the waning moon, as she paced her room to and fro, to and fro, like some restless or tormented animal, and now and then lifted her arms aloft in despair? in malediction? in triumph? in entreaty?—which?

In spite of his brief rest, if rest it was, Ferrars was astir before sunrise: but, even so, he found the doctor awake before him, and his horse in waiting at the side gate.

They drove swiftly and were soon within sight of the Indian Mound.

"Show me first the place where the body was found," Ferrars had said to his guide as they set out, and when the two stood at this spot, which some one had marked with two small stakes, and the doctor had answered some brief questions regarding the road through the fringe of wood, the mound, and the formation of the lake shore further south or away from the town, the detective announced his wish to be left alone to pursue his work in his own way.

"Your guest will be astir early if I am not much mistaken," he said. "And you have Miss Grant to look after, and may be wanted for a dozen reasons before I return. I can easily walk back, and think you will see me at the breakfast hour, which you must on no account delay."

Two hours later, and just as the doctor's man had announced breakfast, the detective returned, and at once joined the two in the dining-room.

He said nothing of his morning excursion, but the doctor's quick eye noted his look of gravity, and a certain preoccupation of manner which Ferrars did not attempt to hide. Before the meal was ended Doctor Barnes was convinced that something was puzzling the detective, and troubling him not a little.

After breakfast, and while Brierly was for the moment absent from the porch where they had seated themselves with their cigars, Ferrars asked—

"Where does the lady live who drove Mr. Doran's black pony yesterday. Is it at an hotel?"

"It is at the Glenville, an aristocratic family hotel on the terrace. She is a Mrs. Jamieson."

"Do you know her?"

"She sent for me once to prescribe for some small ailment not long ago."

"Has she been summoned?"

"She will be."

"If there was any one in the woods, or approaching the mound by the road from the south, she should have seen them, or him; even a boat might have been seen through the trees for some distance southward, could it not?"

"Yes. For two miles from the town the lake is visible from the wood road. Ah! here comes Doran and our constable."

For half an hour the doctor was busy with Doran, the constable, and a number of other men who had or wished to have some small part to play in this second act of the tragedy, the end of which no one could foresee. Then, having dispatched them on their various missions, the doctor set out to inquire after the welfare of Hilda Grant; and Robert Brierly, who could not endure his suspense and sorrow in complete inaction, asked permission to accompany him, thus leaving the detective, who was quite in the mood for a little solitude just then, in possession of the porch, three wicker chairs and his cigar.

But not for long. Before he had smoked and wrinkled his brows, as was his habit when things were not developing to his liking, and pondered ten minutes alone, he heard the click of the front gate, and turned in his chair to see a lady, petite, graceful, and dressed in mourning, coming toward him with quick, light steps. She was looking straight at him as she came, but as he rose at her approach, she stopped short, and standing a few steps from the porch, said crisply—

"Your pardon. I have made a mistake. I am looking for Doctor Barnes."

"He has gone out for a short time only. Will you be seated, madam, and wait?"

She advanced a step and stopped irresolute.

"I suppose I must, unless," coming close to the lower step, "unless you can tell me, sir, what I wish to know."

"If it is a question of medicine, madam, I fear——"

"It is not," she broke in, her voice dropping to a lower note. "It is about the—the inquiry or examination into the death of the poor young man who—but you know, of course."

"I have heard. The inquest is held at one o'clock."

"Ah! And do you know if the—the witnesses have been notified as yet?"

"They are being summoned now. As the doctor's guest I have but lately heard him sending out the papers."

"Oh, indeed!" The lady put a tiny foot upon the step as if to mount, and then withdrew it. "I think, if I may leave a message with you, sir," she said, "I will not wait."

"Most certainly," he replied.

"I chanced to be driving through the wood yesterday when the body was discovered near the Indian Mound, and am told that I shall be wanted as a witness. I do not understand why."

"Possibly a mere form, which is nevertheless essential."

"I had engaged to go out with a yachting party," she went on, "and before I withdraw from the excursion I wish to be sure that I shall really be required. My name is Mrs. Jamieson, and——"

"Then I can assure you, Mrs. Jamieson, that you are, or will be wanted, at least. My friend has sent a summons to a Mrs. Jamieson of the Glenville House."

"That is myself," the lady said, and turned to go. "Of course then I must be at hand."

She nodded slightly and went away, going with a less appearance of haste down the street and so from his sight.

When she was no longer visible the detective resumed his seat, and relighted his cigar, making, as he did so, this very unprofessional comment—

"I hate to lose sight of a pretty woman, until I am sure of the colour of her eyes."

And yet Francis Ferrars had never been called, in any sense, a "ladies' man."

CHAPTER VII
RENUNCIATION

Ferrars had predicted that nothing would be gained by the inquest, and the result proved him a prophet.

Peter Kramer, the poor half-wit who had given the first clue to the whereabouts of the murdered man, was found, and his confidence won by much coaxing, and more sweets and shining pennies, the only coin which Peter would ever recognise as such. But the result was small. Asked had he seen the teacher, the reply was, "Yep." Asked where, "Most by Injun hill." Asked what doing, "Settin' down."

"Had he heard the pistol fired?" asked the doctor.

"Un! Uh! Heard nawthin."

"And whom did you see, Peter, besides the teacher?"

Again the look of affright in the dull eyes, the arm lifted as in self-protection, and the only word they could coax from his lips was, "Ghost!" uttered in evident fear and trembling.

And this was repeated at the inquest. This, and no more, from Peter.

Mrs. Fry, Charles Brierly's landlady, told how the dead man had appeared at breakfast, and her testimony did not accord with the statement of her little daughter.

"Miss Grant has told me of my little girl's mistake," she said. "Mr. Brierly was down-stairs unusually early that morning, and he did not look quite as well as usual. He looked worried, in fact, and ate little. He was always a small eater, and I said something about his eating even less than usual, I can't recall the exact words. Nellie of course, did not observe his worried look, as I did, and quoted me wrong. Mr. Brierly left the house at once after leaving the table. I did not think of it at first, but it came to me this morning that as he did not carry any books with him, he must of course have meant to come back for them, and——" She paused.

"And, of course," suggested the coroner, "he must have had his pistol upon his person when he came down to breakfast? Is that your meaning?"

"Yes, sir."

The weapon, found near the dead man's hand as it had doubtless fallen from it, was there in evidence, as it had been picked up with two of the chambers empty.

That it was not a case of murder for plunder was proven, or so they thought, by the fact that the dead man's watch was found upon his person; his pockets containing a small sum of money, pencils, knives, note book, a small picture case, closed with a spring, and containing Hilda Grant's picture, and a letter from his brother.

Hilda Grant's brief testimony did not agree with that of Mrs. Fry.

"She saw her lover, alive, for the last time on the evening before his death. He was in good spirits, and if there was anything troubling him he gave no sign of it. He was by nature quiet and rather reserved," she said.

"Yes, she knew his habit of sometimes going to the lake shore beyond the town to practice at target-shooting, but when he did not appear at his post at nine o'clock, she never thought to send to the lake shore at first, because he usually returned from his morning exercise before nine o'clock; and so her first thought had been to send to Mrs. Fry's."

When the doctor and Robert were about to leave the scene of the murder, among other instructions given to Doran had been this:

"Don't say anything in town about Mr. Brierly's arrival; you know how curious our people are, and we would have a lot of our curiosity lovers hovering around my place to see and hear and ask questions. Just caution the others, will you?"

Doran held an acknowledged leadership over the men with whom he consorted, and the group willingly preserved silence. Later, when Doctor Barnes explained to Ferrars how he had kept the curious away from his door, and from Brierly, he thought the detective's gratification because of this rather strange, just at first, and in excess of the cause.

"You couldn't have done a better thing," Ferrars had declared. "It's more than I had ventured to hope. Keep Brierly's identity as close as possible until the inquest is called, and then hold it back, and do not put him on the stand until the last."

After Mrs. Fry, the boy Peter and Hilda Grant had been questioned, Samuel Doran took the witness chair, telling of his summons from Miss Grant, of the separation of the group at the Indian Mound, of his meeting with Mrs. Jamieson, of the discovery made by his two companions and of all that followed. And then Mrs. Jamieson was called.

She had entered the place accompanied by an acquaintance from the Glenville, and they had taken, from choice, as it seemed to them, seats in the rear of the jury, and somewhat aloof from the place where Hilda Grant, Mrs. Marcy, and Mrs. Fry sat. Robert Brierly would have taken his place beside Hilda, but the detective interposed.

"Owing to the precautions of the doctor and Mr. Doran, the fact of your relationship has not leaked out. It appears that Mrs. Fry was not informed of your coming until the evening before, or Thursday evening, and she seems to be a very discreet woman. After the inquest you will be free to devote yourself to Miss Grant. Until then, it is my whim, if you like, to keep you incog."

Of course Brierly acquiesced, but more than once he found himself wondering why this should seem to Ferrars needful.

Mrs. Jamieson came quietly to the witnesses' chair, and took her place. There was a little stir as she came forward, for, while she had been for some weeks in Glenville, and had driven much about its pretty country roads and lanes, she had gone, for the most part, more or less closely veiled in fleecy gauzes of black or white. Afoot she was seldom seen beyond the grounds about the family hotel.

To-day, however, the lady had chosen to wear a Parisian looking gown of dull black silk and a tiny capote of the same material rested upon her blonde and abundant hair, while only the filmiest of white illusion veiled, but did not hide, the pretty face from which the blue eyes looked out and about her, gravely but with perfect self-possession.

She told of her morning drive, and while so doing, Ferrars, sitting a little in the rear of the coroner, slipped into his palm a small card closely written upon both sides. Upon one side was written, "Use these as random shots."

And when she spoke of the man whom she had seen going into the wood near the mound, the doctor interposed his first question.

"Can you describe the person at all? His dress, his bearing?"

"Not distinctly," she replied. "He was going from me and his face, of course, I could not see. In fact, as I have before stated, my pony was fresh, and required my attention. Besides, there was really no reason why I should look a second time at the back of a strange person whom I passed at some little distance. As I seem to recall the figure now, it was that of a rather tall, fair-haired man. I can say no more."

"And at what hour was this?"

"It must have been nearing eight o'clock, I fancy, although being out for pleasure I took little notice of the hour."

No further interruptions were made until she had finished the story of the morning's experience, of her meeting with Doran and the others, of the drive to the village, and of her message to Miss Grant.

"Did you know Miss Grant?"

"Only as I had seen her at church, and upon the street or in the school-yard. We had never met, prior to that morning."

"And Charles Brierly? Did you know him?"

"Only by sight. I know few people in Glenville outside of my ho—of the Glenville House."

Both the doctor and Ferrars noted the unfinished word broken off at the first syllable. To the one it was a riddle; to the other it told something which he might find useful later on.

"Mrs. Jamieson," resumed the coroner, after consulting the detective's card, "how far did you drive yesterday before you turned about upon the wood road?"

For a moment the lady seemed to be questioning her memory. Then she replied.

"The distance in miles, or fractions of miles, I could not give. I turned the pony about, I remember, at the place where the road curves toward the lake, at the old mill, near the opening of the wood."

"Ah, then you could see, of course, for some distance up and down the lake shore?"

"I could!"

There was a hint of surprise in her coldly courteous reply.

"And at that point did you see anything, any one in the wood, or along the lake?"

"I certainly saw no person. But—yes, I do remember that there was a boat at the water's edge, not far from the place where I turned homeward. It was a little beyond, or north of me."

"Did you observe whether there were oars in the boat?"

"I saw none, I am quite sure," the lady replied, and this ended her part in the inquiry.

But now there were some youthful, eager and valuable new witnesses, and their combined testimony amounted to this:

When the body of their beloved teacher had been brought home and the first hour of excitement had passed, three boys, who had been among Charles Brierly's brightest and most mischief loving and adventurous pupils, had set out, a full hour in advance of the elder exploring party, and had followed the lake shore and the wood road, one closely skirting the lake shore, another running through the sparse timber and undergrowth about half way up the shallow slope, and the third trotting down the road beyond; the three keeping pretty nearly parallel, until the discovery, by the lad upon the shore, of the boat drawn out of the water, and in the shade of a tree. This had brought the others down to the lake and then caused them to go hastily back. Meeting the party of men, who were not far behind them, the boys had turned back with them, and now there was a crowd of witnesses to corroborate the story of the boat.

It stood, they all affirmed, in the shade of a spreading tree, so as that no sun rays had beaten upon it, and its sides were still damp from recent contact with the water, while it stood entirely upon the land. Two oars, also showing signs of contact with the lake, were in the little boat, blade ends down, and it was evident that its late occupant had disembarked in haste, for, while the stake by which the boat had been secured, stood scarcely three feet away, and the chain and padlock lay over the edge of the little craft, there had been no effort to secure it, and the oars had the look of having been hastily shipped and left thus without further care.

When the matter of the boat had been fully investigated, the coroner and Ferrars conferred together for some moments, and during these moments Mrs. Jamieson and her companion exchanged some whispered words.

Through some mistake, it would seem, these two had been given places which, while aloof from the strange men, and almost in the rear of the jurors, brought them facing the open door of the inner room, where, in full view, the shrouded body of the murdered man lay, and from the first the eyes of the two seemed held and fascinated by the sight of the long, still figure outlined under the white covering.

"Is it possible," whispered the lady witness, "that we must sit here until the end, face to face with that!" She was trembling slightly, as she spoke. "It is making me nervous."

"And no wonder," murmured her friend. "But it must be almost over. I—I confess to some curiosity. This is such a new and unusual sensation, to be here, you know."

"Ugh!"

Mrs. Jamieson turned away, for the coroner was speaking.

"There is one point," he said, "upon which our witnesses differ, and that is the mental condition of the deceased during the twenty-four hours preceding his death. Another witness will now speak upon this matter. Mr. Robert Brierly, the brother of Charles Brierly, will now testify."

As Robert Brierly came out from the rather secluded place he had heretofore occupied, at the suggestion of the detective, all eyes were fixed upon him. There could be no doubt of his relationship to the deceased. It was the same face, but darker and stronger; the same tall form, but broader and more athletic. The eyes of this man were darker and more resolute than those of his dead brother; his hair was browner, too, and where the face of the one had been full of kindliness and gentle dignity, that of this other was strong, spirited and resolute. But, beyond a doubt, these two were brothers.

There was a stir as Brierly made his way forward, paused before the coroner and faced the jury; and then, as his eyes fell upon the two figures in the rear of that body he made a sudden step forward.

"Doctor!" he called quickly, "you are needed here! A lady has fainted!"

For a moment all was forgotten, save the white face that had fallen back upon her friend's shoulder, and that seemed even whiter because of the black garments, and beneath the halo of fair blonde hair.

"It was that," explained the friend, who proved to be a Mrs. Arthur, pointing toward the shrouded figure in the inner room. "She has been growing more and more nervous for some time."

Robert Brierly was the first at her side, but, as the doctor took his place and he drew back a pace, a hand touched his arm.

"Step aside," whispered Ferrars, "where she cannot see you." And without comprehending but answering a look in the detective's eye, he obeyed.

Mrs. Jamieson did not at once recover, and the doctor and Ferrars carried her across the hall and into the room lately occupied by Brierly. As Mrs. Arthur followed them, it seemed to her that the detective, whom of course she did not know as such, was assuming the leadership, and that half a dozen quick words were spoken by him to the doctor, across her friend's drooping head.

"She must be removed immediately," said the doctor a moment after. "Let some one find a carriage or phæton at once." Then, as Ferrars did not move from his place beside the bed where they had placed the unconscious woman, he strode to the chamber door, said a word or two to Doran, who had followed them as far as the door, and came back to his place beside the bed.

Before Mrs. Jamieson had opened her eyes a low wagonette was at the door, and when the lady became conscious and had been raised and given a stimulating draught, she was lifted again by Ferrars and Doctor Barnes and carried to the waiting vehicle, followed by Mrs. Arthur.

"Kindly take the place beside the driver, madam," directed the doctor. "My friend will go with the lady and assist her; it will be best. It is possible that she may faint again." And so they drove away, Mrs. Arthur beside Doran, the driver; and Mrs. Jamieson, still pallid and tremulous, leaning upon the supporting shoulder of Ferrars, silent and with closed eyes.

As he lifted her from the wagonette, and assisted her up the steps and within the door, however, the lady seemed to recover herself with an effort. She had crossed the threshold supported by Ferrars on the one side, and leaning upon her friend's arm upon the other, and at the door of the reception room she turned, saying faintly:

"Let me rest here first. Before we go upstairs, I mean." Then, withdrawing her hand from her friend's arm, she seemed to steady herself, and standing more erect, turned to Ferrars.

"I must not trouble you longer, now, sir. You have been most kind." Her voice faltered, she paused a moment, and then held out her hand. "I should like very much to hear the outcome," she hesitated.

"With your permission," the detective replied quickly, "I will call to ask after your welfare, and to inform you if I can." He turned to go, but she made a movement toward him.

"That poor girl," she said, "I pity her so. Do you know her well, sir?" She was quite herself now, but her voice was still weak and tremulous.

"You have not heard, I see, that she is my cousin."

"No. I would like to call upon her. Will you ask her if I may?" He nodded and she added quickly, "And call, if you please, to-morrow."

Robert Brierly told his story almost without interruption; all that he knew of his brother's life in the village; of his own; of his coming earlier than he was expected, and of his firm belief that his brother had been made the victim of foul play. Possibly killed by mistake, because of some fancied resemblance; for his life, which had been like an open book to all his friends, held no secrets, no "episodes," and enemies he never had one. In short, he could throw no light upon the mystery of his brother's death. Rather, his story made that death seem more mysterious than at first because of the possibilities that it rendered at least probable.

But this evidence had its effect upon a somewhat bucolic jury. That Charles Brierly had been shot by another hand than his own had been very clearly demonstrated, for his brother would have no doubt whatever left upon this point; while he little knew how much the judicious whispers and hints uttered in the right places, and with apparent intent of confidence and secrecy, had to do with the shaping of the verdict, which was as follows:

> "We, the jury, find that the deceased, Charles
> Brierly, died from a bullet wound, fired, accord-
> ing to our belief, by mistake or accident, and at
> the hands of some person unknown."

And now came the question of proof.

"It must be cleared up," said Robert Brierly to the detective. "I am not a rich man, Mr. Ferrars, but all that I have shall be spent at need to bring the truth to light. For I can never rest until I have learned it. It is my duty to my dead brother, father, mother—all."

And late that night, alone in his room he looked out upon the stars hung low upon the eastern horizon and murmured—

"Ah, Ruth, Ruth, we were far enough asunder before, and now—Ah, it was well to have left you your freedom, for now the gulf is widening; it may soon, it will soon be impassable." And he sighed heavily, as a strong man sighs when the tears are very near his eyes and the pain close to his heart.

CHAPTER VIII

TRICKERY

As was quite natural, the three men, thrown so strangely and unexpectedly together at the doctor's cottage, sat up late after the inquest, and discussed the strange death of Charles Brierly in all its bearings. As a result of this they slept somewhat late, except the detective, who let himself out of the house at sunrise, and lighting a cigar, set off for a short walk, up one certain street, and down another. He walked slowly, and looked indolently absorbed in his cigar. But it was a very observant eye that noted, from under the peak of his English cap, the streets, the houses, and the very few stray people whom he passed. It was not the people, though, in whom he was chiefly interested. Ferrars was intently studying the topography of the town, at least of that portion of it which he was then traversing with such seeming aimlessness.

From the doctor's cottage he had sauntered north for several blocks, crossed over, until he reached the upper or terraced street, and followed it until he had reached the southern edge of the village and was in sight of the school-house not far beyond. Turning here he crossed a street or two, and was nearing the house where the dead school teacher had lived, when he saw the front door of the house open, and a woman come out and hasten away in the direction in which he was moving. She hurried on like one intent upon some absorbing errand, and, knowing the house as the late home of Charles Brierly, and the woman as its mistress, Ferrars quickened his steps that he might keep her in sight, and when she turned the corner leading directly to the doctor's cottage he further increased his speed, feeling instinctively that her errand, whatever its nature, would take her there.

He was not far behind her now, and he saw the doctor standing alone upon the side porch, saw the woman enter at the side gate, and the meeting of the two.

Mrs. Fry, with her back towards him, was making excited gestures, and the face of the doctor, visible above her head, changed from a look of mild wonder to such sudden anxiety and amazement that the detective halted at the gate, hesitating, and was seen at that instant by the doctor, who beckoned him on with a look of relief.

"Look here, Ferrars," he began, and then turned to assure himself that Brierly had not arisen, and was not observing them from the office window. "Come this way a few steps," moving away from the porch and halting where the shadow of the wing hid them from view from within the main dwelling. "And now, Mrs. Fry, please tell Mr. Grant what you had begun to tell me. I want his opinion on it. He's not a bad lawyer."

"A good detective'd be the right thing, I think," declared the woman. "It's about Mr. Brierly's room, sir. He had a small bedroom, and another opening out from it, where he used to read and study. You know how they were, doctor!"

The doctor nodded silently.

"Well, last night, you remember, when you brought this gentleman and his brother to my place to look at the rooms. You or he decided not to go up then, but told me to close the rooms, and he would come to-morrow—to-day—that would be."

"Yes, yes!" said the doctor, impatiently, "we remember all that, Mrs. Fry."

"Well, I'd had the rooms locked ever since I heard that he was dead." Mrs. Fry was growing somewhat hazy as to her pronouns. "And I had the key in my pocket. Then, well, after a while I lit the lamp in the sittin' room so's it wouldn't seem so gloomy in the house, and went out and sat on my side stoop, and after a little my neighbour on that side, Mrs. Robson, came acrost the lawn—there aint no fence between, ye know—and we talked for some time, and my little girl fell asleep with her head in my lap.”

“Don’t be too long with the story,” broke in the doctor. “I don’t want it to spoil Mr. Brierly’s breakfast, for he needs it badly.”

“Yes, sir. Well, just about that time—it must have been half-past eight, I guess—and there was plenty of folks all along the street, a boy came running across the lawn and right up to me.

“‘If you please,’ he says, touching his hat rim, ‘Mr. Brierly, down to the doctor’s, forgot to get the key to his brother’s room, and he sent me to get it for him.’ I s’pose I was foolish. I felt hurt, thinkin’ he couldn’t trust me with his brother’s things, an’ so I jest hands out the key and no questions asked.”

A look of sudden alertness shot from the eyes of the detective, and he arrested the doctor’s evident impatience by a quick shake of the head unperceived by the woman, who was addressing her narrative to the doctor, as was natural.

“I s’pose,” she went on, “that I shouldn’t a’ done it, but I didn’t scent anything wrong then. Mrs. Robson went home in a few minutes, and then I roused my little girl up and took her in and put her to bed. She was asleep again a’most as soon as her head touched the pillow, and the night was so pleasant-like that I threw my shawl on my shoulders and went out onto the front stoop. I felt sort o’ lonesome in the house all alone.”

“Of course,” commented Ferrars, seeing the dread of their criticism or displeasure that was manifest in her face as she paused and looked from one to the other. “One naturally would in your place.”

“Yes, I suppose so,” she went on, reassured. “Well, I hadn’t been out there two minutes when that same boy came running up the walk, all out of breath, and says, sort of panting between words, ‘Ma’am, the lady that lives next the engine-house by the corner stopped me just now an’ asked me to come back here an’ beg you to come down there quick! Her little boy’s got himself burned awful!’”

“Ah! I see!” Ferrars spoke low, as if to himself, and his face wore the look of one who is beginning to understand a riddle. “You went, of course?”

“Yes, I went.”

“Go on with the story, please. Tell it all as you have begun. Let us have the details,” and he again nodded toward the doctor, who was regarding him with profound surprise, and put a finger to his lip.

"My sister-in-law lives in the house by the engine-house," Mrs. Fry hurried on, "and knowing how careless she is about keepin' things in the house against such times, I ran back into my bedroom and got a bottle of camphor and a roll of cotton batt. 'Run ahead, boy,' I says to the boy, 'an' tell her I am coming; I must lock up my doors and winders.' 'She's in an awful hurry,' he says, 'cryin' fit to kill. I'll set right down here and watch your house, ma'am; I can do no good there.' The boy spoke so honest, and Mary's boy is such a dear little fellow, that I jest lost my head complete, and ran off down the sidewalk. At the corner I looked back. The boy was sittin' on the doorstep, an' I heard him whistlin'; someway it made me feel quite easy. But when I got to the house and found them all in the sitting-room, and Neddy not hurt at all, but sound asleep on the floor, I was so took back that I just dropped down on a chair and acted like a wild woman. Instead of rushin' back that very minute, I sat there and told how I had been tricked, and scolded about that boy, an' vowed I'd have him well punished, and so on, until Mary reminded me that I'd better get back home and see if the house was all right, or if 'twas only a boy's trick."

"It looked like one, surely," was the detective's easy comment.

"That's what Mr. Jones said. He's my neighbour. He was just going home, and we overtook him. Mary told him about the boy and he laughed and said that some boys had played that sort of trick last summer two or three times, sending people running across the town on some such fool's errand. He thought maybe 'twas some boy that I had offended some way; and then I thought about how crisp I was about givin' the boy Mr. Brierly's key, and it made me feel sort of easier. But Mr. Jones went in with us when we got to my house. We looked all around downstairs and everything was all right. Nellie was fast asleep still, and not a thing had been disturbed. Then we went upstairs, 'just for form's sake,' Mr. Jones said, and looked in all the bedrooms, and even tried Mr. Brierly's door. Everything seemed right, and so Mr. Jones and Mary went away, and I went to bed. But someway I couldn't sleep sound. I felt provoked and angry about that boy, and the more I thought of him, of his being a stranger and all, the uneasier I got. Then I began to imagine I heard queer sounds, and creaking doors, and, right on the heels of all that, came a loud slam that waked Nellie, and made me skip right out of bed."

"A shutter, of course," said the doctor, as she paused for breath.

"Yes, a shutter, and I knew well that every shutter on my house was either shut tight or locked open. I look to that every night, as soon as it's lamp-lighting time; them downstairs I shut, them upstairs I open, sometimes. I knew where that slammin' shutter was by the sound, and it set me to dressing quick. I had opened the shutters on Mr. Brierly's windows that very afternoon, thinking the rooms would not seem quite so dreary and lonesome when his brother came to look through 'em and they was locked open, I knew well! All the same, it was them shutters, or one of 'em, that was clattering then, and I knew it."

"Were you alone in the house, you and your little girl?" asked Ferrars.

"All alone, yes, sir; and I took Nellie with me and went out into the hall——"

"You mean downstairs?"

"Yes, sir. We sleep downstairs. Now, I thought I had seen that everything was right when Mr. Jones and Mary was with me, but when we went into that hall—Doctor—" turning again toward that gentlemen, for she had addressed her later remarks to Ferrars,—"I guess you may remember a shelf just at the foot of the stairs. It's right behind the door, when it stands open, and that's why we hadn't seen it, or I hadn't before. Well, I always set the lamp for Mr. Brierly's room—his bedroom lamp, that is—on that shelf for him every morning, as soon as it had been filled for the night's burning; and the morning he was killed I had put it there as usual, and it had been there ever since. It was there when Mr. Brierly and you two gentlemen called, after the inquest."

A queer little sound escaped the detective's throat, and again he checked the doctor's impatience with that slight movement of the head.

"I don't call myself brave," the woman went on, "but I caught Nellie by the hand—I was carrying my bedroom lamp—and ran up the stairs and straight to Mr. Brierly's door. I don't know what made me do it, but I stooped down to look through the keyhole, and there in the door was the very key I had given to that boy to take to Mr. Brierly's brother."

"What did you do?" asked the doctor, breathlessly.

"I set down my lamp very softly, told Nellie in a whisper not to make a noise, and then very carefully tried the key. It turned in the lock. I didn't dare go in, but I locked the door, left the key in it, and went downstairs and out at the front door. I went around the house and stood under the window of that room. The side window shutter that I had fastened back was swinging loose. I went back to the sitting-room, locking the front door and the doors from the hall into the front room and sitting-room, taking out the key of the front door, and leaving the other keys in the locks, on my side. Then I lit the big lamp, pulled down the curtains, fixed the side door so I could open it quick, and set the big dinner bell close by it. I made Nellie lie down on the lounge with her clothes on, and there I sat till morning. Before daylight I went into the kitchen and moved about very softly to get myself a cup of coffee, and a bite of breakfast for Nellie. I had been careful not to let her see how I was scared, and she went sound asleep right away. As soon as I thought you would be up I awoke my little girl, and left her sitting upon the side stoop, while I came here to you. Mr. Brierly's brother ought to be first to enter that room, and—if there was anyone there last night—they're there yet."

"What room is that which I ought to enter, Mrs. Fry?" said a voice behind them, and turning, all together, they saw Robert Brierly standing at the edge of the porch where it joined the wall of the doctor's room.

"I was afraid of this," muttered Doctor Barnes. But the detective seemed in nowise disconcerted. Neither did he seem inclined to listen, or allow Brierly to listen to a repetition of Mrs. Fry's story.

"You are here just in time, Mr. Brierly," he said, briskly. "Mrs. Fry believes that someone has paid a visit to your brother's room during the night, and as she says, you are the one who should investigate, and I think it ought to be done at once, if you feel up to it."

"I'll be with you in a moment," replied Brierly, promptly, and he went indoors by way of the French windows which had given him egress.

CHAPTER IX

A LETTER

As Robert Brierly entered the house, the detective, now taking the lead as a matter of course, turned toward Mrs. Fry.

"I see that you are anxious to get back home," he said to her. "And it is as well that you go back in advance of us, for people are beginning to move about. Wait for us at the side door." And then, as the woman hastened away, he turned toward the doctor. "You need not feel uneasy because of your guest, Doc.," he said, with his rare and fine smile. "There are times when the physical man is in subjection to the spiritual man, or the will power within him, if you like that better. Brierly has already endured a severe mental strain, I grant, but he's not at the end of his endurance yet. In fact, if he's the journalist, and I begin to think so, he knows how to sustain mental strain long and steadily. You don't fancy he could be persuaded to wait for meat and drink now, do you?"

"My soul, man!" exclaimed Doctor Barnes, "how you do read a man's thoughts! No! Brierly wouldn't stop for anything now. Nor you, either, for that matter, What do you make of this?"

"I can tell you better in an hour from now, I hope. Here's Brierly. Now then, gentlemen, try and look as if this was merely a morning walk. We don't want to excite the curiosity of the neighbours."

There seemed little need of this caution, for they saw no one as they crossed to the quiet street in which Mrs. Fry lived. But Ferrars, who had fallen behind the others, had an observant eye upon all within range, as if, as the doctor afterward declared, he held the very town itself under suspicion.

Mrs. Fry awaited them at the side door, and unlocked the one leading to the front hall and stairway at once.

"I hope one of you has got a pistol," she said, nervously, as they approached the stairs.

"There's no one up there, Mrs. Fry," replied Ferrars. "Never fear." But Mrs. Fry was not so positive. She closed the sitting-room door, all but the merest crack, and stood ready to clap it entirely shut at the first sound of attack and defence from the room above.

Meantime Robert Brierly, who had led the way upstairs, placed a firm hand upon the key, turned it and softly opened the door. Then, for a moment, all three stood still at the threshold, gazing within.

It was Francis Ferrars who spoke the first word, with his hand upon Robert Brierly's shoulder, and his voice little more than a whisper.

"Go inside, Brierly, quickly and quietly." He gave the shoulder under his hand a quick, light, forward pressure, and instinctively, as it seemed, Brierly stepped across the threshold with the other two close at his heels, and, the moment they were inside the room, Ferrars turned and silently withdrew the key from the outer side, closed the door cautiously, and relocked it from within.

"We will do well to dispense with Mrs. Fry, at least for the present," he said, coolly. "It's plain enough there has been mischief here. Mr. Brierly, you saw this room last night, for a moment."

Robert Brierly, who had dropped weakly upon a chair, stopped him with a movement of the hand.

"Mr. Ferrars," he said, "I realise the importance of a right beginning here, and if you will undertake this case—I am not a rich man, you understand—all I have is at your disposal. I could hardly bear to have my brother's rooms searched by strange hands in my absence, but will it not be wise that you should take the lead, and begin as you deem best?"

"Yes," replied the detective, "but your assistance will be helpful."

"Mrs. Fry is coming upstairs," broke in the doctor, who had been standing near the door.

Ferrars sprang across the room, turned the key, and put his head out through the smallest possible opening in the door.

"There's no one here, Mrs. Fry; and nothing missing, that we have observed. It was, no doubt, a boyish trick."

He smiled amiably at the somewhat surprised woman.

"When Mr. Brierly has had time to look about a bit he will of course report to you." And he closed the door in the good woman's astonished face. "Better make no confidants until we know what we have to confide," he said, turning back to survey the room afresh. "Now let us have more light here."

The room in which they were was dimly lighted, for the outer blinds of its three windows had been closed, and all the light afforded them came from the one nearest the front corner, where half the shutter was swinging loosely at the will of the morning breeze. This light, however, enabled them to see that the room was in some confusion, or rather, that it was not in the same neat order in which they had seen it on the previous day.

The writing desk, which later Mrs. Fry declared to have been closed, was now open, and a portion of the contents of its usually neatly arranged pigeon-holes was scattered upon the leaf.

"This," said Brierly, as they approached it, "was closed when I saw it last night."

"I remember," Ferrars nodded, and sat down in the revolving chair before the desk, and, without touching anything, ran his eye carefully over the scattered papers, examined the pigeon-holes, the locks, and even the fine coating of dust.

Upon a round table near the front window were some scattered books, mostly of reference, a pile of unruled manuscript tablets, and a little heap of written sheets. There was a set of bookshelves above the writing-desk, and a wire rack near it was filled with newspapers and magazines.

When Ferrars had carefully noted the appearance of the desk and its contents, he swung slowly around in the swivel chair and gazed all about him without rising. He had noted the books above him with a thoughtful gaze, and he now fixed that same speculative glance upon those upon the table. Then he got up.

"Oblige me by not so much as touching this desk yet," he said, and crossed to the table. "Your brother was a magazinist, Mr. Brierly?" he queried.

"Yes," replied Brierly.

Ferrars turned toward the inner room which the others had not yet approached.

"Ah!" he exclaimed suddenly, and then, in an altered tone, "Here is Mrs. Fry's missing lamp."

His two companions came to the door of the room, where Ferrars was now looking down at the pillows of the bed.

"Brierly," asked Ferrars, as they paused in the doorway, "what had your brother with him in the way of valuables, to your knowledge?"

The young man, who had been looking sharply about the room like one who seeks something which should be there, started slightly.

"Why, he had a somewhat odd and valuable watch, which was given him by our father upon our setting out for Europe. It was like this," and he produced a very beautiful specimen of the watchmaker's art, and held it out for inspection. "He also had a ring set with a fine opal, that was once our mother's, and a locket with her monogram. There were also some odd trifles that he had picked up abroad, saying that they would become his future wife, no doubt."

"And you think these were still in his possession?"

"I do. In writing of Miss Grant not long ago he mentioned as a proof of her refinement and womanly delicacy that she would accept no gifts from him other than books or flowers."

"I think," said Ferrars, gravely, "that we had better have Mrs. Fry in here now, and I want you to do the talking, Brierly. Doctor, if you would ask her to come up, I'll post Mr. Brierly, meantime."

The doctor turned the key in the lock and then hesitated. "I dare say I will not be needed here longer?"

"You!" Ferrars turned upon him quickly. "Is there anything urgent outside?"

"Not especially so—only——"

"Only you fancy yourself _de trop_? If you can spare us the time, we want you right here, doctor. Eh, Mr. Brierly?"

"By all means."

"Then of course I am at your disposal," and the doctor went out in search of Mrs. Fry.

"I wish there were more men with his combined delicacy and good sense," grumbled Ferrars, and then he began to explain to Brierly what was wanted from Mrs. Fry.

When that good woman entered, Ferrars was seated by the furthest window, and Robert Brierly met her at the door.

"Mrs. Fry," he began, "will you kindly look about you, without, of course, disturbing or changing things, and tell us if you see anything that has changed? If you miss anything, or if anything in your opinion, has been tampered with? Look through both rooms carefully, and then give us your opinion."

Mrs. Fry, who had been expecting just such a summons and who fully realised the gravity of the occasion, stood still in her place near the door and looked slowly about her; then she began to walk about the room. Once or twice Brierly, prompted by a glance from the detective, had to warn her against putting a finger upon some object, but she went about with firmly closed lips until she had reached the little sleeping room. Then—

"Well, I declare!" she broke out. "If they haven't even been at the bed!"

Brierly started forward, but Ferrars held up a warning finger.

"And there's that lamp!" she went on, "with the chimney all smoked! Somebody's been carrying it around burning full tilt."

By this time Ferrars was so close beside Brierly that he could breathe a low word in his ear, from time to time, unnoted by the woman as she went peering about.

"You are sure the bed has been disturbed?" Brierly asked.

"Certain of it!"

"And can you guess why?"

"Well, he always kept his pistol under the bolster."

The men started and looked at each other. "What an oversight," murmured the doctor.

"Do you mean," went on the enquiry, "that it was there yesterday morning when you made the bed?"

"I can't say, sir. The fact is, I was awfully afraid of the thing, and when I told him I was, he put it clear under the bolster with his own hand, and said it should stay there, instead of on top, as it used to be at first."

"You don't mean that he left it there during the day?"

"Yes, sir! This one. You see he had two. The one he used to practise with—the one they found—was different. This one was bigger and different somehow, and not like any pistol I ever saw. He told me 'twas a foreign weapon."

"She is right," said Brierly. "My brother brought a pair of duelling pistols from Paris. They were elaborately finished. He gave me one of them." He looked anxiously toward the crushed and displaced pillows. "Shall we not look," he asked, "and find out if anything is there? Will you look, Mr. Ferrars? Or did you?"

Ferrars moved forward. "No, I did not look," he said. "But the weapon is not there; I could almost swear to it. Come—see, all of you."

With a quick light hand he removed the pillows, turned back the sheets and lifted the bolster. There was nothing beneath it, save the impression where the weapon had laid upon the mattress.

The detective turned toward Mrs. Fry. "You are sure it was here usually?" he questioned.

"I have lifted that bolster carefully every day, and have always seen it," she declared. "When I wanted to turn the mattress he always took away the pistol himself."

Ferrars turned away from the bed, and Brierly resumed his rôle of questioner.

"What else do you miss or find disturbed, Mrs. Fry?"

She went back to the outer room after a last slow glance about the chamber.

"There is the lamp, of course," she began. "That was taken from the shelf to give them light. Then the writing-desk has been opened, as you see, and the things on that table have been disturbed, the books shoved about, and the papers moved. I think," going slowly toward the article, "that even the waste basket and the paper holder have been rummaged."

"And do you miss anything here?"

Mrs. Fry shook her head. "I don't s'pose you've searched the writing-desk yet?" she ventured.

"Not yet. And is that all you observe, Mrs. Fry? The bed, the lamp, the desk, table, rack, and basket?"

She went back to the table and pointed out with extended forefinger a couple of burned matches, one upon a corner of the table, one upon the floor almost beneath it.

"They lit that lamp there!" she said. "And they brought their own matches. I never use those 'parlour matches,' as they call 'em!" She bent her head to look closer at the polished surface of the table, and then walked to the open window, where the shutter still swung in the breeze. "It has been awful dusty since yesterday, seems to me, for this time of year. That boy's left his finger prints on this window, as well's on the table there."

"Don't touch them!" It was Ferrars who spoke and so sharply that the woman turned suddenly, but not soon enough to note the swift gesture which directed his exclamation.

"Of course we may rely upon you to keep the fact that my brother's rooms have been entered in this manner from every one, for the present. It may be very important that we do not let it be known beyond the four of us. You have not seen or spoken with any one as yet, I think you said?"

"I haven't, and I won't. I'd do more than that for the sake of your brother, Mr. Brierly, and you've only to tell me what I can do."

"I intend to examine my brother's papers now, Mrs. Fry, before I leave the house, and if we should need you again we will let you know." And Mrs. Fry withdrew, puzzled and wondering much, but with her lips tightly set over the secret she must and would help to preserve.

"She'll keep silent, never fear," said the doctor as the door closed behind her. "And now, Brierly, I must remind you that you will need all your strength, and that I don't like your colour this morning. If you must investigate at once, get it over, for you, even more than Ferrars or I, need your morning coffee and steak."

"That is true," agreed Ferrars. "Brierly, let me ask two questions, and then oblige me by leaving certain marks, which I will point out to you, just as you find them."

"Your questions." Brierly had already seated himself before his brother's desk.

"I have an idea that this old oak writing-desk was not selected by our friend, Mrs. Fry. Am I right?"

"It is my brother's desk; bought for its compact and portable qualities."

"Good! Now, where did your brother usually keep these keepsakes and bits of foreign jewellery?"

"In one of these drawers. He kept them in a lacquered Japanese box."

"Look for them. And, before you begin, oblige me by not touching that letter file above the desk, nor the desk top just below it."

The letter file held only a few bits of paper, apparently notes and memoranda; and upon the flat top of the desk was a bronze ink well, a pen tray, a thin layer of dust and nothing more, except a tiny scrap of paper hardly as big as a thumb nail, which lay directly beneath the letter file. Brierly cast a wandering glance over the desk top and file and set about his task.

There was quite a litter of papers, letters mostly, together with some loose sheets that contained figures, dates, or something begun and cast aside. Below some of the pigeon holes, letters lay as if hastily pulled out, and from one of these little receptacles three or four envelopes protruded, half out, half in—one, a square white envelope, projecting beyond the others. These Brierly pulled forth, and turning them over in his hand, scrutinised their superscriptions. Then slowly he took the square white wrapper from among the others, and drew out the letter it contained. As he began to scan the page of closely lined writing he started, frowned, flushed hotly, and then with a look of fierce anger he thrust the sheet back into its envelope, and turned toward the detective.

"Take that!" he said with a curl of the lip. "Unless I am greatly at fault, it's a document in the case."

Ferrars took the letter from him, and asked, as he thrust it into the pocket of his loose coat without so much as glancing at it, "Do you mind my running over the papers in this rack, Brierly? and looking into the waste basket?"

"Do it, by all means," was the reply as Brierly pulled open the topmost drawer; and then for some time there was silence, save for the rustle of paper or the rasping of a hinge or turning knob.

When Brierly had finished his silent search of the two drawers, he approached the detective with a small lacquered box in his hand.

"The watch and the foreign jewels are gone," he said, holding out the open box. "And what do you think of this? Here are my mother's keepsakes,

Robert Brierly flushed and paled. He opened his lips as if to speak, but the detective's eyes were steadfastly turned away, and he resumed almost at once.

"I blame myself that I did not establish myself here last night, as I at first thought of doing. But it is too late for useless regret. And now, about this boy. Have you, either of you, a thought, a suspicion, as to his identity?"

The doctor shook his head.

"You can't suspect one of the pupils, surely?" hazarded Brierly.

"Be sure that Mrs. Fry knows every pupil in Glenville, by sight, at least; and this lad was a stranger, remember. It was a clever lad who first secured the key to these rooms and then decoyed Mrs. Fry half way across the town perhaps. How long must it have taken her, Doc, to go and come, in haste?"

"Quite half an hour, I should think."

"Well, we will assure ourselves of that later. Now we will suppose that this strange boy was acquainted with these rooms to some extent, and that he was, I fully believe. When Mrs. Fry is out of sight—and we know, from her story, that he was careful that she should be before he left his station upon the front porch—he slips indoors and evidently knows where to look for a lamp, which he does not light until he is inside this room." And Ferrars put a finger upon the match remarked upon by Mrs. Fry. "Now, as Mrs. Fry observed, there has been quite a film of dust in the air for the past twenty-four hours, so that, in spite of the good woman's tidy ways, it has accumulated upon this dark and shining wood." And he put down his finger and called their attention to its prints upon the table at his side.

"When we entered this room," he went on, "and I took it upon myself to look at that window with the swinging blind, under pretence of opening the shutters, I first noted that the visitor had left us a clue to his identity—several clues, indeed. Before seeing these I had thought that the boy was only an advance guard for some one else, but I see I was wrong. It was the boy, and a very keen and clever boy, who entered here alone. See upon this table, upon the window sills, and upon the desk, the prints of one, two, and sometimes all four, small slender fingers."

Ferrars paused a moment, while they examined the dust prints, faint but yet clear, upon the dark wood, and making lines of clearer colour upon the painted brown of the window sills.

"And what," asked Brierly, speaking for the first time since the detective began his explanation—"what was his real object?"

"His real object! Ah, I see you have been observant, and if I am not much mistaken he has left something; but the things he took were taken solely to cover up the real reason of his coming. Mr. Charles Brierly's pistol, his watch, and the foreign bijouterie were so little wanted by this remarkable boy that he will no doubt get rid of them in some way at the first opportunity. All but one thing."

"And that?" asked Brierly, breathlessly.

Ferrars walked over to the writing-desk and signed them to follow. "Observe that letter file!" he said. "There is not much upon it, bills for school books, two or three circulars, and so on, but observe that this file hangs over the top of the desk, so that anything falling from it would touch just here. He moistened the tip of a forefinger, and, touching with it a small bit of paper lying upon the top of the desk and just below the letter file, he lifted it deftly, and they all saw beneath it the dust of the previous day upon the polished surface.

"This," said Ferrars, holding out the bit of paper upon the palm of his hand, "was torn from something pulled from this file since Mrs. Fry dusted the furniture here yesterday morning, after Charles Brierly left the house. See, as the paper was pulled from the file this bit came off, because it was attached at the corner, as you see. It is a fragment from a newspaper. If it had been a letter the paper would not have parted so readily; it would merely have torn through."

It was, indeed, a tiny scrap of newspaper, not of the best quality, and not half an inch from the smoothly-cut corner to the ragged edge, where the file had perforated it.

"The slip of printed paper from which this was torn," said Ferrars, "was the one thing which was taken from this room because it was wanted! The rest were merely carried away as a blind."

"But," asked the doctor, "why did he make this search among the books and papers?"

"To find perhaps this very thing," replied Ferrars. "But his first and most important errand was this." He drew forth the letter given into his hands by Robert Brierly, and held it toward them. "Witness the thing itself. It bears no post-mark, it never did bear one, and it is thrust into the most conspicuous place, doubtless, after some looking about, in search of a better. I do not know its contents but I guess."

A gesture from Brierly cut short his speech. "Read it, both of you," he said, with something like a groan. "And tell me what it means."

Ferrars drew forth the sheet of note paper and slowly unfolded it. For a moment he scrutinised the page with a frown, and then began to read—

> "Mr. Charles Brierly: I don't know why I should
> be drawn into your love affair any further, and I
> have said my last word about your friend, Miss
> G——. One would think that the proofs you have al-
> ready had would be more than enough. She is not
> the first woman, with a pretty face and an inno-
> cent way, who has fooled and tricked a man. Why
> don't you ask her and have it out? You'll find she
> can scratch as well as the rest of her sex. One
> word more, when you have had it out with her, be-
> ware! Especially if she weeps and forgives you.
> Remember the 'woman scorned.'
>
> "Don't write me again. I shall not answer any
> more questions. And, remember your promise, don't
> let her dream that you ever heard of me. I shall
> feel safer. So good-bye and good luck.
>
> Yours, J. B."

Ferrars folded up this strange letter slowly, saying:

"This document has no date and no post office address." He held it in his hand for a moment in silence, looking at it thoughtfully, then. "I should like to retain this," he said, looking at Brierly, "as one of the documents in the case." And as Brierly silently bowed his assent, he added: "Have you formed an opinion concerning this letter?"

"I believe it is a shameful trick," declared Robert Brierly, hotly. "An attempt on the part of some person or persons to injure Miss Grant, who stands to me as a sister henceforth. If I am any judge of womankind, she is as good as she is lovely, and I believe that she mourns my brother's awful death as only a good, true and loving woman can. I wish you could and would say the same, Mr. Ferrars."

"I can say that you have said the only right and manly thing, in my opinion. You don't want to know what I think, however, but what can be done? And, first, this affair must be kept between ourselves. This letter makes it all the more important. If it has been put here to mislead justice and to make trouble, perfect silence regarding it will be the most baffling and perplexing course we can pursue. And it may lead to some further manifestation. The word must go out at once that Mr. Brierly has desired these rooms closed for the present, with everything to remain untouched. Meantime I consider that we have got our hands upon some strong clues, if we can find the way to develop them aright. Don't ask me anything more now, gentlemen. I want time to study over this morning's discoveries, and Mr. Brierly, it is time you breakfasted."

At this moment there came a quick tap at the door, and Mrs. Fry's voice was heard without. At a signal from Ferrars, Doctor Barnes opened the door.

"Gentlemen," began the little woman in eager explanation, "I don't want to interrupt."

"We are just going," said the doctor politely.

"Oh, well, I got to thinking, after I went downstairs, and it came into my mind that I didn't see Miss Grant's picture on the top of the writing-desk up here. Mr. Brierly had had it three weeks or so, and he showed it to me himself and says, 'Mrs. Fry, this picture is in its proper place here in my room. You and Nellie both know and love Miss Grant, and so I may tell you that she is to be my wife some day, God willing.'" The woman's voice broke at the last word, and Robert Brierly made a quick stride back toward the desk. But Ferrars said, unconcernedly, "Thank you, Mrs. Fry; we shall find it in the desk, I fancy," and then he explained to her Mr. Brierly's desire that the rooms remain closed to all curious visitors until further notice, adding that they would close the outside blinds and be downstairs directly; then, shutting the door upon the woman's retreating form, and softly turning the key in the lock again, Ferrars went to the desk, and, catching back Brierly's extended hand, said, "Wait!"

He came closer to the desk and bent to scan at the top shelf.

"Look," he said after a moment, "do you see that line, close to the back, where the dust is not quite so apparent? The picture has been taken from there." He took hold of the back and pulled the desk from the wall a few inches.

"Ah," he exclaimed, "I thought so!" and dropping upon one knee he drew out two pieces of cardboard. "I thought so," he repeated as he arose, and there was a steely gleam in his eyes as he held out to view the two halves of a fine picture of Hilda Grant, torn across the middle as if by a firm and vindictive hand. "This helps me," he said, with a touch of triumph in his voice. "It helps me more than all the rest."

He made a movement as if to put the picture together with the letter which he had put down upon the desk-top, into a capacious inner pocket, and then suddenly withdrew his hand and bestowed them elsewhere, for, thrust into that safe side pocket, so convenient and capacious, was a folded newspaper, from which a "clipping" had been carefully cut, a paper which he had found in the rack near the desk, and had secreted, as he thought, unseen, at his earliest opportunity.

CHAPTER XI
DETAILS

During the day that followed the discoveries in Mrs. Fry's upper chamber, Mr. Ferrars did a variety of things that surprised the brother of Charles Brierly; yes, and the doctor as well, and he said some things that seemed quite incomprehensible. For the detective was somewhat given to half-uttered soliloquy when he knew himself among "safe" people, and could therefore afford to relax his guard. Likewise he failed to say the things which Brierly, at least, expected, and much desired to hear.

His first movement after the three had breakfasted, was to ask for the keys of the cottage chambers, for they had been handed over to Brierly somewhat ostentatiously in the presence of Mrs. Fry and at the foot of the cottage stairs, by the doctor.

"I want to spend another half-hour in those rooms," he said, "and to so leave them that I shall know at once if a human foot has so much as crossed the threshold."

This was all the explanation he chose to make then or upon his return.

Indeed, when he came back he spent all of the remaining time until high noon, smoking alone upon the doctor's neat lawn and along the shady side of the house, excusing himself and guarding against possible intrusion, by remarking that he felt the need of a little solitary self-communion.

At luncheon the question of the burial was discussed, and afterward Brierly announced his intentions to call upon Miss Grant, if the doctor thought her able to receive him.

"I have told Mrs. Marcy to keep the gossips out," Doctor Barnes said gravely, "she's too sensitive, Miss Grant I mean, to hear unfeeling or curious discussions of the case. But a friend who is in sympathy—that's another thing. She'll be better with such company than alone."

When Brierly had set out, the detective threw away his after-dinner cigar.

"Were you called to see the little lady who was taken ill here yesterday, after the close of the inquest?" he asked carelessly. "I forgot to inquire, in my desire to keep Brierly occupied."

The doctor shook his head. "I fancy she only needed time to recover from the effect of her gruesome position. It was a blunder, putting her in plain sight of that shrouded corpse. Those little blue-eyed women are masses of nerves and fine sensibilities—often. I don't see how it came about."

"If you mean the 'blunder' of putting those ladies where they were, it was I who blundered. I arranged to place them there."

"You!" the doctor's eyes opened wide in astonishment. "Then I retract. It was I who have blundered."

"Um—I am not so sure," Ferrars replied slowly, and then the subject as by mutual consent was ignored between them. Ferrars, who seemed for the time at least to have done his thinking, wrote several letters at the doctor's desk, and then prepared to go out.

"I asked permission to call and inquire after Mrs. Jamieson's health, yesterday," he said to the doctor, "and as she has not required your services she may be able to receive me now."

"There is another Esculapius in Glenville," reminded Doctor Barnes.

"So I have heard; but the lady is a person of good taste. She would have called you in if any one." He bowed and went out with a gleam of humour in his eyes.

"It's sometimes hard to guess what Ferrars means when he speaks with that queer look and tone," mused the doctor. "And who would have thought he would care or think of a formal call like this just now! And yet, that little woman is pretty enough to attract a man, I'm sure; and a detective may be as susceptible, I suppose, as another."

Ferrars waited for a few moments in the reception-room of the Glenville House, and was then conducted to the pretty suite occupied by Mrs. Jamieson. He found her half reclining in a long, low chair, with her friend, Mrs. Arthur, still in attendance. She wore a soft, loose robe of black, with billowy gauze-like ruffles, and floating ribbons of the same sable hue, relieved only by a knot of purple wood violets at her throat. Her face was very pale and her eyes, with their changing lights of greyish green and glinting blue, looking larger and deeper than usual because of the dark shadows beneath them, and the waves of her plentiful fair hair falling low and loose upon her forehead.

She welcomed her visitor with a faint half smile, and thanked him again for his kindness of the previous day. She blamed herself for her want of nerve and courage. She inquired after Miss Grant and expressed her sympathy for the bereaved girl, and her desire to see her again, to know her, and serve her if possible; she had shown herself so brave, yet so womanly that day—and then the little lady told of her encounter with Miss Grant in the unfortunate character of messenger or bearer of bad news. She was glad there would be no lack of staunch friends to support the sweet girl in her time of need and trouble, and she finished by sending a pretty message to Hilda, and then without further question or comment concerning the murder or the progress of the case, she let the talk slip into the hands of her friend, and leaned back in her chair like one too weak for further effort, seeing which Ferrars soon withdrew.

"You will not consider this an example of my usual hospitality, I trust," Mrs. Jamieson said, as he bent over her chair to say farewell. "I fear I was not wise in refusing to let them call a physician, but I do dread being in the hands of a doctor. I shall be pleased to hear how this sad case progresses, Mr. Grant, and by the bye, has anything new occurred since the inquest? Any new witnesses or discoveries of any sort?"

But Ferrars shook his head, and murmuring something about time being short, and not taxing her good nature and strength further, he bowed low, and went away.

"It's very good of her," he mused, as he went, "to take such kindly interest in my supposed relative, Miss Grant. But she certainly showed scant interest in the chief actor in the drama, my friend Brierly."

The candles had just been lighted that evening, and Ferrars was once more waiting at the doctor's desk, while Brierly, pale and heavy-eyed, lounged by the long window near, when Dr. Barnes came in, hat in hand.

"As you felt some interest in Mrs. Jamieson's selection of a physician this morning," the latter said, "I will inform you that I have just been summoned to see that lady, professionally, of course," he added, as if by an afterthought, and smiling slightly.

"Thank you. Mrs. Jamieson has vindicated my belief in her good judgment," replied Ferrars, and then he wheeled about in his chair, and put out a detaining hand.

"Don't think I doubt your reserve, doctor," he went on, "when I ask you to avoid or evade, if needful, any discussion of this affair of ours. That is, avoid giving any information, be it ever so trivial." He shot a quick glance toward Brierly, and met the doctor's eye for one swift, momentary glance.

"My visit will be purely professional, and doubtless brief," was the reply, as the speaker passed from the room, and Ferrars smiled, knowing that his friend understood the meaning behind the half jesting words.

A moment later Robert Brierly arose, yawned, and crossed the room to take up his hat.

"This inaction is horrible," he said, drearily. "I must get out. I wish I had walked down with Barnes. Won't you come out with me, Mr. Ferrars?"

The detective dipped his pen in the sand-box, and arose quickly. Then when he had found his hat, and had lowered the light over the writing table, he put a hand upon the other's shoulder.

"I'll go out with you, of course, Brierly," he said, and there was a world of sympathy, as well as complete understanding in his tone. "But first, I want to ask you to show yourself as little as possible upon the streets, for a few days to come at least, and then only in the company of the doctor or myself, and not to go out evenings at all unless similarly attended. It will be irksome, I know, but I believe it important, and I must ask this of you, too, without explanation, for the present at least."

The young man looked at him for a moment, earnestly and in silence.

"Do you ask this for reasons personal to myself, or because it seems to you to be for the interest of the investigation?" he asked slowly.

Ferrars smiled. "You're as able to take care of yourself as any man I know, Brierly," he said, with frank conviction. "It's for the interest of the case that we—and especially you—keep ourselves as much aloof as possible from questions and curiosity. There is another reason which I cannot give just yet."

"As you will. I have put myself and my brother's vindication in your hands, Mr. Ferrars, and I shall do nothing, be sure, to hinder your progress." As they passed out Brierly paused under the shadow of the porch. "May I ask if you have put the same embargo upon Miss Grant?" he questioned.

"I have, yes. Glenville must know what we wish it to know, and not a syllable more."

"Ah! I like that."

"Why?"

"Because it sounds as if you had really found the end of your thread here."

"Oh, yes. The beginning is here. Not of the case, mind; only of the clues. But heaven only knows where it may lead us before we find the end."

"What matters," said the brother of Charles Brierly, with a heavy sigh, "so long as it brings us to the truth!"

CHAPTER XII

FERRISS-GRANT

On the fourth day after Charles Brierly's untimely death, his body was taken to the city and laid beside his parents in the beautiful cemetery where love and grief had already prepared for him and his, a place of final rest.

News of the burial had been sent ahead, and a crowd of friends had assembled at the home of their father's oldest friend and family lawyer, where the body was received as that of a son, and the last rites of affection and respect were performed by the venerable rector who had seen the brothers grow from boys to men.

Doctor Barnes and Hilda Grant, with Mrs. Marcy as chaperone, accompanied the sad-hearted brother upon this journey, and they were somewhat surprised when Ferrars, whom they had thought must go with them in his character of sole relative to the young lady, explained that his presence in Glenville just then was essential to the success of the work he had been called there to do.

"There are so many little things which I want to learn," he said. "In fact, I must know Glenville much better before I can go far in my search, and during your absence I can find the time for making many new acquaintances, and I mean to begin by cultivating your friend Doran, doctor."

They were gone three days, and when they returned they were but a party of three. "Poor Charlie Brierly," as his friends in the city had already begun to call the dead, lay in his last, quiet earthly home, and Robert had remained in the city.

"To settle up his brother's affairs, and put the matter of his death into the hands of the detectives." At least this is what Mr. Doran informed one of the loungers who, seeing the return of the doctor and the two ladies, had remarked upon Brierly's absence.

"Of course he'll have to come back here," Doran had further added. "He ain't touched the things in his brother's rooms yet, they say. But they'll wait better than the other business."

"Umph!" the villager sniffed. "He's let three days slip by without makin' much of a stir. Why on earth ain't they had one o' them fellers down here long before this? They ain't seemed to hurry much."

"Well, you see, at first 'twas more than half believed that the shooting must have been by accident; and then, this is just between you and me, Jones; didn't you ever think that even after that jury's verdict, and the doctor's testimony, they, Doc. and the brother, might have wanted to make sure, by a sort of private and more thorough investigation of the wound, eh?"

"By crackey! Now that you speak of it, I heard Mason say't they was up an' movin' round at the doctor's that livelong night! Yes, sir, I reckon you've hit it!"

"My!" mused Samuel Doran as he moved away from the gossip. "They bite at my yarns like babies on a teethin' ring. Doc. knows his fellow critters, sure enough, and my work's laid out for me, I guess."

For Doran, after due consultation, and upon the doctor's voucher, had been taken a little way into the confidence of the three men, and Ferrars began to foresee in him a reliable helper.

The above brief conversation took place between Doran and Mr. Jones, professional depôt-lounger and occasional worker at odd jobs, while the doctor was putting Hilda and Mrs. Marcy into a waiting carriage, and when he had seen it drive away up town, Doran came forward and addressed him in a tone quite audible to the bystanders.

"You see, I didn't forget the carriage, Doc. Hope Miss Grant ain't none the worse for her sad sort of journey." And then as the two walked away from the platform together, and he saw the doctor's eyes glancing from side to side, Doran went on. "Looking for Mr. Grant, Doc.? Well, I guess you won't see him; not before supper-time, anyhow. Fact is, I guess he's sort of fancy struck on that pretty-faced widow down at the Glenville House, and he's taken her out behind my greys this afternoon. I don't know as I blame him any; she is a dainty little wid."

The doctor stared at him in amazement at his first words, and then broke into a hearty laugh over the last.

"Upon my word, Doran, you will be able to write a new dictionary of abbreviations some day! Doran's Original! A dainty wid. is very good in its way; only, is she a 'wid.'?"

"That's what they say at the Glenville. Widow and rich."

At the next corner Doran halted. "Have to tear myself away," he said, amiably. "See you later," and the two men separated.

"Well, old man, how have you fared during the lull in your business?" asked Doctor Barnes, as his man came to meet him. "You don't look overworked."

"I ain't been, neither, sah. Your Mr. Grant or Ferrars, I ain't rightly got his name, I guess, sir, he 'pears ter like the cooks down to the Glenville better than me. I ain't had no bother with him since you left, sir, 'cept to make up his bed."

"I know. He has found some friends there, I fancy, Jude. Any news or messages?" and the doctor became at once absorbed in his neglected business.

Ferrars made his appearance at "supper time" as Doran had described the evening meal, and the two men had much to discuss. When Jude had placed the last dishes and retired, the detective, who thus far had been listening to the doctor's account of the journey and the sad funeral obsequies, looked up and said: "I suppose you have heard of my wanderings, doctor, and how I have forsaken poor Jude? The fact is, I have found plenty of leisure, and Mrs. Jamieson, when one comes to know her a little, is a very ab—interesting woman. The sort of woman, in fact, whose society I now and then enjoy. I have not neglected my duty, however, but there is absolutely nothing new. And, by the bye, I must see Miss Grant this evening; after that, if you are at liberty, we must have a talk. I have decided upon a change of plan, of which you must know."

He had left a note for Miss Grant, which advised her of his intended call as soon as she should have become rested and refreshed. He was glad to find her so strong and so composed, and he came at once to the business in hand.

"Miss Grant," he began, "as I said in my note, I have something to propose to you which has presented itself to me as the best course during your absence; and, to begin, let me ask, have you still full confidence in me as a detective, and as a man whom you may trust?"

She lifted her fine clear eyes to his face and kept them there while she replied.

"I felt that I could trust you, Mr. Ferrars, when we first met. There has been no change in that feeling unless it may be the change to a larger measure of trust and confidence."

"Thank you." And now the cool detective flushed like a schoolboy. "I shall try hard to deserve your good opinion, and it encourages me to broach my singular proposal. I believe it will enable me to get on easier and with more rapidity if you will permit me to continue for an indefinite time in the rôle which I did not at first choose for myself, and I ask you if I may still remain, in the eyes of Glenville, as now, in the character of your cousin."

"To remain—in Glenville?"

"When Doctor Barnes sent for me, advising me that I might arrive in the character of your cousin, it was, of course, with the idea that this masquerade would be a brief one, and it was undertaken because the doctor knew how it would hamper if not really balk, my attempts to unravel this mystery if I were known as a detective. I cannot explain now, but I ask you to believe that, being here, I am now convinced that in laying aside this character I should put out of my hands my best weapon, the most direct means of following up and ferreting out a crime which I fully believe will prove to have been—that is, if we succeed in finding out the truth—a crime with a far-reaching plot behind it, and the cause of which most of us have not even remotely dreamed of."

"You have said enough. All is in your hands. Be what you will and must, the better to prove to the world that Charles Brierly, my husband in the sight of heaven, died as he lived, an upright gentleman and martyr, and not the suicide or the victim of a righteous vengeance that most people would for ever declare him if the truth is not made known."

"Understand," he urged, "that if you consent to this, you, as well as myself, will have a part to play, and an active part, perhaps, in the drama we are about to begin. Remember, you will have to keep up the deception for weeks, possibly months; and to go and come at my desire."

"Do you mean," she asked, breathlessly, "that you may need my help?"

"I do need your help!"

"Oh!" she cried, letting go her splendid self-restraint for the moment.

"You don't know what you are doing for me! To be active, to do something, instead of sitting still and eating my heart out in suspense. It will save me from madness perhaps. What could a true relative do for me more than you are doing and will do. You are my cousin!" And she put out her two hands to him with a new look of energy and resolve in her face. As he took the two slim hands in both his own and looked in her eyes, suddenly so aroused and purposeful, he saw for the first time, the full strength and force of will and nature behind that fair face and gentle bearing, the high spirit and courage animating the slender frame.

"Thank you," he said, simply, as he released her hands. "I feel that I can indeed rely upon you at need. You have the strength; can you have the patience as well? At present I can tell you very little. You will have to take much upon trust."

"I have anticipated that."

"For example, it is my inflexible rule never to reveal the name of a suspected person until I have at least partial proof of guilt, enough to warrant an arrest. But you have a right to such confidence as I can give, and so, if you have a question to ask, and I think you have, let me answer it if I can."

"Oh, I thank you." She came a step nearer. "I ask myself one question, over and over; that there was no guilty secret in my poor boy's life and death, I know. Where, then, can be the motive?"

"The motive, ah! When we know that, we shall be at the beginning of the end of the matter. Sit down, Miss Grant, and I will put the case before you as I now see it."

She sank into the nearest seat without a word.

"As to the manner of the murder," he went on, "this is my conclusion. Some one, an enemy who hated or feared him, has informed himself of Mr. Charles Brierly's habits, and made himself familiar with the woods along the lake shore. Your friend, I learn, has practised target-shooting for some time. Have you ever thought that he might have had a reason for so doing?"

"Good heavens! No!"

"Well, that is only a suggestion. But this much is certain, the deed was premeditated, and carefully planned. I have satisfied myself that the assassin, approaching from the south, made almost the circuit of that long mound, after making sure that no one was near, in order to reach the point, scarcely twelve feet from the place where the body was found, from which to fire the fatal shot."

"My God!"

"It was a bold venture, but not so dangerous as might at first appear. I find that from a point half way to the top of the mound one might be quite concealed from any one down by the lake shore while taking a long look up and down the road. And, in case of approach, there is at the south end of the mound a clump of bushes and young trees, where one could easily remain concealed while awaiting the victim or the passing of an interloper. From the town to a point not far south of the knoll or mound, as your people call it, the ground between the road and lake has been partially cleared of undergrowth for the comfort of picnickers and fishing parties, I am told."

"Yes." She sighed wonderingly. "But beyond that, a person wishing to be unseen from the lake or road could easily hide among the brush and trees. I believe all this was carefully studied and carried out, and that, five minutes after the shots were fired, the slayer was on his way southward to some point where a confederate waited, with some means of conveying themselves to a safe distance."

"Ah!" she whispered. "The boat?"

"Yes, the boat. It was a part of the plot, and rowed to that point by the confederate, I believe, for the purpose of misleading justice. Doran, who is an able helper, learned this morning that a farm hand, who was driving his stock across the road to drink at the lake, saw a man in a boat rowing up towards Glenville at half-past seven that morning."

"Oh! And can you follow them? Is the trail strong enough?"

"I think so. And there are other clues. There is much to be done here in Glenville first of all. At the inquest the testimony was purposely left vague and uncertain at some points."

"And why?"

"Because, somewhere, not far away, there is a person who is watching developments, and who may leave some track unsevered if he can be made to think we are off the scent. I mean to know my Glenville very well before I leave it, and some of its people too. And here you can help me as soon as you are strong enough."

"I am strong enough now. What more can I do?"

"You remember the foolish boy and his fright when questioned?"

"Of course."

"Well, as his teacher, can you not win his confidence until his fear is overcome? That boy has not told all he knows."

"He is very dull, I fear. He said he saw a ghost."

"Well, we must know the nature of that ghost, and why it has closed his lips so effectually. Seriously I hope much from that lad."

"Then be sure I will do my best."

"You see, I am taking you at your word. And there's one more thing. I have been told that strangers go oftenest to the Glenville when in town. Now it behoves me to know the latest comers, and the newcomers there, and chance having given me opportunity to break the ice by being polite to Mrs. Jamieson, I have improved the moments. I don't mean that I am studying the lady for any sinister purpose, but one can see that she is quite a social leader in the house, and through her I have already come to know several of the other inmates. Mrs. Jamieson very much desires to know you, and if you will allow her to call, as under the circumstances she desires to do, and if you will return that call—in short, put yourself upon the footing of an acquaintance—it will really help me greatly."

For a long moment Hilda did not speak, then "I will do as you wish, of course," she said, but the note of eager readiness had gone out of her voice. "But I cannot even think of that woman without living over again our first meeting and the awful blow her news dealt me. Will I ever outlive the hurt of it?"

"It hurt her, too; I am sure of that. She is a keenly sensitive woman. She went from your schoolroom really ill, so her friend has told me."

"I can well believe that. She looked ill when she came to me. And who can wonder?" her tone softening. "Mrs. Jamieson is certainly kind, and why should we not be friends? She is a lady, refined and charming. Don't think me unreasonable, Mr. Ferrars. I shall be pleased to receive her, of course."

"Thank you. And remember, that for the present Francis Ferrars becomes Ferriss, Ferriss-Grant. You'll not forget your part!"

"I will not forget," she answered. And when he was gone she smiled a sad little womanly smile. "After all, a detective is but a man, and that petite, soft-spoken, dainty blonde woman is just the sort to fascinate a big-hearted, strong man like Francis Ferrars."

CHAPTER XIII
THE "LAKE COUNTY HERALD."

"Has Doran been here, doctor?"

These were the detective's first words when he entered the sanctum upon his return from the Marcy cottage, and before his host could do more than shake his head, Ferrars dropped into a seat beside him and went on in a lower tone.

"The fact is, doctor, I've got myself interested in a thing which, after all, may lead me astray. Do you take the _Lake County Herald_?"

"Upon my word!" ejaculated the doctor. "I do; yes. Want to peruse the sheet?"

"I don't suppose you file them?" went on Ferrars.

"File the _Herald_! No, I fire them, or Jude does."

"I wish you had not. The fact is I want very much to get hold of a copy dated November last, the 27th. Do you recall the bit of paper I took from Charles Brierly's desk-top to demonstrate that something had been hastily pulled from the letter file by that clever boy of whom Mrs. Fry could tell so little?"

"Yes; surely." The doctor now began to look seriously interested.

"Well, the stolen paper was a newspaper clipping, cut from the _Herald_ of November 27th last."

"Upon my word! But there, I won't ask questions."

"You need not. Did you not observe me looking over the papers in the rack?"

"Yes."

"Possibly you saw me with a paper in my hand soon after?"

The doctor stared and shook his head. "I've no eye for sleight-of-hand," he grumbled.

"Decidedly not, for I folded up that paper and thrust it in a breast pocket before your very eyes. I kept that tiny bit, too, which I picked up on my forefinger. It fitted into a column from which a piece had been cut, and that's how I know that the stolen article came from that paper. Very simple, after all, you see!"

"For you, yes."

"The fact that the clipping was thought worth stealing, makes me fancy it worth a perusal. I tried for it here in town, in a quiet way, but failed. Then I appealed to Doran, and he has written to Lake, to the editor, whom he happens to know."

"It would be hard to find hereabouts a man of any importance whatever whom Sam Doran does not know. He grew up in Lake County, and has held half the offices in the county's gift."

"There may be a clue for us in that clipping. I discovered another thing in that room. The dead man wrote, or began, a letter to his brother. I learned this from a scrap, dated and addressed, which I found in the waste basket, and I am led to believe the letter was re-written, or rather begun anew, and sent, from the fact that a fresh blotter showed a fragment of Brierly's name, and the city address. That letter, if mailed, must have passed him as he came down. Did he mention getting it?"

Doctor Barnes shook his head.

"He said nothing about such a letter," he replied. "Does he know about this—this newspaper business?"

"Not a word. No one knows it but yourself. If it should prove to be a clue in my hands, it may be better, it will be better, I am sure, to keep it at present between us two. I think, however, that I may decide to show Miss—my cousin—that anonymous letter, and tell her something about that mysterious boy and his visit to her lover's rooms." And then Ferrars turned from this subject to explain to the doctor his present plans. How he had determined to continue his masquerade, and to remain for a time in

Glenville; and, though Mrs. Jamieson's name was not uttered, the doctor found himself wondering, as had Hilda Grant, if the detective had not found the place attractive for personal, as well as business reasons; and if a detective's heart must needs be of adamant after all.

Next morning Samuel Doran, who knew the detective only as "Hilda Grant's cousin and a right good fellow," drove ostentatiously to the door to take "Mr. Grant" for a drive.

"I've had a line from Joe Howlett," he began the moment they were upon the road. "He was just setting out for a run out of town, but he says he told the boys to look up that paper and send it along. So, I guess we'll see it soon, if it's in existence." And Doran chirrupped to his team and promptly changed the subject. He did not know why this man beside him so much wished to obtain a six-months-old copy of a country newspaper, and he did not trouble himself to worry or wonder. "It was none of his business," he would have said if questioned, and Samuel Doran attended to his own business exclusively and was by so much the more a reliable helper when, his aid being asked, the business of his neighbour became his own.

Ferrars was learning to know his man, and he knew that the time might soon come when Doran would be his closest confidant and strongest assistant in Glenville.

"We look for Brierly in a day or two," the detective said, casually, as they bowled along. "He will bring a professional gentleman with him," and he turned his head and the eyes of the two met. Ferrars had found that Doran could extract much meaning from a few words, at need.

"Something in the detective line, for instance? 'S that it?"

"That explanation will do for Glenville, Doran."

"Cert. Glenville ought to know it, too. We've been thinking 'twas about time one of 'em appeared," and Doran grinned.

Ferrars smiled, well satisfied. He knew that the dignified family lawyer and friend, who was coming to Glenville with Robert Brierly by his own desire, would be promptly accepted as the tardy and eagerly looked for "sleuth" who would "solve the mystery" at once and with the utmost ease.

And that is what happened.

The two men arrived a day earlier than they had been expected, and the moment Robert Brierly found himself alone with Ferrars he drew from his pocket a letter, saying, as he unfolded it with gentle, careful touch:

"This letter, Mr. Ferrars, is the last written me by my brother. It was in the city, passing me on the way, before I had arrived here, and I found it, among others, at the office. I have not spoken of it even to the doctor. Read it, please."

Ferrars took the letter and read:

"MY DEAR ROB.,—Since writing you, I have found in an old newspaper, quite by accident, something which has almost set my head to spinning. I know what you will say to that, old boy. It brings up something out of the past; something of which I may have to tell you and which should have been told you before. It's the only thing, concerning myself that is, which you do not know as well as I, and if I have not confided this to you, it was because I almost feared to. But then, why try to explain and excuse on paper when we are to meet, please God, so soon. Brother mine, what if that flood tide which comes, they say, to each, once in life, was on its way to you and to me? Well, it shall not separate us, Rob.; not by my will. But stop. I shall grow positively oracular if I keep on, (no one ever could understand an oracle, you know) and so, till we meet, adieu.

"BROTHER CHARLIE."

When Ferrars had read this strange missive once, he sat for a moment as if thinking, and then deliberately re-read it slowly, and with here and there a pause; when at last he handed it back to Brierly, he asked:

"Do you understand that letter?"

"No more than I do the riddle of the sphinx, Ferrars," he leaned forward eagerly as he put a question, and his eyes were apprehensive, though his voice was firm. "Do you connect that letter in any way with my brother's death?"

For a moment the detective was silent, thinking of the newspaper and the missing clipping. Then he replied slowly as if considering between the words.

"Of course it's possible, Mr. Brierly, but as yet I cannot give an opinion. If you will trust that letter to me for a few days, however, perhaps I may see more clearly. It's a surprise, I'll admit. I had fully decided in my own mind that howsoever much the murderer may have premeditated and planned, his victim was wholly unaware of an en— of his danger."

"You were about to say, of an enemy!"

"Yes. It is what I have been saying before seeing that letter." He put out his hand, and as Brierly placed the letter in it, he added, "Let us not discuss this further. Does your friend, Mr. Myers, know of it?"

"Not a word."

"Then for the present let it rest between us."

Two days after this interview Doran dropped in at the doctor's office, and before he left had managed to put a newspaper, folded small, into the hands of the detective, quite unperceived by the other occupants of the room. For while since Brierley's return, accompanied by his friend, these two had occupied together the rooms at Mrs. Fry's, the doctor's cottage was still headquarters for them all, while Ferrars now had solitary possession of the guest chamber, formerly assigned to Brierly.

Mr. Myers was a shrewd lawyer, as well as a faithful family friend. He had felt from the first that there was mystery as well as crime behind the death of Charles Brierly, who had been near and dear to him, as dear as an own son, for the two families had been almost as one ever since John Myers and the elder Brierly, who had been school friends and fellow students, finally entered together the career of matrimony.

There had been no children in the Myers homestead, and the two lads soon learned to look upon the Myers' house as their second home, and

"Uncle" John Myers had ranked, in their regard, only second to their well beloved father. So that when the young men were left alone, in a broken and desolate home, that other door opened yet wider, and claimed them by right of affection.

Mr. Myers had been taken to the scene of the murder, had visited Hilda Grant, and by his own desire had examined the books, papers, and manuscripts in Charles Brierly's rooms, and on the day of Doran's call, a longer drive than he had yet taken had been arranged. He was going, accompanied by Brierly and driven by Doran, to look at the skiff, still unclaimed and waiting upon the lake shore below the town.

Ferrars, much to Doran's regret, had declined to accompany them from the first, and when he found himself in possession of the coveted newspaper, he joined the others in their desire that Doctor Barnes should take the fourth seat in the light surrey behind Doran's pet span; and the day being fine, and business by no means pressing, that gentleman consented.

CHAPTER XIV
A GHOST

When Ferrars found himself alone he lost no time in locking his chamber door and beginning his study of ancient news.

Taking the newly arrived paper from beneath his pillow, where he had hastily thrust it, he spread out the mutilated copy beside it and speedily located the clipping which should explain, or interpret, Charles Brierly's last letter.

Putting the perforated paper over the other, as the quickest means to the end, he drew a pencil mark around the paragraph which appeared in the vacant space, and then, without pausing to read it, he reversed the two sheets and repeated the operation.

This done, he took up the marked paper and sat down to read and digest the secret.

"It won't take long to tell which side of this precious square of paper contains the thing I want, I fancy," he meditated, as he smoothed out the sheet.

The printed paragraph outlined by his pencil was hardly three inches in length, and he read it through with a growing look of comprehension upon his face. "I wonder if that can be it?" he said to himself at the end. And then he slowly turned the paper and read the pencil-marked lines upon the other side.

When he had perused the brief lines over, his brow knit itself into a frown, and he re-read them, with his face still darkened by it. Then he uttered a short laugh, and laid the paper down across his knee.

"I wonder if the other fellow will know which side was which!" he muttered. "I'm blest if I do!" He sat for half an hour with the paper upon his knee, looking off into space, and wrinkling his brow in thought. Then he got up and put the two papers carefully away.

"I'm very thankful that I did not speak of this to Brierly," he thought as he went out and locked his door behind him. "It would be only another straw—yes, a whole weight of them, added to his load of doubt and trouble."

The two paragraphs read as follows, the first being an advertisement, with the usual heading, and in solid nonpareil type:—

> "Charlie: A. has found you out. He will not give me your address. Be on guard at all times, for there is danger. All will be forgiven if you will come back, and F. will help you to avoid A. You are not safe where you are. The city is better, and we cannot feel at ease knowing the risk you are running. At least stay where you are. Your brother or some friend ought to know. For your own sake do not treat this warning as you did A.'s other threat. He means it. Still at G. Street.
>
> "M."

The second paragraph was in the form of a would-be facetious editorial paragraph, and ran thus:—

> "Not to have a fortune is sad enough, but to go up and down in the land a millionaire and never know it is wretchedness indeed. Many are the foreign fortunes seeking American heirs, if we are to believe the advertising columns, and the heirs seeking fortunes are as the sands of the sea in number.
>
> "There have been the Frayles, and the Jans, and a long retinue of lost heirs to waiting estates, and now it appears that the great Paisley fortune

> rusts in idleness and shamelessly accumulates,
> while the heirs of a certain Hugo Paisley, an En-
> glishman who was last heard from in the Canadas
> many years ago, are much to be desired now that
> the home supply of English bred Paisley stock is
> run out."

There was more to this screed below the line which marked the lower end of the clipping, but it contained no further reference to the Paisleys, merely dilating in a would-be humorous manner upon the degenerating influence of the foreign legacy upon the American citizen. But the advertisement upon the other side had been cut out in full, and exactly at the beginning and end.

It was puzzling and disappointing in the extreme. Ferrars had really looked upon this cut newspaper as his strongest card when he should have found the missing fragment, and now———! He thought and wondered, and re-read letter and clipping again and again, but to no good purpose, and at last he locked away the puzzling documents and went out to make a morning call upon Mrs. Jamieson.

That evening he talked first with Robert Brierly and then with the family lawyer, and to both he put the same direct questions, "What could they tell him of the early history of the Brierlys? of Mrs. Brierly's family and ancestors? Had they any relatives in England or Scotland, say? Were there any old family papers in the possession of either?"

Of Robert Brierly he also asked if, to his knowledge, his brother had had at any time a love affair—not serious, but amusing, perhaps—a student's flirtation, even. Also, when and for how long, if at all, had the brothers been separated since their schooldays?

And Brierly had replied that he knew very little of his father's ancestors, beyond the fact that his grandfather Brierly was a Virginia gentleman, and his father an only son. The family, so far as he knew, had been Virginians for three generations, and what more, pray, could an American ask? As for his mother, she had been a Miss Louise Cotterrell of Baltimore, her father a railway magnate of renown. In her desk, very much as she had left it, in a closed-up room in the old house, were bundles of old letters and ancient family papers, so his father had once told him; he had meant to examine them some time, but had not yet so done. If Ferrars desired it he would do this soon.

So far as his dead brother was concerned, Brierly was sure there had never been a love affair of even the most ephemeral sort. In fact, Charles had always been shy of women, and used to shirk his social duties as much as possible. Hilda Grant was, without doubt, his first and only love. As to their separations, there had been several. To begin, Charlie had been in college a year after he (Robert) had been graduated, and the following year, "because the boy had seemed run down and in need of rest and change," he had spent a few months upon a ranch in Wyoming with a college friend. Then the two had made their European tour, and since, their only long separations had been when his work as journalist had taken him away from the city, sometimes for weeks, until Charlie had taken this school as a relief from his theological studies.

From Mr. Myers he could only learn that the father and mother of Robert and Charles Brierly were of good families, well known in their respective states, and both, he believed, "were as distinctly Americans as the war of the Revolution could make any American citizen of English descent." As to Charlie Brierly, Myers "didn't believe the boy had ever looked twice at a girl until he met with that lovely, sad-eyed sweetheart who, it was plain, was wearing out her heart in silent grief for him."

Then Ferrars went to see his supposed cousin, and asked her to review, mentally, her latest talks with her lover, and to see if she could not recall some mention of a discovery, a surprise, a perplexity possibly, which he wished to lay before his brother when he should come. But she shook her head sadly.

"Was he, to her knowledge, in the habit of collecting odd things from the newspapers?"

She shook her head. "He did not think very highly of our daily papers, and seldom if ever read beyond the news of the day. The scandals and criminal reports he abhorred," she said.

"And he never alluded in any way to his family history, you say? Think, was there no mention of family facts or names?"

She looked up after some moments of thought. "I can only recall one thing which, after all, does not contain information, except as regards the two brothers. Charlie was speaking of the difference of their temperaments.

Robert, he said, was intensely practical, living in and enjoying most, the present, and by anticipation, the future, while he

(Charlie) was a dreamer, loving the past, and idealising its history. To illustrate, he told how, as boys, he loved to hear his mother, whom I fancy he resembled, tell the tales she had heard at her grandmother's knee, of the early days, the French convents, the Indians, the colonists, the quaint living, the speech, which had for him such charms, while Robert would only hear of the fighting and would run away from the ancestral history."

Hilda, grown accustomed to his numerous queries and scant explanations, was not surprised at Ferrars' hurried departure at the end of the catechism, and he went back to the doctor's cottage with just one faint little possibility as a reward for all this interviewing. He had known Mr. Myers in the city, as a successful detective is apt to know an able lawyer, well by reputation and personally a little, and he was glad to find in him a friend to the Brierlys, dead and living.

Going back that night he said to himself:

"It's of no use to try to go on like this; a confidant will save me a lot of time, and Myers is the man. I can't call upon the doctor; he's got his profession, and he belongs here. Myers can make my business and Brierly's his at need. Besides, he's a lawyer and won't be knocked entirely out by my wild theorising, and he's the one man who can get access to the ancestral documents at need."

He found the lawyer still upon the doctor's piazza, and without the least attempt at explanation invited him into his own room, where they were still closeted when, at midnight, Robert Brierly went slowly toward the Fry cottage, and the doctor, who never got his full quota of sleep, went yawning off to bed.

Mr. Myers spent five days in Glenville, and then went back to the city, taking Robert Brierly with him, "for a purpose," as he said to the doctor and Ferrars. "He can come back in a day or two if he chooses," the lawyer added, "but in truth, Robert, unless you're needed here, which I doubt, you'll be better at work. Mr. 'Ferriss-Grant,' here, will summon you at need."

When they were on board the train, and the lawyer had exhausted the morning paper, he drew close to his companion in that confidential attitude travellers fall into when they do not converse for the entertainment of all on board, and said:

"Robert, I want to tell you why I so insisted upon your company back to the city. I want you to rouse yourself, to open your house, and when you first have looked over your father's and mother's private and business papers, I want you to turn over to me all such as are not too sacred for other eyes than yours; all letters, journals—if there are such—all, in fact, that deal in any way with your family, friends, and family history."

Brierly turned to look in his face.

"This is some of Ferrars' planning," he said.

"It is, and it has my hearty endorsement. Don't ask questions. Frank Ferrars knows what he is about."

"No doubt of it. I only wish I did."

"You'll know at the right time. And if it will be a comfort to you, I'll admit that, while I am to a certain degree in his confidence, I know no more what or whom he suspects than you do, for he won't accuse without proof of guilt, however much he suspects or believes. But I know this, Ferrars is convinced that the secret of your brother's death lies in the past."

"And in whose past?"

"In his own, in that of your family, or of Hilda Grant."

At the beginning of the following week Hilda Grant resumed her duties as school mistress, the place of Charles Brierly being filled by a young student from the city.

Mrs. Jamieson, meantime, had called upon Hilda, the call had been returned, and the two were now upon quite a friendly and sympathetic footing; it was not long before the fair, black-robed little figure was quite familiar to the children, to whom she gave generously sweets, pleasant words and smiles.

Sometimes she met Ferrars, who would look in now and then at the recess or noon hour to keep up his cousinly character, and Hilda Grant's clear eyes saw, day by day, the blue eyes of the pretty widow taking on a new look and noted that, while she was at all other times full of easy, charming chat, the approach of "Mr. Grant," would close the pretty lips and cause the white eyelids to quiver and fall.

The understanding between Hilda and the detective was now almost perfect, and one day, Ferrars, having asked her if she had ever heard Mrs.

Jamieson speak of leaving Glenville, or name her place of residence, Hilda replied—

"I have heard her express herself as well pleased with Glenville, and I think she is in no haste to go. In truth, Mr. Ferrars, I am beginning to feel that, in seeing this lady as a means toward a selfish end, we, or I, have done wrong. That she is a woman of the world, and has seen much of good society, is evident, but she has lived, of late, a lonely and much secluded life, she tells me, her late husband having been a somewhat exacting invalid for two years before his death; and forgive me for my great frankness, I fear that because of your absorption in this trouble of mine, you have not thought or observed, how 'much' your acquaintance is becoming to Mrs. Jamieson. One woman can read another as a man cannot, and I must not let you serve me at the cost of another's happiness perhaps."

"Miss Grant, is this a riddle?"

"Mr. Ferrars, no. Must I say plainly, then, that you are making yourself quite too interesting to this lady?"

Ferrars turned his face away for a moment. Then he replied slowly, as if choosing his words with difficulty.

"My friend, I believe time will prove you the mistaken one. I cannot take this flattering idea of yours to myself and venture to believe in it, but should it have the smallest foundation in reality, rest your conscience upon this candid declaration. The lady cannot feel more interest in my unworthy self than I in her; from the first moment almost I have taken an interest in Mrs. Jamieson, such as I have seldom felt for any woman. Shall we let the subject rest here? Be sure I shall not let any personal interest conflict with, or supersede, the work I came here to do."

In later years Hilda remembered these words.

During the next two weeks the wheels of progress, so far as Ferrars' work was concerned, moved slowly, and even rested, or seemed so to do.

To be baffled in a small town, and by a small boy, was something new and surprising in the experience of detective Ferrars, but so it was. Work as he would, finesse as he might, he could find no trace of the boy,

"about half grown, with dark eyes and hair, freckles, a polite way with him, and a cap pulled over his eyes," and this was the best description Mrs. Fry could give of the strange lad.

"If Mrs. Fry was not the honest woman she is," said the doctor, "I should call that boy a myth. How could he come and go so utterly unseen by all Glenville."

Samuel Doran, who still believed that "Mr. Grant" was Mr. Grant, and thought it most natural that he should turn his attention to the mystery surrounding the murder of "his cousin's lover," thought otherwise.

"Pshaw!" he objected, "look at the raff of half-grown boys racing up and down these streets from sunset to pretty late bedtime, for kids, and how much different does one boy look from another in the dark? Mrs. Fry herself only saw him out in the twilight."

Ferrars reserved his criticism and opinions for the time.

Doran had taken upon himself the investigation of the "boat puzzle," as he called it, for the skiff remained, after many days, still drawn up, unmoored and unclaimed, by the lake shore; and at last, by dint of much driving up and down the lake shore road and interviewing of boat owners, he brought to Ferrars this unsatisfactory solution.

Two weeks before the murder the skiff had been owned by a certain Jerry Small, hunter and fisherman by choice, blacksmith by profession. On a certain day a man dressed in outing costume had entered Small's shop, asked about the boat, and made him such a liberal offer for it, that Jerry had at once closed with him. The shop stood upon the outskirts of the town and close to the lake. The man had said that he was coming out from the city in a few days for a few weeks in the country, meaning to secure board, if possible, near the lake shore. If Mr. Small did not mind, the boat might stay where it was until his return; the money was paid down, and Small engaged to care for the boat.

One day, after much agitation, Small decided that it must have been the day of the murder that he missed the boat; and one of his "kids" told him that "a gentleman with flannel clothes and whiskers" took away the boat "right early," and neither boat nor man had ever reappeared.

Then Ferrars tore his hair and fumed at the long delay only to learn that Jerry Small had left his house on the day after the murder to attend a sick brother, and had returned just two days ago.

"It's of no use," fumed the detective to Doctor Barnes; "I shall put a couple of fellows I know in the Jerry Small vicinity; it's right in their line of work, and probably they'll find the man and boy together—in Timbuctoo."

"And you will remain in Glenville, eh?" queried the doctor, grinning openly.

"Yes," with an answering grin, which somehow the doctor did not quite understand. "I'll stay—for a while longer."

As they sat at lunch next day a small boy brought Ferrars a note from the teacher.

"Come to me at once.—H. G."

That was all it said, and Ferrars lost no time in obeying the summons.

"You may not see much in my news," Hilda said, as she closed the door upon intruders. "But I have got Peter's story out of him at last."

"The foolish boy? Ah, that is something after all, at least, I hope it will prove so. Well?"

"It was slow work, for the boy has been terribly frightened. His story is most absurd."

"No matter, tell it in your own way."

"He says still that he saw a ghost—a live ghost. That it arose out of the bushes and waved its arms at him. It was dressed 'all in white like big sheets,' Peter said, and its face was black, with white eyes. It spoke to him 'very low and awful,' and told him to lie down and put his face to the ground until it went back into its grave. If he looked, or even told that he had seen a ghost, the grave would open and swallow him too. Then it held up a 'shiny big knife' and he tumbled over in sheer fright. After a long time he began to crawl toward the road; and when he at last looked around and saw no ghost anywhere, he ran as fast as he could. I am afraid," Hilda added, "that you'll think as I do, that some of the school boys have played the poor child a trick, or else that he has imagined it all. It's too absurd to credit. Still, as you made a point of being told at once of whatever I might learn from Peter, I kept my promise. I'm afraid I've spoiled your luncheon." She finished with a wan little half smile.

The detective's face was very grave and he did not speak at once.

"Is it possible," she ejaculated, "that you find anything in the boy's story?"

Ferrars leaned forward and took her hand. "Miss Grant," he said gravely, "I believe that poor foolish Peter saw Charles Brierly's murderer."

He got up quickly. "Do you think the boy could be got to show you where he saw this apparition?"

"I asked him that. He thinks he might dare to go if he were protected by 'big mans.'"

"Then, arrange to leave your school for a short time, at, say two o'clock. I shall get Doran and his surrey. Have the boy ready——"

"Pardon me, I will say nothing to Peter. The surrey will be enough, he is wild to ride."

"That will be best then. I shall lose no time. I have a strong reason for wishing to see the precise place where this ghost appeared."

The sight of the surrey filled poor foolish Peter with delight, and he rode on in high glee, sitting between Hilda and Ferrars, whom he had learned to know, and like, and trust. When they were abreast of the hill Hilda bent over him.

"Now, Peter, tell me just where you saw that ghost."

Instantly the boy's face blanched and he cowered in his seat, but Ferrars with gentle firmness interfered. Peter would show him the place, and then he would drive away the ghosts. Ghosts were afraid of grown men, he averred. And at last, hesitating much, and full of fears, Peter was finally persuaded, yielding at last to Doran's offer to let him sit in front "and drive one of the horses."

As they reached the lower end of the Indian Mound, the boy's lips began to quiver and one arm went up before his face, while he extended the other toward the thickest of brushwood before described by Ferrars.

"That's where," he whimpered. "It comed up out there."

"From among the bushes?"

"Ye-us."

"Did it have any feet?"

"Oh-oh! Only head and arms—ugh!"

"Turn around, Doran," said Ferrars sharply, and then in a lower tone to Hilda, "I shall go to the city to-night."

When Hilda reached her room, at the close of the school, she found this letter awaiting her, "left," Mrs. Marcy said, "by her cousin":

> "DEAR COUSIN,—Even if you had been disengaged,
> I could have told you nothing except that what
> I have learned to-day impels me to look a lit-
> tle more closely to the other end of my line. For
> there is another end.

"Now that I shall have the two men on duty in the south end of the county, and with the doctor and Doran alert in G——, not to mention yourself, I can go where I have felt that I should be for the past week or more. Will you keep me informed of the slightest detail that in any way concerns our case? And will you do me one individual favour? I trust Mrs. J—— may not leave this place until I see you all again, but should she do so, will you inform me of her intention at once? You see that I am quite frank. I should deeply regret it, if she went away before I could see her again. De-stroy this.

"Yours hopefully,
"FERRARS."

CHAPTER XV

REBELLION

May had passed, and June roses were in late bloom. The city was horrid with the warm sun-filtered air after a summer shower, and Robert Brierly looked pale and languid as he stepped from an elevator, in one of the great department houses wherein Ferrars had his bachelor quarters, and walked slowly to his door.

Possibly it was the warmth of a very warm June, or there may have been other causes. At any rate Frank Ferrars' face wore an almost haggard look in spite of the welcoming smile with which he held out his hand to greet his friend, for friends these two had grown to be during the past weeks. Friends warm and true and strong, in spite of the fact that the mystery surrounding the death of Charlie Brierly remained as much of a mystery as on the day when foolish Peter Kramer led the detective to the scene of his ghostly encounter.

There were dark lines beneath the keen gray eyes, which, Rob Brierly had declared, "compelled a man's trust," and the smooth, shaven cheek was almost hectic, symptoms which, in Ferrars, denoted, among other things, loss of sleep.

There was a moment of silence, after the men had exchanged greetings, and it seemed, almost, that each was covertly studying the other, and then

Brierly tossed down his straw hat, and pulling a chair directly in front of that in which the detective lounged, said, abruptly:

"I shouldn't like to quarrel with you, Ferrars, but I've something on my mind, and I'm here to have it out with you."

"Oh! Then I am in it?" the detective spoke nonchalantly, carelessly almost, and as the other seemed hesitating for a word, he added: "Give us the first round, old man. I'm apprehensive."

"H—m! You look it. Ferrars, do you know that for weeks, ever since my return from Glenville, in fact, I have been under constant surveillance?"

"Constant sur——. Excuse me, it's not polite to repeat, Brierly, but what do you mean?"

"What I say. It's plain enough, somebody is watching me, following me day and night."

"Pshaw! You don't mean that, man!"

"But I do. And that is not all," he leaned forward and fixed his eyes upon those of his _vis-à-vis_ as if watching for the effect of his words. "I have been slowly discovering that I am being controlled—constrained—in many ways."

"Upon my word!" Ferrars was leaning back in his chair with his face a mask, expressing nothing but grave attention. "Make it plainer, Brierly."

"I will. I'll make it so plain that there will be no room for misunderstanding. When I first came back from Glenville, I did not go out much, especially evenings, but when I did, I began to fancy that I was spied upon, followed, and, after a time, I became sure of it."

"Stop! When did you observe this first?"

"I think it was on the third night after my return. I was going down to the Lyceum Club rooms, when something caused me to glance at a fellow on the other side of the street. You know my eyes are good!"

"Unusually so."

"Well, I came out in a very short time, alone, and the same fellow was lounging so close to the entrance that I recognised him at once."

"A bungler, evidently."

"Perhaps. Well, I met two men whom I know, just outside, and they dragged me back with them. When at last I left the place, I started to walk home, and when I got upon the quieter streets I soon became conscious of some one keeping so evenly opposite me across the street, that I began to watch, and as the fellow glided, as quickly as possible under a street lamp, I recognised the same man."

"And you have seen him since?"

"Himself or another. A disguise is easy at night. I have been watched, at any rate, and followed again and again."

"Ah! And could you imagine his motive?"

"No." A look that was almost of anger crossed Brierly's face. "But I have wondered if it was the same as yours, and Myers, when you have contrived to keep me from going here and there, or doing this or that, unless accompanied by one or the other of you two."

He bent forward again after this utterance. His eyes seemed to challenge an answer.

But it did not come. Ferrars only sat with that look of grave inquiry still upon his face. He knew the man before him.

"Ferrars," exclaimed Brierly, when he saw that no answer, no defence, was to be made, "will you look me in the face and say that you, and Myers also, have not connived to keep me under your eyes? to accompany me when that was practicable, and to prevent my going when it was not? I can recall several occasions when——"

He stopped short, checked in his utterance by a sudden, subtle change in the face of Ferrars, who had not stirred so much as an eyelid, but who spoke at once quietly, but with a certain tone of finality, of decision.

"Brierly, do you believe that James Myers is your friend, in the full meaning of the word?"

"I do! It is not that I doubt, or that——"

"And do you believe," went on Ferrars, putting aside his protest with a peremptory gesture: "do you believe that, while thus far I seem to have failed in unravelling the mystery in which your brother's death seems enshrouded, I have given it my most faithful study, my time, thought, effort and labour? That, in short, I have been true to your interest at all times?"

"I know it. You have been all that and more. You must hear me, Ferrars. And I beg that you will answer me. Why am I watched, thwarted, cajoled? Why do you and Myers fear to let me out of your sight? A few weeks ago you found, or seemed to find, your chief interest in Glenville; you looked for clues, for developments, there; and yet, you have not visited Glenville since you left it so suddenly. Even your own personal interest has not drawn you there for a single day."

"By my 'personal interest' you mean what, Brierly?"

"You know what I mean. Pardon me, and do not misunderstand me. I could not fail to see that you were interested in Mrs. Jamieson, and why not?" While Brierly spoke, the detective arose and began to pace the floor with lowered eyelids and slow tread. Brierly watching him, was silent a moment, then he seemed to pull himself together and to speak with enforced calmness. "Ferrars, do you know what thought has taken possession of my brain until I cannot shake it off?"

"Assuredly not," going on with his promenade. "But I shall be glad to hear."

"I have begun to fear—yes, to fear—that you have found some reason for suspecting me, and that your horribly acute logic has even caused Myers to doubt too."

"Man!" Ferrars swung about and suddenly faced him. "Much meditation has surely made you mad. Now, in heaven's name, so far as may be, let us understand each other. First, you are utterly wrong."

"Ah!"

"Next, you speak of Mrs. Jamieson, and of my 'personal interest.' I admit, willingly, that I am interested in that lady. But my personal feelings and interests must be subservient for a time to your business."

"Pardon me."

"And now, I did leave Glenville to follow you, and see that you did not spoil my plans by any rashness."

"You are talking a puzzle!"

"Let me talk it out then, for you have forced my hand. But for this I should have gone on as before. And I did not dream that Mr. Myers and I were playing our game so stupidly, so openly; nor that you, owing to your present preoccupation, would prove so astute."

"You have not bungled, be sure of that. You have been most wonderfully keen and clever, but it was this very preoccupation, as you call it, my abnormal sensitiveness, in fact, which made me study your every word and set me searching for its hidden meaning; and so I could not fail to see that you were handling me, hedging me about, for some purpose."

"Ah! You have said the word, Brierly." Ferrars resumed his seat opposite the other, and his tone became once more composed. "We were trying to 'hedge you about,' to put up a wall between you and the assassin who killed your brother. Wait! Let me say it all. It is little enough. Do you remember telling me of an 'assault' upon your brother, made by footpads, not long before he came to Glenville?"

"Yes."

"It was that which gave me my first real clue. It confirmed one of the few theories that seem to fit, or cover, the case so far as known; but it wanted confirmation. I found nothing in Glenville that was in any way opposed to this theory which I was growing to believe in, but, on the other hand, I found nothing there to strengthen it. When you left that place, I meant to follow soon. Meantime I had confided my theory to Mr. Myers, who promised not to lose sight of you before I should arrive."

"But why? Why?"

"Because I then believed, as I do now, that that attack upon your brother last summer was the first act in the tragedy which has robbed you of him. I believed the plot to be far-reaching. It may be a case of vengeance, a family feud. The motive is yet to be discovered, but I will admit to you that I have had, from the first, a reason to think that the affair has not yet ended; and so, as soon as I could, I followed you to town. It was well that I did so. Before I had been your shadow forty-eight hours, I had proof that you were being otherwise watched and followed."

"Great heavens! And that is why——" He stopped short and bowed his head.

"That is why Myers and I have been such officious friends, why we have advised, remarked, and why I have tried to trace to his lair the man who has been your very frequent shadow."

"And you think he is——"

"The assassin himself or his tool."

"Good heavens! And you cannot guess his motive?"

"We might guess, of course, half a dozen motives. What I have hoped to find was something, some fact in your family history, your father's life, or your mother's, perhaps, that would fit into one of these guesses or theories, and make of it a probability."

And then the two went all over the array of possible reasons and motives, and Brierly again protested his lack of any knowledge which might serve as the feeblest of guides to the truth.

"There's one other thing," said Brierly, at last. "I want to know if the new man, whom Myers took on soon after you came to town, is one of your sleuths? He has annoyed me more than once by his persistent attentions."

Ferrars smiled. "I never supposed you a reader of the penny dreadful, Brierly," he said, "and 'sleuth' is a word which makes the actual detective smile, and which is not known to the professional vocabulary. Hicks is my man; yes. And he has followed you by day and night when you have not had the company of either Myers or myself."

Robert Brierly threw back his head and folded his arms. After a moment of silence he got up and stood before the detective.

"Ferrars," he said, "I owe you and my absent friend an abject apology for my unworthy suspicions, my impatience under restraint. And now, I beg of you, let this end. I am warned, and I do not think myself a rash man. I believe I can protect myself, and how can I endure the thought that I must be hedged about by this constant guardianship, which may last indefinitely? Withdraw Hicks, and give your own valuable time to better things. Rather than go about knowing myself so fenced in and guarded, I will lock myself up in the attic, and remain a recluse and invisible. Heavens, man! am I so stupid or cowardly a man not to be able to cope with an enemy whom I know to be in ambush at my very heels?"

CHAPTER XVI
OUT OF REACH

Much as Ferrars regretted Brierly's discovery, he was not much surprised by it, nor could he avoid or refuse an explanation. Robert Brierly was not a child. He was a strong man, and a brave one; and Ferrars, putting himself in the other's place, felt at once the force of his words, the right of his position; and, after a day or two, he withdrew Hicks from his post. At the same time he observed with surprise and some misgiving that the shadow was no longer on duty. With two trusty and able men, by turns, always on watch within sight of the Myers place, no glimpse of him had been seen for more than a week.

And then, like a lightning flash from a clear sky, the blow fell.

It was Sunday evening, and in the aristocratic uptown street where the Myers lived there reigned a Sabbath quiet, for the habitues of the little park beyond had left it with the fading twilight, and had already passed on their way townward.

Robert Brierly had been indoors since morning, and now, shortly after Mr. and Mrs. Myers had walked down the tree-shaded street, toward the church on the avenue three blocks away, he came out upon the broad front portico and stood for a moment looking idly up and down.

There had been concessions on both sides, since that interview between Brierly and Ferrars in which the former had demanded an explanation;

and the withdrawal of Hicks had been but one of the results; another had been a promise, given by Brierly, whereby he pledged himself not to walk the city streets alone after dark, but if unaccompanied to take a cab, there being a stand only two blocks away, in the direction of the park.

These cabs, when wanted, were to be called by one of the servants, and to take him from the door; but on this Sunday night, as Brierly looked up and down with a growing wish to drive about town and have a talk with Ferrars, he remembered that on Sunday the servants were allowed to go out; all save one who must remain in charge, and decided that it would be absurd to stand there "like a prisoner bound by invisible chains" and wait for a chance to bring either carriage or policeman. He had received on the previous evening letters from Glenville, from Hilda and Doctor Barnes, and his curiosity had been aroused by the contents of both. He had not seen the detective for four days, and he fancied that he, too, would have had news from the little lakeside town; more explicit and satisfactory news, doubtless, than that contained in his own letters.

"How absurd!" he muttered, apropos of his own thoughts. "No doubt I'll meet a hack before I reach the corner," and he lighted a cigar and went down the steps, glancing, from sheer force of habit, for the street at that moment seemed quite empty, up and down, as he went toward the cab stand.

"I was sure of it," he said again, as he neared the corner, at the end of the block farthest from his home. "There they are, both of them."

He was looking ahead, where a cab was coming at a slow trot toward him, while around the corner, still nearer, a policeman had just appeared.

As the two men approached each other the officer, who had been looking toward the approaching cab, turned his face toward Brierly, just as he was passing under the glare of a street lamp, and stopped short.

"Excuse me, sir; this is Mr. Brierly, I believe?"

Brierly nodded.

"Mr. Brierly, may I have a few words with you? I have been lately put upon this beat, sir; changed from the next lower one; and there is something you ought, for your own safety, to know. Will you walk a few steps with me? I hardly like to stop; I ought to be at the next corner right now, in fact."

Brierly looked toward the approaching cab. "The truth is," he said, "I want very much to get that cab down town; otherwise——"

"Oh, I'll fix that, sir." And the officer took a step out from the curbstone and, standing under the glare of the light just above, held up his hand, and whistled shrilly. "Follow us a few steps, Johnny," he said to the driver. "You are wanted down town." Then, turning toward Brierly,

"If you'll just step across the street after me, I'll tell you what you ought to know. It's a short story." And he crossed the street briskly, and paused on the opposite side to await the other.

"You see, sir," he began, as Brierly joined him, "we can walk slow for a few steps here, where all's quiet."

Brierly paused to look back. The cab was turning at the corner, and it followed them, at a snail's pace, and close behind, down the still and shady side-street. "You see, I've been noticing, for a couple of weeks, or maybe more, a fellow who just seemed to patrol the street next below this, almost as faithfully as I did, and for quite a time I wondered why; and thus I began to watch him, till I found that his promenades always took him round the corner, and seemed to bring him up right opposite the house you live in. I guess I ought to step a little brisker, sir; somebody's coming. The man was not very tall, and thick set like, and if I hadn't taken notice of him, at the first, almost, I might not have recognised him, for he changed his clothes almost every trip; sometimes dressing common, sometimes quite swell; but I knew him every time."

"Make it as short as you can, officer; we're almost at the corner."

"All right, sir." The man glanced back. "Your cab's here, all right, sir. I was just going to tell you how we came to arrest the fellow."

"Ah!" Brierly smiled in the dusk. It had puzzled Ferrars or seemed to, the sudden cessation of the spy's visits, and now he would be able to enlighten the detective. "You have him, then? This shall be worth something to you."

"I don't want a reward for doing a plain duty, sir. Just walk on ahead for a step; somebody's coming."

Preoccupied with the story, and without glancing behind, Brierly did as he was told, and had advanced not ten paces from the corner, when there was a swift blow, a fall and a cry, three pistol shots in swift succession, and the rattle of wheels; all so close together that the time could have been counted in seconds.

"Brierly! Are you badly hurt?" The revolver fell from the fingers of the man who had prevented the second blow, and put to flight the sham policeman, who had so deftly contrived his appearance, with the aid of the cab, between the rounds of the policeman proper, the latter now came up panting, his footsteps hastened by the shrill call of the whistle in the hands of the new or latest comer. And then the inmates of the neighbouring houses rushed out, and, for the moment, there was confusion, consternation and clamour.

"Is he dead?"

"How did it happen?"

"Was it a sandbag?"

"To think of a holdup on this street!"

"There was a carriage, I'm sure."

And then the policeman was flashing his lantern about among them, as he bade them stand back, and the rescuer, who looked like a workman in his Sunday clothes, looked up, from the place where he knelt, supporting the head and shoulders of the unconscious man, and said:

"Gentlemen, this is Mr. Brierly, Robert Brierly of 1030 C—— Avenue; the Myers house, only two blocks away. He must be taken home at once. Has any one a cot? No, he must be carried." For at the name of the Myers house, a gentleman had proffered his carriage at once. "And, officer, call up help. If possible, that cab must be traced. Send to the stand just above and find out what cabs have left it within the past quarter hour. Let some one go ahead and bring Doctor Glessner from just opposite 1030. He's at home."

"How did it happen?" asked Mr. Myers, two hours later, when the injured man—his wounded head carefully dressed—lay, still dazed and in a precarious condition, in his darkened room, with a trained nurse in attendance.

Ferrars having seen his friend in his own room, and in the hands of the doctors, had not waited for their verdict, but had set off to put in motion his plan for hunting down the would-be murderer, and he had but now returned, full of anxiety for the fate of the sufferer.

"How did it happen? After all our precautions, too!"

"It's easy to tell how it happened," replied Ferrars with some bitterness. "It happened, first, because the enemy outwitted me, in spite of my cordon of guards; and, second, because Brierly lost patience and exposed himself."

"But how?"

"I can only give you my theory for that. He was alone in the house, eh?"

"Yes. We were both out when he went."

"He wanted, doubtless, to go to town. There was no servant at hand whom he wished to send, so he walked toward the hack stand, or so I suppose. At the corner he met a policeman, as he thought, of course, and so, for a moment did I. They stopped, spoke together, and the sham policeman hailed an empty cab that was close at hand; then they crossed the street, the cab following, and the policeman seemed to be doing the talking, as I saw when they passed under the light at the corner. I had suspected some new plot, from the fact that the spy had so suddenly disappeared, and I had watched your place, in person, for the past three nights."

"Oh! And that is why we have seen so little of you?"

"In part. Well, I made up my mind, when they walked away together down that tree-shaded cross-street, that there was something wrong. I was on the opposite side, and concluded to close up, seeing that the cab was getting very near and edging close to their side, against all rules of the road. I had got half way across, and was just behind the cab, when I saw Brierly step ahead of the other, and then came the blow. As I sprang forward the cabby gave a loud hiss and the scoundrel saw me, and sprang for the cab with his arm still uplifted for another blow. I fired twice running, the third time turning long enough to send another shot at him as he entered the carriage door. Then he was off. I think he was hit, once at least."

"He will be caught, don't you think so? A cab driving like mad through those quiet streets?"

"No. He will not be caught, I fear."

"But why?"

"Because he will have had a second vehicle, a carriage, no doubt, not far away, and he will leave the cab, which will slacken up for a moment for that, and then dash on."

"How can you know that?"

"Because, when I find that I am dealing with a clever rascal I ask, what would I do in his place? And that is what I would have done."

"Well, well!" The lawyer sighed. "Poor Robert."

"If he only had been less impatient!" exclaimed Ferrars.

"If we had been wiser, and had not left him! The boy was in a peculiarly restless mood. Even my wife had observed that since morning."

"And why since morning?"

The lawyer looked at him gravely for a moment. "Did you ever hear of Ruth Glidden?" he asked.

"The orphan heiress? Of course; through the society columns of the newspapers."

"Ruth Glidden and the Brierly boys grew up as the best of friends and neighbours. The elders of the two families were friends equally warm. I believe in my soul that Glidden would gladly have seen his daughter marry one of the Brierly boys. And if things had run smooth—but there! Brierly was accounted a rich man, and he was until less than a year before his death, when the failure of the F. and S. Railway Company, and the North-Western Land concern, within three months of each other, left him a heavy loser. Even then, if Glidden had been alive all might have been well. But he died, two years before Brierly's death, and Ruth went to live with her purse-proud aunt, her father's sister. The two families had resided for years, side by side, on this avenue."

"And where is Miss Glidden now?" asked Ferrars.

"Here in this city since the day before yesterday. She and her aunt have been abroad for a year, but I believe that they care for each other, though Robert is so proud, and that is not all. The brothers have each a few thousand dollars still, and it appears that shortly before his death, Charlie—he was always a methodical fellow—instructed his brother, in case of his sudden death, to make over all of his share to Miss Hilda Grant. Robert told me of this upon his return with the body, and he also said that all he possessed should go, if needful, to the clearing up of this murder mystery."

"It may be needful," sighed Ferrars. "I fear it will be."

"Then, good-bye to Robert's hopes! With it he might make a lucky hit; might have a chance. Without it"—he shrugged his shoulders—"what can even so bright a journalist, as he undoubtedly is, do to win a fortune quickly. And he won't accept help, even from me, his father's oldest friend."

"No," said Ferrars, gloomily. "Of course not How could he? Mr. Myers, I'll be honest and tell you that I'm afraid we've struck a blank wall. Things look dark on all hands, just now, for poor Brierly."

"What! Do you think the clue, the case, is lost then?"

"Not lost. Oh, no. Only, I fear, out of reach."

CHAPTER XVII
RUTH GLIDDEN

Francis Ferrars sat in his sanctum, one could scarcely call it an office, although he received here, now and again, visitors of many sorts on business bent. For, since his coming to America, five years before, to find the heiress of Sir Hillary Massinger, he had read many another riddle, and now, as at first, he worked independently, but with the difference that he now undertook only such cases as especially attracted him by reason of their strangeness, or of the worth, or need, of the client.

Two letters lay before him, and as he pondered, frowning from time to time, he would take up one or the other and re-read a passage, and compress his lips and give vent to his thoughts in fragmentary sentences. For he had grown, because of much solitude, to think aloud when his thoughts grew troublesome, voicing the pros and cons of a case, and seeming to find this an aid to clearness of thought.

"It's a most baffling thing," he declared, taking up for the third time a letter in the strong upright hand of Doctor Barnes. "I wonder just what the man meant by penning this," and once more he ran his eye over this paragraph which occurred at the end of a long letter:

> "Mrs. Jamieson has not forgotten you. She asks after you now and then, when we meet, and de-sires to be remembered to you. She is not looking

```
well, and, I fancy, finds Glenville duller than at
first."
```

"I'll wager she does not think of me any oftener than I of her. And she can't know how ardently I long to stand before her and look into those changeful, blue-green eyes of hers. What strangely handsome eyes they are—And say—Ah! how will those eyes look then, I wonder?"

Presently he turns the sheet and reads again:

```
"I think you did well to instruct your two men
here to make use of, and place confidence in Dor-
an. He's a host in himself. And what do you think
of the tramp they have traced to the vicinity of
that boat on the morning of the murder? He was
seen, it appears, by at least three."
```

"Umph!" laying down the letter. "If you were here, my dear Barnes, I would tell you frankly—I feel just like being brutally frank with some one—that I have no doubt that the tramp is a link—there seems to be so many of them, and all detached—a link—and that he approached the boat in that tramp disguise, after separating from his confederate at some more distant point. Bah! It looks simple enough. Confederate leaves vehicle—or two horses, possibly—they could slip off the saddles and hobble them in a thicket, where they would look, to the passer-by, like a pair of grazing animals, or they might have used a wagon, travelling thus like two innocent bucolics. Then how plain to me, the assassin goes through the woods, watchfully, like an Indian. The tramp boatman patrols the shore, to signal to the other when the victim appears; or, should the assassin on shore be unable to creep upon his prey, the assassin in the boat may row boldly near, and, at the signal from the other, telling him there is a clear coast, fire upon the victim. If he is sure of his aim, how easy! And if seen by the victim, well—'Dead men tell no tales.'"

He muses silently awhile now, puts down the doctor's letter, and takes up the other.

"This," he murmurs, "is tantalising." And then he read from a letter, signed "Hilda G——."

```
"Mrs. Jamieson begins to complain of the dull-
ness of this place, in spite of the fact that
she has had a visit from her husband's brother,
```

a Mr. Carl Jamieson. He did not make a long visit, and I saw but little of him. He is something
of a cripple, a sufferer from rheumatism, and just
back from the hot springs. I met him but once.
He looks and talks like an Englishman, and has a
dark eye that betokens, if I am a judge of eyes,
a bad temper. I give you these details knowing
that all concerning the little blonde lady is of
interest to you."

"Of interest!" he muttered "I should think so! Doubly so, now that there's so little else of interest, or——" He stopped short, and wheeled about in his chair. His office-boy had swung open his door, and was saying:

"A lady to see you, sir." And Ferrars arose to confront a visitor, a brunette so tall and lissom, so glowing with the rich hues of health and beauty, so clear of eye, and direct of gaze, that Ferrars could not at first find his usually obedient tongue, and then she spoke.

"Mr. Ferrars!" her voice was a low, rich contralto. "I am Miss Ruth Glidden, and I have come to you to seek information concerning the awful death of my friend, Charles Brierly. Pray let me explain myself at once."

Ferrars bowed, placed her a chair, and closed the half-open door.

"The Brierlys and my own people were old friends, and Robert and Charles Brierly were my childhood playmates. I arrived home, ten days ago, after a year spent in Europe, and learned, soon, of Charlie's sad fate. While this shock was still fresh upon me, I heard of Robert's narrow escape from a like attack. Mr. and Mrs. Myers are my dear friends. I have spent much of the past week under their roof, and——" There was a little catch of the breath, and then she went bravely on. "And I have had a long, frank talk, first with Mrs. Myers, and then with her husband. He has told me all that he could tell. He has assured me that you are wholly to be trusted and relied upon, and, knowing my wishes—my intentions, in fact—Mr. Myers has advised me to come to you."

"And in what way can I serve you, Miss Glidden?"

"Please understand me. I have heard the story; that there are clues, but broken and disconnected ones; that you know what should be done, but that there is a barrier in the way of the doing. Mr. Ferrars, as a true friend of Robert Brierly, I ask you to tell me what that barrier is? I have a right to know." The rich tints of olive and rose had faded from her rounded cheek, leaving it pale. But the dark eyes were still steadily intense in their regard.

As Ferrars was about to reply, after a moment of silent meditation, the door opened, and the boy came in again, softly and silently, and placed upon the desk a handful of letters, just arrived; laying a finger upon the topmost one, and glancing up at his employer, thus signifying that here was his excuse for entering at such a moment.

The letter was marked "immediate," and the handwriting was that of James Myers.

With a murmured apology, the detective opened it, and read—

> "MY DEAR FERRARS,—During the day you will no doubt receive a call from Miss Glidden. I cannot dictate your course, but I write this to say that no friend of Brierly's has a better right to the truth—all of it—nor a stronger will and greater power to aid. Of her ability to keep a secret you can judge when you meet her.
>
> "Yours,
> "JAMES MYERS."

When he had read this letter Ferrars silently proffered it to his visitor, and in silence she accepted and read it.

"I was strongly inclined to accede to your request, after, first, asking one question," he said, when she gave the letter back, still without speaking. "And now, having read this, I am quite ready to tell you what I can."

"And the question?"

"I will ask it, but have no right to insist upon the answer. Have you any motive, beyond the natural desire to understand the case, in coming to me?"

She leaned slightly toward him and kept her earnest eyes steadily upon his face as she replied, "I cannot believe that you credit me with coming here, on such an errand, simply because I wish to know. I do wish to know as much as possible, but let me first tell you, plainly, my motives and why I have assumed such a right or privilege. To begin, I am told that Robert Brierly will not be able to think or act for himself for some time to come."

"That, unhappily, is true."

"And how does this affect your position?"

"It is unfortunate for me, of course. The case has reached a point when I can hardly venture far unauthorised, and yet no moment should be lost. The time has come when skilled investigations, covering many weeks, perhaps, as well as long journeys, are necessary. We need also the constant watchfulness of a number of clever shadowers."

"And this requires—it will incur great expense?" she asked, quickly.

"Is it not so?"

Ferrars bowed gravely.

"Mr. Ferrars," she began, and there was a sudden subtle change in her voice. "I am going to speak to you as a woman seldom speaks to a man, for I trust you, and we must understand each other. Two years ago, when I was leaving my old home for my aunt's house, having still a half year of study before me, with the year abroad, already planned, to follow, Robert Brierly came to bid me good-bye, and this is what he said; I remember every word: 'Ruth, we have been playmates for ten years, and dear friends for almost ten years more. Now I am a man, and poor, and you a budding woman, soon to be launched into society, and an heiress. I would be a scoundrel to seek to bind you to any promise now, so I leave you free to see the world and to know your own heart. I have not a fortune, but if labour and effort will bring it about I hope to be able to offer you a fit home some day, for I love you, and I shall not change. I want you to be happy, Ruth, more than all else, and so I say, go out into the world, dear, and if you find in it a good man whom you love, that is enough. But, remember this, as long as you remain Ruth Glidden, I shall hope to win you when I can do so and still feel myself a man, for I do not fear your wealth, Ruth, only I must first show myself to possess the ability to win my way, on your own level.'

She paused a moment, and bent her face upon her hand. Then she resumed, almost in a whisper. "He would not let me speak. He knew too well that he had always been very dear to me, and he feared to take advantage of my inexperience. I loved and honoured him for that, and every day and every hour since that moment I have looked upon myself as his promised wife, and have been supremely happy in the thought. And now——" There was a little pause and a sobbing catch of the breath— "Have I not the right, Mr. Ferrars, to put out my hand and help in this work? To say what I came here to say? My fortune is ample. It is mine alone. I am of age, and my own mistress. Take me into your confidence, to the utmost, make me your banker, and push on the work. Robert Brierly may be helpless for weeks or months longer. Charlie Brierly was a brother to me. No one has a stronger right to do this thing."

"Miss Glidden, have you thought or been told that——"

"That Robert may die? Yes. But I will never believe it. And, even so, there is yet more reason why this work should not be dropped, why no moment should be lost." She paused again, battling now for self-control; then—"There is one other thing," she resumed. "Mr. Myers has told me of the young lady, poor Charlie's _fiancée_. Will you tell me her name? He did not speak it, I am sure, and I want to write to her, to know her."

"That will be a kindly deed, for she, too, is an orphan. Her name is Hilda Grant."

"Hilda! Hilda Grant! Tell me, how does she look?"

"A brown-haired, grey-eyed, sweet-faced young woman, with a clear, healthy pallor and a rich colour in her lips alone. The hair is that golden brown verging upon auburn; she is tall, or seems so, because of her slight, almost fragile, gracefulness."

"Ah! Thank you, thank you. This is my own Hilda Grant, who was my schoolmate and dearest friend, and who cut me because she was poor, and buried herself in some rustic school-house. She shall not stay there. She shall come to me."

"I fancy she will hardly be induced to leave Glenville now."

"I must see her. She will come up to see Robert, surely!"

"She is only waiting to know when she may see him."

"Of course. And now, it is agreed, is it not? You will take me as a silent partner?"

"Since Mr. Myers sanctions it I cannot refuse. Besides, I see you are quite capable of instituting a new search, if I did."

"I will not deny it." And they smiled, each in the other's face.

"Perhaps," he said, now grave again, "when I have told you all my ideas, theories, and plans, you will not be so ready to risk a small fortune, for, unless I am greatly in error, you will think what I am about to propose, after I have reviewed the entire situation, the wildest bit of far-fetched imagining possible, especially as I cannot, even to you, describe, name, or in any manner characterise the person, or persons, whom I wish to follow up, for months it may be, and because the slender threads by which

I connect them with the few facts and clues we have, would not hold in the eyes of the most visionary judge and jury in the land."

"It will hold in my eyes. Do you think I have not informed myself concerning you and your work? Is not Elias Lord my banker, and Mrs. Bathurst _persona grata_ in my aunt's home? I am ready to listen, Mr. Ferrars."

CHAPTER XVIII
SUDDEN FLITTINGS

For two weeks Ruth Glidden stood at the right hand of Mrs. Myers, and supplemented the trained nurse in the sick room.

At first she only entered while the patient slept, but after a few days the stupor began to lessen, and the flightiness, with which it had alternated, to decrease. And then one day he knew them, and, by the doctor's orders, the nurse withdrew and Ruth came to the bedside and sat down beside him.

"Robert, dear," she said, smiling down upon him, "you have very nearly let that wretched footpad spoil the good looks of the only lover I ever had, and to prevent further mischief I am come to take care of you." She said very little more then, but gradually the patient found himself being ruled by her nod, and liking the tyranny; so that when he was told that he was going away to try what change of air and scene would do for his maltreated head, he listened to her while she told him a tale which seemed to interest her much, and through which the names Ferrars, Myers, Hilda, and the pronouns "they" and "them" often occurred. And then it came about that, supported to a carriage and transferred then to a swinging cot, he was taken on board a Pullman sleeper, and, with nurse and attendant, was whirled away southward.

Two days later, James Myers said good-bye to wife and friends and set sail, on board the good ship _Etruria en route_ for Europe.

"Yes," he said to an acquaintance whom he met at the wharf. "I've wanted to make the trip, you know, for a long time, and now a matter of business, the looking up of certain titles and records, makes the journey needful, and I can combine pleasure and business." And then he turned away to say a few last words to Francis Ferrars before the signal sounded, and he must say good-bye to his anxious wife, to serious-faced Ruth Glidden.

"And now," said the detective to Ruth, "the next flitting will be toward Glenville."

Before the end of that week Mrs. Myers, who stood staunchly by Ruth, and would not hear of her going alone, Ruth herself, and a keen-eyed maid—not the one who had accompanied the young heiress home from Europe, but another supplied by Mr. Ferrars—all arrived at Glenville, and took quarters at the Glenville House, where Hilda Grant soon sought her friend, and promised herself much comfort in her society.

At first, Miss Glidden did not seem to desire acquaintances, and Mrs. Jamieson complained that she found herself almost deserted, Hilda was so preoccupied with her newly-arrived friend. But this was soon changed.

Miss Glidden and her party had at first been placed in quarters which the young lady did not find to her taste. There must be a pleasanter chamber for her friend, Mrs. Myers, and a reception room for their joint use, and it ended in her securing the little parlour suite adjoining that of Mrs. Jamieson.

For a time even this close proximity did not seem to break the ice, and while having been introduced by Hilda, the two ladies were for some days strangers still.

For reasons which Ferrars might have explained if he would, Hilda Grant had not visited Robert Brierly while he lay under the care of doctor and nurse, and now that they were together, the two girls, having first exchanged fullest personal confidences, had much to say about Robert and his dead brother.

At the end of their first confidential talk Ruth had said: "Apropos of this, Hilda, my dear, let me remind you that I have not outgrown my dislike of being quizzed or questioned by the simply curious, for the sake of curiosity. I know what a small town is, and so, I warn you not to let the dear inhabitants know that I am more than a friend of your own. To proclaim me a friend of the Brierlys as well, will be just to expose us both to the inquisitive, and to set vivid imaginations at work."

Hilda's eyes studied her face a moment. "I think you will not be troubled. My acquaintances all know that I do not willingly talk on that terrible subject. Even Mrs. Jamieson, who saw its fearful beginning and who is with me often, seldom speaks of it to me."

"The pretty widow? Mr. Ferrars, pardon me, your cousin, spoke of her more than once," and Ruth cast a keen side glance at her friend's face.

"And she speaks of him, now and then."

"As which?"

"As my cousin; for so she believes him to be."

"And you think them mutually interested? I must really see more of my pretty neighbour."

Miss Glidden and her party had been a week in Glenville when "Mr. Ferriss-Grant" arrived, and spent a few days in the village, making his home at the doctor's cottage, and passing most of his time with Hilda and her friends. Mrs. Jamieson had now made better progress with her fair and stately neighbour, and they might have been seen strolling toward the school-house together, or driving along the terrace road—for Mrs. Jamieson had declared that the tragedy of the lake shore had spoiled the lakeside road for her—in Doran's pony carriage, and, sometimes with "Miss Grant's cousin" for charioteer.

One evening the little party sauntered away from the pretty hotel together to walk to Hilda's home and sit for an hour upon Mrs. Marcy's broad and shaded piazza, which Mrs. Jamieson declared so charmingly secluded, after the chatter and movement, the coming and going upon that of the Glenville House.

They had been taking tea with Mrs. Myers and Ruth, Hilda, Mrs. Jamieson, and the sham cousin, who seemed to rather enjoy his _rôle_, if one might judge by his manner, and they seemed inclined to pass the remainder of the evening together.

They had not been long seated upon the vine-shaded piazza when Doctor Barnes came up the walk and dropped down upon the upper step, like one quite at home. It was now more than two weeks since Robert

Brierly had been carried southward and the people of Glenville, for the most part, had heard most discouraging reports from the invalid, most of them given forth by the doctor, or "Sam" Doran, who, by the way, had been for the past month entertaining a warmly welcomed and much quoted "first cousin" from "out west."

The doctor held a letter in his hand, and seeing this, Miss Grant's cousin asked carelessly:

"Any news of general interest in that blue envelope, doctor?"

They could not see the doctor's face, but his voice was very grave when he replied, "I'm sorry to say yes. Our friend down south is in a very bad way."

"Mr. Brierly?" exclaimed Mrs. Jamieson. "Oh, doctor, tell us the worst." And then she murmured to Ruth, who sat near her, "Miss Grant's friend, you know, but of course you do. I have grown as much interested in his welfare, somehow, as if he were not really a stranger, whom I never saw but once."

The doctor had left his place, and crossed to the open window, through which the lamp-light shone upon the open letter.

"I think I can see to read it," he said, and bent over the sheet. "The writer says:

"I fear our friend will not see many more Florida suns; will not be here with us long. The change has been surprisingly rapid, and the heart is now seriously implicated. Do not be surprised if ill news comes at an early day."

He folded the letter. "Ill news should always be briefly told," he said.

When the ladies came in, that night, having parted from the two gentlemen who had escorted them as far as the piazza steps, they found Miss Glidden's maid hovering in the passage, near her mistress's door.

"Miss Glidden, ladies," she began in evident agitation, "I have been terribly frightened. Some one has been in your room, and, I fear, in that of this lady also. I sat, for an hour, on the back piazza with two of the housemaids, and when I came up, only a few steps from this room, some one slipped out from Mrs. Jamieson's door and round the corner toward the south hall. I did not think about it until I had gone into your room to make all ready for the night, and then I saw the closet door open, and the things upon your table pulled about as if some one had hurried much, and had left, when they found it was not a sleeping room. Then I thought of the next room, of the person coming out so still and so sly——"

Miss Glidden pushed past the maid, and opened her own door. "Look in your room, Mrs. Jamieson," she said, "and see if you have really been robbed before we alarm the house. Susan, go with her."

Mrs. Jamieson found that her door was indeed unlocked, and her inner room showed plainly that a hasty hand had searched, here and there.

"It's lucky that I never leave money where it can be got at," she said to Ruth, when she had taken in the full extent of the mischief, "and that I haven't taken my jewel box from the hotel safe for three days. Even my purse was in my chatelaine with me. I find absolutely nothing gone. But my boxes, my frocks, my boots and wraps, even, have been pulled about. It's very strange. The thief must have been frightened away before anything was taken."

"Perhaps," suggested Miss Glidden, "the person wanted clothing, and heard Susan coming down the hall."

It was very strange, but, although they called the landlord, and told him privately of the invasion, and though there was a quiet but strict investigation, nothing came of it, and no one was even suspected.

"It was certainly some one from outside, who slipped in through some open door in the dark, while every one was out upon the piazzas, or in the grounds. These halls are not lighted until quite dark, sometimes, I find. I am thankful that you met with no loss, ladies," said mine host.

Next morning Mrs. Myers declared herself more than ready to leave Glenville. The thought of being in a house where an intruder found it so easy to make free with a lady's wardrobe, was not pleasant, and she hoped Ruth would not ask her to spend another week in the town. In fact she only stipulated for a fortnight's visit with her friend, Miss Grant, upon which Ruth promised that they would really go very soon, although she was enjoying herself.

Three days later a party of the Glenville's guests set off, after an early breakfast, for a long drive and a day's fishing, at a spot some miles distant and near the north end of the lake, at a famous picnic ground. Mrs. Jamieson was one of the merry crew, and she urged Ruth Glidden to join them, as did the others, all; but Ruth "never fished and detested picnics;" besides, the other people, she declared, were for the most part utter strangers, and Hilda and "Mr. Grant" were not invited.

When Mrs. Jamieson came back with the rest of the tired merrymakers she knocked at Ruth's door to announce her return.

There was no response, and she entered her own rooms where she found, conspicuously placed, a note. It was in a strong masculine hand, and she opened it quickly, looking first at the name at the bottom of the sheet. It was F. Grant.

She caught her breath, and sat down to read, wondering still and her heart beating strangely.

> "DEAR MADAM"—so ran the note—"You will be surprised, I know, to hear of our so sudden departure. Poor Brierly is dead, and we start to-day by the four o'clock express, hoping thus to reach the city before the party from the south arrive there. They started, we learn, on Tuesday morning. Mrs. Myers and Miss Glidden have kindly accompanied us, that my cousin may have the comfort of her friends' companionship, and the protection of the elder lady, whose guest she will be. In the haste of departure I am commissioned to say what they would have gladly said in person. For myself, while I trust we may meet again, and soon, may I presume to ask—in the event of your going away from Glenville, for my cousin has said it was possible—that you will let the doctor know where we may in future address you? In the hope of seeing you again, at an early date, I am,
>
> "Sincerely and hopefully,
> "F. Grant."

An hour later she sent for Doctor Barnes, who came promptly.

"Doctor," she began, as soon as he had entered her room, and closed the door. "I won't try to deceive you. I have had twinges of neuralgia to-day, and my bottle is quite empty. But I want, most of all, to hear more about this sudden flitting. They have left me just a line of farewell. Of course I know about poor Mr. Brierly. There's no doubt of his death."

"Not the least in the world, I regret to say."

"It is very sad, but I suppose they were prepared for the news."

"Yes."

"Now tell me about Miss Grant. Is she not coming back to her school?"

"I don't quite know. Her cousin, who is a very successful man in business, goes abroad soon, and he would like to have her among her friends. Miss Glidden is anxious to keep her for a time at least. I believe she, Miss Grant, had a few words with Doran. I fancy it will end in her resignation."

"Then how I wish she would come abroad, if not with her cousin, then with me. For I shall go soon, I quite think. In fact there are business matters, of my husband's, money matters that require my presence. I must write to Miss Grant."

"Then address her at the Loremer House for the present. Miss Glidden has a suite of rooms there."

A week later Mrs. Jamieson, accompanied by her friend, Mrs. Arthur, looked in upon Doctor Barnes.

"I have come to say good-bye, doctor," said the former. "I leave here in the morning. My brother-in-law, who is on his way eastward, after a second hurried western trip, will be in the city to-morrow; I meet him there, and we sail in three days. Mr. Grant has written me that the ladies are all out of the city, so I shall not see them, but he thinks they will all be in London before the end of summer."

Thus of all the active dramatis personæ of our story, but few were left in Glenville by mid-July.

"And so the pretty widow's gone," said Samuel Doran to the doctor, the day after this final flitting. "Looks like Glenville couldn't be a healthy place in July. Even my 'first cousin from out west' skipped out sort of sudden yesterday; couldn't stay another minute."

"You don't look heartbroken," suggested the doctor.

"Oh, I can spare him. Anyhow, I guess 'twas time he went. Powerful eater, that first cousin of mine," and Doran grinned from ear to ear.

CHAPTER XIX
THROUGH THE MAIL

From James Myers, Att'y, to Wendell Haynes, solicitor, with offices in Middle Temple Lane, off Fleet Street, which is London's legal heart and brain and life. Fleet Street, with such a history past, present, and to come, as may never be written in full by all the story-telling pens combined in this greatest literary centre, and working harmoniously; no, not in the space of a lifetime. Drafted in the office of the American lawyer, two days before his setting sail from New York, bound for London; and it was received, owing to stress of weather, five days before its writer set foot on British ground; and read by its recipient with no little surprise.

This is what it contained:

```
"WENDELL HAYNES, Esq.,
"Middle Temple Lane, etc., London.

"DEAR SIR,—After four years I find myself in the
act of reminding you of my continued existence,
and of your promise of proffered help, should a
day come when you, on that side, could aid me, on
this, because of what you chose to consider your
debt to me. To proceed: in two days I set out
for England, and it will take me, upon my arriv-
al, many days, perhaps, to find out what you, with
```

your knowledge of places and people, and your
easy access to the records, can do in half a day,
no doubt. I feel sure that I can rely upon you to
do for me this personal favour, which is not in
the direct line of your business routine, perhaps, but is quite within your ability, I trust
and hope; and without taxing too much your time
and energy. And now to business.

"I have reason to think that a certain Paisley
estate over there awaits an heir; and that one
Hugo Paisley, or his heirs, have been advertised
for. To know the exact status of the case, and
something about the people with whom I may have
to deal, at once, upon my arrival, will help me
much. And it is to ask for this information at
your hands that I now address you, and, being
sure of your will to aid me, as well as confident
of your ability, I shall trust to hear that which
I so much wish to know, upon my arrival in London, and from you.

"I sail by the _Etruria_ and shall stop at
Brown's.

"Yours sincerely,
"JAS. MYERS."

Wendell Haynes, solicitor, smiled as he read this missive. He had a
most vivid remembrance of his first and only visit to America, and of his
meeting with James Myers, quite by accident and shortly after his arrival in
Chicago, which city had seemed, to the visitor, a more amazing thing than
the howling wilderness which he had been in daily expectation of seeing,
would have appeared to him.

In his efforts to run down a friend from the suburbs, Myers had
consulted a hotel register, and seeing the name of the English lawyer,
written by its owner just under his eye, he had first looked at the man, and
then at the name, and, upon learning that he was an utter stranger to the
city, and to the ways of its legal fraternity, he had presented his card.

Solicitor Haynes had visited America and the "States" to investigate
what had appeared to be an effort, on the part of American agents, to

cheat the widow of a certain English ranch owner out of her just rights and lawful income, and the assistance rendered by Mr. Myers had earned him the lasting and earnestly expressed gratitude of his brother attorney, who asked for nothing better than an opportunity to repay the favour in kind, and no time was lost in the doing of it; so that when James Myers arrived at Brown's, and put his name upon the big register, the following letter was promptly handed him across the clerk's desk:

```
"JAMES MYERS, Esq.,
"Brown's Hotel, London.

"DEAR SIR,—Your favour of ... was very welcome,
affording me, as it did, some small opportunity to
return a very little of what I owe you for many
past courtesies and most valuable service, and I
have lost no time in looking up the information
you desire.

"There is a large estate, that of the Paisleys of
Illchester, awaiting the next of kin, who should
be, so far as is known, the descendants of one
Hugo Paisley who left this country nearly eighty
years ago, and whose heirs, male or female, are
entitled to inherit. There has been an effort made
to hear from these heirs, and, strange to say,
there has been no reply, nor has any other claim-
ant appeared of lesser degree. If you will call
upon me upon your arrival I will give you all
details and addresses so far as known to me, and
shall be very glad if I can be of yet further
use.

"Yours sincerely,
"W. D. HAYNES."
```

"You see," said Solicitor Haynes, at the close of an hour's talk with Lawyer Myers, "thus far all is quite clearly traced, and there is no doubt of the rights of the Hugo Paisley heirs—if such are to be found, and if they can prove their heirship."

"And the family, here in England, is quite extinct, then?"

"In the direct male line, yes. There may be cousins, or more distant relatives, but the father of Hugo Paisley had four children, the three eldest being boys, the youngest a girl. This girl married young and died childless. The elder son married, had one son, who did not live to become of age, and himself died before he had reached his forty-second year. Then the second son, Martin, inherited, and the last of his descendants died not quite two years ago, a widow and of middle age, I hear."

"And there have been no claimants?"

"None, I am told. The case was advertised, both here and in the United States, but with no results as yet, unless——" The solicitor stopped short and looked keenly at his visitor. "Something," he said, "has surprised, and I could almost imagine, disappointed you."

"You are quite sure of this?" the other urged, unheeding the last words.

"There have been no claimants, near or remote?"

"Absolutely none." The solicitor looked again, questioningly, into the face of his _vis-à-vis_, and then something like surprise came into his own. "Upon my soul, Mr. Myers, if I were to express an opinion upon your state of mind, I should say—yes, upon my word I should say that you were disappointed, absurd as that would seem."

"Disappointed—how?"

"Because, by Jove, there have not been any applicants or claimants for Hugo Paisley's money."

"Well, you wouldn't be far wrong. I am surprised, at any rate, and I shall have to admit that this fact disarranges my plans, stops my hand, as it were." He got up and took his hat from the table. "I came here with the intention of telling you a rather long story, in the hope of enlisting your interest, perhaps your aid. Now, I find that I must defer the story, and go at once and cable to friends at home."

He wasted no more words, but, promising to dine with his friend later, hurried back to his hotel, where he found a cablegram awaiting him.

Previous to his departure from New York, Ferrars had given him a code by which to frame any needful cable messages, concerning the business of the journey, or the people whom it concerned. The detective had warned all of the little group, now so closely bound together by mutual interest and in the same endeavour, to be constantly on guard against spies.

"Unless I am greatly mistaken," he said, "every effort will be made to keep in view all who are known to be connected with the Brierlys and their interests, and the fact that we are fighting an unknown quantity makes it the more necessary that we use double caution. We don't want another 'blow in the dark,' any of us; and, above all, we do not want to be followed across the water, and shadowed when there."

The wisdom of this was admitted, for, since the attack upon Robert Brierly, the unseen foe had become a bugbear indeed to Hilda and Ruth; and they abetted Ferrars in all possible ways, no longer questioning and with growing confidence in his leadership, in spite of the seeming absence of results.

The cable message which Mr. Myers read was worded as follows:

> "Jas. Myers, etc., etc.
>
> "H. has seen brother, who is watching affairs, un-able to sail at present; letter follows.
>
> "F."

These were the words; their meaning, according to the chart, was this:

> "Hilda has seen the western tourist. He is watch-ing us, and we will not attempt to sail until he is off the scent.
>
> "F."

Half an hour later this message went speeding back to New York, and from thence westward:

> "To F. Ferrars, etc., etc.
>
> "Case all right; way clear; no claimants."

Which meant precisely what it said.

A few days later two letters passed each other in mid-ocean. The one westward-bound read thus:

> "MY DEAR FERRARS,—It will not take me long to tell all that I have to tell concerning my mission. As I had anticipated, Mr. Wendell Haynes was more than ready to assist, and had the few facts I now give you already tabulated and await-ing me. Here they are in the order of your writ-ten queries:
>
> "1st. The Paisley fortune is no hoax. There is

a fine country seat, a factory, a town house, and various stocks, bonds and city investments amounting in all to above a million in American dollars.

"2nd. The English Paisleys are quite extinct, and the claim to the whole estate can surely be established by our claimant.

"3rd. And this may change all your plans possibly, and will startle you quite as much as it has me. There has been no effort made by any one to claim or get possession of the property, and there is no clue to such a person if he, she, or they exist. This balks us. How shall I proceed? Was ever a trail so completely hidden?

"Mr. Haynes has placed himself, and his knowledge and resources—both being extensive—entirely at our disposal. If you still think well of the advertising plan, wire me. I am idle until I hear from you, and mean to employ myself doing London, which will render my part of the enforced waiting very pleasant.

"By the by, I omitted to say that there have been but two 'notices' published. No unseemly haste, you observe. Awaiting your reply, I am,

"Yours sincerely,
"JAS. MYERS."

The letter which passed this midway was from Ferrars, and contained some information.

"DEAR SIR AND FRIEND"—it began—

"This finds us all in the city, the ladies at the flats, and myself in the old quarters, with which you have lately grown familiar. I fancied that we were quite snugly placed and could pass our period of waiting your summons with some ease of mind. Your house, which looks as untenanted and forbidding as possible, has been viewed, your caretaker says, by a 'party' who, from the description, I take to be the man whom we have termed the 'westerner,' and who was seen for a day or two in Glenville.

"But I have been rudely aroused from my comfortable sense of security. Yesterday Miss Grant and Miss Glidden were down town, and were driven out of the avenue by a long political parade. Driving down a cross street their coachman turned up Clark Street, only to find that another contingent was moving into that street, at the upper corner of the block. It was moving toward them, and the man quickly reined his horses close to the curb to await the passage of the line. Directly opposite the carriage was the sign, so frequent upon that street, of three balls, and while Miss Hilda gazed with some idle curiosity at the, to her, strange sight, a man came out tucking something into his waistcoat as he stepped down upon the pavement, glanced about him, and, without seeming to observe the carriage, or its occupants, walked quickly away. She had seen him, twice at least, at the Glenville, and she knew him at once. She ordered the driver home by a round-about road, but she is certain that the man was the same whom we thought a spy or worse. The most disagreeable feature of this is that I have not yet seen the man, watch as I would, and if he is watching us, he has the advantage. If the worst comes to the worst we shall have to spread out and go aboard our boat, when the time comes, singly and in disguise.

"Evening—

"Since writing the above I have visited the place of the three gilt balls and have found, at last, 'a straight tip.'

"The fellow had just redeemed a watch, pawned three days ago. It was a very pathetic story that we got out of the warm-hearted pawnbroker. The young man was overjoyed to be able to claim his watch so soon, for it was a keepsake given him by his dead father, and he 'prized it beyond words.' The watch was a fine foreign made affair, and on the inside was engraved Charles A. 'Braily' or

'Brierly'; he could not remember exactly. So, you see, the probability is that we have stumbled upon the watch stolen from Brierly's room in Glenville, which the fellow first pawned, from necessity perhaps, and then hastened to redeem, having taken the alarm in some way. He may even have been made aware that a description of the stolen watch and jewels had been lodged with the police. But all this is guessing. I am still confident that we shall find the solution of our problem on the other side of the Atlantic. Miss Glidden is still bent upon crossing, and your wife is her willing abettor. As for the fifth member of our party, he is at present like wax in our hands. Mind I say our, not mine alone.

"There is nothing new from Glenville—how could there be—now? I need not tell you about ourselves; Mrs. Myers, I know, keeps you well up in our personal history. And so, good luck to you. From yours in good hope,

"F. S. FERRARS."

Two days later this letter reached Ferrars.

"Glenville, July—
"FERRIS GRANT, ESQ.

"DEAR SIR,—Yesterday, too late for the mail, I struck luck, at least I hope you will call it luck. It came through our 'girl,' that is, the young woman who presides in my kitchen; she has a chum in the kitchen of the Glenville, and last evening they were exchanging confidences upon my back porch. It appears—I'm going to cut the story short—it appears that the night clerk is a kodak fiend, and a month or two ago the fellow,

> after being guyed about his poor work until he got rattled, vowed he'd contrive to get a picture of every person who set foot in that house for the next month to come, and that they should be the judges as to whether the pictures were good or not. Now it turns out that our traveller from out west was one of the victims of this rash vow, and when I found it out I lost no time in getting that picture. The fellow likes to drive my hors-es, and he always owes me a pretty good bill. I enclose to you this masterpiece of art. As you never saw him, to your knowledge, and as I had one glimpse, you will be glad, I dare say, to be told that the Glenville House people think it a good likeness.
>
> "There's nothing else in the way of news, and so, good luck to you, and a good voyage.
>
> "SAMUEL DORAN."

When Francis Ferrars had looked long at the picture enclosed in Doran's letter he started, and ejaculated, in the short, jerky fashion in which he used habitually to commune with himself, "That face!—I've seen it before—but where?" And then he suddenly seemed to see himself approaching the City Hall, and noting, as he walked on, this same face.

It was the habit of the detective to see all that came within his range of vision, as he went about, but he might not have retained a memory so distinct if he had not, in leaving the very same place, encountered the man again, his position slightly shifted, but his attitude as before, that of one who waits, or watches.

For some moments he looked thoughtfully at the picture, which was that of a dark and bearded man wearing a double eyeglass, and then he placed it under a strong magnifier, and looked again.

"Ah!" he finally exclaimed, "I was sure of it! The man is in disguise!"

He took the picture at once to the ladies' sitting room, and held it before the eyes of Hilda Grant.

"Do you know it?" he asked.

"That!" She caught it from his hand, and held it toward the light. "It is the man whom——" She paused, looking at Ferrars, inquiringly.

"Whom you saw at the pawnshop?"

"Yes. And——"

"And at Glenville?"

"Yes, at the hotel."

"And he was tall, you say, and broad-shouldered?"

"Yes."

"Strong looking, in fact. As if——" He checked himself at sight of the intent look upon Ruth Glidden's face, and she took the word from his lips.

"As if," she repeated, icily, "he could shoot straight, or strike a man down in the dark." She arose and took the picture. "It is a bad face," she said, with decision.

"It is a disguised face," replied Ferrars. "Nevertheless, I think I shall know it, even without the beard and thick, bushy wig. Let me see?" He took a piece of paper, and a pencil, and placing the photograph before him, began to sketch in the head, working from the nose, mouth, eyes and facial outlines outward, and drawing, instead of the thick, pointed beard, a thin-lipped mouth and smooth chin. Then, when the young ladies had studied this, he copied in the moustache of the photograph.

"It belongs to the face," he observed, as he worked; "and probably grew there."

Late that night, as the detective sat alone in his room with a pile of just completed letters before him, he again drew the photograph from its envelope and studied it with wrinkling brow.

"If you are the man," he said, with slow moving lips that grew into hard, stern lines as he spoke—"If you are the man I will find you! If you have struck the first blow—and it's very possible—you also struck the second. But the work is not yet finished, and, unless my patience and skill desert me, the last stroke shall be mine."

CHAPTER XX

A WOMAN'S HEART

The blow dealt Robert Brierly by the sham policeman had been a severe one, and at first it had been feared that he would recover, if at all, with his fine intellect dulled if not altogether shattered. But the best medical skill, aided by a fine constitution, and above all, the new impulse given his lately despondent spirits by the appearance at his bedside of Ruth Glidden, her eyes filled with love, and pity and resolve, all had combined to bring about good results, and so, one evening, not quite two months after that blow in the dark, he found himself sitting in an easy chair, very pale and much emaciated but, save for this, and his exceeding bodily weakness, quite himself again. Indeed a more buoyant and hopeful self than he had been for many a day, and with good reason.

At first, and for one week, his mind had been a blank, then delirium had claimed and swayed him, until one day the crisis came, and with it a sudden clearing of mind and brain.

Through it all Ruth had been beside him, and now she called the doctor aside and spoke with the grave frankness of a woman whose all is at stake, and who knows there is no time for formalities.

"Doctor, tell me the truth. He will know me now, and he must not see me unless—unless I tell him I have come to stay. Will a shock, such a shock, render his chances more critical? The surprise and——" She turned away her face. "Doctor, you know!"

Then the good physician, who had nursed her through her childish ills, and closed her father's eyes in death, put a fatherly hand upon her shoulder. "There must be absolutely no emotion," he said. "But a happy surprise, just now, if it comes with gentleness, and firmness—that tender firmness to which the weak so instinctively turns—will do him good, not harm. Only, it must be for just a moment, and he must not speak. My dear, I believe I can trust you."

He called away the nurse and beckoned Ruth to follow him. Then he went straight to the bedside, where the sick man lay, so pale and deathlike, beneath his linen bandages.

"Robert," he said, slowly. "Listen, and do not speak. I bring you a friend who will not be denied; you know who it is. You must not attempt to speak, Rob, for your own sake. If I thought you would not obey me I would shut her out even now." And with the last word upon his lips he was gone and Ruth stood in his place.

Involuntarily the wounded man opened his lips, but she put a soft finger upon them, and shook her head. She was very pale, but the voice, which was the merest murmur, yet how distinct to his ears, was quite controlled.

"Robert, you are not to speak. I have promised that for us both. I have been near you since the first, and I am going to stay until—until I can trust you to others. And, Rob, you must get well for my sake. You must, dear, or you'll make me wear mourning all my days for the only lover I have ever had. Don't fail me, my dear." She bent above him, placed her soft, cool hand upon his own, pressed a kiss upon his brow, and the next moment the doctor stood in her place, and was saying, "Don't be uneasy, Rob, old man; that was a real live dream, which will come back daily, so long as you are good, and remember, sir, you have two tyrants now."

And so it proved.

When Brierly was at last fit to be removed to that safe and comfortable haven—not too far from the doctor's watchful care—which they fictitiously named the South, Ruth bade him good-bye one day, with a tear in her eye, and a smile upon her lip.

"You will soon be a well man now," she said to him. "And when that time comes, and the tyrant Ferrars permits it, you will come to me, of course." And with the rare meaning smile he knew and loved so well, and so well understood, she left him, to bestow her cheering presence upon Hilda Grant and Glenville.

And now, on a fine midsummer night, thinner than of old, and paler, with a scar across his left temple, and a languor of body which he was beginning to find irksome because of the revived activity of the lately clouded and heavy brain, Brierly sat in a pleasant upper room of a certain hospitable suburban villa, the only south he had known since they bore him away from the Myers' home, and whirled him away from the city on a suburban train, to stop, within the same hour, and leave him, safely guarded, in this snug retreat.

"You see," the detective was saying, "I had found this series of tiny clues, and thought all was plain sailing, until that mysterious boy paid his visit to your brother's room and left almost as much as he took away. That forced me to reconstruct my theory somewhat, and set me to wondering just what status Miss Grant held in the game our unknown assassin was playing. For I will do the young lady, and myself, the justice to say that I never for a moment doubted her. That fling at her gave me, however, a key to the character of the unknown." He was silent a moment, then, "After all," he said, "it was you who gave me my first suggestion of the truth."

"How? when I had no conception of it?"

"By telling of that attack upon your brother the winter before his coming here."

"I do not recall it."

"I suppose not; but in telling me of your brother's career, before his going to Glenville, you spoke of an accident which occurred to him, an accident which was eventually the cause of his going to Glenville. I made a note of this, and, later, questioned Mr. Myers. He told me of the attack at the mouth of an alley. How two men assailed your brother, and only his presence of mind in shouting as he struck, and striking hard and with skilled fists, saved him from death at their hands; how he warded off, and held, the fellow with the bludgeon, but was cut by the other's knife. I might not have been so much impressed by these details, perhaps, had I not learned that your brother was returning from a visit of charity to the sick, a visit which he had paid regularly for some time. Then I thought I saw light upon the subject."

"Yes." Brierly bent toward the detective, a keen light in his eyes. "I have been very dull, Ferrars, but I have had time for much thinking of late. I think that, at last, I begin to understand."

"And what do you understand?" A slow smile was overspreading the detective's face.

"That my brother and I have had a common enemy. That nothing short of both our lives will satisfy him; that the attack upon Charley, nearly a year ago, was the beginning—that, having taken his life, they are now upon a still hunt for mine—and that, but for you, they would have completed their work that evening when, chafing, like the fool I was, under restraint, I set out alone, and met——"

"A policeman." Ferrars' lips were grave, but his eyes smiled. "It was a close squeak, Brierly. The fellow very nearly brained you. And now"— and he drew his chair closer, and his face at once became grave almost to sternness—"we want to end this game; there is too much risk in it for you."

"You need not fear for me, Ferrars. From this moment I go forward, or follow, as you will, blindly; you have only to command. What must I do?"

"Prepare to go aboard the _Lucania_ five days from date in the disguise of what do you imagine?"

"A navvy possibly."

"No. I know the boat's captain, luckily, and I know that a party of Salvation Army officers are to sail that day for England. We will go aboard, all of us, in the salvation uniform and doff it later, if we choose."

"You say all of us?"

"I mean Mrs. Myers, who goes to join her husband and see London and Paris; Miss Glidden, who goes because she wills to go and because she believes that Miss Grant can be best diverted from her sorrow, and strengthened for her future life, by such a journey, Miss Grant, _ergo_, and our two selves." He leaned back and watched his _vis-à-vis_ narrowly from underneath drooping lashes. He was giving his client's docility a severe test, and he knew it.

As for Robert, he remained so long silent that the detective, relaxing his gaze, resumed—

"I won't ask you to take too much upon trust, Brierly. Our present position, briefly told, is this. We are nearing the climax, but we cannot force it. One point of the game remains still in the enemy's hands. And the scene is shifted to England—to London, to be literal. The next move must be made by the other side. It will be made over there, and we must be at hand when the card is played. If all ends as I hope and anticipate, your presence in London will be imperative, almost. As for the ladies, Miss Grant's presence may be needed, as a witness perhaps, and certainly nothing could be better for her than the companionship of her friend, Miss Ruth, and the motherly kindness of Mrs. Myers, just now."

Robert Brierly turned his face away, and clinched his hands in desperation. He was thinking of Ruth, and an inward battle was raging between strong love and stubborn pride.

"And now," went on the other, as if all unheeding, "concerning the disguises. I have told you of the person seen by our spies at the Glenville House, for a brief time?"

Brierly bowed assent.

"He, this man, was only described to me, but seen by Miss Grant."

"Oh!" Brierly started.

"Lately, we have received, through the good offices of Mr. Doran, a picture of this man—it's growing late and I'll give the details at another time—I have believed this man to be one of your enemies, quite possibly the one."

"One of them?"

"Yes. And large and muscular enough he is, to have been your assailant, and——"

"And my brother's murderer?"

"In my opinion they are not the same. But we must not go into this. Some one has kept us—that is, yourself, Miss Grant and myself, in the character of her cousin—under constant watch, almost. There must have been tools, but this man I believe to be the chief, on this side."

"Great heavens! How many are there, then?"

"Honestly, I do not yet know. The answer to that is in Europe. But this man—he has been shadowed since Miss Grant saw him on Clark Street— has already sailed for England. My man escorted him, after a modest and retiring fashion, to New York, and saw him embark. I propose that we go east by different routes. The ladies one way, you and I by another. They will hardly imagine us all flitting by water, and their spies will hardly be prepared for a sea voyage, even should one of us be 'piped' to the wharf.

Of one thing I must warn you; you are not to set foot in London, nor to put yourself in evidence anywhere as a tourist, until you are assured that you may walk abroad in safety. To know you were in England would be to render your opponents desperate, indeed."

"You have only to command. I am as wax in the potter's hand henceforth. And now I ask you on the eve of this long journey why my brother and myself are thus hunted. How we stand in the way of these enemies of ours I cannot imagine."

"That I am ready to tell you, since you ask no more. You stand between your enemies and a fortune."

"Impossible!"

"I knew you would say that. But wait." Ferrars rose abruptly. "I shall not see you again before we leave for New York," he said, taking up his hat. "Come with me across the way, I must say good-bye to the ladies; they——"

"Do they understand?"

"Yes."

Mrs. Myers and her two charges were pleasantly bestowed just across the street, in one of the cosy and tree-encircled cottages of the aristocratic little suburb, in which the party had found a retreat. And all three were still upon the broad piazza when the two men appeared.

No other occupants of the house were visible, and before long Robert Brierly found that, by accident or design, the detective, Mrs. Myers, and Hilda, had withdrawn to the further end of the long veranda, and that Ruth Glidden had crossed to his side, and now stood before him, leaning lightly against a square pillar, and so near that he could not well rise without disturbing her charming pose.

Before he could open his lips she was speaking.

"Robert, don't get up. Please do not. There is something I must say to you. I have seen the trouble, the anxiety in your face to-night. I know what Mr. Ferrars has been saying to you; at least I can guess, and I understand."

"Ruth!"

"Don't speak. Let me finish, Rob. If I didn't know you so thoroughly, if the whole of your big, noble heart had not been laid bare to me, as never before, during your illness, I should not dare, would lack the courage to say what I will say, for your sake, as well as for mine." She caught her breath sharply, and before he could command the words he would have spoken, she hurried on.

"Don't think that I do not know how you look upon this journey abroad, in my company, and now——" She paused again. "This is very hard to say, Rob, and I am not saying it well, but you will not misunderstand me, I know that; and I can't lose your friendship, Rob, dear, and the pleasure your company will be to me, if we can set out understanding ourselves and each other. You have let Charlie's death and the money loss this search may bring you, crush out all hope, and you have been steeling yourself to give me up; to forget me. But do you think I will let you do this? I know your pride, dear. I love you for it. But why must it separate us utterly? You are not the only man in this world who must win his way first, and whose wife must wait. I have waited, and I shall wait, always if need be. But it need not be. You will be the King Cophetua to my beggar maid yet. Oh, I know. I am afraid of nothing but your horrible self doubt, your fear of being——"

"Of being called a fortune hunter, Ruth."

"Well, you shall not be called that, sir knight of the proud, proud crest. Listen! You must be to me the Robert of old; not avoiding me, but my friend who understands me. We are both free to go abroad, and with a chaperone, as we are going, would not be _de rigueur_ otherwise; and this subject is not to be referred to again, until the quest upon which we are starting—yes, I say we—is at an end.

"Who knows what may happen between our going and our home-coming? At the worst, I am still your friend, and shall never be more to any other man." She was about to move away, but he sprang up and caught her hands.

"Ruth! You have given me new life. And you have shamed me. It is of you I have thought, when I have tried to tear myself away and leave you free to choose another."

"Robert, for shame. Shall you 'choose another' then?"

"Never! You know that!"

"If I did not I should never have spoken as I have just now."

"But there are so many who might give you everything."

"There is only one who can give me my heart's desire."

"Ruth, my darling, if I were rich, or if you were poor, no man should ever win you from me. But the world must never call Ruth Glidden's husband a fortune hunter."

"It never shall. Never!"

"And so, you see——"

"I see the folly of what I have said. What do we care for dame Grundy? And why should you and I be foolish hypocrites, deceiving no one? In my heart of hearts I have been your promised wife always. I think I have the little ring with which we were betrothed when we were ten years old. We will go abroad as lovers, Rob, and if you cannot offer me a fortune—it must be a very large one to satisfy me—before we return, I shall give all mine to the London poor, and you will have to support me the rest of my days. What folly, Robert, what wickedness, to let mere money matters come between you and me!"

CHAPTER XXI
QUARRELSOME HARRY

The _Lucania_ had been in port forty-eight hours, and Mrs. Myers and her party had been snugly quartered in one of London's most charming rural nooks, at Hampton Court, with Robert Brierly close at hand, before Ferrars ventured to visit the city.

Mr. Myers had discreetly remained in London, going from thence to meet his friends at Hampton Court, but Ferrars, for reasons which he did not explain, went to the city, as soon as he had assured himself of the comfort and safety of his party, this assurance including the provision of a watchful aid, who kept guard whenever Robert Brierly, himself now well convinced of the need of caution, ventured abroad.

Leaving Mr. Myers thus to enjoy an evening with his wife and friends, Ferrars hastened to "the city," where every stone seemed familiar, and many faces were those of friends or foes, well known and well remembered. To escape recognition his own countenance had been simply but sufficiently hidden behind a disguise of snowy hair and rubicund visage, both assumed as soon as he had parted from the group at Hampton Court, for Ferrars realised that the battle was now on, and he had no idea of giving the foe the chance possibility of an encounter. He was well known at Scotland Yard, as well as to the chief of the department of police, and it was to one of these officials that he made his way, for he had two reasons of his own for hastening on, in advance of the party.

Not long before leaving the "States," he had received a dainty notelet. It could not have been called a letter. It came through the hands of Doctor Barnes, and it was signed, "Lotilia K. Jamieson."

It is late afternoon when Ferrars reaches Oxford Street, after his interview with several official personages, during which he has bestowed upon each a number of typewritten cards, bearing what seems to be a brief descriptive list, and as many photographs, faithful and enlarged copies of the "snap shot" furnished him by the hand of Samuel Doran.

He alights from an omnibus at the end of Regent Street, and stands, for a moment, looking down Oxford Street. He is not in haste, for he lets cabs and omnibuses rattle by him, or stand, waiting for fares, and walks slowly on and on. A mile and a quarter of shops, that is Oxford Street, but Ferrars foots it sturdily. Past the Circus, beyond the region of Soho, and he slackens his pace and consults a tiny memorandum book. Who ever saw Frank Ferrars produce a letter or card, for reference, in the streets of a crowded city? Then he smiles and paces on.

Bloomsbury. He is walking slowly now, and under his low-drawn hat his eyes are very alert.

And now he is in that portion of Bloomsbury where, earlier, very early in the century, the wealthy, and those of high degree resided. It is comfortable and middle class now, and our pedestrian passes a certain pleasant semi-detached house—not large, but eminently respectable—with a stealthy, lingering glance, pausing, before he has walked quite beyond it, as if to note some object of fleeting interest. Two or three times, within the hour, he passes that house, now on this side, now on that; once on the top of an omnibus, once in a cab, and driving very slowly, and as close as possible.

It is fairly dusk when he slowly ascends the well scrubbed steps, with the reluctant air of a man by no means sure of himself. He carries a small package beneath his arm, and a card between the fingers of his left hand, to which he shifts the package as he rings the bell.

"I beg your pardon, young Miss." It is a sour-faced damsel of uncertain age who melts perceptibly under this adjective. "Will you tell me if Mrs.—Mrs.——" He peers near-sightedly at the card he holds, and slowly pronounces a name.

"No, sir; this is not the place."

"But, doesn't the lady stop here, Miss? It's some'res in this here block, and somehow they've forgot the number, you see. Is there a lady guest maybe, or a boarder belike?"

But the maid, quite melted now, shakes her head, and tells him that beside her mistress, whom she names, and her mistress' niece, who stops with them, "off and on," there are no ladies in the house.

The detective blunders on down the street, and, when the lamps are lit he passes the house again. The lamps are lighted in the little dining room now, and through a window which projects upon the corner, he can see a table set for two. And now at last he is rewarded, for a maid enters and places something upon the table; a lady follows, glances at the table, walks to the window, and turns, with a quick, imperious gesture, toward the maid; a little lady, with a fair face, pale, fleecy hair and wearing a flowing silken gown of some soft violet shade. She sweeps past the maid and seats herself at the head of the table, while the young person—it is the same who attended so lately at the door—comes forward to close the curtain. Slowly it is drawn together, shutting in the lights, the table and the violet-clad figure, but not until the watcher outside has caught a glimpse of a man, tall and, yes, handsome, in a dark fierce fashion, who is entering at the door on the other side of the room.

The watcher passes on. He has seen, once more, the woman who has, according to his own confession, aroused in him "a profound interest." And he has also seen, whom and what? A brother? A lover? A rival, perhaps? Ferrars hails a passing cab now, and is driven swiftly towards his room in the Strand, and as he rolls along, this comment, which may mean much or little, passes his lips.

"So my little lady has doffed her mourning. I wonder what that may mean?"

"I'm very sorry, Ferrars, but I fear there's a great disappointment in store for you."

"A disappointment! How? And in what respect, Mr. Myers?"

Ferrars was seated opposite Mr. Myers in the office of Wendell Haynes, solicitor, in Middle Temple Lane, where he had hastened on the morning after his little adventure in Bloomsbury, and so prompt and eager had he been that he had encountered the American lawyer at the very threshold,

Mr. Myers having just arrived, with equal haste and promptness, from Hampton Court.

Solicitor Haynes and the English detective were not unknown to each other, and when they had exchanged greetings, the solicitor left the others together in his inner office. He was, by this time, fully acquainted with all the facts, so far as they were known to Mr. Myers, and he left them with a promise to rejoin them soon, when they should have compared notes and gone over the ground already known to the busy solicitor.

There was a look of suppressed eagerness upon the face of Ferrars, as he seated himself opposite the shrewd American lawyer. His face, his manner, his very silence and alertness as he held himself erect upon his chair, a picture of calm force, long suppressed, but now out of leash and ready for anything—anything except inaction; and that, his very attitude seemed to say was past.

Mr. Myers had waited a moment, after they were left alone together, for Ferrars to speak the first word, but the latter only sat still and waited, and the lawyer, with characteristic directness, spoke straight to the point. He had what he felt to be bad news to impart, and he did not delay or play with words in the doing it.

But if he had expected disappointment or any change to cross that keenly questioning face, he looked in vain. Ferrars only sat leaning slightly toward him, waited a moment, and repeated his last words.

"In what manner? How disappointed?" And then, as the lawyer still hesitated, he went on. "You find the case as it should be, eh?"

"The case! Oh, yes!"

"Are there any flaws?"

"No," broke in the lawyer.

"Any unexpected delays?"

"No."

"Any new claimants?"

"No, Ferrars. The Hugo Paisley will case is one of the simplest and clearest of its kind. The last incumbent surely must have had a wonderfully clear idea of how to do the thing he meant to do. Once the claim is proven, and he makes that work easy, there need be no delays, no chancery, no holding back for big fees. The agents in the case are paid according to their expedition, and have every incentive to haste. With the proofs in hand the heir could step at once into his fortune, a matter of £200,000."

"An American millionaire, eh?" Ferrars smiled. "That, then, is quite as it should be, especially as the young lady is here. Well, then, you advertised, according to your report?"

"Yes, we advertised. A very craftily worded document calculated to arouse the dilatory claimants to prompt action."

"And, did it not?"

"It did, yes."

"Then, in heaven's name why must I be disappointed in any way?"

"Because I fear the claimant—we have seen but one—is not the person you hoped to find."

Ferrars actually smiled. "Describe the person," he said.

Without speaking, the lawyer held out to him across the table a visiting card, a lady's card, correct according to the London mode of the hour, and bearing a name which Ferrars read aloud with no sign of emotion in his face.

"Mrs. Gaston Latham." He looked up with the card still between his fingers. "Is she the solitary heir?"

"No; there are two children; girls of twelve and nine."

"And her proofs?"

"Seem to be perfect, making her the next in line of succession after——"

"After the Brierlys, of course."

Mr. Myers nodded and the detective looked down again at the address upon the card.

"Lives in the city, I see! Are the children with her here?"

"Only the younger, I am told. The elder has 'an infirmity,' and is at present in an institution. It seems a great cross to the mother; in fact her anxiety and distress, because of this child, have made her almost indifferent about this business of the fortune. In short"—and here the lawyer glanced askance at his _vis-à-vis_—"I'm afraid she is not the—the sort of claimant you have expected to see. And there seems to be no one of the other sex in the family."

"Well, well!" Ferrars threw himself back in the big office chair, assuming an easy and almost careless attitude.

"Tell me all about her, Myers. Is she old, or young? Handsome or not?"

The face of the lawyer was overspread with a cynical smile. He had expected to see disappointment, consternation, perhaps, in the face of the detective, when he heard that the English claimant to the Paisley fortune was a woman lorn and lone. His heart was in the work they were engaged upon. Robert Brierly's interests were his own; but, still, this cool, emotionless detective, whom he liked well, had more than once piqued and puzzled him. He believed that Ferrars was quite prepared to meet with, and hear of, quite another sort of claimant, and he was now looking to see him at last stirred out of his provoking calm.

"Mrs. Gaston Latham is not a claimant to whom one could object, upon the ground of unfitness. She would make a very handsome and gracious dispenser of the Paisley thousands."

"Too bad that she will never get them!" And Ferrars smiled.

"She is a woman of medium height, and rather—well—plump, and while her hair is snowy white, she does not look a day over forty. She has the fine, fresh English colour, blue eyes, that require the aid of strong eyeglasses, and a voice that is very high-pitched for an Englishwoman, and that sounds, I am sorry to say—for she's really a very intelligent and winning little lady—somewhat affected at times. She dresses in soft grays and pale lavenders, as you may be interested to know." And here the lawyer smiled broadly.

"That," commented Ferrars, with no cessation of his own gravely indifferent manner, "for a 'plump' woman, is a great mistake. A plump person should never assume light colours." And then the eyes of the two men met, and over each face there slowly crept a smile that grew into a laugh.

"Upon my soul, Ferrars," exclaimed the elder, "I believe you have heard of this Mrs. Latham!"

"Not to make a mystery of it, Mr. Myers, I'll explain that I have heard of Mrs. Latham. But, I give you my word, I did not look to find her the claimant. You have heard us, some, or all, speak of Mrs. Jamieson!"

The lawyer nodded and a smile of meaning crossed his face.

"Well, I have lately learned that she might be found at a certain number in Bloomsbury, and addressed, in case of her temporary absence, in care of Mrs. Gaston Latham, an old family friend."

"I see!" The lawyer was silent a moment. Then he looked the detective frankly in the face. "To be perfectly candid with you, Ferrars," he said, "I have thought that you looked to see a different sort of claimant, more than one perhaps, and that this lady could not, by any possibility, be the expected one. I fancied this would trouble, perhaps hinder, if not quite balk you."

"Honestly, Myers, I have wondered not a little what sort of claimant I should meet, and I am neither surprised nor disappointed. I see what is in your mind; you looked to see the conclusion of the game here and soon, eh?"

"I admit it."

"And I hoped it. I do hope it. We must strike our final blow now if ever. We can depend upon Mr. Haynes."

"Entirely."

"And you have fully enlightened him?"

"To the extent of my own knowledge?"

"Then let's call him in, and I will put my cards upon the table. We shall need his help, but I'll explain that later."

When the English solicitor had joined them, Ferrars briefly reviewed the events surrounding and connected with the death of Charles Brierly, and the attempt upon Robert's life; and when he was sure that they understood each other, thus far, and that the English lawyer was deeply interested in the case and had committed himself to it, he summed up the situation thus.

"You will see, of course, that I might make a bold stroke and arrest my suspects at once; or, at least, as soon as we could lay our hands upon them, but the case is a complicated one, and having it in my power to make our quarry commit themselves altogether, I do not intend to leave them a loophole of escape. I have not been entirely open with you; you must take my word for some things. I have put the Scotland Yard men on the lookout for our man; I do not know his name, but I think they will have no trouble in finding him, by acting upon my hints. There is much which even I do not understand, in his connection with the case. I do not believe him to be the master spirit, and I want to let him have his fling over here."

"Do you mean," broke in the solicitor, "that you do not intend to arrest him, as soon as found?"

"He must be kept under close espionage, when traced, but so long as he does not leave London, he must be left quite free to come and go at will. There is much that is still hazy, concerning his appearance in Glenville, and I look to him to lead me to another—to the other, in fact."

"And," urged the solicitor, "do you feel safe in venturing this? May he not shun those places?"

"Listen! The man's name I do not know, but I know what he is. There are plotting villains in this world, who might scheme forever and still be often penniless. This man is a gambler. In Chicago he pawned the watch stolen from Charles Brierly's room, knowing that there was risk in so doing, but desperate for the money it would bring. He won soon after, and aware of danger ahead, for he had good reason to think himself followed over there, he at once redeemed his pledge. He does not dream that we are here, and the finances at headquarters, I have reason to think, are running low. To play he must have money, and when he has lost he will either pledge or sell the remainder of the jewels stolen from the writing desk. They were of considerable value, as I have discovered."

"Ah!" Mr. Myers looked up quickly.

"Oh, that's no secret. Hilda Grant saw the jewels, and knew their value."

"May I ask why you presume that all the stolen jewels are in this man's possession?" asked the solicitor.

"Because they were stolen, in the first place, not for plunder's sake, but to mislead; and the party who took them lost no time, I am sure, in passing them on, and out of the town. It is hardly likely they would have divided them."

"Then you look upon this man as in truth little more than a cat's paw?"

"In some respects, yes. He does not take this view, however, and now I want to hear all about your interview with this lady, Mrs. Gaston Latham."

"According to your instructions," said Mr. Myers, "I remained in the background. Mr. Haynes was the spokesman."

Ferrars turned toward the solicitor, who began at once.

"There is really very little to tell. Of course I quite understand that the claimant was to be held off, and the next interview to take place in your presence."

Ferrars shook his head. "I fear we must change our plans somewhat. The fact is," here he glanced up and met the eye of Mr. Haynes, a queer smile lighting his own, "I have found just now, that I knew a lady who seems to be a friend of this Mrs. Gaston Latham, and an inmate of her house in Bloomsbury. Now it might be a little awkward for me to appear before my—the lady in question, as the opponent of her friend. In fact, I must not appear in the matter—not yet, at any rate. And, upon my word, Mr. Myers, since our friend has taken up the _rôle_ of Spokesman-in-chief, you and I will both stand aside, just at first. May we count upon you?"

"I shall need some coaching, of course," suggested the solicitor.

"Of course; and that you shall have at once. But first, when is she to call again?"

"When I give the word."

"Give it at once, then; to-morrow at 2 p.m. Tell her to come alone. You can arrange for us to hear the interview, I dare say?"

The solicitor swung about in his big chair. "You see those two doors?" he asked, quite needlessly pointing at the two doors, at opposite corners of the inner wall, "They open upon my private chamber of horrors. Formerly there was a partition, and two smaller rooms The partition has been removed. In the morning I will have my man move that tall bookcase across the door at the right. The door, behind it, can then stand open, and you can hear very well. I will have my desk and the chairs moved nearer that corner. Will that do?"

"Excellently; only I must see the lady in some way."

"Then, if you will come in some slight disguise, you can sit at my clerk's desk, over by that window, with your back to the light. I will dismiss you, and you can go out to join Mr. Myers, through the left-hand door."

They inspected the inner room, and Ferrars, gauging the distance with his quick eye, made a suggestion or two regarding the placing of the desks, and the visitor's chair, and then they sat down to discuss the part the solicitor must take in the coming interview.

That evening when Ferrars strolled into his room after an early dinner, he found a note from a certain police inspector, in whose charge he had left the hunt, or rather, the watch for the suspected stranger. The note contained a summons, brief and peremptory, and he hastened to present himself before Inspector Hirsch.

"We have found your man," were the inspector's first words, when the detective was left alone with him. "And it was an easy trick, too, for all your fears to the contrary. I tell you, Ferrars, when a sport who lives only to gamble and bet on horses, comes back to London after any long absence, he's sure to go to one of a dozen flush places I can name, as soon as he can get there. And, if he's heeled he'll go to them all. Just give him time. I didn't neglect the houses of mine uncle, but I also sent a squad around to these other places."

"And you found him?"

"We found him. And that's not all. We have found a name for him."

"Good! What is it?"

"He goes by the name of 'Quarrelsome Harry' among his kind. Harry Levey is the way he writes it."

Ferrars pondered a moment "M—m—I'm not surprised," he said finally. "I was sure he was that kind. What's his specialty besides being quarrelsome?"

"Cards, and crooked bookmaking, I fancy. But Smithson, who seems to have known him of old, says he's up to most sorts of shady business, when his luck's down."

And the inspector went on describing the search for "Quarrelsome Harry" who had been "spotted" at a time when he was in a fair way to prove his right to his sobriquet. For he had been losing money all the previous night, and had sought his room in a dingy house in Soho, in a very black mood.

Here, so the shadow had reported, "Quarrelsome Harry" had remained until late noonday, emerging then to lunch at a coffee-house, and to take his way, for what purpose the watcher could only guess, to Houndsditch, where he seemed quite at home among the Jews in several cafés and "club rooms," where he tarried for a greater or shorter time, and seemed to be looking for some one—some one whom he did not find, it would seem, for he left the neighbourhood as he came, alone and with a lowering face.

"Looking for a loan, I'll wager," declared Ferrars. "By to-morrow he'll be visiting my uncle. I'll have to leave him to your men to-night, I suppose, Hirsch, but to-morrow I will go on guard myself."

He made a note of the Soho street and number, where Harry Levey had lodged, and then he took out his cigar case and the two men sat down together to talk about London, and compare notes. For they were old acquaintances, and could find much to say, one to another.

An hour later, when Ferrars arose to go, the inspector looked at his watch.

"By Jove! Frank, you don't mind my calling you that, eh? It seems like old times, half a dozen years ago. Say, it's almost the hour for the Swiss to report. He's on duty now looking after your man; wait till he comes in. Hobson must already have gone to relieve him, if he can find him. Harry was airing himself along the embankment when last heard from."

It was nearing ten o'clock, but Ferrars resumed his seat and his cigar very willingly, and Inspector Hirsch set out a very pretty decanter of something which he described, while pouring it into the glasses, as both light and pleasant.

At half-past ten "the Swiss," as rank an Englishman as ever ignored his h's, came in beaming.

He had left "'Arry," as he familiarly called the man he had been set to guard, in a front seat in the gallery of the Vaudeville theatre in the Strand, and Hobson was sitting just three seats away, and nearest the

"halley."

"'E's got a sort of green lookin' young duffer with 'im," went on the Swiss, "and they seem to be goin' to 'ave a night of it."

Ferrars got up quickly. "Come out with me, inspector," he said. "I may want you to call off your man. And, say, let me have one of your badges. It may come handy."

CHAPTER XXII
IN NUMBER NINE

As the inspector and Ferrars approached the theatre they were obliged to slacken their pace, for, although the performance must have been well on its way, there was a crowd about the entrance.

"It's a first night for some new 'stars,' now that I think of it, and you'll find a lot of the sporting gentry here whenever a new and pretty face, that has had the right kind of advertising, is billed. That accounts for our friend's presence here, of course," said the inspector.

They made slowly their way toward the entrance, and as they reached it, and were about to pass within the brilliantly lighted vestibule, Inspector Hirsch grasped his companion's arm and pulled him back within the shadow of a friendly bill board.

"H'sh!" he whispered. "Here's Hobson!" He drew Ferrars still further out of the crowd. "He must have lost his man, or else—hold on, Ferrars; I'll speak to him." And he glided into the crowd and Ferrars saw him pause by the side of a flashily-dressed young fellow, who seemed utterly absorbed in trying to revive a smouldering cigar stump. He gave no sign of recognition as the inspector paused beside him, and seemed engrossed with his cigar and his own thoughts, but Inspector Hirsch was back in a moment with a grin upon his face.

"Your man has tired of the Vaudeville," he said, "and Hobson got close enough behind him—the other chap's still with him, too—to hear them planning to go on to the Savoy for a short time. Harry's evidently doing the theatres with his 'young duffer,' as the Swiss calls the fellow, and will probably pluck him if nothing intervenes." He looked hard at Ferrars. "My man won't lose sight of them. Want to go on to the Savoy?"

"By all means," replied Ferrars, and they set out, noting, as they skirted the crowd, that Hobson was no longer visible.

Crossing the street, they hastened their steps, and upon arriving at the Savoy, took up their station near the entrance once more. The crowd here was not dense, and they had not long to wait before two men approached from the direction of the Vaudeville, walking slowly, and entered the vestibule of the Savoy.

The taller of the two was broad shouldered, dark and handsome, after a coarse fashion, while the other was smaller, with a weak face and uncertain manner. Both were in evening dress, and when they entered the theatre Ferrars and the inspector followed.

"I can stay with you an hour longer," said the latter. "Then I must go about my own affairs."

Ferrars nodded. He was watching "Quarrelsome Harry" closely, and after a time, as that personage began to look about as if in search of some expected face, he procured an opera glass, and with its aid began to sweep the house.

Then, suddenly, he started, and, after a long look at a certain point in the dress circle, he turned quickly toward the inspector.

"Do you know any one in authority here?" he asked.

"I know the head usher over there; or, rather, he knows me."

"That will do. Just call him, won't you? Introduce me. Tell him I'm after a crook who is up to mischief here, and ask him to help me."

After a time this was accomplished, and soon after the inspector took his leave.

And now came the entre-acte, and a number of ladies left their places and went, some to the cloak-room, some to the foyer. The two men in whom Ferrars was interested went out among many others, and Ferrars followed. In the refreshment room they took places at the side, and the detective, contrary to his usual plan, passed them, and took a place midway between that occupied by the two men and a certain table, further down, where a party of six were seated.

To the waiter, who came to serve him, Ferrars said: "Send me your chief waiter," and slipped a coin into his willing hand.

When the chief waiter came, the two exchanged some whispered sentences, and then, as the man withdrew, our detective addressed himself to his light repast. He had been careful to keep himself unseen, so far as Harry Levey was concerned; and he had now chosen his seat behind a pillar, which hid him from view, while he still could, by moving slightly, look around it.

It was while taking one of his frequent peeps around this pillar that Ferrars saw "Quarrelsome Harry" tear a leaf from a small pocket-book and write a few words upon it, doing this in the most unobtrusive manner possible, with the bit of paper upon his knee.

Since they had exchanged those few whispered words together, Ferrars and the head waiter had not lost sight of each other, and now a slight movement of the brows brought the man to Ferrars' table.

"Now," whispered the detective, "and be sure you are not observed."

The man nodded and passed on, seeming to scan, with equal interest, each table as he passed it. Nevertheless, he saw a note slipped into the hand of a vacant faced young waiter, and a few words of instruction given. Then the young man turned away, and began to move slowly toward the opposite side of the room.

A little beyond Ferrars' table he encountered the head waiter, present arbiter of his destiny.

"Kit," said this personage, in a low tone, "slip that note you carry into my hand and wait behind the screen yonder until I give it back to you. Quick! No nonsense, man; and mum's the word!"

As between a stranger with a liberal tip, and the august commander of the dining-room corps, Kit did not hesitate, and a moment later the head waiter dropped the note into Ferrars' palm with one hand, while he placed a bottle of wine beside his plate with the other.

Putting the bit of paper between the two leaves of the menu card, Ferrars boldly read its pencilled message.

> "Drive to the Café Royal. Ask to be shown to No. 9. I will join you there soon."

A moment later this note was placed, by Kit, beside the plate of the one for whom it was intended. The next, Ferrars, having tossed off his glass of light wine, arose and sauntered out of the refreshment room.

But he did not return to the theatre. Instead, he took a cab and was driven to the Café Royal.

Here again he sought out a person in authority, to whom he exhibited his star, and a card from Inspector Hirsch, and was at once shown to No. 8.

"If questions are asked," he said, as he slipped a goodly fee into the hand of authority, "remember that No. 8 is vacant, but is engaged for an hour later."

Left to himself, Ferrars moved a chair close to the wall between himself and number nine. It was but a flimsy barrier of wood and he nodded his approval, turned down the jet of gas, until it was the merest speck, and sat himself down to wait. But not for long; soon he heard the next door open, a sweeping, rustling sound, and the scraping of a chair. Then a bright light flashed up, the door closed, and all was still for a short time.

Then, again the door opened, there was a heavy step, low voices, and Ferrars knew that he might, if he would, lay his hand upon those whom he had sought so long, and, for a time, it had seemed, so hopelessly.

"Are we quite alone here, do you suppose?" It was a man's voice, strong and somewhat gruff. "Let us see." And he rang the bell. The man who had admitted Ferrars, and who had no mind to fall out with the police, responded, and at once showed conclusively that the adjoining rooms, Nos. 8 and 10, were quite deserted, although, he admitted, he had locked No. 8 in order to secure it for a party at midnight; whereupon wine was ordered and he was at once dismissed.

"Well," began the heavier voice again, "why in the name of goodness haven't you pushed things more? I told you, from the first, that all was safe. There will be no crossing the big pond now. How long do you mean to dally?"

"We can't dally now," replied the lighter voice. "Didn't you see the notice in the papers? They are calling for the heirs. I don't understand it, but they tell me that unless we come forward now, the matter will be referred to some other court, and then there must be a long delay. No, I must produce those papers now, and if there should be any question, any flaw——"

"Pshaw!"

"Or if they should call for further proof of identity, you know. Suppose some one should be found, at the last moment, acquainted with her!"

"Bosh! How foolish!"

"Or who remembered me!"

"I tell you this is folly! Latham's first wife died so long ago, and at a Swedish spa. And she never had many friends. As for relatives, well, we know there are none now."

"Sometimes I fear the children will remember; that it will all come back to them, some day."

"I tell you this is simply idiotic; the time has come, and everything is in train. You have all the papers, certificate of marriage, copy of will, and who is to prove that the first Mrs. Latham died, and that she was the last of the Paisley line, on this side, or the other? You were married abroad, you have all her family papers and her jewels. Her children call you mother."

"And hate me!"

"Well, that won't cut any figure. Besides, we must have money. You and I have put our little all into this scheme. How much longer can we live decently unless you claim this estate soon? I must have money! Do you mean to see your brother starve?"

"Hush! You are not my brother, remember that; only my brother-in-law."

"All right. How lucky that Latham's brother never came back. Now, what did you especially want to say to-night?"

"This. I must meet those lawyers to-morrow."

"Oh! And I as nearest male kin, must be your escort, and support you through the trying ordeal."

"Not at all. I am especially requested to come alone."

"The d——!"

"But they will want corroborative testimony, and I want to beg of you not to take anything to-morrow, and not to stay out the rest of the night. Much depends upon the impression we make. And if we should fail——"

"We can't fail; or you can't. Aren't you next-of-kin?"

Ferrars got up and crept noiselessly to the door. He had heard enough, and he had much to do. A new enquiry to open up. He knew that he should find Hobson, who had not been dismissed, outside and near, and he meant to leave "Quarrelsome Harry" to him once more.

"Look after him sharp, Hobson," he said, when he had found the man in the outer room. "And ask the inspector to have a warrant ready in the morning. We must arrest him to-morrow. He is to be taken for conspiracy and attempted murder. That will do for a beginning." And leaving the pair in No. 9 to their plotting, and to the watchful care of Hobson, Ferrars hastened from the place.

CHAPTER XXIII
TWO INTERVIEWS

And now let us turn the clock back a few hours, that we may relate how Hilda and Ruth made the well-laid plans of Ferrars of no effect, so far as himself and another were concerned.

Mr. Myers had left the ladies of his party safe in their snug quarters at Hampton Court, and went early to the city to meet Ferrars, as has already been related; but if he expected them to remain in _statu quo_ on such a day, and in easy reach of Bond Street, it speaks ill for his knowledge of women, especially of Ruth Glidden, who knew her London well, and who—when Mrs. Myers began to long to see the inside of Howells and James, and their royal array of painted and other rare china, and Hilda looked yearningly over the guide-books for the city—took matters into her own hands.

There was no reason why they should not go to town, especially, so she privately informed Mrs. Myers, as Hilda was moping. She could guide them anywhere where they might wish to go.

And this is how the three ladies came to be seen at Marshall and Snelgrove's, linen drapers, so called; at Redmayne's and Redfern's, and at Jay's, for Hilda's sombre bedecking. Jay's has been called the "mourning warehouse" of the world, not because Jay keeps on tap a perennial and unfailing supply of tears, but because "all they (feminine) that mourn" may be suitably clad—at enormous expense, by the way—by Jay and Co.

And here it was that our little party, sweeping into one of the superb parlours where models display Jay's sombre wares, came face to face with Mrs. Jamieson, who, seated upon a broad divan, was gazing at a little blonde, of her own size and colouring, who displayed for her benefit a flowing tea-gown of soft, black silk, lighted up here and there with touches of gleaming white.

Of course there were greetings and exclamations, and such converse as may be held in so public a place; and Ruth, who, somehow, made herself spokesman for the party, exclaimed that they had "just run over for that little outing, and because Hilda needed the change. Oh, yes, they were well escorted; Mr. Myers was with them, and also Mr. Grant."

At the name, which was the only one by which she knew Ferrars, Mrs. Jamieson flushed and paled, and the smile with which she received this news was slightly tremulous. And then she told them how she was stopping, for a short time, with a friend in Bloomsbury. Her husband's business affairs, that had called her so suddenly back to England, were now almost settled. And then she should leave London for a time. She had been thinking of a place in Surrey; she hoped to be in possession soon, and then surely they would not return too soon for a visit to her among the Surrey Downs? And where were they stopping?

Upon which Ruth confided the fact that they were not yet in permanent quarters. They must be settled soon; however, meantime, etc., etc., etc.

They parted soon, and it was only when they were riding homeward that it occurred to them that Robert Brierly's name had not been spoken, and that Ferrars, perhaps, would not be best pleased to know of their unpremeditated excursion.

As for the little widow, she went back to Bloomsbury in a state of excitement unusual for her.

To know that "Ferriss Grant" was in London, and that she might see him soon, set her pulses beating, and her brain teeming with plans for their meeting. What had brought him to London just now? What, indeed, save herself? Unless—and here she paled, and her little hands were clenched till the black gloves burst across the dainty palms—unless it were Ruth Glidden.

What was Ruth Glidden to the Grants? she asked herself futilely, and why were they together? And then for ten minutes Mrs. Jamieson wished she had never seen Ferriss Grant.

"I was very well content until then," she assured herself. "And my future seemed all arranged; and now——" she longed to meet him, and yet—

"If he had but waited, or if I had not been so hesitating! Now I must go on, and he must not know. A month later and I might have received them all in my sweet Surrey home, have met him with full hands, and there would have been no need of explanation, while now!" She struck her hands together, and set her lips in firm lines. "I must see him once, and then we need not meet until all is arranged. If I only knew where to send a note."

She had been absent since luncheon, and upon her arrival at home she found this brief note awaiting her:

"MRS. JAMIESON.

"DEAR MADAM,—Being in London for a short time only, and with little leisure, I take the liberty of asking if I may call upon you in the morning, at the unfashionable hour of eleven o'clock?

"Yours respectfully,
"FERRISS GRANT."

It was late when she reached Bloomsbury, and she had little time to dress for dinner and the evening, for she was going out again, but she replied to this note, bidding him come, and assuring him of his welcome at any hour. Then, reluctantly, and with a look of distaste, amounting almost to repugnance upon her face, she began to dress for the evening.

When Ferrars reached his rooms, after leaving the café, his lips were set, and his eyes gleamed dangerously, for a little time he paced the floor, and then, impelled by some thought, he looked to see if any letters had arrived during his absence. Yes, there they were, half a dozen of them. He glanced at their superscriptions, and then opened a little perfumed and black-bordered envelope. It was Mrs. Jamieson's reply to his note of the afternoon, and he read it and put it down slowly.

"I shall be prompt," he said to himself, "to keep that appointment, and I wonder whether its outcome will make me more or less her friend. If it will alter or modify my plans; and if, having met this once I shall have the courage, the hardihood to meet her again, and to say what I must say if we meet." He put down the little note and took up the one next in interest.

The handwriting was that of Ruth Glidden, and the stationery that of a fashionable Piccadilly dressmaker.

```
"DEAR MR. F."—so ran the note—

"I am aware that you did not wish us, any of us,
to be seen of men in London until certain things
were accomplished, and I take upon myself all
the blame of the little journey we, Mrs. Myers,
Hilda, and myself, took this afternoon. We felt
quite safe in visiting a few shops 'for ladies
only,' but at the third we met Mrs. Jamieson.
This may, or may not, be of moment to you. At all
events, I have eased my conscience, and Hilda's,
by letting you know. Nothing of any moment was
said on either side, and no questions were asked.

"Yours penitently,
"RUTH G."
```

Over this womanlike note Ferrars wrinkled his brows, and finally smiled.

"I had not meant that they should meet until—but pshaw! What does it matter? Everything seems urging me on and shaping my course. So be it! It is time for the last stroke, and to-morrow, before this hour, I shall be a free man, or a failure."

Ferrars was prompt in his appearance at the Bloomsbury cottage, and Mrs. Jamieson had been for a long half-hour awaiting him alone in the little drawing-room Her face was somewhat pale, and there was a hint of agitation in her greeting, and a shade of gravity in his.

She talked of Hilda, and was full of pleasure at their meeting; and by and by she spoke of Ruth, her beauty, her grace, and style. Was it true that she was an heiress? And was she not, in some way, related to Miss Hilda and himself. Or perhaps to the Brierlys?

It was the first mention of that name by either, and Ferrars, looking into her eyes, answered:

"She bore the same relation to Robert Brierly that Hilda bore to Charles. They had been lovers since childhood."

"How sad, strange, and romantic! How pitiful!"

"The sadness outweighs the romance, and it is strange that the same hand should have struck at the happiness of both their friends. I have asked myself," he went on musingly, "what would be the fate of the destroyer of so much happiness, if these two girls could be made judge and jury, with the slayer at their mercy."

"Ugh!" The lady shuddered and turned her face away. "The thought is unnatural!"

"I don't know; women have been dread enemies before now, and are generally good haters. They make great criminals, too. But I fancy a woman must always betray——"

"Mercy!" She crossed the room suddenly to change the position of a translucent screen through which the sun had begun to filter. "You are positively gruesome, Mr. Grant! Let us change the subject. Or, first let me ask if they have found any trace of the cr— the person?"

"The clues have been very unsatisfactory for the most part. But the ladies both hope to see justice done yet. We all hope it, in fact."

"And what is most lacking?"

"From the first, the motive seemed most difficult to discover. But we won't dwell upon this longer now, Mrs. Jamieson."

"Ah! And I was just getting up courage to ask you to tell me what had been done, what progress had been made; I was so near to being a witness, you know, and——"

"And of course you are interested, I quite understand that. If you really care to hear, Mrs. Jamieson, I will tell you the whole story when next we meet. It is quite interesting. I will tell you that and other things." He arose and stood before her. "I must not tarry now. Shall you be at liberty this afternoon?"

"I am so sorry. I am promised to my hostess. She thinks I live too secluded a life. But I am about to make a change." She brightened visibly as she told of her Surrey prospects, and her hope of seeing his party, and himself, there. And then her smile faded.

"I fear I may not see you again for at least a fortnight. I have promised Mrs. Latham, my hostess, that I would go over to Paris with her. She has been very good to me," she faltered. "How long shall you remain in England?" she added.

"More than a fortnight at least."

"I shall see you again?"

"Mrs. Jamieson, never doubt it." He was drawing on a glove, as he uttered the words, and across the busy fingers he looked into her eyes.

"It was to see you that I came to England, and so——" he bowed low,

"till we meet." He caught up his hat and stick, and before she could put out a hand had bowed himself from the room, and she heard his quick receding step across the little vestibule.

For many moments after, she sat where she had sunk down at his sudden going, and presently the slow tears fell upon the hands that supported her bowed face.

For years she had been an unhappy woman, living an unloved, unloving life. Then ambition and hope had taken hold of her mind, and she had tested herself, and found, in that small body, the strength to dare much, and to risk much; and now—how she thrilled at the thought—wealth, success, and love; all would come to her together. What else could his words mean? She had only to be courageous and firm for a little while. To be patient for a few more days, and then—— She sprang to her feet and flung her arms aloft. She wanted to shout for triumph.

"Victory!" she said aloud. "Is there another woman in all the world who can say that she has conquered fate, and gained all the good she has worked and wished for?"

And just then, the maid's voice broke in upon her dream.

"Madam, the charwoman is here for the money. Do you still wish me to give her the little suit?"

The woman turned as suddenly as if Nemesis had spoken.

"Yes!" she said, and the voice was husky, and the face almost terror stricken.

"Ruth."

Robert Brierly came up the piazza steps, where Ruth sat alone, and dropped upon the topmost one, at her feet. "I have just received a note from Ferrars."

Ruth looked up from her bit of needlework. There was a note of suppressed excitement in his tone, which she was quick to observe.

"He seems to have changed his mind," Brierly went on, "and bids me come up with Myers."

"To-day?" The work fell from her hands.

"Now. In half an hour."

"But Robert, after all his caution!"

"Let me read the note, dear," he said, unfolding the sheet he had held in his hand. "It is very brief and pointed:

> "'DEAR BRIERLY,—Come up with Myers, and be sure that you are not observed when you enter Haynes' office. He will know what to do with you. If I have not been an awful bungler—and I don't think I have this time—you will stand a free man to-night, able to go up and down the earth without menace from the assassin's knife, and will have come into your own, which means a fortune.

> "'FERRARS.'"

"Ruth," he spoke softly, "Do you know what that means?"

"Better than you do, perhaps." She spoke hurriedly, as if to gain time, and her cheeks were already aflame. "Your mind was so entirely set upon finding Charlie's murderer, Rob, that they thought it best not to risk a new anxiety by telling you too much about the other; besides, there could be nothing certain, you know, until Mr. Myers had investigated. You had a hint of it."

"Oh, to be sure. And I have not been quite blind to their kindly cunning. Will it be a very great fortune, Ruthie?" He caught her hand, and held it fast.

"Very!"

"Because if it is, I intend to come back and lay it all at your feet, formally, abjectly, and with utmost speed."

Ruth wrestled away the imprisoned hand and gave her chair a backward push.

"Robert Brierly, if you dare to come to me and offer me a fortune, a hateful old English fortune—that I despise; if you only ask me to accept you after you are sure of that money, I won't! I will not! Never!"

"Ruthie!" She sprang up, but he was before her. "Oh, you can't escape now. I intend to propose to you this minute. I'll run no risks, after such a threat as that. Ruth, if you run away, I will shout it after you, and Mrs. Myers and Hilda are half way down the stairs now. Quick, Ruth, dear, will you marry me? I sha'n't let you go until you say yes."

And then, in spite of herself, Ruth's laughter bubbled over.

"You stupid! As if we hadn't been engaged for years! At least I have."

Half an hour later when Mr. Myers and Brierly came out upon the piazza together they found Ruth awaiting them there, equipped for a journey.

"Why, Ruth," said the lawyer, "are you going to the city?"

"I am going with you!" the girl replied firmly. "You need not argue. I mean to go. And Mr. Ferrars will not object. He will need me."

CHAPTER XXIV

MRS. GASTON LATHAM

Solicitor Wendell Haynes sat at his desk, at half past two, seemingly busy, while across the room, at a smaller desk, sat a second person, with his shoulder toward the outer door, and a screen partially concealing him. From the inner room came the low hum of voices. At the side of the room where the clerk's desk stood, and the tall bookcase towered before the concealed door, the curtains were lowered; but there was a strong light upon the solicitor's corner, and upon the chair, placed near his desk, manifestly, for a visitor.

When Ferrars appeared without the disguise he was expected to wear, the solicitor wondered. But the detective explained in a few words. He had made certain discoveries which would enable him to end a very unpleasant piece of business at once, he hoped. And his disguise would only hamper him.

"I must ask you, however, to add something to your _rôle_," he said finally, and at once made plain what more would be required of the solicitor.

As for Ruth Glidden, she had waited in dignified silence, and much to the wonder of the politely reserved solicitor, until Ferrars appeared, and then she went straight to his side.

"Mr. Ferrars," she said, so low that the others caught only the soft murmur, "It came to me, almost at the last moment, that a woman might not be amiss here now if she comes alone. You can trust me, surely?"

Ferrars gave her a sudden look of gratitude. "Thank you for showing me my own brutality," he replied. "I can trust you, and I do thank you; there could have been no one else." And Ruth went back to the inner room smiling a little, as she met her lover's eye.

To guard against all emergencies, the detective had left with the inspector a card telling him, and his men, where a telegram would reach him at different hours of the day, and at a quarter past two a message arrived, bearing the signature of the Swiss.

"Q. H. and a lady on the way to meet you now."

So it ran, and having read it, Ferrars asked:

"Is your boy safe, Mr. Haynes? and trusty?"

"Quite. I find him really valuable."

"Then please instruct him to go and bring a brace of policemen, as soon as he has shown the next arrivals in." And he held out the telegram by way of explanation, adding, as the solicitor read and returned it, "The man is coming, too. I can't just see why. But we will soon know. By the way, that door on the north side, in the inner room; where does it lead one?"

"Into a side hall, connecting with the other."

"I thought so. Then, as soon as they are in, I will just slip out, myself, and see my man, who won't be far from your door, you may be sure, once his quarry is inside. He will be needed, perhaps, to serve the warrant, which he carries, ready for an emergency. Hist!"

There was the sound of an opening door, and, as Ferrars seated himself, the office boy entered and announced the two visitors.

The lady, who entered and bowed in stately fashion to the solicitor, was all in gray, except where, here and there, a bit of violet protruded. The hair, which was white, rather than gray, was worn low about the ears, and rolled back from the centre of the forehead, giving an effect of length to the face. The eyes looked dark, behind their gold rimmed glasses, and seemed set far back, in dark hollows. The mouth was slightly sunken, but the cheeks and chin, though pale, were sound and smooth, and the brow showed a scarcely perceptible wrinkle, beneath a veil of gray gauze spotted with black. She had a plump figure, its fulness accentuated by her rustling gray silk gown, with its spreading mantle glittering with steel beads, and finished with a thick, outstanding ruche at the neck. Atop of the high coifed white hair, sat a dainty Parisian bonnet, all gray beads and violets, and the small hands were daintily gloved, in pearl gray.

"I have taken the liberty of bringing my husband's brother, Mr. Haynes," she said, as she advanced into the room, "Mr. Harry Latham."

The tall, dark fellow behind her advanced, and proffered a hand with an air of easy geniality.

"Mrs. Latham," he explained, "fancied I might be of some use by way of identification. I hope my presence is not _de trop_; if so————"

"You are very welcome, sir. Sit down, pray, and we will begin our little inquiry. You have brought the papers, Mrs. Latham?"

Mrs. Latham, who had been looking with something like disapproval upon her aristocratic face, toward the partly visible person behind the screen, turned toward the speaker, and, as she advanced to lay a packet of papers, produced from a little bag, upon the desk, the solicitor called out, as if by her suggestion, "Richards, I shall not need you for an hour or more." And before the lady could turn toward him again, the man at the desk had vanished through the door just at his back.

Glancing toward this closed door, the lady seated herself, and drew the packet toward her. "I suppose we may begin with these?" she said, untying the packet with deft fingers, and laying the papers one by one upon the desk before the solicitor, as she talked. "I think all the needed proofs are here; my marriage certificate, and that of my mother as well; other family papers that may, or may not, be of use—letters relating to family matters and to the Paisleys of an earlier day—a copy of the will of Hugo Paisley the first, letters announcing the deaths of various members of the family; also a copy of my grandfather's will. I think you will find them quite correct, and conclusive." She stopped, and looked at him inquiringly. "You will need to examine them, of course, if only for form's sake?" she asked, somewhat crisply.

"Possibly, yes. All in good time, madam." The solicitor took up one of the papers, and glanced at the first words.

"I would like to ask," now spoke Harry Latham, "how soon—supposing of course all things are correct, and Mrs. Latham's claim proved—how soon can she take personal and complete possession of the property? I am a busy man, myself, and my time——"

"I fancy you will not be needed after to-day," broke in Mr. Haynes, somewhat abruptly. "As to the property, once the claim is proven there need not be a day's delay. The late incumbent was a very far-seeing person." He turned abruptly to Mrs. Latham. "Madam, may I ask why you were not more prompt in putting forward your claim to so fine an estate?"

She turned toward him with a slow smile.

"That is a most natural question. I did not at first imagine myself a claimant; a certain Hugo Paisley, the younger, or his heirs, was before me in the line of succession, and I have waited to see if they would not be heard from. I had no wish to claim that which might not have been mine."

"And you are satisfied now that no such heirs exist? Of course this must be proven."

"Of course, I have been at some pains, and to much expense, to learn if there were such heirs. With the help of friends we made inquiry in the United States, where Hugo went years ago. He was never heard of again."

"And was your search rewarded by definite news?"

"By an accident we learned of a member of the family, and through him traced all the remaining ones. They were three, a mother, the great granddaughter of Hugo Paisley, and two sons. The mother has been dead some years. They were not a rugged family."

"Consumption," came from the dark man at her elbow.

"Yes, consumption. The two sons died within a few months of each other."

"I see. And of course you have the proofs of death?"

"They can readily be proved at need," the lady coldly answered.

"Then there remains but one more question, where you are concerned. Supposing your claim to be disputed, could you prove beyond a doubt that you are the Bessie Cramer, who was the last descendant in this country of the Paisleys, your mother having been a Paisley?"

"Of course!"

"And you are then able to furnish proof that there was no other Mrs. Gaston Latham? That Gaston Latham married only one wife?"

A loud laugh broke upon this speech, and the man arose.

"Would the word of Gaston's only brother be of any worth as a witness to the marriage, the only marriage of his only brother? Fortunately I knew Miss Bessie Cramer as a slim young girl. I was a boy in roundabouts then."

Solicitor Haynes arose, and looked gravely down upon his client, ignoring the man's words, and even his presence.

"I must tell you, Mrs. Latham, that there has been a claim set up by the American heirs."

"There are no heirs!" warmly.

"Only yesterday I had a visit from an American gentleman, a Mr. Myers, attorney-at-law. Do you know of him?"

"I know no Americans, and very little of the country."

"Then you have never crossed the ocean?"

"No, indeed! It's quite enough for me to cross the channel."

"Mr. Myers has presented a claim." The solicitor's eyes were narrowing.

"For whom?"

"For—a—I think the name is Brierly; as I was about to say, having made an appointment with you, I thought it best that you should meet him." He touched the bell at his side, as he spoke the last word.

"But," interposed the man, "this is some old claim, or else a fraud! The Brierlys are dead!" The last words harshly guttural.

The office boy had entered now, and Mr. Haynes quietly gave his order.

"See if Mr. Myers is in number seventeen, William."

"Mr. Haynes," said Mrs. Latham, with a touch of haughtiness, "Why should I need to see this man? These deaths can be proved."

The solicitor bowed formally. "So much the worse for Mr. Myers and his claim," he said. "Of course you must meet him; there's no other alternative. He is a gentleman, and he certainly believes in his claim."

"He's not up to date, then," interposed the brother-in-law, somewhat coarsely, and even as he spoke the door opened, and Mr. Myers, having taken his way around by the side hall, entered, hat in hand.

CHAPTER XXV
THE LAST STROKE

As the solicitor turned toward the newcomer, the man and woman exchanged glances, and while he was still confident, not to say defiant, he looked to the unobservant solicitor with a nervous, apprehensive glance, and leaning toward her would have whispered a word of his anxiety; but she shook her head, and the next moment the solicitor was naming them to each other and, as Mr. Myers paused before the lady, continued with the utmost directness—

"Mr. Myers, this lady denies the existence of any and all American heirs. She fears you may have been deceived. Do you know this man Brierly to be living at present?"

"I believe him to be living."

"Mr. Myers," said the lady, sweetly, "I am very sorry to think or say it, but you have certainly been grossly tricked! If you have seen a would-be claimant, you have seen a fraudulent one. How long, may I ask, since you left America?"

"I have been in England for some time, and I will admit, madam, that I do not quite understand this case in all its details. Still, may it not be possible that you have been misled? There seem to have been complications." He checked himself, and appeared to be considering his next words, then he resumed—"I think I can help to clear up this misunderstanding. I brought with me here a young man lately from the United States. He claims to have seen a Mr. Brierly very recently. With your permission I will ask him to join us."

The Lathams again exchanged swift glances, and the man gave his head a quick negative shape. But the solicitor went promptly to the door. They did not hear the brief order he gave the boy, and he did not come back at once.

"Who is this young American who has seen the invisible? And how came he here to-day?" asked the man, who was now frowning heavily and moving restlessly in his seat. "What is his name?"

Mr. Myers had picked up a book off the desk, and was turning its pages slowly. He seemed hardly to hear the fellow's words.

"He's a very bright young fellow," he said, musingly. "I don't think he would be easily deceived. He's quite a clever detective, in his way." He was studying the pair from under bent brows. Just then Mr. Latham's hat fell from his hands to the floor, and before he had recaptured it, the solicitor had entered, followed by a serious-faced young man, whom he carelessly named to the two strangers.

"Mr. Grant."

The lady's hand went suddenly to her heart, and her face was ashen beneath the dotted veil.

"Are you ill, madam?"

"A twinge," she faltered.

"It's neuralgia," declared the man, drawing his chair toward her. "She's subject to these sharp attacks. Better, Bessie?"

She nodded, and fixed her eyes upon "Mr. Grant," to whom Mr. Myers was saying:

"This lady, Grant, is positive that the Brierlys, of whom you have talked to me, are not now living. There has been tricking somewhere, and deception. Will you help us to understand one another?" The lawyer's face had grown very grave.

Francis Ferrars seated himself directly before the woman, whose eyes never left his face now, and were growing visibly apprehensive.

"There has been more than tricking, worse than deceit here, and if I am to make it clear to you, madam, I must begin at the beginning. So far, at least, as I know it."

The woman bent her head slightly. "Go on," said the man. He had never seen Ferrars either in _propria persona_, or as Ferriss Grant.

The detective began with a brief sketch of the Brierly brothers, and then described, vividly, the discovery of Charles Brierly's dead body beside the lake at Glenville. He paused here, and his voice grew stern as he resumed—

"I had never seen Charles Brierly in life, but, standing beside his dead body, looking down into that face so lately inspired by a manly, strong soul, I knew that here was murder. There was no possibility of accident, and such men, I know, do not cheat death by meeting him half way. It was a murder, and yet he had no enemies, they said.

"The case interested me from the first, and when I had seen the sorrow of the fair girl he loved, and who loved him, I gave myself eagerly to the work of seeking the author of this most cowardly blow.

"That night I walked the streets of Glenville alone, and, passing a certain fashionable boarding house, I saw, in a room lighted only by the late moonbeams, the shadow of a woman, who paced the floor with her bare arms tossing aloft in a pantomime of agony, or shame."

He glanced about him. The two lawyers were standing side by side near the door, erect and stern. The man in the chair opposite was affecting an incredulous indifference. The room was intensely still when the voice ceased and no one stirred or spoke.

"Next morning, early, I viewed the scene of the crime, and I saw how easily the destroyer might have crept upon an unsuspecting victim, owing to the formation of the shore, the shelter of the trees and shrubs, and the protection of the curving Indian Mound. There had been showers two days before, and in certain spots, where the sun did not penetrate, the earth was still moist. Under a huge tree, just where the slayer might have stood, I found the print of a dainty shoe, or rather, the pointed toe of it. In two other sheltered places I found parts of other footprints, and, a little off the road, in a clump of underbrush, I found two well-formed footprints, all alike, small, and pointed at the toe. But I found something more in that hazel thicket. I found my first convincing, convicting clue. It was just a shred, a thread of a black mourning veil, such as widows wear. Later I found a poor simpleton who had been in the wood on the morning of the murder, and who had been horribly terrified. For a time he would only cry out that he had seen a ghost, but by and by he grew more communicative, and from what he then said—for he described the 'ghost' at last as a thing all white with a black face—I knew how to account for a white fragment which I found not far from the black one. A hired carriage had passed over that lakeside road on that fatal morning, and I learned that the lap cover with it was

'large and white.' Large enough to cover a woman of small stature, who, with a black veil drawn close across her features, and rising suddenly from among that clump of hazel, could easily terrify a simpleton into leaving the place where his presence was a menace."

He paused a moment, but he might as well have been looking upon carven statues. No one stirred, no one spoke, and he resumed his fateful story.

"Then came the inquest. I believed, even then, that I knew the hand that took Charles Brierly's life. But I did not know the motive, and, until I did, my case was a weak one. Besides, a woman sometimes strikes and still deserves our pity and protection. 'I must know the motive,' I said, and waited. Then, at the inquest, as Robert Brierly, the brother of the dead man, whose presence in the town was known to only a few, came forward to testify, a woman, who did not know him, and whom he did not know, fainted at sight of him, and was taken out of court. Then I knew the motive."

"Ah-h-h!" A queer sighing sound escaped the lips of the woman still sitting stonily erect before him; but he hurried on.

"But knowledge is not always proof—in a court of law—and I must have proof. That night a woman, dressed as a boy, by courage and cunning combined, forced her way into the rooms so lately occupied by Charles Brierly. Fear of detection had begun its work upon her mind, and she went, most of all, to try and throw justice off the track. In Brierly's desk she left a letter, very conspicuously placed, an anonymous letter, so framed as to throw suspicion upon the dead man's betrothed. This again showed the woman's hand. She also carried away a watch, a pistol, and some foreign jewellery and dainty _bric-a-brac_, to make the work seem that of a thief; and last, she found, upon a letter file, a newspaper clipping, which she also carried away. If she had left that I might have overlooked its value. As it was, I found the paper from which it had been cut, secured a second copy, and discovered my clue to the tangle. It was an advertisement for the heirs of one Hugo Paisley, and I soon found that the Brierly brothers were the sought-for heirs. Then I knew that Robert Brierly's life was also menaced, and I warned him, and tried to set a guard about him.

"In the meantime a boat had been found, not far from the scene of the shooting; it had been seen on the lake that morning, and its occupant was a spy, keeping watch up and down the road, and the hillsides, while his confederate carried out their programme of death. I had already fixed upon the woman, and now we began to look for the man."

Just here the man calling himself Latham got up stiffly, and moved toward the window near the clerk's desk, where he leaned against the casement, as if looking down upon the street. No one seemed to notice him, and the narrator went on:

"And now I had to find my final convincing proofs of the motive and the deed. The brothers Brierly were, all unknown to themselves, the heirs to the Paisley estates, and of Hugo Paisley, by descent. Through some error the murderers of Charles Brierly had been led to think him the sole living member of the family, and when Robert Brierly stood forth at the inquest, the woman who had shot down his brother with hand and heart of steel, fell fainting at the sight of him, and, perhaps, at the thought of her wasted crime.

"And now it was a drawn game, in which both sides were forced to move with caution, and, for a time, I could only watch the woman, on the one hand, and the safety of Robert Brierly on the other, for he now stood between the plotters and their goal.

"But despite my watchfulness, the second blow fell, and the first time Robert Brierly ventured upon the city street alone, after dark, he was struck down, almost at his own door. It was a dangerous injury, and, lest the assassins should find a way to complete their work, we took him away, as soon as he could be moved."

The woman was sitting very erect now, her eyes smouldering behind the gleaming glasses, her hands tightly clinched upon her knee.

"I knew that we must force the issue, then," Ferrars went on. "And Mr. Myers came over here to substantiate his client's claim to the Paisley estates, and to look up the pedigree, the past and present history, of the other claimants. How well he succeeded need not here be told. He did succeed."

Mrs. Latham had risen to her feet, and, for a moment, seemed struggling for composure, and the power to speak clearly.

"All this," she said then, "which is very strange, does not explain why you dispute my claim in favour of a dead man. As for this murder—if you have proved what you charge——"

"One moment," Ferrars broke in. "Let me add, in that connection, that one night one of my agents, in the character of a burglar, entered this woman's room at her hotel in Glenville. She found in a trunk, the veil from which the black fragment, found on the bush, was torn; and also a suit of boy's clothes. The veil she brought away, the clothes were given away to a poor woman only this morning, and she sold them to my agent. As for the man, he has been traced by the stolen watch and jewelled ornaments. He tried to sell, and did pawn, them in Chicago, in New York, and here in London. In fact the chain of evidence is complete; nothing more is needed to convict these two."

The woman's face was white and set. "After all," she said in a hollow voice, "you have not proved that the Paisley estate is not mine by right. Mr. Brierly, the elder, being dead!"

"Even so, the second wife of Gaston Latham cannot inherit, and her brother, even in the character of brother-in-law, cannot share the inheritance. One moment," for the woman seemed about to speak. "Let me end this. Last night, in room number eight at a certain café, I heard the plotters in conference, and I know that the daughter of Mrs. Cramer, who would have inherited after the Brierlys, is dead. The game is up, Mr. Harry Levey. You and your sister have aimed two heavy strokes at the happiness of two noble women, and the lives of two good men, but the final stroke is mine! And now, Mrs. Jamieson, if that is——" He did not finish the sentence. The man Levey had drawn closer and closer to the inner door, while Ferrars spoke, and now with a swift spring he hurled himself against it, plunged forward and would have fallen had not Ferrars, always alert, bounded after him, and caught him as he fell. For the inner door had opened suddenly, at his touch, and when Ferrars drew the now struggling man backward, and away from it, the others in the room saw, in the doorway, a man and woman side by side.

At sight of Robert Brierly's face the woman, who had faced the ordeal of denunciation and conviction almost without a quiver, threw up her hands, and uttering a shrill scream, a cry of mortal terror and anguish, fell forward upon her face.

Then came a moment of excited movement, which would have been confusion but for the quick wit of Ruth Glidden, and the coolness and energy of the detective.

While the entrapped villain was struggling like a fiend in the grasp of four strong men, Ruth knelt beside the fallen woman and lifted her head.

The next moment two or three officers came hastening in, and Ferrars and Brierly, seeing their captive in safe hands, came together to her aid. She looked up at them with a questioning face.

"Did you know?" she asked, her face full of horror. "Did you know her?"

Ferrars nodded, and as the officers led their captive, cursing and blustering, out at one door, he lifted the senseless woman, and carried her to the couch in the inner room.

"Bring water!" Ruth commanded, "and leave her to me."

As the two men closed the door between them and the two so strangely different women, Brierly laid a hand upon the detective's shoulder.

"Ferrars," he said, "what did Ruth mean? Who is that terrible woman? And how is she concerned in your story? It is time I should know the truth."

"Quite time. That woman is Mrs. Jamieson, or the person you knew under that name. She is cleverly disguised, but I expected some such trick. She went to 'the States' to rid herself of you and your brother; and she took that man, who is really her own brother, and who tried to kill you, as her fellow criminal."

"And did she——" Brierly stopped, shuddering.

"She shot your brother; there is not a doubt of it."

"My God! And I thought——" They were alone in the office, and Brierly dropped weakly into the nearest chair and dropped his face upon his hands.

"You thought," finished Ferrars, "that I was interested in the woman. I was. I suspected her from the very first, and so did Hilda Grant."

In the inner room, Mrs. Jamieson opened her eyes and looked up to meet the gaze of the fair woman who was in all things what she was not.

Ruth bent over her, a glass of water in her hand.

"Drink this, Mrs. Jamieson," she said simply.

A shudder like a death throe shook the recumbent form. She lifted herself by one elbow, and caught at the glass, drinking greedily. Then, still holding the glass, she said slowly:

"Then you know me?"

"Yes."

"How?"

"By your voice, a little, but mostly by what Mr. Ferrars said."

"Mr. Ferrars!" she gasped. "Do you mean him?"

"I mean the man you have called Grant. Did you never guess that he was a detective?"

"And he knew!" The woman arose to her full height and again, as on a night long since, and in another country, her arms were tossed above her head, as Ruth nodded her answer, and for a moment her face was awful to look upon, so tortured, so despairing, so full of wrath and wretchedness and soul torture and heart agony, for women can love and suffer, though their souls be steeped in crime.

Ruth, who had taken the half emptied glass from her hand as she struggled to her feet, now put it down, and, startled by her look and manner, moved toward the door, but the woman, her face ghastly, cried

"Stop!" with such agonised entreaty that the girl drew back.

"Don't!—I can't see him yet—Wait!—Let me——" She sank weakly back upon the couch, and Ruth noted, while turning away for a moment, how her hand toyed with her dainty watchguard, in seeming self forgetfulness, drawing forth the little watch, a moment later, and looking at it, as if the time was now of importance. Then she threw herself back against the cushions.

"My—vinaigrette—my bag!" she moaned between gasping breaths.

The little bag had been left in the outer office, where it had fallen from her lap, and Ruth opened the door of communication a little way and asked for it, saying, as Ferrars came toward her, "Not yet."

As Ruth turned back, she heard a sharp little click, like the quick shutting of a watch case, and when she held out the vinaigrette, Mrs. Jamieson was swallowing the remainder of the water in the glass.

"Your salts, Mrs. Jamieson."

The woman looked up with a wild scared look in her eyes, and held out, for an instant, the little jewelled watch.

"For years," she said, in a slow, strange monotone, "I have faced and feared danger, and failure. For years I have been prepared! Because of my cowardice, and my conscience, I have always kept a way of escape." Her fingers fluttered aimlessly and the watch fell upon her lap. Her last words seemed to come through stiffening lips. Her face grew suddenly ghostly gray. Ruth sprang toward the door.

"Don't let him come yet." With these words the dying woman seemed to collapse, and sank limply back into the cushions; her head drooped, her chin dropped.

Ruth flung open the door with a cry of terror, and the four men—for the two lawyers had returned from their escort duty—gathered about the couch. They saw a shudder pass over the limp frame. The fingers fluttered again feebly, there was a spasmodic stiffening of the figure—and that was the end.

Four weeks later, a group of people were standing upon the deck of a homeward bound steamer, about to set out upon her ocean voyage. They were five in number, and they were welcoming, each in turn, the man who had just joined them.

There had been a quiet wedding, a few days before, at a little English church, and Ruth Glidden had become Ruth Brierly as simply as if she were not an heiress, and her newly made husband not the owner of English lands, houses, stocks, and factories, that changed him into a millionaire.

"I could see no good reason for delay," Brierly was saying, as he grasped the hand of Ferrars, whose congratulations had been hearty and sincere. "Neither of us have need to consult aught save our own wishes; and besides our nearest friends are with us."

"Besides," interposed the smiling woman at his side, "we have been an encumbrance upon Mr. and Mrs. Myers for so long—and it was really the only conventional way to relieve them of so many charges. And then"—and here she lowered her tone, and glanced toward Hilda Grant, who, having already greeted Ferrars, was standing a little aloof—"we can now make a home for Hilda, and have a double claim on her."

"In all of which you have done well," smiled Ferrars. "My only regret is that I must bring into this parting moment an unpleasant element, but you may as well hear it from me." He beckoned the others to approach; and, when they were close about him, said, speaking low and gravely:

"'Quarrelsome Harry' has escaped the punishment of the law."

"Escaped!" It was Mr. Myers who repeated the word. "Do you mean——?"

"I mean that he is dead. He was shot while trying to escape. He had feigned illness so well that they were taking him to the hospital department. He tried a rush and a surprise, but it ended fatally for him. He was shot while resisting re-arrest."

"It is better so," said Mr. Myers. "They have been their own executioners. What could the law have added to their punishment?"

"Only the law's delays," said Ferrars, and then he turned to Hilda Grant.

"This is not a long good-bye," he said gently. "At least I hope not. I shall be back in 'the States' soon. And, may I not still find a cousin there? Or must I stand again outside the barrier alone?"

"You will always find an affectionate cousin," said Hilda, putting out her hand.

And now it was time to leave the ship. All around them was the hurry of delayed farewells, the bustle of late comers, the shifting of baggage, smiles, tears, last words.

Ferrars would remain for a time in London, but he knew, as he answered to the call "all ashore," that when he returned to the United States he would find in one of her fair western cities, a warm welcome and a lasting friendship.

The plot, by which the beautiful tigress-hearted woman whom they had known as Mrs. Jamieson had hoped to achieve riches, was cleverly planned. The real claimant had died in a remote place, and there were no near friends to look after her interests, or those of her young children. And then Harry Levey's sister, beautiful, and an adventuress, from choice, like her brother, had beguiled Gaston Latham, and had, by frequent changes of abode, by cunning, and by fraud, merged her own personality into that of the former wife. Then had come the baffling discovery of heirs in America, the plotting and scheming to remove them from their path—and the shameful end.

"Ferrars is a strange fellow," said Robert Brierly to his wife, one moonlight night, as they sat together, and somewhat aloof from the others on deck. "Do you know he was the sole attendant, except for her servants, at that woman's burial. He went in a carriage alone. Was it from sentiment, or sympathy, think you?"

It was the first time the dead woman had been spoken of, by either, since that trying day of her exposure and death, and Ruth was silent a moment, before she answered; the awful scene coming vividly before her. Then she put her hand within her husband's arm, and said, slowly, softly:

"It was because he is a good man; because she was a woman without a friend, and because she loved him."

There was a long silence, and it was Ruth who next spoke.

"Have you ever thought, or hoped, that the friendship and trust that has grown out of Hilda's relation to Mr. Ferrars might, sometime, end in something more?"

"No, dear, and this is why: Yesterday, Ferrars said to me 'There is a friend over in Glenville whom I hope you will not forget. Let him be your guest. And, if the day should come when your sweet sister that was to be should enter society and be sought by others, give the doctor his chance. He has loved her from the first.'"

Ruth sighed.

"Hilda is too young to go through the world loveless and alone. Yes, and too sweet. And the doctor is a noble man. But all this we may safely leave to the future, and to their own hearts."

The End

◆ WEATHER ◆

The Daily Record

The Record Is First
IN CIRCULATION — NEWS
PHOTOS — ADVERTISING
COMICS & NEA FEATURES

VOLUME 5   TELEPHONES 3117, 3118   DUNN, N. C., WEDNESDAY AFTERNOON, JANUARY 26, 1955   FIVE CENTS PER COPY

U. S. PLANES WARN RED CHINA

Ike's Decision Repudiation Of Old Policy

Group Gives Approval To Ike's Request

* AVA, SORE AT FRANKIE, TAKES OFF FOR BRAZIL

The Truth About Ava Gardner

These Little Things
BY ROGER ADAMS

Marilyn, Joe Reported In Hiding Today

Atomic Weapons To Defend U.S.

Dunn Lions To Hear Patterson Thursday

Lillington Mill Is Enlarged

12 Divorce Cases Slated For Trial

Socialite Divorced On Adultery Charge

Shepard To Leave Erwin Pastorate

Health Hero Hiding From Angry Wives

+ Record Roundup +

Hildreth Heads Merchants

THE CALL OF THE WILD

BY JACK LONDON

"Old longings nomadic leap,
Chafing at custom's chain;
Again from its brumal sleep
Wakens the ferine strain."

CHAPTER 1
INTO THE PRIMITIVE

Buck did not read the newspapers, or he would have known that trouble was brewing, not alone for himself, but for every tide-water dog, strong of muscle and with warm, long hair, from Puget Sound to San Diego. Because men, groping in the Arctic darkness, had found a yellow metal, and because steamship and transportation companies were booming the find, thousands of men were rushing into the Northland. These men wanted dogs, and the dogs they wanted were heavy dogs, with strong muscles by which to toil, and furry coats to protect them from the frost.

Buck lived at a big house in the sun-kissed Santa Clara Valley. Judge Miller's place, it was called. It stood back from the road, half hidden among the trees, through which glimpses could be caught of the wide cool veranda that ran around its four sides. The house was approached by gravelled driveways which wound about through wide-spreading lawns and under the interlacing boughs of tall poplars. At the rear things were on even a more spacious scale than at the front. There were great stables, where a dozen grooms and boys held forth, rows of vine-clad servants' cottages, an endless and orderly array of outhouses, long grape arbors, green pastures, orchards, and berry patches. Then there was the pumping plant for the artesian well, and the big cement tank where Judge Miller's boys took their morning plunge and kept cool in the hot afternoon.

And over this great demesne Buck ruled. Here he was born, and here he had lived the four years of his life. It was true, there were other dogs, There could not but be other dogs on so vast a place, but they did not count. They came and went, resided in the populous kennels, or lived obscurely in the recesses of the house after the fashion of Toots, the Japanese pug, or Ysabel, the Mexican hairless,—strange creatures that rarely put nose out of doors or set foot to ground. On the other hand, there were the fox terriers, a score of them at least, who yelped fearful promises at Toots and Ysabel looking out of the windows at them and protected by a legion of housemaids armed with brooms and mops.

But Buck was neither house-dog nor kennel-dog. The whole realm was his. He plunged into the swimming tank or went hunting with the Judge's sons; he escorted Mollie and Alice, the Judge's daughters, on long twilight or early morning rambles; on wintry nights he lay at the Judge's feet before the roaring library fire; he carried the Judge's grandsons on his back, or rolled them in the grass, and guarded their footsteps through wild adventures down to the fountain in the stable yard, and even beyond, where the paddocks were, and the berry patches. Among the terriers he stalked imperiously, and Toots and Ysabel he utterly ignored, for he was king,—king over all creeping, crawling, flying things of Judge Miller's place, humans included.

His father, Elmo, a huge St. Bernard, had been the Judge's inseparable companion, and Buck bid fair to follow in the way of his father. He was not so large,—he weighed only one hundred and forty pounds,—for his mother, Shep, had been a Scotch shepherd dog. Nevertheless, one hundred and forty pounds, to which was added the dignity that comes of good living and universal respect, enabled him to carry himself in right royal fashion. During the four years since his puppyhood he had lived the life of a sated aristocrat; he had a fine pride in himself, was even a trifle egotistical, as country gentlemen sometimes become because of their insular situation. But he had saved himself by not becoming a mere pampered house-dog. Hunting and kindred outdoor delights had kept down the fat and hardened his muscles; and to him, as to the cold-tubbing races, the love of water had been a tonic and a health preserver.

And this was the manner of dog Buck was in the fall of 1897, when the Klondike strike dragged men from all the world into the frozen North. But Buck did not read the newspapers, and he did not know that Manuel, one of the gardener's helpers, was an undesirable acquaintance. Manuel had one besetting sin. He loved to play Chinese lottery. Also, in his gambling, he had one besetting weakness—faith in a system; and this made his damnation certain. For to play a system requires money, while the wages of a gardener's helper do not lap over the needs of a wife and numerous progeny.

The Judge was at a meeting of the Raisin Growers' Association, and the boys were busy organizing an athletic club, on the memorable night of Manuel's treachery. No one saw him and Buck go off through the orchard on what Buck imagined was merely a stroll. And with the exception of a solitary man, no one saw them arrive at the little flag station known as College Park. This man talked with Manuel, and money chinked between them.

"You might wrap up the goods before you deliver 'm," the stranger said gruffly, and Manuel doubled a piece of stout rope around Buck's neck under the collar.

"Twist it, an' you'll choke 'm plentee," said Manuel, and the stranger grunted a ready affirmative.

Buck had accepted the rope with quiet dignity. To be sure, it was an unwonted performance: but he had learned to trust in men he knew, and to give them credit for a wisdom that outreached his own. But when the ends of the rope were placed in the stranger's hands, he growled menacingly. He had merely intimated his displeasure, in his pride believing that to intimate was to command. But to his surprise the rope tightened around his neck, shutting off his breath. In quick rage he sprang at the man, who met him halfway, grappled him close by the throat, and with a deft twist threw him over on his back. Then the rope tightened mercilessly, while Buck struggled in a fury, his tongue lolling out of his mouth and his great chest panting futilely. Never in all his life had he been so vilely treated, and never in all his life had he been so angry. But his strength ebbed, his eyes glazed, and he knew nothing when the train was flagged and the two men threw him into the baggage car.

The next he knew, he was dimly aware that his tongue was hurting and that he was being jolted along in some kind of a conveyance. The hoarse shriek of a locomotive whistling a crossing told him where he was. He had travelled too often with the Judge not to know the sensation of riding in a baggage car. He opened his eyes, and into them came the unbridled anger of a kidnapped king. The man sprang for his throat, but Buck was too quick for him. His jaws closed on the hand, nor did they relax till his senses were choked out of him once more.

"Yep, has fits," the man said, hiding his mangled hand from the baggageman, who had been attracted by the sounds of struggle. "I'm takin' 'm up for the boss to 'Frisco. A crack dog-doctor there thinks that he can cure 'm."

Concerning that night's ride, the man spoke most eloquently for himself, in a little shed back of a saloon on the San Francisco water front.

"All I get is fifty for it," he grumbled; "an' I wouldn't do it over for a thousand, cold cash."

His hand was wrapped in a bloody handkerchief, and the right trouser leg was ripped from knee to ankle.

"How much did the other mug get?" the saloon-keeper demanded.

"A hundred," was the reply. "Wouldn't take a sou less, so help me."

"That makes a hundred and fifty," the saloon-keeper calculated; "and he's worth it, or I'm a squarehead."

The kidnapper undid the bloody wrappings and looked at his lacerated hand. "If I don't get the hydrophoby—"

"It'll be because you was born to hang," laughed the saloon-keeper. "Here, lend me a hand before you pull your freight," he added.

Dazed, suffering intolerable pain from throat and tongue, with the life half throttled out of him, Buck attempted to face his tormentors. But he was thrown down and choked repeatedly, till they succeeded in filing the heavy brass collar from off his neck. Then the rope was removed, and he was flung into a cagelike crate.

There he lay for the remainder of the weary night, nursing his wrath and wounded pride. He could not understand what it all meant. What did they want with him, these strange men? Why were they keeping him pent up in this narrow crate? He did not know why, but he felt oppressed by the vague sense of impending calamity. Several times during the night he sprang to his feet when the shed door rattled open, expecting to see the Judge, or the boys at least. But each time it was the bulging face of the saloon-keeper that peered in at him by the sickly light of a tallow candle. And each time the joyful bark that trembled in Buck's throat was twisted into a savage growl.

But the saloon-keeper let him alone, and in the morning four men entered and picked up the crate. More tormentors, Buck decided, for they were evil-looking creatures, ragged and unkempt; and he stormed and raged at them through the bars. They only laughed and poked sticks at him, which he promptly assailed with his teeth till he realized that that was what they wanted. Whereupon he lay down sullenly and allowed the crate to be lifted into a wagon. Then he, and the crate in which he was imprisoned, began a passage through many hands. Clerks in the express office took charge of him; he was carted about in another wagon; a truck carried him, with an assortment of boxes and parcels, upon a ferry steamer; he was trucked off the steamer into a great railway depot, and finally he was deposited in an express car.

For two days and nights this express car was dragged along at the tail of shrieking locomotives; and for two days and nights Buck neither ate nor drank. In his anger he had met the first advances of the express messengers with growls, and they had retaliated by teasing him. When he flung himself against the bars, quivering and frothing, they laughed at him and taunted him. They growled and barked like detestable dogs, mewed, and flapped their arms and crowed. It was all very silly, he knew; but therefore the more outrage to his dignity, and his anger waxed and waxed. He did not mind the hunger so much, but the lack of water caused him severe suffering and fanned his wrath to fever-pitch. For that matter, high-strung and finely sensitive, the ill treatment had flung him into a fever, which was fed by the inflammation of his parched and swollen throat and tongue.

He was glad for one thing: the rope was off his neck. That had given them an unfair advantage; but now that it was off, he would show them. They would never get another rope around his neck. Upon that he was resolved. For two days and nights he neither ate nor drank, and during those two days and nights of torment, he accumulated a fund of wrath that boded ill for whoever first fell foul of him. His eyes turned blood-shot, and he was metamorphosed into a raging fiend. So changed was he that the

Judge himself would not have recognized him; and the express messengers breathed with relief when they bundled him off the train at Seattle.

Four men gingerly carried the crate from the wagon into a small, high-walled back yard. A stout man, with a red sweater that sagged generously at the neck, came out and signed the book for the driver. That was the man, Buck divined, the next tormentor, and he hurled himself savagely against the bars. The man smiled grimly, and brought a hatchet and a club.

"You ain't going to take him out now?" the driver asked.

"Sure," the man replied, driving the hatchet into the crate for a pry.

There was an instantaneous scattering of the four men who had carried it in, and from safe perches on top the wall they prepared to watch the performance.

Buck rushed at the splintering wood, sinking his teeth into it, surging and wrestling with it. Wherever the hatchet fell on the outside, he was there on the inside, snarling and growling, as furiously anxious to get out as the man in the red sweater was calmly intent on getting him out.

"Now, you red-eyed devil," he said, when he had made an opening sufficient for the passage of Buck's body. At the same time he dropped the hatchet and shifted the club to his right hand.

And Buck was truly a red-eyed devil, as he drew himself together for the spring, hair bristling, mouth foaming, a mad glitter in his blood-shot eyes. Straight at the man he launched his one hundred and forty pounds of fury, surcharged with the pent passion of two days and nights. In mid air, just as his jaws were about to close on the man, he received a shock that checked his body and brought his teeth together with an agonizing clip. He whirled over, fetching the ground on his back and side. He had never been struck by a club in his life, and did not understand. With a snarl that was part bark and more scream he was again on his feet and launched into the air. And again the shock came and he was brought crushingly to the ground. This time he was aware that it was the club, but his madness knew no caution. A dozen times he charged, and as often the club broke the charge and smashed him down.

After a particularly fierce blow, he crawled to his feet, too dazed to rush. He staggered limply about, the blood flowing from nose and mouth and ears, his beautiful coat sprayed and flecked with bloody slaver. Then the man advanced and deliberately dealt him a frightful blow on the nose.

All the pain he had endured was as nothing compared with the exquisite agony of this. With a roar that was almost lionlike in its ferocity, he again hurled himself at the man. But the man, shifting the club from right to left, coolly caught him by the under jaw, at the same time wrenching downward and backward. Buck described a complete circle in the air, and half of another, then crashed to the ground on his head and chest.

For the last time he rushed. The man struck the shrewd blow he had purposely withheld for so long, and Buck crumpled up and went down, knocked utterly senseless.

"He's no slouch at dog-breakin', that's wot I say," one of the men on the wall cried enthusiastically.

"Druther break cayuses any day, and twice on Sundays," was the reply of the driver, as he climbed on the wagon and started the horses.

Buck's senses came back to him, but not his strength. He lay where he had fallen, and from there he watched the man in the red sweater.

"'Answers to the name of Buck,'" the man soliloquized, quoting from the saloon-keeper's letter which had announced the consignment of the crate and contents. "Well, Buck, my boy," he went on in a genial voice, "we've had our little ruction, and the best thing we can do is to let it go at that. You've learned your place, and I know mine. Be a good dog and all 'll go well and the goose hang high. Be a bad dog, and I'll whale the stuffin' outa you. Understand?"

As he spoke he fearlessly patted the head he had so mercilessly pounded, and though Buck's hair involuntarily bristled at touch of the hand, he endured it without protest. When the man brought him water he drank eagerly, and later bolted a generous meal of raw meat, chunk by chunk, from the man's hand.

He was beaten (he knew that); but he was not broken. He saw, once for all, that he stood no chance against a man with a club. He had learned the lesson, and in all his after life he never forgot it. That club was a revelation. It was his introduction to the reign of primitive law, and he met the introduction halfway. The facts of life took on a fiercer aspect; and while he faced that aspect uncowed, he faced it with all the latent cunning of his nature aroused. As the days went by, other dogs came, in crates and at the ends of ropes, some docilely, and some raging and roaring as he had come; and, one and all, he watched them pass under the dominion of the man in the red sweater. Again and again, as he looked at each brutal performance, the lesson was driven home to Buck: a man with a club was a lawgiver, a master to be obeyed, though not necessarily conciliated. Of this last Buck was never guilty, though he did see beaten dogs that fawned upon the man, and wagged their tails, and licked his hand. Also he saw one dog, that would neither conciliate nor obey, finally killed in the struggle for mastery.

Now and again men came, strangers, who talked excitedly, wheedlingly, and in all kinds of fashions to the man in the red sweater. And at such times that money passed between them the strangers took one or more of the dogs away with them. Buck wondered where they went, for they never came back; but the fear of the future was strong upon him, and he was glad each time when he was not selected.

Yet his time came, in the end, in the form of a little weazened man who spat broken English and many strange and uncouth exclamations which Buck could not understand.

"Sacredam!" he cried, when his eyes lit upon Buck. "Dat one dam bully dog! Eh? How moch?"

"Three hundred, and a present at that," was the prompt reply of the man in the red sweater. "And seem' it's government money, you ain't got no kick coming, eh, Perrault?"

Perrault grinned. Considering that the price of dogs had been boomed skyward by the unwonted demand, it was not an unfair sum for so fine an animal. The Canadian Government would be no loser, nor would its despatches travel the slower. Perrault knew dogs, and when he looked at Buck he knew that he was one in a thousand—"One in ten t'ousand," he commented mentally.

Buck saw money pass between them, and was not surprised when Curly, a good-natured Newfoundland, and he were led away by the little weazened man. That was the last he saw of the man in the red sweater, and as Curly and he looked at receding Seattle from the deck of the *Narwhal*, it was the last he saw of the warm Southland. Curly and he were taken below by Perrault and turned over to a black-faced giant called François. Perrault was a French-Canadian, and swarthy; but François was a French-Canadian half-breed, and twice as swarthy. They were a new kind of men to Buck (of which he was destined to see many more), and while he developed no affection for them, he none the less grew honestly to respect them. He speedily learned that Perrault and François were fair men, calm and impartial in administering justice, and too wise in the way of dogs to be fooled by dogs.

In the 'tween-decks of the *Narwhal*, Buck and Curly joined two other dogs. One of them was a big, snow-white fellow from Spitzbergen who had been brought away by a whaling captain, and who had later accompanied a Geological Survey into the Barrens. He was friendly, in a treacherous sort of way, smiling into one's face the while he meditated some underhand trick, as, for instance, when he stole from Buck's food at the first meal. As Buck sprang to punish him, the lash of François's whip sang through the air, reaching the culprit first; and nothing remained to Buck but to recover the bone. That was fair of François, he decided, and the half-breed began his rise in Buck's estimation.

The other dog made no advances, nor received any; also, he did not attempt to steal from the newcomers. He was a gloomy, morose fellow, and he showed Curly plainly that all he desired was to be left alone, and further, that there would be trouble if he were not left alone. "Dave" he was called, and he ate and slept, or yawned between times, and took interest in nothing, not even when the *Narwhal* crossed Queen Charlotte Sound and rolled and pitched and bucked like a thing possessed. When Buck and Curly grew excited, half wild with fear, he raised his head as though annoyed, favored them with an incurious glance, yawned, and went to sleep again.

Day and night the ship throbbed to the tireless pulse of the propeller, and though one day was very like another, it was apparent to Buck that the weather was steadily growing colder. At last, one morning, the propeller was quiet, and the *Narwhal* was pervaded with an atmosphere of excitement. He felt it, as did the other dogs, and knew that a change was at hand. François leashed them and brought them on deck. At the first step upon the cold surface, Buck's feet sank into a white mushy something very like mud. He sprang back with a snort. More of this white stuff was falling through the air. He shook himself, but more of it fell upon him. He sniffed it curiously, then licked some up on his tongue. It bit like fire, and the next instant was gone. This puzzled him. He tried it again, with the same result. The onlookers laughed uproariously, and he felt ashamed, he knew not why, for it was his first snow.

CHAPTER 2
THE LAW OF CLUB AND FANG

Buck's first day on the Dyea beach was like a nightmare. Every hour was filled with shock and surprise. He had been suddenly jerked from the heart of civilization and flung into the heart of things primordial. No lazy, sun-kissed life was this, with nothing to do but loaf and be bored. Here was neither peace, nor rest, nor a moment's safety. All was confusion and action, and every moment life and limb were in peril. There was imperative need to be constantly alert; for these dogs and men were not town dogs and men. They were savages, all of them, who knew no law but the law of club and fang.

He had never seen dogs fight as these wolfish creatures fought, and his first experience taught him an unforgetable lesson. It is true, it was a vicarious experience, else he would not have lived to profit by it. Curly was the victim. They were camped near the log store, where she, in her friendly way, made advances to a husky dog the size of a full-grown wolf, though not half so large as she. There was no warning, only a leap in like a flash, a metallic clip of teeth, a leap out equally swift, and Curly's face was ripped open from eye to jaw.

It was the wolf manner of fighting, to strike and leap away; but there was more to it than this. Thirty or forty huskies ran to the spot and surrounded the combatants in an intent and silent circle. Buck did not comprehend that silent intentness, nor the eager way with which they were licking their chops. Curly rushed her antagonist, who struck again and leaped aside. He met her next rush with his chest, in a peculiar fashion that tumbled her off her feet. She never regained them, This was what the onlooking huskies had waited for. They closed in upon her, snarling and yelping, and she was buried, screaming with agony, beneath the bristling mass of bodies.

So sudden was it, and so unexpected, that Buck was taken aback. He saw Spitz run out his scarlet tongue in a way he had of laughing; and he saw François, swinging an axe, spring into the mess of dogs. Three men with clubs were helping him to scatter them. It did not take long. Two minutes from the time Curly went down, the last of her assailants were clubbed off. But she lay there limp and lifeless in the bloody, trampled snow, almost literally torn to pieces, the swart half-breed standing over her and cursing horribly. The scene often came back to Buck to trouble him in his sleep. So that was the way. No fair play. Once down, that was the end of you. Well, he would see to it that he never went down. Spitz ran out his tongue and laughed again, and from that moment Buck hated him with a bitter and deathless hatred.

Before he had recovered from the shock caused by the tragic passing of Curly, he received another shock. François fastened upon him an arrangement of straps and buckles. It was a harness, such as he had seen the grooms put on the horses at home. And as he had seen horses work, so he was set to work, hauling François on a sled to the forest that fringed the valley, and returning with a load of firewood. Though his dignity was sorely hurt by thus being made a draught animal, he was too wise to rebel. He buckled down with a will and did his best, though it was all new and strange. François was stern, demanding instant obedience, and by virtue of his whip receiving instant obedience; while Dave, who was an experienced wheeler, nipped Buck's hind quarters whenever he was in error. Spitz was the leader, likewise experienced, and while he could not always get at Buck, he growled sharp reproof now and again, or cunningly threw his weight in the traces to jerk Buck into the way he should go. Buck learned easily, and under the combined tuition of his two mates and François made remarkable progress. Ere they returned to camp he knew enough to stop at "ho," to go ahead at "mush," to swing wide on the bends, and to keep clear of the wheeler when the loaded sled shot downhill at their heels.

"T'ree vair' good dogs," François told Perrault. "Dat Buck, heem pool lak hell. I tich heem queek as anyt'ing."

By afternoon, Perrault, who was in a hurry to be on the trail with his despatches, returned with two more dogs. "Billee" and "Joe" he called them, two brothers, and true huskies both. Sons of the one mother though they were, they were as different as day and night. Billee's one fault was his excessive good nature, while Joe was the very opposite, sour and introspective, with a perpetual snarl and a malignant eye. Buck received them in comradely fashion, Dave ignored them, while Spitz proceeded to thrash first one and then the other. Billee wagged his tail appeasingly, turned to run when he saw that appeasement was of no avail, and cried (still appeasingly) when Spitz's sharp teeth scored his flank. But no matter how Spitz circled, Joe whirled around on his heels to face him, mane bristling, ears laid back, lips writhing and snarling, jaws clipping together as fast as he could snap, and eyes diabolically gleaming—the incarnation of belligerent fear. So terrible was his appearance that Spitz was forced to forego disciplining him; but to cover his own discomfiture he turned upon the inoffensive and wailing Billee and drove him to the confines of the camp.

By evening Perrault secured another dog, an old husky, long and lean and gaunt, with a battle-scarred face and a single eye which flashed a warning of prowess that commanded respect. He was called Sol-leks, which means the Angry One. Like Dave, he asked nothing, gave nothing, expected nothing; and when he marched slowly and deliberately into their midst, even Spitz left him alone. He had one peculiarity which Buck was unlucky enough to discover. He did not like to be approached on his blind side. Of this offence Buck was unwittingly guilty, and the first knowledge he had of his indiscretion was when Sol-leks whirled upon him and slashed his shoulder to the bone for three inches up and down. Forever after Buck avoided his blind side, and to the last of their comradeship had no more trouble. His only apparent ambition, like Dave's, was to be left alone; though, as Buck was afterward to learn, each of them possessed one other and even more vital ambition.

That night Buck faced the great problem of sleeping. The tent, illumined by a candle, glowed warmly in the midst of the white plain; and when he, as a matter of course, entered it, both Perrault and François bombarded him with curses and cooking utensils, till he recovered from his consternation and fled ignominiously into the outer cold. A chill wind was blowing that nipped him sharply and bit with especial venom into his wounded shoulder. He lay down on the snow and attempted to sleep, but the frost soon drove him shivering to his feet. Miserable and disconsolate, he wandered about among the many tents, only to find that one place was as cold as another. Here and there savage dogs rushed upon him, but he bristled his neck-hair and snarled (for he was learning fast), and they let him go his way unmolested.

Finally an idea came to him. He would return and see how his own team-mates were making out. To his astonishment, they had disappeared. Again he wandered about through the great camp, looking for them, and again he returned. Were they in the tent? No, that could not be, else he would not have been driven out. Then where could they possibly be? With drooping tail and shivering body, very forlorn indeed, he aimlessly circled the tent. Suddenly the snow gave way beneath his fore legs and he sank down. Something wriggled under his feet. He sprang back, bristling and snarling, fearful of the unseen and unknown. But a friendly little yelp reassured him, and he went back to investigate. A whiff of warm air ascended to his nostrils, and there, curled up under the snow in a snug ball, lay Billee. He whined placatingly, squirmed and wriggled to show his good will and intentions, and even ventured, as a bribe for peace, to lick Buck's face with his warm wet tongue.

Another lesson. So that was the way they did it, eh? Buck confidently selected a spot, and with much fuss and waste effort proceeded to dig a hole for himself. In a trice the heat from his body filled the confined space and he was asleep. The day had been long and arduous, and he slept soundly and comfortably, though he growled and barked and wrestled with bad dreams.

Nor did he open his eyes till roused by the noises of the waking camp. At first he did not know where he was. It had snowed during the night and he was completely buried. The snow walls pressed him on every side, and a great surge of fear swept through him—the fear of the wild thing for the trap. It was a token that he was harking back through his own life to the lives of his forebears; for he was a civilized dog, an unduly civilized dog, and of his own experience knew no trap and so could not of himself fear it. The muscles of his whole body contracted spasmodically and instinctively, the hair on his neck and shoulders stood on end, and with a ferocious snarl he bounded straight up into the blinding day, the snow flying about him in a flashing cloud. Ere he landed on his feet, he saw the white camp spread out before him and knew where he was and remembered all that had passed from the time he went for a stroll with Manuel to the hole he had dug for himself the night before.

A shout from François hailed his appearance. "Wot I say?" the dog-driver cried to Perrault. "Dat Buck for sure learn queek as anyt'ing."

Perrault nodded gravely. As courier for the Canadian Government, bearing important despatches, he was anxious to secure the best dogs, and he was particularly gladdened by the possession of Buck.

Three more huskies were added to the team inside an hour, making a total of nine, and before another quarter of an hour had passed they were in harness and swinging up the trail toward the Dyea Cañon. Buck was glad to be gone, and though the work was hard he found he did not particularly despise it. He was surprised at the eagerness which animated the whole team and which was communicated to him; but still more surprising was the change wrought in Dave and Sol-leks. They were new dogs, utterly transformed by the harness. All passiveness and unconcern had dropped from them. They were alert and active, anxious that the work should go well, and fiercely irritable with whatever, by delay or confusion, retarded that work. The toil of the traces seemed the supreme expression of their being, and all that they lived for and the only thing in which they took delight.

Dave was wheeler or sled dog, pulling in front of him was Buck, then came Sol-leks; the rest of the team was strung out ahead, single file, to the leader, which position was filled by Spitz.

Buck had been purposely placed between Dave and Sol-leks so that he might receive instruction. Apt scholar that he was, they were equally apt teachers, never allowing him to linger long in error, and enforcing their teaching with their sharp teeth. Dave was fair and very wise. He never nipped Buck without cause, and he never failed to nip him when he stood in need of it. As François's whip backed him up, Buck found it to be cheaper to mend his ways than to retaliate. Once, during a brief halt, when he got tangled in the traces and delayed the start, both Dave and Sol-leks flew at him and administered a sound trouncing. The resulting tangle was even worse, but Buck took good care to keep the traces clear thereafter; and ere the day was done, so well had he mastered his work, his mates about ceased nagging him. François's whip snapped less frequently, and Perrault even honored Buck by lifting up his feet and carefully examining them.

It was a hard day's run, up the Cañon, through Sheep Camp, past the Scales and the timber line, across glaciers and snowdrifts hundreds of feet deep, and over the great Chilcoot Divide, which stands between the salt water and the fresh and guards forbiddingly the sad and lonely North. They made good time down the chain of lakes which fills the craters of extinct volcanoes, and late that night pulled into the huge camp at the head of Lake Bennett, where thousands of goldseekers were building boats against the break-up of the ice in the spring. Buck made his hole in the snow and slept the sleep of the exhausted just, but all too early was routed out in the cold darkness and harnessed with his mates to the sled.

That day they made forty miles, the trail being packed; but the next day, and for many days to follow, they broke their own trail, worked harder, and made poorer time. As a rule, Perrault travelled ahead of the team, packing the snow with webbed shoes to make it easier for them. François, guiding the sled at the gee-pole, sometimes exchanged places with him, but not often. Perrault was in a hurry, and he prided himself on his knowledge of ice, which knowledge was indispensable, for the fall ice was very thin, and where there was swift water, there was no ice at all.

Day after day, for days unending, Buck toiled in the traces. Always, they broke camp in the dark, and the first gray of dawn found them hitting the trail with fresh miles reeled off behind them. And always they pitched camp after dark, eating their bit of fish, and crawling to sleep into the snow. Buck was ravenous. The pound and a half of sun-dried salmon, which was his ration for each day, seemed to go nowhere. He never had enough, and suffered from perpetual hunger pangs. Yet the other dogs, because they weighed less and were born to the life, received a pound only of the fish and managed to keep in good condition.

He swiftly lost the fastidiousness which had characterized his old life. A dainty eater, he found that his mates, finishing first, robbed him of his unfinished ration. There was no defending it. While he was fighting off two or three, it was disappearing down the throats of the others. To remedy this, he ate as fast as they; and, so greatly did hunger compel him, he was not above taking what did not belong to him. He watched and learned. When he saw Pike, one of the new dogs, a clever malingerer and thief, slyly steal a slice of bacon when Perrault's back was turned, he duplicated the performance the following day, getting away with the whole chunk. A great uproar was raised, but he was unsuspected; while Dub, an awkward blunderer who was always getting caught, was punished for Buck's misdeed.

This first theft marked Buck as fit to survive in the hostile Northland environment. It marked his adaptability, his capacity to adjust himself to changing conditions, the lack of which would have meant swift and terrible death. It marked, further, the decay or going to pieces of his moral nature, a vain thing and a handicap in the ruthless struggle for existence. It was all well enough in the Southland, under the law of love and fellowship, to respect private property and personal feelings; but in the Northland, under the law of club and fang, whoso took such things into account was a fool, and in so far as he observed them he would fail to prosper.

Not that Buck reasoned it out. He was fit, that was all, and unconsciously he accommodated himself to the new mode of life. All his days, no matter what the odds, he had never run from a fight. But the club of the man in the red sweater had beaten into him a more fundamental and primitive code. Civilized, he could have died for a moral consideration, say the defence of Judge Miller's riding-whip; but the completeness of his decivilization was now evidenced by his ability to flee from the defence of a moral consideration and so save his hide. He did not steal for joy of it, but because of the clamor of his stomach. He did not rob openly, but stole secretly and cunningly, out of respect for club and fang. In short, the things he did were done because it was easier to do them than not to do them.

His development (or retrogression) was rapid. His muscles became hard as iron, and he grew callous to all ordinary pain. He achieved an internal as well as external economy. He could eat anything, no matter how loathsome or indigestible; and, once eaten, the juices of his stomach extracted the last least particle of nutriment; and his blood carried it to the farthest reaches of his body, building it into the toughest and stoutest of tissues. Sight and scent became remarkably keen, while his hearing developed such acuteness that in his sleep he heard the faintest sound and knew whether it heralded peace or peril. He learned to bite the ice out with his teeth when it collected between his toes; and when he was thirsty and there was a thick scum of ice over the water hole, he would break it by rearing and striking it with stiff fore legs. His most conspicuous trait was an ability to scent the wind and forecast it a night in advance. No matter how breathless the air when he dug his nest by tree or bank, the wind that later blew inevitably found him to leeward, sheltered and snug.

And not only did he learn by experience, but instincts long dead became alive again. The domesticated generations fell from him. In vague ways he remembered back to the youth of the breed, to the time the wild dogs ranged in packs through the primeval forest and killed their meat as they ran it down. It was no task for him to learn to fight with cut and slash and the quick wolf snap. In this manner had fought forgotten ancestors. They quickened the old life within him, and the old tricks which they had stamped into the heredity of the breed were his tricks. They came to him without effort or discovery, as though they had been his always. And when, on the still cold nights, he pointed his nose at a star and howled long and wolflike, it was his ancestors, dead and dust, pointing nose at star and howling down through the centuries and through him. And his cadences were their cadences, the cadences which voiced their woe and what to them was the meaning of the stiffness, and the cold, and dark.

Thus, as token of what a puppet thing life is, the ancient song surged through him and he came into his own again; and he came because men had found a yellow metal in the North, and because Manuel was a gardener's helper whose wages did not lap over the needs of his wife and divers small copies of himself.

CHAPTER 3
THE DOMINANT PRIMORDIAL BEAST

The dominant primordial beast was strong in Buck, and under the fierce conditions of trail life it grew and grew. Yet it was a secret growth. His newborn cunning gave him poise and control. He was too busy adjusting himself to the new life to feel at ease, and not only did he not pick fights, but he avoided them whenever possible. A certain deliberateness characterized his attitude. He was not prone to rashness and precipitate action; and in the bitter hatred between him and Spitz he betrayed no impatience, shunned all offensive acts.

On the other hand, possibly because he divined in Buck a dangerous rival, Spitz never lost an opportunity of showing his teeth. He even went out of his way to bully Buck, striving constantly to start the fight which could end only in the death of one or the other. Early in the trip this might have taken place had it not been for an unwonted accident. At the end of this day they made a bleak and miserable camp on the shore of Lake Le Barge. Driving snow, a wind that cut like a white-hot knife, and darkness had forced them to grope for a camping place. They could hardly have fared worse. At their backs rose a perpendicular wall of rock, and Perrault and François were compelled to make their fire and spread their sleeping robes on the ice of the lake itself. The tent they had discarded at Dyea in order to travel light. A few sticks of driftwood furnished them with a fire that thawed down through the ice and left them to eat supper in the dark.

Close in under the sheltering rock Buck made his nest. So snug and warm was it, that he was loath to leave it when François distributed the fish which he had first thawed over the fire. But when Buck finished his ration and returned, he found his nest occupied. A warning snarl told him that the trespasser was Spitz. Till now Buck had avoided trouble with his enemy, but this was too much. The beast in him roared. He sprang upon Spitz with a fury which surprised them both, and Spitz particularly, for his whole experience with Buck had gone to teach him that his rival was an unusually timid dog, who managed to hold his own only because of his great weight and size.

François was surprised, too, when they shot out in a tangle from the disrupted nest and he divined the cause of the trouble. "A-a-ah!" he cried to Buck. "Gif it to heem, by Gar! Gif it to heem, the dirty t'eef!"

Spitz was equally willing. He was crying with sheer rage and eagerness as he circled back and forth for a chance to spring in. Buck was no less eager, and no less cautious, as he likewise circled back and forth for the advantage. But it was then that the unexpected happened, the thing which projected their struggle for supremacy far into the future, past many a weary mile of trail and toil.

An oath from Perrault, the resounding impact of a club upon a bony frame, and a shrill yelp of pain, heralded the breaking forth of pandemonium. The camp was suddenly discovered to be alive with skulking furry forms,—starving huskies, four or five score of them, who had scented the camp from some Indian village. They had crept in while Buck and Spitz were fighting, and when the two men sprang among them with stout clubs they showed their teeth and fought back. They were crazed by the smell of the food. Perrault found one with head buried in the grub-box. His club landed heavily on the gaunt ribs, and the grub-box was capsized on the ground. On the instant a score of the famished brutes were scrambling for the bread and bacon. The clubs fell upon them unheeded. They yelped and howled under the rain of blows, but struggled none the less madly till the last crumb had been devoured.

In the meantime the astonished team-dogs had burst out of their nests only to be set upon by the fierce invaders. Never had Buck seen such dogs.

It seemed as though their bones would burst through their skins. They were mere skeletons, draped loosely in draggled hides, with blazing eyes and slavered fangs. But the hunger-madness made them terrifying, irresistible. There was no opposing them. The team-dogs were swept back against the cliff at the first onset. Buck was beset by three huskies, and in a trice his head and shoulders were ripped and slashed. The din was frightful. Billee was crying as usual. Dave and Sol-leks, dripping blood from a score of wounds, were fighting bravely side by side. Joe was snapping like a demon. Once, his teeth closed on the fore leg of a husky, and he crunched down through the bone. Pike, the malingerer, leaped upon the crippled animal, breaking its neck with a quick flash of teeth and a jerk, Buck got a frothing adversary by the throat, and was sprayed with blood when his teeth sank through the jugular. The warm taste of it in his mouth goaded him to greater fierceness. He flung himself upon another, and at the same time felt teeth sink into his own throat. It was Spitz, treacherously attacking from the side.

Perrault and François, having cleaned out their part of the camp, hurried to save their sled-dogs. The wild wave of famished beasts rolled back before them, and Buck shook himself free. But it was only for a moment. The two men were compelled to run back to save the grub, upon which the huskies returned to the attack on the team. Billee, terrified into bravery, sprang through the savage circle and fled away over the ice. Pike and Dub followed on his heels, with the rest of the team behind. As Buck drew himself together to spring after them, out of the tail of his eye he saw Spitz rush upon him with the evident intention of overthrowing him. Once off his feet and under that mass of huskies, there was no hope for him. But he braced himself to the shock of Spitz's charge, then joined the flight out on the lake.

Later, the nine team-dogs gathered together and sought shelter in the forest. Though unpursued, they were in a sorry plight. There was not one who was not wounded in four or five places, while some were wounded grievously. Dub was badly injured in a hind leg; Dolly, the last husky added to the team at Dyea, had a badly torn throat; Joe had lost an eye; while Billee, the good-natured, with an ear chewed and rent to ribbons, cried and whimpered throughout the night. At daybreak they limped warily back to camp, to find the marauders gone and the two men in bad tempers. Fully half their grub supply was gone. The huskies had chewed through the sled lashings and canvas coverings. In fact, nothing, no matter how remotely eatable, had escaped them. They had eaten a pair of Perrault's moose-hide moccasins, chunks out of the leather traces, and even two feet of lash from the end of François's whip. He broke from a mournful contemplation of it to look over his wounded dogs.

"Ah, my frien's," he said softly, "mebbe it mek you mad dog, dose many bites. Mebbe all mad dog, sacredam! Wot you t'ink, eh, Perrault?"

The courier shook his head dubiously. With four hundred miles of trail still between him and Dawson, he could ill afford to have madness break out among his dogs. Two hours of cursing and exertion got the harnesses into shape, and the wound-stiffened team was under way, struggling painfully over the hardest part of the trail they had yet encountered, and for that matter, the hardest between them and Dawson.

The Thirty Mile River was wide open. Its wild water defied the frost, and it was in the eddies only and in the quiet places that the ice held at all. Six days of exhausting toil were required to cover those thirty terrible miles. And terrible they were, for every foot of them was accomplished at the risk of life to dog and man. A dozen times, Perrault, nosing the way broke through the ice bridges, being saved by the long pole he carried, which he so held that it fell each time across the hole made by his body. But a cold snap was on, the thermometer registering fifty below zero, and each time he broke through he was compelled for very life to build a fire and dry his garments.

Nothing daunted him. It was because nothing daunted him that he had been chosen for government courier. He took all manner of risks, resolutely thrusting his little weazened face into the frost and struggling on from dim dawn to dark. He skirted the frowning shores on rim ice that bent and crackled under foot and upon which they dared not halt. Once, the sled broke through, with Dave and Buck, and they were half-frozen and all but drowned by the time they were dragged out. The usual fire was necessary to save them. They were coated solidly with ice, and the two men kept them on the run around the fire, sweating and thawing, so close that they were singed by the flames.

At another time Spitz went through, dragging the whole team after him up to Buck, who strained backward with all his strength, his fore paws on the slippery edge and the ice quivering and snapping all around. But behind him was Dave, likewise straining backward, and behind the sled was François, pulling till his tendons cracked.

Again, the rim ice broke away before and behind, and there was no escape except up the cliff. Perrault scaled it by a miracle, while François prayed for just that miracle; and with every thong and sled lashing and the last bit of harness rove into a long rope, the dogs were hoisted, one by one, to the cliff crest. François came up last, after the sled and load. Then came the search for a place to descend, which descent was ultimately made by the aid of the rope, and night found them back on the river with a quarter of a mile to the day's credit.

By the time they made the Hootalinqua and good ice, Buck was played out. The rest of the dogs were in like condition; but Perrault, to make up lost time, pushed them late and early. The first day they covered thirty-five miles to the Big Salmon; the next day thirty-five more to the Little Salmon; the third day forty miles, which brought them well up toward the Five Fingers.

Buck's feet were not so compact and hard as the feet of the huskies. His had softened during the many generations since the day his last wild ancestor was tamed by a cave-dweller or river man. All day long he limped in agony, and camp once made, lay down like a dead dog. Hungry as he was, he would not move to receive his ration of fish, which François had to bring to him. Also, the dog-driver rubbed Buck's feet for half an hour each night after supper, and sacrificed the tops of his own moccasins to make four moccasins for Buck. This was a great relief, and Buck caused even the weazened face of Perrault to twist itself into a grin one morning, when François forgot the moccasins and Buck lay on his back, his four feet waving appealingly in the air, and refused to budge without them. Later his feet grew hard to the trail, and the worn-out foot-gear was thrown away.

At the Pelly one morning, as they were harnessing up, Dolly, who had never been conspicuous for anything, went suddenly mad. She announced her condition by a long, heartbreaking wolf howl that sent every dog bristling with fear, then sprang straight for Buck. He had never seen a dog go mad, nor did he have any reason to fear madness; yet he knew that here was horror, and fled away from it in a panic. Straight away he raced, with Dolly, panting and frothing, one leap behind; nor could she gain on him, so great was his terror, nor could he leave her, so great was her madness. He plunged through the wooded breast of the island, flew down to the lower end, crossed a back channel filled with rough ice to another island, gained a third island, curved back to the main river, and in desperation started to cross it. And all the time, though he did not look, he could hear her snarling just one leap behind. François called to him a quarter of a mile away and he doubled back, still one leap ahead, gasping painfully for air and putting all his faith in that François would save him. The dog-driver held the axe poised in his hand, and as Buck shot past him the axe crashed down upon mad Dolly's head.

Buck staggered over against the sled, exhausted, sobbing for breath, helpless. This was Spitz's opportunity. He sprang upon Buck, and twice his teeth sank into his unresisting foe and ripped and tore the flesh to the bone. Then François's lash descended, and Buck had the satisfaction of watching Spitz receive the worst whipping as yet administered to any of the teams.

"One devil, dat Spitz," remarked Perrault. "Some dam day heem keel dat Buck."

"Dat Buck two devils," was François's rejoinder. "All de tam I watch dat Buck I know for sure. Lissen: some dam fine day heem get mad lak hell an' den heem chew dat Spitz all up an' spit heem out on de snow. Sure. I know."

From then on it was war between them. Spitz, as lead-dog and acknowledged master of the team, felt his supremacy threatened by this strange Southland dog. And strange Buck was to him, for of the many Southland dogs he had known, not one had shown up worthily in camp and on trail. They were all too soft, dying under the toil, the frost, and starvation. Buck was the exception. He alone endured and prospered, matching the husky in strength, savagery, and cunning. Then he was a masterful dog, and what made him dangerous was the fact that the club of the man in the red sweater had knocked all blind pluck and rashness out of his desire for mastery. He was preeminently cunning, and could bide his time with a patience that was nothing less than primitive.

It was inevitable that the clash for leadership should come. Buck wanted it. He wanted it because it was his nature, because he had been gripped tight by that nameless, incomprehensible pride of the trail and trace—that pride which holds dogs in the toil to the last gasp, which lures them to die joyfully in the harness, and breaks their hearts if they are cut out of the harness. This was the pride of Dave as wheel-dog, of Sol-leks as he pulled with all his strength; the pride that laid hold of them at break of camp, transforming them from sour and sullen brutes into straining, eager, ambitious creatures; the pride that spurred them on all day and dropped them at pitch of camp at night, letting them fall back into gloomy unrest and uncontent. This was the pride that bore up Spitz and made him thrash the sled-dogs who blundered and shirked in the traces or hid away at harness-up time in the morning. Likewise it was this pride that made him fear Buck as a possible lead-dog. And this was Buck's pride, too.

He openly threatened the other's leadership. He came between him and the shirks he should have punished. And he did it deliberately. One night there was a heavy snowfall, and in the morning Pike, the malingerer, did not appear. He was securely hidden in his nest under a foot of snow. François called him and sought him in vain. Spitz was wild with wrath. He raged through the camp, smelling and digging in every likely place, snarling so frightfully that Pike heard and shivered in his hiding-place.

But when he was at last unearthed, and Spitz flew at him to punish him, Buck flew, with equal rage, in between. So unexpected was it, and so shrewdly managed, that Spitz was hurled backward and off his feet. Pike, who had been trembling abjectly, took heart at this open mutiny, and sprang upon his overthrown leader. Buck, to whom fair play was a forgotten code, likewise sprang upon Spitz. But François, chuckling at the incident while unswerving in the administration of justice, brought his lash down upon Buck with all his might. This failed to drive Buck from his prostrate rival, and the butt of the whip was brought into play. Half-stunned by the blow, Buck was knocked backward and the lash laid upon him again and again, while Spitz soundly punished the many times offending Pike.

In the days that followed, as Dawson grew closer and closer, Buck still continued to interfere between Spitz and the culprits; but he did it craftily, when François was not around, With the covert mutiny of Buck, a general insubordination sprang up and increased. Dave and Sol-leks were unaffected, but the rest of the team went from bad to worse. Things no longer went right. There was continual bickering and jangling. Trouble was always afoot, and at the bottom of it was Buck. He kept François busy, for the dog-driver was in constant apprehension of the life-and-death struggle between the two which he knew must take place sooner or later; and on more than one night the sounds of quarrelling and strife among the other dogs turned him out of his sleeping robe, fearful that Buck and Spitz were at it.

But the opportunity did not present itself, and they pulled into Dawson one dreary afternoon with the great fight still to come. Here were many men, and countless dogs, and Buck found them all at work. It seemed the ordained order of things that dogs should work. All day they swung up and down the main street in long teams, and in the night their jingling bells still went by. They hauled cabin logs and firewood, freighted up to the mines, and did all manner of work that horses did in the Santa Clara Valley. Here and there Buck met Southland dogs, but in the main they were the wild wolf husky breed. Every night, regularly, at nine, at twelve, at three, they lifted a nocturnal song, a weird and eerie chant, in which it was Buck's delight to join.

With the aurora borealis flaming coldly overhead, or the stars leaping in the frost dance, and the land numb and frozen under its pall of snow, this song of the huskies might have been the defiance of life, only it was pitched in minor key, with long-drawn wailings and half-sobs, and was more the pleading of life, the articulate travail of existence. It was an old song, old as the breed itself—one of the first songs of the younger world in a day when songs were sad. It was invested with the woe of unnumbered generations, this plaint by which Buck was so strangely stirred. When he moaned and sobbed, it was with the pain of living that was of old the pain of his wild fathers, and the fear and mystery of the cold and dark that was to them fear and mystery. And that he should be stirred by it marked the completeness with which he harked back through the ages of fire and roof to the raw beginnings of life in the howling ages.

Seven days from the time they pulled into Dawson, they dropped down the steep bank by the Barracks to the Yukon Trail, and pulled for Dyea and Salt Water. Perrault was carrying despatches if anything more urgent than those he had brought in; also, the travel pride had gripped him, and he purposed to make the record trip of the year. Several things favored him in this. The week's rest had recuperated the dogs and put them in thorough trim. The trail they had broken into the country was packed hard by later journeyers. And further, the police had arranged in two or three places deposits of grub for dog and man, and he was travelling light.

They made Sixty Mile, which is a fifty-mile run, on the first day; and the second day saw them booming up the Yukon well on their way to Pelly. But such splendid running was achieved not without great trouble and vexation on the part of François. The insidious revolt led by Buck had destroyed the solidarity of the team. It no longer was as one dog leaping in the traces. The encouragement Buck gave the rebels led them into all kinds of petty misdemeanors. No more was Spitz a leader greatly to be feared. The old awe departed, and they grew equal to challenging his authority. Pike robbed him of half a fish one night, and gulped it down under the protection of Buck. Another night Dub and Joe fought Spitz and made him forego the punishment they deserved. And even Billee, the good-natured, was less good-natured, and whined not half so placatingly as in former days. Buck never came near Spitz without snarling and bristling menacingly. In fact, his conduct approached that of a bully, and he was given to swaggering up and down before Spitz's very nose.

The breaking down of discipline likewise affected the dogs in their relations with one another. They quarrelled and bickered more than ever among themselves, till at times the camp was a howling bedlam. Dave and Sol-leks alone were unaltered, though they were made irritable by the unending squabbling. François swore strange barbarous oaths, and stamped the snow in futile rage, and tore his hair. His lash was always singing among the dogs, but it was of small avail. Directly his back was turned they were at it again. He backed up Spitz with his whip, while Buck backed up the remainder of the team. François knew he was behind all the trouble, and Buck knew he knew; but Buck was too clever ever again to be caught red-handed. He worked faithfully in the harness, for the toil had become a delight to him; yet it was a greater delight slyly to precipitate a fight amongst his mates and tangle the traces.

At the mouth of the Tahkeena, one night after supper, Dub turned up a snowshoe rabbit, blundered it, and missed. In a second the whole team was in full cry. A hundred yards away was a camp of the Northwest Police, with fifty dogs, huskies all, who joined the chase. The rabbit sped down the river, turned off into a small creek, up the frozen bed of which it held steadily. It ran lightly on the surface of the snow, while the dogs ploughed through by main strength. Buck led the pack, sixty strong, around bend after bend, but he could not gain. He lay down low to the race, whining eagerly, his splendid body flashing forward, leap by leap, in the wan white moonlight. And leap by leap, like some pale frost wraith, the snowshoe rabbit flashed on ahead.

All that stirring of old instincts which at stated periods drives men out from the sounding cities to forest and plain to kill things by chemically propelled leaden pellets, the blood lust, the joy to kill—all this was Buck's, only it was infinitely more intimate. He was ranging at the head of the pack, running the wild thing down, the living meat, to kill with his own teeth and wash his muzzle to the eyes in warm blood.

There is an ecstasy that marks the summit of life, and beyond which life cannot rise. And such is the paradox of living, this ecstasy comes when one is most alive, and it comes as a complete forgetfulness that one is alive. This ecstasy, this forgetfulness of living, comes to the artist, caught up and out of himself in a sheet of flame; it comes to the soldier, war-mad on a stricken field and refusing quarter; and it came to Buck, leading the pack, sounding the old wolf-cry, straining after the food that was alive and that fled swiftly before him through the moonlight. He was sounding the deeps of his nature, and of the parts of his nature that were deeper than he, going back into the womb of Time. He was mastered by the sheer surging of life, the tidal wave of being, the perfect joy of each separate muscle, joint, and sinew in that it was everything that was not death, that it was aglow and rampant, expressing itself in movement, flying exultantly under the stars and over the face of dead matter that did not move.

But Spitz, cold and calculating even in his supreme moods, left the pack and cut across a narrow neck of land where the creek made a long bend around. Buck did not know of this, and as he rounded the bend, the frost wraith of a rabbit still flitting before him, he saw another and larger frost wraith leap from the overhanging bank into the immediate path of the rabbit. It was Spitz. The rabbit could not turn, and as the white teeth broke its back in mid air it shrieked as loudly as a stricken man may shriek. At sound of this, the cry of Life plunging down from Life's apex in the grip of Death, the full pack at Buck's heels raised a hell's chorus of delight.

Buck did not cry out. He did not check himself, but drove in upon Spitz, shoulder to shoulder, so hard that he missed the throat. They rolled over and over in the powdery snow. Spitz gained his feet almost as though he had not been overthrown, slashing Buck down the shoulder and leaping clear. Twice his teeth clipped together, like the steel jaws of a trap, as he backed away for better footing, with lean and lifting lips that writhed and snarled.

In a flash Buck knew it. The time had come. It was to the death. As they circled about, snarling, ears laid back, keenly watchful for the advantage, the scene came to Buck with a sense of familiarity. He seemed to remember it all,—the white woods, and earth, and moonlight, and the thrill of battle. Over the whiteness and silence brooded a ghostly calm. There was not the faintest whisper of air—nothing moved, not a leaf quivered, the visible breaths of the dogs rising slowly and lingering in the frosty air. They had made short work of the snowshoe rabbit, these dogs that were ill-tamed wolves; and they were now drawn up in an expectant circle. They, too, were silent, their eyes only gleaming and their breaths drifting slowly upward. To Buck it was nothing new or strange, this scene of old time. It was as though it had always been, the wonted way of things.

Spitz was a practised fighter. From Spitzbergen through the Arctic, and across Canada and the Barrens, he had held his own with all manner of dogs and achieved to mastery over them. Bitter rage was his, but never blind rage. In passion to rend and destroy, he never forgot that his enemy was in like passion to rend and destroy. He never rushed till he was prepared to receive a rush; never attacked till he had first defended that attack.

In vain Buck strove to sink his teeth in the neck of the big white dog. Wherever his fangs struck for the softer flesh, they were countered by the fangs of Spitz. Fang clashed fang, and lips were cut and bleeding, but Buck could not penetrate his enemy's guard. Then he warmed up and enveloped Spitz in a whirlwind of rushes. Time and time again he tried for the snow-white throat, where life bubbled near to the surface, and each time and every time Spitz slashed him and got away. Then Buck took to rushing, as though for the throat, when, suddenly drawing back his head and curving in from the side, he would drive his shoulder at the shoulder of Spitz, as a ram by which to overthrow him. But instead, Buck's shoulder was slashed down each time as Spitz leaped lightly away.

Spitz was untouched, while Buck was streaming with blood and panting hard. The fight was growing desperate. And all the while the silent and wolfish circle waited to finish off whichever dog went down. As Buck grew winded, Spitz took to rushing, and he kept him staggering for footing. Once Buck went over, and the whole circle of sixty dogs started up; but he recovered himself, almost in mid air, and the circle sank down again and waited.

But Buck possessed a quality that made for greatness—imagination. He fought by instinct, but he could fight by head as well. He rushed, as though attempting the old shoulder trick, but at the last instant swept low to the snow and in. His teeth closed on Spitz's left fore leg. There was a crunch of breaking bone, and the white dog faced him on three legs. Thrice he tried to knock him over, then repeated the trick and broke the right fore leg. Despite the pain and helplessness, Spitz struggled madly to keep up. He saw the silent circle, with gleaming eyes, lolling tongues, and silvery breaths drifting upward, closing in upon him as he had seen similar circles close in upon beaten antagonists in the past. Only this time he was the one who was beaten.

There was no hope for him. Buck was inexorable. Mercy was a thing reserved for gentler climes. He manœuvred for the final rush. The circle had tightened till he could feel the breaths of the huskies on his flanks. He could see them, beyond Spitz and to either side, half crouching for the spring, their eyes fixed upon him. A pause seemed to fall. Every animal was motionless as though turned to stone. Only Spitz quivered and bristled as he staggered back and forth, snarling with horrible menace, as though to frighten off impending death. Then Buck sprang in and out; but while he was in, shoulder had at last squarely met shoulder. The dark circle became a dot on the moon-flooded snow as Spitz disappeared from view. Buck stood and looked on, the successful champion, the dominant primordial beast who had made his kill and found it good.

CHAPTER 4
WHO HAS WON TO MASTERSHIP

"Eh? Wot I say? I spik true w'en I say dat Buck two devils." This was François's speech next morning when he discovered Spitz missing and Buck covered with wounds. He drew him to the fire and by its light pointed them out.

"Dat Spitz fight lak hell," said Perrault, as he surveyed the gaping rips and cuts.

"An' dat Buck fight lak two hells," was François's answer. "An' now we make good time. No more Spitz, no more trouble, sure."

While Perrault packed the camp outfit and loaded the sled, the dog-driver proceeded to harness the dogs. Buck trotted up to the place Spitz would have occupied as leader; but François, not noticing him, brought Sol-leks to the coveted position. In his judgment, Sol-leks was the best lead-dog left. Buck sprang upon Sol-leks in a fury, driving him back and standing in his place.

"Eh? eh?" François cried, slapping his thighs gleefully. "Look at dat Buck. Heem keel dat Spitz, heem t'ink to take de job."

"Go 'way, Chook!" he cried, but Buck refused to budge.

He took Buck by the scruff of the neck, and though the dog growled threateningly, dragged him to one side and replaced Sol-leks. The old dog did not like it, and showed plainly that he was afraid of Buck. François was obdurate, but when he turned his back Buck again displaced Sol-leks, who was not at all unwilling to go.

François was angry. "Now, by Gar, I feex you!" he cried, coming back with a heavy club in his hand.

Buck remembered the man in the red sweater, and retreated slowly; nor did he attempt to charge in when Sol-leks was once more brought forward. But he circled just beyond the range of the club, snarling with bitterness and rage; and while he circled he watched the club so as to dodge it if thrown by François, for he was become wise in the way of clubs. The driver went about his work, and he called to Buck when he was ready to put him in his old place in front of Dave. Buck retreated two or three steps. François followed him up, whereupon he again retreated. After some time of this, François threw down the club, thinking that Buck feared a thrashing. But Buck was in open revolt. He wanted, not to escape a clubbing, but to have the leadership. It was his by right. He had earned it, and he would not be content with less.

Perrault took a hand. Between them they ran him about for the better part of an hour. They threw clubs at him. He dodged. They cursed him, and his fathers and mothers before him, and all his seed to come after him down to the remotest generation, and every hair on his body and drop of blood in his veins; and he answered curse with snarl and kept out of their reach. He did not try to run away, but retreated around and around the camp, advertising plainly that when his desire was met, he would come in and be good.

François sat down and scratched his head. Perrault looked at his watch and swore. Time was flying, and they should have been on the trail an hour gone. François scratched his head again. He shook it and grinned sheepishly at the courier, who shrugged his shoulders in sign that they were beaten. Then François went up to where Sol-leks stood and called to Buck. Buck laughed, as dogs laugh, yet kept his distance. François unfastened Sol-leks's traces and put him back in his old place. The team stood harnessed to the sled in an unbroken line, ready for the trail. There was no place for Buck save at the front. Once more François called, and once more Buck laughed and kept away.

"T'row down de club," Perrault commanded.

François complied, whereupon Buck trotted in, laughing triumphantly, and swung around into position at the head of the team. His traces were fastened, the sled broken out, and with both men running they dashed out on to the river trail.

Highly as the dog-driver had forevalued Buck, with his two devils, he found, while the day was yet young, that he had undervalued. At a bound Buck took up the duties of leadership; and where judgment was required, and quick thinking and quick acting, he showed himself the superior even of Spitz, of whom François had never seen an equal.

But it was in giving the law and making his mates live up to it, that Buck excelled. Dave and Sol-leks did not mind the change in leadership. It was none of their business. Their business was to toil, and toil mightily, in the traces. So long as that were not interfered with, they did not care what happened. Billee, the good-natured, could lead for all they cared, so long as he kept order. The rest of the team, however, had grown unruly during the last days of Spitz, and their surprise was great now that Buck proceeded to lick them into shape.

Pike, who pulled at Buck's heels, and who never put an ounce more of his weight against the breast-band than he was compelled to do, was swiftly and repeatedly shaken for loafing; and ere the first day was done he was pulling more than ever before in his life. The first night in camp, Joe, the sour one, was punished roundly—a thing that Spitz had never succeeded in doing. Buck simply smothered him by virtue of superior weight, and cut him up till he ceased snapping and began to whine for mercy.

The general tone of the team picked up immediately. It recovered its old-time solidarity, and once more the dogs leaped as one dog in the traces. At the Rink Rapids two native huskies, Teek and Koona, were added; and the celerity with which Buck broke them in took away François's breath.

"Nevaire such a dog as dat Buck!" he cried. "No, nevaire! Heem worth one t'ousan' dollair, by Gar! Eh? Wot you say, Perrault?"

And Perrault nodded. He was ahead of the record then, and gaining day by day. The trail was in excellent condition, well packed and hard, and there was no new-fallen snow with which to contend. It was not too cold. The temperature dropped to fifty below zero and remained there the whole trip. The men rode and ran by turn, and the dogs were kept on the jump, with but infrequent stoppages.

The Thirty Mile River was comparatively coated with ice, and they covered in one day going out what had taken them ten days coming in. In one run they made a sixty-mile dash from the foot of Lake Le Barge to the White Horse Rapids. Across Marsh, Tagish, and Bennett (seventy miles of lakes), they flew so fast that the man whose turn it was to run towed behind the sled at the end of a rope. And on the last night of the second week they topped White Pass and dropped down the sea slope with the lights of Skaguay and of the shipping at their feet.

It was a record run. Each day for fourteen days they had averaged forty miles. For three days Perrault and François threw chests up and down the main street of Skaguay and were deluged with invitations to drink, while the team was the constant centre of a worshipful crowd of dog-busters and mushers. Then three or four western bad men aspired to clean out the town, were riddled like pepper-boxes for their pains, and public interest turned to other idols. Next came official orders. François called Buck to him, threw his arms around him, wept over him. And that was the last of François and Perrault. Like other men, they passed out of Buck's life for good.

A Scotch half-breed took charge of him and his mates, and in company with a dozen other dog-teams he started back over the weary trail to Dawson. It was no light running now, nor record time, but heavy toil each day, with a heavy load behind; for this was the mail train, carrying word from the world to the men who sought gold under the shadow of the Pole.

Buck did not like it, but he bore up well to the work, taking pride in it after the manner of Dave and Sol-leks, and seeing that his mates, whether they prided in it or not, did their fair share. It was a monotonous life, operating with machine-like regularity. One day was very like another. At a certain time each morning the cooks turned out, fires were built, and breakfast was eaten. Then, while some broke camp, others harnessed the dogs, and they were under way an hour or so before the darkness fell which gave warning of dawn. At night, camp was made. Some pitched the flies, others cut firewood and pine boughs for the beds, and still others carried water or ice for the cooks. Also, the dogs were fed. To them, this was the one feature of the day, though it was good to loaf around, after the fish was eaten, for an hour or so with the other dogs, of which there were fivescore and odd. There were fierce fighters among them, but three battles with the fiercest brought Buck to mastery, so that when he bristled and showed his teeth they got out of his way.

Best of all, perhaps, he loved to lie near the fire, hind legs crouched under him, fore legs stretched out in front, head raised, and eyes blinking dreamily at the flames. Sometimes he thought of Judge Miller's big house in the sun-kissed Santa Clara Valley, and of the cement swimming-tank, and Ysabel, the Mexican hairless, and Toots, the Japanese pug; but oftener he remembered the man in the red sweater, the death of Curly, the great fight with Spitz, and the good things he had eaten or would like to eat. He was not homesick. The Sunland was very dim and distant, and such memories had no power over him. Far more potent were the memories of his heredity that gave things he had never seen before a seeming familiarity; the instincts (which were but the memories of his ancestors become habits) which had lapsed in later days, and still later, in him, quickened and become alive again.

Sometimes as he crouched there, blinking dreamily at the flames, it seemed that the flames were of another fire, and that as he crouched by this other fire he saw another and different man from the half-breed cook before him. This other man was shorter of leg and longer of arm, with muscles that were stringy and knotty rather than rounded and swelling. The hair of this man was long and matted, and his head slanted back under it from the eyes. He uttered strange sounds, and seemed very much afraid of the darkness, into which he peered continually, clutching in his hand, which hung midway between knee and foot, a stick with a heavy stone made fast to the end. He was all but naked, a ragged and fire-scorched skin hanging part way down his back, but on his body there was much hair. In some places, across the chest and shoulders and down the outside of the arms and thighs, it was matted into almost a thick fur. He did not stand erect, but with trunk inclined forward from the hips, on legs that bent at the knees. About his body there was a peculiar springiness, or resiliency, almost catlike, and a quick alertness as of one who lived in perpetual fear of things seen and unseen.

At other times this hairy man squatted by the fire with head between his legs and slept. On such occasions his elbows were on his knees, his hands clasped above his head as though to shed rain by the hairy arms. And beyond that fire, in the circling darkness, Buck could see many gleaming coals, two by two, always two by two, which he knew to be the eyes of great beasts of prey. And he could hear the crashing of their bodies through the undergrowth, and the noises they made in the night. And dreaming there by the Yukon bank, with lazy eyes blinking at the fire, these sounds and sights of another world would make the hair to rise along his back and stand on end across his shoulders and up his neck, till he whimpered low and suppressedly, or growled softly, and the half-breed cook shouted at him, "Hey, you Buck, wake up!" Whereupon the other world would vanish and the real world come into his eyes, and he would get up and yawn and stretch as though he had been asleep.

It was a hard trip, with the mail behind them, and the heavy work wore them down. They were short of weight and in poor condition when they made Dawson, and should have had a ten days' or a week's rest at least. But in two days' time they dropped down the Yukon bank from the Barracks, loaded with letters for the outside. The dogs were tired, the drivers grumbling, and to make matters worse, it snowed every day. This meant a soft trail, greater friction on the runners, and heavier pulling for the dogs; yet the drivers were fair through it all, and did their best for the animals.

Each night the dogs were attended to first. They ate before the drivers ate, and no man sought his sleeping-robe till he had seen to the feet of the dogs he drove. Still, their strength went down. Since the beginning of the winter they had travelled eighteen hundred miles, dragging sleds the whole weary distance; and eighteen hundred miles will tell upon life of the toughest. Buck stood it, keeping his mates up to their work and maintaining discipline, though he, too, was very tired. Billee cried and whimpered regularly in his sleep each night. Joe was sourer than ever, and Sol-leks was unapproachable, blind side or other side.

But it was Dave who suffered most of all. Something had gone wrong with him. He became more morose and irritable, and when camp was pitched at once made his nest, where his driver fed him. Once out of the harness and down, he did not get on his feet again till harness-up time in the morning. Sometimes, in the traces, when jerked by a sudden stoppage of the sled, or by straining to start it, he would cry out with pain. The driver examined him, but could find nothing. All the drivers became interested in his case. They talked it over at meal-time, and over their last pipes before going to bed, and one night they held a consultation. He was brought from his nest to the fire and was pressed and prodded till he cried out many times. Something was wrong inside, but they could locate no broken bones, could not make it out.

By the time Cassiar Bar was reached, he was so weak that he was falling repeatedly in the traces. The Scotch half-breed called a halt and took him out of the team, making the next dog, Sol-leks, fast to the sled. His intention was to rest Dave, letting him run free behind the sled. Sick as he was, Dave resented being taken out, grunting and growling while the traces were unfastened, and whimpering broken-heartedly when he saw Sol-leks in the position he had held and served so long. For the pride of trace and trail was his, and, sick unto death, he could not bear that another dog should do his work.

When the sled started, he floundered in the soft snow alongside the beaten trail, attacking Sol-leks with his teeth, rushing against him and trying to thrust him off into the soft snow on the other side, striving to leap inside his traces and get between him and the sled, and all the while whining and yelping and crying with grief and pain. The half-breed tried to drive him away with the whip; but he paid no heed to the stinging lash, and the man had not the heart to strike harder. Dave refused to run quietly on the trail behind the sled, where the going was easy, but continued to flounder alongside in the soft snow, where the going was most difficult, till exhausted. Then he fell, and lay where he fell, howling lugubriously as the long train of sleds churned by.

With the last remnant of his strength he managed to stagger along behind till the train made another stop, when he floundered past the sleds to his own, where he stood alongside Sol-leks. His driver lingered a moment to get a light for his pipe from the man behind. Then he returned and started his dogs. They swung out on the trail with remarkable lack of exertion, turned their heads uneasily, and stopped in surprise. The driver was surprised, too; the sled had not moved. He called his comrades to witness the sight. Dave had bitten through both of Sol-leks's traces, and was standing directly in front of the sled in his proper place.

He pleaded with his eyes to remain there. The driver was perplexed. His comrades talked of how a dog could break its heart through being denied the work that killed it, and recalled instances they had known, where dogs, too old for the toil, or injured, had died because they were cut out of the traces. Also, they held it a mercy, since Dave was to die anyway, that he should die in the traces, heart-easy and content. So he was harnessed in again, and proudly he pulled as of old, though more than once he cried out involuntarily from the bite of his inward hurt. Several times he fell down and was dragged in the traces, and once the sled ran upon him so that he limped thereafter in one of his hind legs.

But he held out till camp was reached, when his driver made a place for him by the fire. Morning found him too weak to travel. At harness-up time he tried to crawl to his driver. By convulsive efforts he got on his feet, staggered, and fell. Then he wormed his way forward slowly toward where the harnesses were being put on his mates. He would advance his fore legs and drag up his body with a sort of hitching movement, when he would advance his fore legs and hitch ahead again for a few more inches. His strength left him, and the last his mates saw of him he lay gasping in the snow and yearning toward them. But they could hear him mournfully howling till they passed out of sight behind a belt of river timber.

Here the train was halted. The Scotch half-breed slowly retraced his steps to the camp they had left. The men ceased talking. A revolver-shot rang out. The man came back hurriedly. The whips snapped, the bells tinkled merrily, the sleds churned along the trail; but Buck knew, and every dog knew, what had taken place behind the belt of river trees.

CHAPTER 5
THE TOIL OF TRACE AND TRAIL

Thirty days from the time it left Dawson, the Salt Water Mail, with Buck and his mates at the fore, arrived at Skaguay. They were in a wretched state, worn out and worn down. Buck's one hundred and forty pounds had dwindled to one hundred and fifteen. The rest of his mates, though lighter dogs, had relatively lost more weight than he. Pike, the malingerer, who, in his lifetime of deceit, had often successfully feigned a hurt leg, was now limping in earnest. Sol-leks was limping, and Dub was suffering from a wrenched shoulder-blade.

They were all terribly footsore. No spring or rebound was left in them. Their feet fell heavily on the trail, jarring their bodies and doubling the fatigue of a day's travel. There was nothing the matter with them except that they were dead tired. It was not the dead-tiredness that comes through brief and excessive effort, from which recovery is a matter of hours; but it was the dead-tiredness that comes through the slow and prolonged strength drainage of months of toil. There was no power of recuperation left, no reserve strength to call upon. It had been all used, the last least bit of it. Every muscle, every fibre, every cell, was tired, dead tired. And there was reason for it. In less than five months they had travelled twenty-five hundred miles, during the last eighteen hundred of which they had had but five days' rest. When they arrived at Skaguay they were apparently on their last legs. They could barely keep the traces taut, and on the down grades just managed to keep out of the way of the sled.

"Mush on, poor sore feets," the driver encouraged them as they tottered down the main street of Skaguay. "Dis is de las'. Den we get one long res'. Eh? For sure. One bully long res'."

The drivers confidently expected a long stopover. Themselves, they had covered twelve hundred miles with two days' rest, and in the nature of reason and common justice they deserved an interval of loafing. But so many were the men who had rushed into the Klondike, and so many were the sweethearts, wives, and kin that had not rushed in, that the congested mail was taking on Alpine proportions; also, there were official orders. Fresh batches of Hudson Bay dogs were to take the places of those worthless for the trail. The worthless ones were to be got rid of, and, since dogs count for little against dollars, they were to be sold.

Three days passed, by which time Buck and his mates found how really tired and weak they were. Then, on the morning of the fourth day, two men from the States came along and bought them, harness and all, for a song. The men addressed each other as "Hal" and "Charles." Charles was a middle-aged, lightish-colored man, with weak and watery eyes and a mustache that twisted fiercely and vigorously up, giving the lie to the limply drooping lip it concealed. Hal was a youngster of nineteen or twenty, with a big Colt's revolver and a hunting-knife strapped about him on a belt that fairly bristled with cartridges. This belt was the most salient thing about him. It advertised his callowness—a callowness sheer and unutterable. Both men were manifestly out of place, and why such as they should adventure the North is part of the mystery of things that passes understanding.

Buck heard the chaffering, saw the money pass between the man and the Government agent, and knew that the Scotch half-breed and the mail-train drivers were passing out of his life on the heels of Perrault and François and the others who had gone before. When driven with his mates to the new owners' camp, Buck saw a slipshod and slovenly affair, tent half stretched, dishes unwashed, everything in disorder; also, he saw a woman. "Mercedes" the men called her. She was Charles's wife and Hal's sister—a nice family party.

Buck watched them apprehensively as they proceeded to take down the tent and load the sled. There was a great deal of effort about their manner, but no businesslike method. The tent was rolled into an awkward bundle three times as large as it should have been. The tin dishes were packed away unwashed. Mercedes continually fluttered in the way of her men and kept up an unbroken chattering of remonstrance and advice. When they put a clothes-sack on the front of the sled, she suggested it should go on the back; and when they had put it on the back, and covered it over with a couple of other bundles, she discovered overlooked articles which could abide nowhere else but in that very sack, and they unloaded again.

Three men from a neighboring tent came out and looked on, grinning and winking at one another.

"You've got a right smart load as it is," said one of them; "and it's not me should tell you your business, but I wouldn't tote that tent along if I was you."

"Undreamed of!" cried Mercedes, throwing up her hands in dainty dismay. "However in the world could I manage without a tent?"

"It's springtime, and you won't get any more cold weather," the man replied.

She shook her head decidedly, and Charles and Hal put the last odds and ends on top the mountainous load.

"Think it'll ride?" one of the men asked.

"Why shouldn't it?" Charles demanded rather shortly.

"Oh, that's all right, that's all right," the man hastened meekly to say. "I was just a-wonderin', that is all. It seemed a mite top-heavy."

Charles turned his back and drew the lashings down as well as he could, which was not in the least well.

"An' of course the dogs can hike along all day with that contraption behind them," affirmed a second of the men.

"Certainly," said Hal, with freezing politeness, taking hold of the gee-pole with one hand and swinging his whip from the other. "Mush!" he shouted. "Mush on there!"

The dogs sprang against the breast-bands, strained hard for a few moments, then relaxed. They were unable to move the sled.

"The lazy brutes, I'll show them," he cried, preparing to lash out at them with the whip.

But Mercedes interfered, crying, "Oh, Hal, you mustn't," as she caught hold of the whip and wrenched it from him. "The poor dears! Now you must promise you won't be harsh with them for the rest of the trip, or I won't go a step."

"Precious lot you know about dogs," her brother sneered; "and I wish you'd leave me alone. They're lazy, I tell you, and you've got to whip them to get anything out of them. That's their way. You ask any one. Ask one of those men."

Mercedes looked at them imploringly, untold repugnance at sight of pain written in her pretty face.

"They're weak as water, if you want to know," came the reply from one of the men. "Plum tuckered out, that's what's the matter. They need a rest."

"Rest be blanked," said Hal, with his beardless lips; and Mercedes said, "Oh!" in pain and sorrow at the oath.

But she was a clannish creature, and rushed at once to the defence of her brother. "Never mind that man," she said pointedly. "You're driving our dogs, and you do what you think best with them."

Again Hal's whip fell upon the dogs. They threw themselves against the breast-bands, dug their feet into the packed snow, got down low to it, and put forth all their strength. The sled held as though it were an anchor. After two efforts, they stood still, panting. The whip was whistling savagely, when once more Mercedes interfered. She dropped on her knees before Buck, with tears in her eyes, and put her arms around his neck.

"You poor, poor dears," she cried sympathetically, "why don't you pull hard?—then you wouldn't be whipped." Buck did not like her, but he was feeling too miserable to resist her, taking it as part of the day's miserable work.

One of the onlookers, who had been clenching his teeth to suppress hot speech, now spoke up:—

"It's not that I care a whoop what becomes of you, but for the dogs' sakes I just want to tell you, you can help them a mighty lot by breaking out that sled. The runners are froze fast. Throw your weight against the gee-pole, right and left, and break it out."

A third time the attempt was made, but this time, following the advice, Hal broke out the runners which had been frozen to the snow. The overloaded and unwieldy sled forged ahead, Buck and his mates struggling frantically under the rain of blows. A hundred yards ahead the path turned and sloped steeply into the main street. It would have required an experienced man to keep the top-heavy sled upright, and Hal was not such a man. As they swung on the turn the sled went over, spilling half its load through the loose lashings. The dogs never stopped. The lightened sled bounded on its side behind them. They were angry because of the ill treatment they had received and the unjust load. Buck was raging. He broke into a run, the team following his lead. Hal cried "Whoa! whoa!" but they gave no heed. He tripped and was pulled off his feet. The capsized sled ground over him, and the dogs dashed on up the street, adding to the gayety of Skaguay as they scattered the remainder of the outfit along its chief thoroughfare.

Kind-hearted citizens caught the dogs and gathered up the scattered belongings. Also, they gave advice. Half the load and twice the dogs, if they ever expected to reach Dawson, was what was said. Hal and his sister and brother-in-law listened unwillingly, pitched tent, and overhauled the outfit. Canned goods were turned out that made men laugh, for canned goods on the Long Trail is a thing to dream about. "Blankets for a hotel" quoth one of the men who laughed and helped. "Half as many is too much; get rid of them. Throw away that tent, and all those dishes,—who's going to wash them, anyway? Good Lord, do you think you're travelling on a Pullman?"

And so it went, the inexorable elimination of the superfluous. Mercedes cried when her clothes-bags were dumped on the ground and article after article was thrown out. She cried in general, and she cried in particular over each discarded thing. She clasped hands about knees, rocking back and forth broken-heartedly. She averred she would not go an inch, not for a dozen Charleses. She appealed to everybody and to everything, finally wiping her eyes and proceeding to cast out even articles of apparel that were imperative necessaries. And in her zeal, when she had finished with her own, she attacked the belongings of her men and went through them like a tornado.

This accomplished, the outfit, though cut in half, was still a formidable bulk. Charles and Hal went out in the evening and bought six Outside dogs. These, added to the six of the original team, and Teek and Koona, the huskies obtained at the Rink Rapids on the record trip, brought the team up to fourteen. But the Outside dogs, though practically broken in since their landing, did not amount to much. Three were short-haired pointers, one was a Newfoundland, and the other two were mongrels of indeterminate breed. They did not seem to know anything, these newcomers. Buck and his comrades looked upon them with disgust, and though he speedily taught them their places and what not to do, he could not teach them what to do. They did not take kindly to trace and trail. With the exception of the two mongrels, they were bewildered and spirit-broken by the strange savage environment in which they found themselves and by the ill treatment they had received. The two mongrels were without spirit at all; bones were the only things breakable about them.

With the newcomers hopeless and forlorn, and the old team worn out by twenty-five hundred miles of continuous trail, the outlook was anything but bright. The two men, however, were quite cheerful. And they were proud, too. They were doing the thing in style, with fourteen dogs. They had seen other sleds depart over the Pass for Dawson, or come in from Dawson, but never had they seen a sled with so many as fourteen dogs. In the nature of Arctic travel there was a reason why fourteen dogs should not drag one sled, and that was that one sled could not carry the food for fourteen dogs. But Charles and Hal did not know this. They had worked the trip out with a pencil, so much to a dog, so many dogs, so many days, Q.E.D. Mercedes looked over their shoulders and nodded comprehensively, it was all so very simple.

Late next morning Buck led the long team up the street. There was nothing lively about it, no snap or go in him and his fellows. They were starting dead weary. Four times he had covered the distance between Salt Water and Dawson, and the knowledge that, jaded and tired, he was facing the same trail once more, made him bitter. His heart was not in the work, nor was the heart of any dog. The Outsides were timid and frightened, the Insides without confidence in their masters.

Buck felt vaguely that there was no depending upon these two men and the woman. They did not know how to do anything, and as the days went by it became apparent that they could not learn. They were slack in all things, without order or discipline. It took them half the night to pitch a slovenly camp, and half the morning to break that camp and get the sled loaded in fashion so slovenly that for the rest of the day they were occupied in stopping and rearranging the load. Some days they did not make ten miles. On other days they were unable to get started at all. And on no day did they succeed in making more than half the distance used by the men as a basis in their dog-food computation.

It was inevitable that they should go short on dog-food. But they hastened it by overfeeding, bringing the day nearer when underfeeding would commence. The Outside dogs, whose digestions had not been trained by chronic famine to make the most of little, had voracious appetites. And when, in addition to this, the worn-out huskies pulled weakly, Hal decided that the orthodox ration was too small. He doubled it. And to cap it all, when Mercedes, with tears in her pretty eyes and a quaver in her throat, could not cajole him into giving the dogs still more, she stole from the fish-sacks and fed them slyly. But it was not food that Buck and the huskies needed, but rest. And though they were making poor time, the heavy load they dragged sapped their strength severely.

Then came the underfeeding. Hal awoke one day to the fact that his dog-food was half gone and the distance only quarter covered; further, that for love or money no additional dog-food was to be obtained. So he cut down even the orthodox ration and tried to increase the day's travel. His sister and brother-in-law seconded him; but they were frustrated by their heavy outfit and their own incompetence. It was a simple matter to give the dogs less food; but it was impossible to make the dogs travel faster, while their own inability to get under way earlier in the morning prevented them from travelling longer hours. Not only did they not know how to work dogs, but they did not know how to work themselves.

The first to go was Dub. Poor blundering thief that he was, always getting caught and punished, he had none the less been a faithful worker. His wrenched shoulder-blade, untreated and unrested, went from bad to worse, till finally Hal shot him with the big Colt's revolver. It is a saying of the country that an Outside dog starves to death on the ration of the husky, so the six Outside dogs under Buck could do no less than die on half the ration of the husky. The Newfoundland went first, followed by the three short-haired pointers, the two mongrels hanging more grittily on to life, but going in the end.

By this time all the amenities and gentlenesses of the Southland had fallen away from the three people. Shorn of its glamour and romance, Arctic travel became to them a reality too harsh for their manhood and womanhood. Mercedes ceased weeping over the dogs, being too occupied with weeping over herself and with quarrelling with her husband and brother. To quarrel was the one thing they were never too weary to do. Their irritability arose out of their misery, increased with it, doubled upon it, outdistanced it. The wonderful patience of the trail which comes to men who toil hard and suffer sore, and remain sweet of speech and kindly, did not come to these two men and the woman. They had no inkling of such a patience. They were stiff and in pain; their muscles ached, their bones ached, their very hearts ached; and because of this they became sharp of speech, and hard words were first on their lips in the morning and last at night.

Charles and Hal wrangled whenever Mercedes gave them a chance. It was the cherished belief of each that he did more than his share of the work, and neither forbore to speak this belief at every opportunity. Sometimes Mercedes sided with her husband, sometimes with her brother. The result was a beautiful and unending family quarrel. Starting from a dispute as to which should chop a few sticks for the fire (a dispute which concerned only Charles and Hal), presently would be lugged in the rest of the family, fathers, mothers, uncles, cousins, people thousands of miles away, and some of them dead. That Hal's views on art, or the sort of society plays his mother's brother wrote, should have anything to do with the chopping of a few sticks of firewood, passes comprehension; nevertheless the quarrel was as likely to tend in that direction as in the direction of Charles's political prejudices. And that Charles's sister's tale-bearing tongue should be relevant to the building of a Yukon fire, was apparent only to Mercedes, who disburdened herself of copious opinions upon that topic, and incidentally upon a few other traits unpleasantly peculiar to her husband's family. In the meantime the fire remained unbuilt, the camp half pitched, and the dogs unfed.

Mercedes nursed a special grievance—the grievance of sex. She was pretty and soft, and had been chivalrously treated all her days. But the present treatment by her husband and brother was everything save chivalrous. It was her custom to be helpless. They complained. Upon which impeachment of what to her was her most essential sex-prerogative, she made their lives unendurable. She no longer considered the dogs, and because she was sore and tired, she persisted in riding on the sled. She was pretty and soft, but she weighed one hundred and twenty pounds—a lusty last straw to the load dragged by the weak and starving animals. She rode for days, till they fell in the traces and the sled stood still. Charles and Hal begged her to get off and walk, pleaded with her, entreated, the while she wept and importuned Heaven with a recital of their brutality.

On one occasion they took her off the sled by main strength. They never did it again. She let her legs go limp like a spoiled child, and sat down on the trail. They went on their way, but she did not move. After they had travelled three miles they unloaded the sled, came back for her, and by main strength put her on the sled again.

In the excess of their own misery they were callous to the suffering of their animals. Hal's theory, which he practised on others, was that one must get hardened. He had started out preaching it to his sister and brother-in-law. Failing there, he hammered it into the dogs with a club. At the Five Fingers the dog-food gave out, and a toothless old squaw offered to trade them a few pounds of frozen horse-hide for the Colt's revolver that kept the big hunting-knife company at Hal's hip. A poor substitute for food was this hide, just as it had been stripped from the starved horses of the cattlemen six months back. In its frozen state it was more like strips of galvanized iron, and when a dog wrestled it into his stomach it thawed into thin and innutritious leathery strings and into a mass of short hair, irritating and indigestible.

And through it all Buck staggered along at the head of the team as in a nightmare. He pulled when he could; when he could no longer pull, he fell down and remained down till blows from whip or club drove him to his feet again. All the stiffness and gloss had gone out of his beautiful furry coat. The hair hung down, limp and draggled, or matted with dried blood where Hal's club had bruised him. His muscles had wasted away to knotty strings, and the flesh pads had disappeared, so that each rib and every bone in his frame were outlined cleanly through the loose hide that was wrinkled in folds of emptiness. It was heartbreaking, only Buck's heart was unbreakable. The man in the red sweater had proved that.

As it was with Buck, so was it with his mates. They were perambulating skeletons. There were seven all together, including him. In their very great misery they had become insensible to the bite of the lash or the bruise of the club. The pain of the beating was dull and distant, just as the things their eyes saw and their ears heard seemed dull and distant. They were not half living, or quarter living. They were simply so many bags of bones in which sparks of life fluttered faintly. When a halt was made, they dropped down in the traces like dead dogs, and the spark dimmed and paled and seemed to go out. And when the club or whip fell upon them, the spark fluttered feebly up, and they tottered to their feet and staggered on.

There came a day when Billee, the good-natured, fell and could not rise. Hal had traded off his revolver, so he took the axe and knocked Billee on the head as he lay in the traces, then cut the carcass out of the harness and dragged it to one side. Buck saw, and his mates saw, and they knew that this thing was very close to them. On the next day Koona went, and but five of them remained: Joe, too far gone to be malignant; Pike, crippled and limping, only half conscious and not conscious enough longer to malinger; Sol-leks, the one-eyed, still faithful to the toil of trace and trail, and mournful in that he had so little strength with which to pull; Teek, who had not travelled so far that winter and who was now beaten more than the others because he was fresher; and Buck, still at the head of the team, but no longer enforcing discipline or striving to enforce it, blind with weakness half the time and keeping the trail by the loom of it and by the dim feel of his feet.

It was beautiful spring weather, but neither dogs nor humans were aware of it. Each day the sun rose earlier and set later. It was dawn by three in the morning, and twilight lingered till nine at night. The whole long day was a blaze of sunshine. The ghostly winter silence had given way to the great spring murmur of awakening life. This murmur arose from all the land, fraught with the joy of living. It came from the things that lived and moved again, things which had been as dead and which had not moved during the long months of frost. The sap was rising in the pines. The willows and aspens were bursting out in young buds. Shrubs and vines were putting on fresh garbs of green. Crickets sang in the nights, and in the days all manner of creeping, crawling things rustled forth into the sun. Partridges and woodpeckers were booming and knocking in the forest. Squirrels were chattering, birds singing, and overhead honked the wild-fowl driving up from the south in cunning wedges that split the air.

From every hill slope came the trickle of running water, the music of unseen fountains. All things were thawing, bending, snapping. The Yukon was straining to break loose the ice that bound it down. It ate away from beneath; the sun ate from above. Air-holes formed, fissures sprang and spread apart, while thin sections of ice fell through bodily into the river. And amid all this bursting, rending, throbbing of awakening life, under the blazing sun and through the soft-sighing breezes, like wayfarers to death, staggered the two men, the woman, and the huskies.

With the dogs falling, Mercedes weeping and riding, Hal swearing innocuously, and Charles's eyes wistfully watering, they staggered into John Thornton's camp at the mouth of White River. When they halted, the dogs dropped down as though they had all been struck dead. Mercedes dried her eyes and looked at John Thornton. Charles sat down on a log to rest. He sat down very slowly and painstakingly what of his great stiffness. Hal did the talking. John Thornton was whittling the last touches on an axe-handle he had made from a stick of birch. He whittled and listened, gave monosyllabic replies, and, when it was asked, terse advice. He knew the breed, and he gave his advice in the certainty that it would not be followed.

"They told us up above that the bottom was dropping out of the trail and that the best thing for us to do was to lay over," Hal said in response to Thornton's warning to take no more chances on the rotten ice. "They told us we couldn't make White River, and here we are." This last with a sneering ring of triumph in it.

"And they told you true," John Thornton answered. "The bottom's likely to drop out at any moment. Only fools, with the blind luck of fools, could have made it. I tell you straight, I wouldn't risk my carcass on that ice for all the gold in Alaska."

"That's because you're not a fool, I suppose," said Hal. "All the same, we'll go on to Dawson." He uncoiled his whip. "Get up there, Buck! Hi! Get up there! Mush on!"

Thornton went on whittling. It was idle, he knew, to get between a fool and his folly; while two or three fools more or less would not alter the scheme of things.

But the team did not get up at the command. It had long since passed into the stage where blows were required to rouse it. The whip flashed out, here and there, on its merciless errands. John Thornton compressed his lips. Sol-leks was the first to crawl to his feet. Teek followed. Joe came next, yelping with pain. Pike made painful efforts. Twice he fell over, when half up, and on the third attempt managed to rise. Buck made no effort. He lay quietly where he had fallen. The lash bit into him again and again, but he neither whined nor struggled. Several times Thornton started, as though to speak, but changed his mind. A moisture came into his eyes, and, as the whipping continued, he arose and walked irresolutely up and down.

This was the first time Buck had failed, in itself a sufficient reason to drive Hal into a rage. He exchanged the whip for the customary club. Buck refused to move under the rain of heavier blows which now fell upon him. Like his mates, he was barely able to get up, but, unlike them, he had made up his mind not to get up. He had a vague feeling of impending doom. This had been strong upon him when he pulled in to the bank, and it had not departed from him. What of the thin and rotten ice he had felt under his feet all day, it seemed that he sensed disaster close at hand, out there ahead on the ice where his master was trying to drive him. He refused to stir. So greatly had he suffered, and so far gone was he, that the blows did not hurt much. And as they continued to fall upon him, the spark of life within flickered and went down. It was nearly out. He felt strangely numb. As though from a great distance, he was aware that he was being beaten. The last sensations of pain left him. He no longer felt anything, though very faintly he could hear the impact of the club upon his body. But it was no longer his body, it seemed so far away.

And then, suddenly, without warning, uttering a cry that was inarticulate and more like the cry of an animal, John Thornton sprang upon the man who wielded the club. Hal was hurled backward, as though struck by a falling tree. Mercedes screamed. Charles looked on wistfully, wiped his watery eyes, but did not get up because of his stiffness.

John Thornton stood over Buck, struggling to control himself, too convulsed with rage to speak.

"If you strike that dog again, I'll kill you," he at last managed to say in a choking voice.

"It's my dog," Hal replied, wiping the blood from his mouth as he came back. "Get out of my way, or I'll fix you. I'm going to Dawson."

Thornton stood between him and Buck, and evinced no intention of getting out of the way. Hal drew his long hunting-knife. Mercedes screamed, cried, laughed, and manifested the chaotic abandonment of hysteria. Thornton rapped Hal's knuckles with the axe-handle, knocking the knife to the ground. He rapped his knuckles again as he tried to pick it up. Then he stooped, picked it up himself, and with two strokes cut Buck's traces.

Hal had no fight left in him. Besides, his hands were full with his sister, or his arms, rather; while Buck was too near dead to be of further use in hauling the sled. A few minutes later they pulled out from the bank and down the river. Buck heard them go and raised his head to see, Pike was leading, Sol-leks was at the wheel, and between were Joe and Teek. They were limping and staggering. Mercedes was riding the loaded sled. Hal guided at the gee-pole, and Charles stumbled along in the rear.

As Buck watched them, Thornton knelt beside him and with rough, kindly hands searched for broken bones. By the time his search had disclosed nothing more than many bruises and a state of terrible starvation, the sled was a quarter of a mile away. Dog and man watched it crawling along over the ice. Suddenly, they saw its back end drop down, as into a rut, and the gee-pole, with Hal clinging to it, jerk into the air. Mercedes's scream came to their ears. They saw Charles turn and make one step to run back, and then a whole section of ice give way and dogs and humans disappear. A yawning hole was all that was to be seen. The bottom had dropped out of the trail.

John Thornton and Buck looked at each other.

"You poor devil," said John Thornton, and Buck licked his hand.

CHAPTER 6
FOR THE LOVE OF A MAN

When John Thornton froze his feet in the previous December his partners had made him comfortable and left him to get well, going on themselves up the river to get out a raft of saw-logs for Dawson. He was still limping slightly at the time he rescued Buck, but with the continued warm weather even the slight limp left him. And here, lying by the river bank through the long spring days, watching the running water, listening lazily to the songs of birds and the hum of nature, Buck slowly won back his strength.

A rest comes very good after one has travelled three thousand miles, and it must be confessed that Buck waxed lazy as his wounds healed, his muscles swelled out, and the flesh came back to cover his bones. For that matter, they were all loafing,—Buck, John Thornton, and Skeet and Nig,— waiting for the raft to come that was to carry them down to Dawson. Skeet was a little Irish setter who early made friends with Buck, who, in a dying condition, was unable to resent her first advances. She had the doctor trait which some dogs possess; and as a mother cat washes her kittens, so she washed and cleansed Buck's wounds. Regularly, each morning after he had finished his breakfast, she performed her self-appointed task, till he came to look for her ministrations as much as he did for Thornton's. Nig, equally friendly, though less demonstrative, was a huge black dog, half bloodhound and half deerhound, with eyes that laughed and a boundless good nature.

To Buck's surprise these dogs manifested no jealousy toward him. They seemed to share the kindliness and largeness of John Thornton. As Buck grew stronger they enticed him into all sorts of ridiculous games, in which Thornton himself could not forbear to join; and in this fashion Buck romped through his convalescence and into a new existence. Love, genuine passionate love, was his for the first time. This he had never experienced at Judge Miller's down in the sun-kissed Santa Clara Valley. With the Judge's sons, hunting and tramping, it had been a working partnership; with the Judge's grandsons, a sort of pompous guardianship; and with the Judge himself, a stately and dignified friendship. But love that was feverish and burning, that was adoration, that was madness, it had taken John Thornton to arouse.

This man had saved his life, which was something; but, further, he was the ideal master. Other men saw to the welfare of their dogs from a sense of duty and business expediency; he saw to the welfare of his as if they were his own children, because he could not help it. And he saw further. He never forgot a kindly greeting or a cheering word, and to sit down for a long talk with them ("gas" he called it) was as much his delight as theirs. He had a way of taking Buck's head roughly between his hands, and resting his own head upon Buck's, of shaking him back and forth, the while calling him ill names that to Buck were love names. Buck knew no greater joy than that rough embrace and the sound of murmured oaths, and at each jerk back and forth it seemed that his heart would be shaken out of his body so great was its ecstasy. And when, released, he sprang to his feet, his mouth laughing, his eyes eloquent, his throat vibrant with unuttered sound, and in that fashion remained without movement, John Thornton would reverently exclaim, "God! you can all but speak!"

Buck had a trick of love expression that was akin to hurt. He would often seize Thornton's hand in his mouth and close so fiercely that the flesh bore the impress of his teeth for some time afterward. And as Buck understood the oaths to be love words, so the man understood this feigned bite for a caress.

For the most part, however, Buck's love was expressed in adoration. While he went wild with happiness when Thornton touched him or spoke to him, he did not seek these tokens. Unlike Skeet, who was wont to shove her nose under Thornton's hand and nudge and nudge till petted, or Nig, who would stalk up and rest his great head on Thornton's knee, Buck was content to adore at a distance. He would lie by the hour, eager, alert, at Thornton's feet, looking up into his face, dwelling upon it, studying it, following with keenest interest each fleeting expression, every movement or change of feature. Or, as chance might have it, he would lie farther away, to the side or rear, watching the outlines of the man and the occasional movements of his body. And often, such was the communion in which they lived, the strength of Buck's gaze would draw John Thornton's head around, and he would return the gaze, without speech, his heart shining out of his eyes as Buck's heart shone out.

For a long time after his rescue, Buck did not like Thornton to get out of his sight. From the moment he left the tent to when he entered it again, Buck would follow at his heels. His transient masters since he had come into the Northland had bred in him a fear that no master could be permanent. He was afraid that Thornton would pass out of his life as Perrault and François and the Scotch half-breed had passed out. Even in the night, in his dreams, he was haunted by this fear. At such times he would shake off sleep and creep through the chill to the flap of the tent, where he would stand and listen to the sound of his master's breathing.

But in spite of this great love he bore John Thornton, which seemed to bespeak the soft civilizing influence, the strain of the primitive, which the Northland had aroused in him, remained alive and active. Faithfulness and devotion, things born of fire and roof, were his; yet he retained his wildness and wiliness. He was a thing of the wild, come in from the wild to sit by John Thornton's fire, rather than a dog of the soft Southland stamped with the marks of generations of civilization. Because of his very great love, he could not steal from this man, but from any other man, in any other camp, he did not hesitate an instant; while the cunning with which he stole enabled him to escape detection.

His face and body were scored by the teeth of many dogs, and he fought as fiercely as ever and more shrewdly. Skeet and Nig were too good-natured for quarrelling,—besides, they belonged to John Thornton; but the strange dog, no matter what the breed or valor, swiftly acknowledged Buck's supremacy or found himself struggling for life with a terrible antagonist. And Buck was merciless. He had learned well the law of club and fang, and he never forewent an advantage or drew back from a foe he had started on the way to Death. He had lessoned from Spitz, and from the chief fighting dogs of the police and mail, and knew there was no middle course. He must master or be mastered; while to show mercy was a weakness. Mercy did not exist in the primordial life. It was misunderstood for fear, and such misunderstandings made for death. Kill or be killed, eat or be eaten, was the law; and this mandate, down out of the depths of Time, he obeyed.

He was older than the days he had seen and the breaths he had drawn. He linked the past with the present, and the eternity behind him throbbed through him in a mighty rhythm to which he swayed as the tides and seasons swayed. He sat by John Thornton's fire, a broad-breasted dog, white-fanged and long-furred; but behind him were the shades of all manner of dogs, half-wolves and wild wolves, urgent and prompting, tasting the savor of the meat he ate, thirsting for the water he drank, scenting the wind with him, listening with him and telling him the sounds made by the wild life in the forest, dictating his moods, directing his actions, lying down to sleep with him when he lay down, and dreaming with him and beyond him and becoming themselves the stuff of his dreams.

So peremptorily did these shades beckon him, that each day mankind and the claims of mankind slipped farther from him. Deep in the forest a call was sounding, and as often as he heard this call, mysteriously thrilling and luring, he felt compelled to turn his back upon the fire and the beaten earth around it, and to plunge into the forest, and on and on, he knew not where or why; nor did he wonder where or why, the call sounding imperiously, deep in the forest. But as often as he gained the soft unbroken earth and the green shade, the love for John Thornton drew him back to the fire again.

Thornton alone held him. The rest of mankind was as nothing. Chance travellers might praise or pet him; but he was cold under it all, and from a too demonstrative man he would get up and walk away. When Thornton's partners, Hans and Pete, arrived on the long-expected raft, Buck refused to notice them till he learned they were close to Thornton; after that he tolerated them in a passive sort of way, accepting favors from them as though he favored them by accepting. They were of the same large type as

Thornton, living close to the earth, thinking simply and seeing clearly; and ere they swung the raft into the big eddy by the saw-mill at Dawson, they understood Buck and his ways, and did not insist upon an intimacy such as obtained with Skeet and Nig.

For Thornton, however, his love seemed to grow and grow. He, alone among men, could put a pack upon Buck's back in the summer travelling. Nothing was too great for Buck to do, when Thornton commanded. One day (they had grub-staked themselves from the proceeds of the raft and left Dawson for the head-waters of the Tanana) the men and dogs were sitting on the crest of a cliff which fell away, straight down, to naked bed-rock three hundred feet below. John Thornton was sitting near the edge, Buck at his shoulder. A thoughtless whim seized Thornton, and he drew the attention of Hans and Pete to the experiment he had in mind. "Jump, Buck!" he commanded, sweeping his arm out and over the chasm. The next instant he was grappling with Buck on the extreme edge, while Hans and Pete were dragging them back into safety.

"It's uncanny," Pete said, after it was over and they had caught their speech.

Thornton shook his head. "No, it is splendid, and it is terrible, too. Do you know, it sometimes makes me afraid."

"I'm not hankering to be the man that lays hands on you while he's around," Pete announced conclusively, nodding his head toward Buck.

"Py Jingo!" was Hans's contribution. "Not mineself either."

It was at Circle City, ere the year was out, that Pete's apprehensions were realized. "Black" Burton, a man evil-tempered and malicious, had been picking a quarrel with a tenderfoot at the bar, when Thornton stepped good-naturedly between. Buck, as was his custom, was lying in a corner, head on paws, watching his master's every action. Burton struck out, without warning, straight from the shoulder. Thornton was sent spinning, and saved himself from falling only by clutching the rail of the bar.

Those who were looking on heard what was neither bark nor yelp, but a something which is best described as a roar, and they saw Buck's body rise up in the air as he left the floor for Burton's throat. The man saved his life by instinctively throwing out his arm, but was hurled backward to the floor with Buck on top of him. Buck loosed his teeth from the flesh of the arm and drove in again for the throat. This time the man succeeded only in partly blocking, and his throat was torn open. Then the crowd was upon Buck, and he was driven off; but while a surgeon checked the bleeding, he prowled up and down, growling furiously, attempting to rush in, and being forced back by an array of hostile clubs. A "miners' meeting," called on the spot, decided that the dog had sufficient provocation, and Buck was discharged. But his reputation was made, and from that day his name spread through every camp in Alaska.

Later on, in the fall of the year, he saved John Thornton's life in quite another fashion. The three partners were lining a long and narrow poling-boat down a bad stretch of rapids on the Forty-Mile Creek. Hans and Pete moved along the bank, snubbing with a thin Manila rope from tree to tree, while Thornton remained in the boat, helping its descent by means of a pole, and shouting directions to the shore. Buck, on the bank, worried and anxious, kept abreast of the boat, his eyes never off his master.

At a particularly bad spot, where a ledge of barely submerged rocks jutted out into the river, Hans cast off the rope, and, while Thornton poled the boat out into the stream, ran down the bank with the end in his hand to snub the boat when it had cleared the ledge. This it did, and was flying down-stream in a current as swift as a mill-race, when Hans checked it with the rope and checked too suddenly. The boat flirted over and snubbed in to the bank bottom up, while Thornton, flung sheer out of it, was carried down-stream toward the worst part of the rapids, a stretch of wild water in which no swimmer could live.

Buck had sprung in on the instant; and at the end of three hundred yards, amid a mad swirl of water, he overhauled Thornton. When he felt him grasp his tail, Buck headed for the bank, swimming with all his splendid strength. But the progress shoreward was slow; the progress down-stream amazingly rapid. From below came the fatal roaring where the wild current went wilder and was rent in shreds and spray by the rocks which thrust through like the teeth of an enormous comb. The suck of the water as it took the beginning of the last steep pitch was frightful, and Thornton knew that the shore was impossible. He scraped furiously over a rock, bruised across a second, and struck a third with crushing force. He clutched its slippery top with both hands, releasing Buck, and above the roar of the churning water shouted: "Go, Buck! Go!"

Buck could not hold his own, and swept on down-stream, struggling desperately, but unable to win back. When he heard Thornton's command repeated, he partly reared out of the water, throwing his head high, as though for a last look, then turned obediently toward the bank. He swam powerfully and was dragged ashore by Pete and Hans at the very point where swimming ceased to be possible and destruction began.

They knew that the time a man could cling to a slippery rock in the face of that driving current was a matter of minutes, and they ran as fast as they could up the bank to a point far above where Thornton was hanging on. They attached the line with which they had been snubbing the boat to Buck's neck and shoulders, being careful that it should neither strangle him nor impede his swimming, and launched him into the stream. He struck out boldly, but not straight enough into the stream. He discovered the mistake too late, when Thornton was abreast of him and a bare half-dozen strokes away while he was being carried helplessly past.

Hans promptly snubbed with the rope, as though Buck were a boat. The rope thus tightening on him in the sweep of the current, he was jerked under the surface, and under the surface he remained till his body struck against the bank and he was hauled out. He was half drowned, and Hans and Pete threw themselves upon him, pounding the breath into him and the water out of him. He staggered to his feet and fell down. The faint sound of Thornton's voice came to them, and though they could not make out the words of it, they knew that he was in his extremity. His master's voice acted on Buck like an electric shock, He sprang to his feet and ran up the bank ahead of the men to the point of his previous departure.

Again the rope was attached and he was launched, and again he struck out, but this time straight into the stream. He had miscalculated once, but he would not be guilty of it a second time. Hans paid out the rope, permitting no slack, while Pete kept it clear of coils. Buck held on till he was on a line straight above Thornton; then he turned, and with the speed of an express train headed down upon him. Thornton saw him coming, and, as Buck struck him like a battering ram, with the whole force of the current behind him, he reached up and closed with both arms around the shaggy neck. Hans snubbed the rope around the tree, and Buck and Thornton were jerked under the water. Strangling, suffocating, sometimes one uppermost and sometimes the other, dragging over the jagged bottom, smashing against rocks and snags, they veered in to the bank.

Thornton came to, belly downward and being violently propelled back and forth across a drift log by Hans and Pete. His first glance was for Buck, over whose limp and apparently lifeless body Nig was setting up a howl, while Skeet was licking the wet face and closed eyes. Thornton was himself bruised and battered, and he went carefully over Buck's body, when he had been brought around, finding three broken ribs.

"That settles it," he announced. "We camp right here." And camp they did, till Buck's ribs knitted and he was able to travel.

That winter, at Dawson, Buck performed another exploit, not so heroic, perhaps, but one that put his name many notches higher on the totem-pole of Alaskan fame. This exploit was particularly gratifying to the three men; for they stood in need of the outfit which it furnished, and were enabled to make a long-desired trip into the virgin East, where miners had not yet appeared. It was brought about by a conversation in the Eldorado Saloon, in which men waxed boastful of their favorite dogs. Buck, because of his record, was the target for these men, and Thornton was driven stoutly to defend him. At the end of half an hour one man stated that his dog could start a sled with five hundred pounds and walk off with it; a second bragged six hundred for his dog; and a third, seven hundred.

"Pooh! pooh!" said John Thornton; "Buck can start a thousand pounds."

"And break it out? and walk off with it for a hundred yards?" demanded Matthewson, a Bonanza King, he of the seven hundred vaunt.

"And break it out, and walk off with it for a hundred yards," John Thornton said coolly.

"Well," Matthewson said, slowly and deliberately, so that all could hear, "I've got a thousand dollars that says he can't. And there it is." So saying, he slammed a sack of gold dust of the size of a bologna sausage down upon the bar.

Nobody spoke. Thornton's bluff, if bluff it was, had been called. He could feel a flush of warm blood creeping up his face. His tongue had tricked him. He did not know whether Buck could start a thousand pounds. Half a ton! The enormousness of it appalled him. He had great faith in Buck's strength and had often thought him capable of starting such a load; but never, as now, had he faced the possibility of it, the eyes of a dozen men fixed upon him, silent and waiting. Further, he had no thousand dollars; nor had Hans or Pete.

"I've got a sled standing outside now, with twenty fiftypound sacks of flour on it," Matthewson went on with brutal directness; "so don't let that hinder you."

Thornton did not reply. He did not know what to say. He glanced from face to face in the absent way of a man who has lost the power of thought and is seeking somewhere to find the thing that will start it going again. The face of Jim O'Brien, a Mastodon King and old-time comrade, caught his eyes. It was as a cue to him, seeming to rouse him to do what he would never have dreamed of doing.

"Can you lend me a thousand?" he asked, almost in a whisper.

"Sure," answered O'Brien, thumping down a plethoric sack by the side of Matthewson's. "Though it's little faith I'm having, John, that the beast can do the trick."

The Eldorado emptied its occupants into the street to see the test. The tables were deserted, and the dealers and gamekeepers came forth to see the outcome of the wager and to lay odds. Several hundred men, furred and mittened, banked around the sled within easy distance. Matthewson's sled, loaded with a thousand pounds of flour, had been standing for a couple of hours, and in the intense cold (it was sixty below zero) the runners had frozen fast to the hard-packed snow. Men offered odds of two to one that Buck could not budge the sled. A quibble arose concerning the phrase "break out." O'Brien contended it was Thornton's privilege to knock the runners loose, leaving Buck to "break it out" from a dead standstill. Matthewson insisted that the phrase included breaking the runners from the frozen grip of the snow. A majority of the men who had witnessed the making of the bet decided in his favor, whereat the odds went up to three to one against Buck.

There were no takers. Not a man believed him capable of the feat. Thornton had been hurried into the wager, heavy with doubt; and now that he looked at the sled itself, the concrete fact, with the regular team of ten dogs curled up in the snow before it, the more impossible the task appeared. Matthewson waxed jubilant.

"Three to one!" he proclaimed. "I'll lay you another thousand at that figure, Thornton. What d'ye say?"

Thornton's doubt was strong in his face, but his fighting spirit was aroused—the fighting spirit that soars above odds, fails to recognize the impossible, and is deaf to all save the clamor for battle. He called Hans and Pete to him. Their sacks were slim, and with his own the three partners could rake together only two hundred dollars. In the ebb of their fortunes, this sum was their total capital; yet they laid it unhesitatingly against Matthewson's six hundred.

The team of ten dogs was unhitched, and Buck, with his own harness, was put into the sled. He had caught the contagion of the excitement, and he felt that in some way he must do a great thing for John Thornton. Murmurs of admiration at his splendid appearance went up. He was in perfect condition, without an ounce of superfluous flesh, and the one hundred and fifty pounds that he weighed were so many pounds of grit and virility. His furry coat shone with the sheen of silk. Down the neck and across the shoulders, his mane, in repose as it was, half bristled and seemed to lift with every movement, as though excess of vigor made each particular hair alive and active. The great breast and heavy fore legs were no more than in proportion with the rest of the body, where the muscles showed in tight rolls underneath the skin. Men felt these muscles and proclaimed them hard as iron, and the odds went down to two to one.

"Gad, sir! Gad, sir!" stuttered a member of the latest dynasty, a king of the Skookum Benches. "I offer you eight hundred for him, sir, before the test, sir; eight hundred just as he stands."

Thornton shook his head and stepped to Buck's side.

"You must stand off from him," Matthewson protested. "Free play and plenty of room."

The crowd fell silent; only could be heard the voices of the gamblers vainly offering two to one. Everybody acknowledged Buck a magnificent animal, but twenty fifty-pound sacks of flour bulked too large in their eyes for them to loosen their pouch-strings.

Thornton knelt down by Buck's side. He took his head in his two hands and rested cheek on cheek. He did not playfully shake him, as was his wont, or murmur soft love curses; but he whispered in his ear. "As you love me, Buck. As you love me," was what he whispered. Buck whined with suppressed eagerness.

The crowd was watching curiously. The affair was growing mysterious. It seemed like a conjuration. As Thornton got to his feet, Buck seized his mittened hand between his jaws, pressing in with his teeth and releasing slowly, half-reluctantly. It was the answer, in terms, not of speech, but of love. Thornton stepped well back.

"Now, Buck," he said.

Buck tightened the traces, then slacked them for a matter of several inches. It was the way he had learned.

"Gee!" Thornton's voice rang out, sharp in the tense silence.

Buck swung to the right, ending the movement in a plunge that took up the slack and with a sudden jerk arrested his one hundred and fifty pounds. The load quivered, and from under the runners arose a crisp crackling.

"Haw!" Thornton commanded.

Buck duplicated the manœuvre, this time to the left. The crackling turned into a snapping, the sled pivoting and the runners slipping and grating several inches to the side. The sled was broken out. Men were holding their breaths, intensely unconscious of the fact.

"Now, MUSH!"

Thornton's command cracked out like a pistol-shot. Buck threw himself forward, tightening the traces with a jarring lunge. His whole body was gathered compactly together in the tremendous effort, the muscles writhing and knotting like live things under the silky fur. His great chest was low to the ground, his head forward and down, while his feet were flying like mad, the claws scarring the hard-packed snow in parallel grooves. The sled swayed and trembled, half-started forward. One of his feet slipped, and one man groaned aloud. Then the sled lurched ahead in what appeared a rapid succession of jerks, though it never really came to a dead stop again...half an inch...an inch... two inches... The jerks perceptibly diminished; as the sled gained momentum, he caught them up, till it was moving steadily along.

Men gasped and began to breathe again, unaware that for a moment they had ceased to breathe. Thornton was running behind, encouraging Buck with short, cheery words. The distance had been measured off, and as he neared the pile of firewood which marked the end of the hundred yards, a cheer began to grow and grow, which burst into a roar as he passed the firewood and halted at command. Every man was tearing himself loose, even Matthewson. Hats and mittens were flying in the air. Men were shaking hands, it did not matter with whom, and bubbling over in a general incoherent babel.

But Thornton fell on his knees beside Buck. Head was against head, and he was shaking him back and forth. Those who hurried up heard him cursing Buck, and he cursed him long and fervently, and softly and lovingly.

"Gad, sir! Gad, sir!" spluttered the Skookum Bench king. "I'll give you a thousand for him, sir, a thousand, sir—twelve hundred, sir."

Thornton rose to his feet. His eyes were wet. The tears were streaming frankly down his cheeks. "Sir," he said to the Skookum Bench king, "no, sir. You can go to hell, sir. It's the best I can do for you, sir."

Buck seized Thornton's hand in his teeth. Thornton shook him back and forth. As though animated by a common impulse, the onlookers drew back to a respectful distance; nor were they again indiscreet enough to interrupt.

CHAPTER 7

THE SOUNDING OF THE CALL

When Buck earned sixteen hundred dollars in five minutes for John Thornton, he made it possible for his master to pay off certain debts and to journey with his partners into the East after a fabled lost mine, the history of which was as old as the history of the country. Many men had sought it; few had found it; and more than a few there were who had never returned from the quest. This lost mine was steeped in tragedy and shrouded in mystery. No one knew of the first man. The oldest tradition stopped before it got back to him. From the beginning there had been an ancient and ramshackle cabin. Dying men had sworn to it, and to the mine the site of which it marked, clinching their testimony with nuggets that were unlike any known grade of gold in the Northland.

But no living man had looted this treasure house, and the dead were dead; wherefore John Thornton and Pete and Hans, with Buck and half a dozen other dogs, faced into the East on an unknown trail to achieve where men and dogs as good as themselves had failed. They sledded seventy miles up the Yukon, swung to the left into the Stewart River, passed the Mayo and the McQuestion, and held on until the Stewart itself became a streamlet, threading the upstanding peaks which marked the backbone of the continent.

John Thornton asked little of man or nature. He was unafraid of the wild. With a handful of salt and a rifle he could plunge into the wilderness and fare wherever he pleased and as long as he pleased. Being in no haste, Indian fashion, he hunted his dinner in the course of the day's travel; and if he failed to find it, like the Indian, he kept on travelling, secure in the knowledge that sooner or later he would come to it. So, on this great journey into the East, straight meat was the bill of fare, ammunition and tools principally made up the load on the sled, and the time-card was drawn upon the limitless future.

To Buck it was boundless delight, this hunting, fishing, and indefinite wandering through strange places. For weeks at a time they would hold on steadily, day after day; and for weeks upon end they would camp, here and there, the dogs loafing and the men burning holes through frozen muck and gravel and washing countless pans of dirt by the heat of the fire. Sometimes they went hungry, sometimes they feasted riotously, all according to the abundance of game and the fortune of hunting. Summer arrived, and dogs and men packed on their backs, rafted across blue mountain lakes, and descended or ascended unknown rivers in slender boats whipsawed from the standing forest.

The months came and went, and back and forth they twisted through the uncharted vastness, where no men were and yet where men had been if the Lost Cabin were true. They went across divides in summer blizzards, shivered under the midnight sun on naked mountains between the timber line and the eternal snows, dropped into summer valleys amid swarming gnats and flies, and in the shadows of glaciers picked strawberries and flowers as ripe and fair as any the Southland could boast. In the fall of the year they penetrated a weird lake country, sad and silent, where wildfowl had been, but where then there was no life nor sign of life—only the blowing of chill winds, the forming of ice in sheltered places, and the melancholy rippling of waves on lonely beaches.

And through another winter they wandered on the obliterated trails of men who had gone before. Once, they came upon a path blazed through the forest, an ancient path, and the Lost Cabin seemed very near. But the path began nowhere and ended nowhere, and it remained mystery, as the man who made it and the reason he made it remained mystery. Another time they chanced upon the time-graven wreckage of a hunting lodge, and amid the shreds of rotted blankets John Thornton found a long-barrelled flint-lock. He knew it for a Hudson Bay Company gun of the young days in the Northwest, when such a gun was worth its height in beaver skins packed flat, And that was all—no hint as to the man who in an early day had reared the lodge and left the gun among the blankets.

Spring came on once more, and at the end of all their wandering they found, not the Lost Cabin, but a shallow placer in a broad valley where the gold showed like yellow butter across the bottom of the washing-pan. They sought no farther. Each day they worked earned them thousands of dollars in clean dust and nuggets, and they worked every day. The gold was sacked in moose-hide bags, fifty pounds to the bag, and piled like so much firewood outside the spruce-bough lodge. Like giants they toiled, days flashing on the heels of days like dreams as they heaped the treasure up.

There was nothing for the dogs to do, save the hauling in of meat now and again that Thornton killed, and Buck spent long hours musing by the fire. The vision of the short-legged hairy man came to him more frequently, now that there was little work to be done; and often, blinking by the fire, Buck wandered with him in that other world which he remembered.

The salient thing of this other world seemed fear. When he watched the hairy man sleeping by the fire, head between his knees and hands clasped above, Buck saw that he slept restlessly, with many starts and awakenings, at which times he would peer fearfully into the darkness and fling more wood upon the fire. Did they walk by the beach of a sea, where the hairy man gathered shellfish and ate them as he gathered, it was with eyes that roved everywhere for hidden danger and with legs prepared to run like the wind at its first appearance. Through the forest they crept noiselessly, Buck at the hairy man's heels; and they were alert and vigilant, the pair of them, ears twitching and moving and nostrils quivering, for the man heard and smelled as keenly as Buck. The hairy man could spring up into the trees and travel ahead as fast as on the ground, swinging by the arms from limb to limb, sometimes a dozen feet apart, letting go and catching, never falling, never missing his grip. In fact, he seemed as much at home among the trees as on the ground; and Buck had memories of nights of vigil spent beneath trees wherein the hairy man roosted, holding on tightly as he slept.

And closely akin to the visions of the hairy man was the call still sounding in the depths of the forest. It filled him with a great unrest and strange desires. It caused him to feel a vague, sweet gladness, and he was aware of wild yearnings and stirrings for he knew not what. Sometimes he pursued the call into the forest, looking for it as though it were a tangible thing, barking softly or defiantly, as the mood might dictate. He would thrust his nose into the cool wood moss, or into the black soil where long grasses grew, and snort with joy at the fat earth smells; or he would crouch for hours, as if in concealment, behind fungus-covered trunks of fallen trees, wide-eyed and wide-eared to all that moved and sounded about him. It might be, lying thus, that he hoped to surprise this call he could not understand. But he did not know why he did these various things. He was impelled to do them, and did not reason about them at all.

Irresistible impulses seized him. He would be lying in camp, dozing lazily in the heat of the day, when suddenly his head would lift and his ears cock up, intent and listening, and he would spring to his feet and dash away, and on and on, for hours, through the forest aisles and across the open spaces where the niggerheads bunched. He loved to run down dry watercourses, and to creep and spy upon the bird life in the woods. For a day at a time he would lie in the underbrush where he could watch the partridges drumming and strutting up and down. But especially he loved to run in the dim twilight of the summer midnights, listening to the subdued and sleepy murmurs of the forest, reading signs and sounds as man may read a book, and seeking for the mysterious something that called—called, waking or sleeping, at all times, for him to come.

One night he sprang from sleep with a start, eager-eyed, nostrils quivering and scenting, his mane bristling in recurrent waves. From the forest came the call (or one note of it, for the call was many noted), distinct and definite as never before,—a long-drawn howl, like, yet unlike, any noise made by husky dog. And he knew it, in the old familiar way, as a sound heard before. He sprang through the sleeping camp and in swift silence dashed through the woods. As he drew closer to the cry he went more slowly, with caution in every movement, till he came to an open place among the trees, and looking out saw, erect on haunches, with nose pointed to the sky, a long, lean, timber wolf.

He had made no noise, yet it ceased from its howling and tried to sense his presence. Buck stalked into the open, half crouching, body gathered compactly together, tail straight and stiff, feet falling with unwonted care. Every movement advertised commingled threatening and overture of friendliness. It was the menacing truce that marks the meeting of wild beasts that prey. But the wolf fled at sight of him. He followed, with wild leapings, in a frenzy to overtake. He ran him into a blind channel, in the bed of the creek where a timber jam barred the way. The wolf whirled about, pivoting on his hind legs after the fashion of Joe and of all cornered husky dogs, snarling and bristling, clipping his teeth together in a continuous and rapid succession of snaps.

Buck did not attack, but circled him about and hedged him in with friendly advances. The wolf was suspicious and afraid; for Buck made three of him in weight, while his head barely reached Buck's shoulder. Watching his chance, he darted away, and the chase was resumed. Time and again he was cornered, and the thing repeated, though he was in poor condition, or Buck could not so easily have overtaken him. He would run till Buck's head was even with his flank, when he would whirl around at bay, only to dash away again at the first opportunity.

But in the end Buck's pertinacity was rewarded; for the wolf, finding that no harm was intended, finally sniffed noses with him. Then they became friendly, and played about in the nervous, half-coy way with which fierce beasts belie their fierceness. After some time of this the wolf started off at an easy lope in a manner that plainly showed he was going somewhere. He made it clear to Buck that he was to come, and they ran side by side through the sombre twilight, straight up the creek bed, into the gorge from which it issued, and across the bleak divide where it took its rise.

On the opposite slope of the watershed they came down into a level country where were great stretches of forest and many streams, and through these great stretches they ran steadily, hour after hour, the sun rising higher and the day growing warmer. Buck was wildly glad. He knew he was at last answering the call, running by the side of his wood brother toward the place from where the call surely came. Old memories were coming upon him fast, and he was stirring to them as of old he stirred to the realities of which they were the shadows. He had done this thing before, somewhere in that other and dimly remembered world, and he was doing it again, now, running free in the open, the unpacked earth underfoot, the wide sky overhead.

They stopped by a running stream to drink, and, stopping, Buck remembered John Thornton. He sat down. The wolf started on toward the place from where the call surely came, then returned to him, sniffing noses and making actions as though to encourage him. But Buck turned about and started slowly on the back track. For the better part of an hour the wild brother ran by his side, whining softly. Then he sat down, pointed his nose upward, and howled. It was a mournful howl, and as Buck held steadily on his way he heard it grow faint and fainter until it was lost in the distance.

John Thornton was eating dinner when Buck dashed into camp and sprang upon him in a frenzy of affection, overturning him, scrambling upon him, licking his face, biting his hand—"playing the general tomfool," as John Thornton characterized it, the while he shook Buck back and forth and cursed him lovingly.

For two days and nights Buck never left camp, never let Thornton out of his sight. He followed him about at his work, watched him while he ate, saw him into his blankets at night and out of them in the morning. But after two days the call in the forest began to sound more imperiously than ever. Buck's restlessness came back on him, and he was haunted by recollections of the wild brother, and of the smiling land beyond the divide and the run side by side through the wide forest stretches. Once again he took to wandering in the woods, but the wild brother came no more; and though he listened through long vigils, the mournful howl was never raised.

He began to sleep out at night, staying away from camp for days at a time; and once he crossed the divide at the head of the creek and went down into the land of timber and streams. There he wandered for a week, seeking vainly for fresh sign of the wild brother, killing his meat as he travelled and travelling with the long, easy lope that seems never to tire. He fished for salmon in a broad stream that emptied somewhere into the sea, and by this stream he killed a large black bear, blinded by the mosquitoes while likewise fishing, and raging through the forest helpless and terrible. Even so, it was a hard fight, and it aroused the last latent remnants of Buck's ferocity. And two days later, when he returned to his kill and found a dozen wolverenes quarrelling over the spoil, he scattered them like chaff; and those that fled left two behind who would quarrel no more.

The blood-longing became stronger than ever before. He was a killer, a thing that preyed, living on the things that lived, unaided, alone, by virtue of his own strength and prowess, surviving triumphantly in a hostile environment where only the strong survived. Because of all this he became possessed of a great pride in himself, which communicated itself like a contagion to his physical being. It advertised itself in all his movements, was apparent in the play of every muscle, spoke plainly as speech in the way he carried himself, and made his glorious furry coat if anything more glorious. But for the stray brown on his muzzle and above his eyes, and for the splash of white hair that ran midmost down his chest, he might well have been mistaken for a gigantic wolf, larger than the largest of the breed. From his St. Bernard father he had inherited size and weight, but it was his shepherd mother who had given shape to that size and weight. His muzzle was the long wolf muzzle, save that it was larger than the muzzle of any wolf; and his head, somewhat broader, was the wolf head on a massive scale.

His cunning was wolf cunning, and wild cunning; his intelligence, shepherd intelligence and St. Bernard intelligence; and all this, plus an experience gained in the fiercest of schools, made him as formidable a creature as any that roamed the wild. A carnivorous animal living on a straight meat diet, he was in full flower, at the high tide of his life, overspilling with vigor and virility. When Thornton passed a caressing hand along his back, a snapping and crackling followed the hand, each hair discharging its pent magnetism at the contact. Every part, brain and body, nerve tissue and fibre, was keyed to the most exquisite pitch; and between all the parts there was a perfect equilibrium or adjustment. To sights and sounds and events which required action, he responded with lightning-like rapidity. Quickly as a husky dog could leap to defend from attack or to attack, he could leap twice as quickly. He saw the movement, or heard sound, and responded in less time than another dog required to compass the mere seeing or hearing. He perceived and determined and responded in the same instant. In point of fact the three actions of perceiving, determining, and responding were sequential; but so infinitesimal were the intervals of time between them that they appeared simultaneous. His muscles were surcharged with vitality, and snapped into play sharply, like steel springs. Life streamed through him in splendid flood, glad and rampant, until it seemed that it would burst him asunder in sheer ecstasy and pour forth generously over the world.

"Never was there such a dog," said John Thornton one day, as the partners watched Buck marching out of camp.

"When he was made, the mould was broke," said Pete.

"Py jingo! I t'ink so mineself," Hans affirmed.

They saw him marching out of camp, but they did not see the instant and terrible transformation which took place as soon as he was within the secrecy of the forest. He no longer marched. At once he became a thing of the wild, stealing along softly, cat-footed, a passing shadow that appeared and disappeared among the shadows. He knew how to take advantage of every cover, to crawl on his belly like a snake, and like a snake to leap and strike. He could take a ptarmigan from its nest, kill a rabbit as it slept, and snap in mid air the little chipmunks fleeing a second too late for the trees. Fish, in open pools, were not too quick for him; nor were beaver, mending their dams, too wary. He killed to eat, not from wantonness; but he preferred to eat what he killed himself. So a lurking humor ran through his deeds, and it was his delight to steal upon the squirrels, and, when he all but had them, to let them go, chattering in mortal fear to the treetops.

As the fall of the year came on, the moose appeared in greater abundance, moving slowly down to meet the winter in the lower and less rigorous valleys. Buck had already dragged down a stray part-grown calf; but he wished strongly for larger and more formidable quarry, and he came upon it one day on the divide at the head of the creek. A band of twenty moose had crossed over from the land of streams and timber, and chief among them was a great bull. He was in a savage temper, and, standing over six feet from the ground, was as formidable an antagonist as even Buck could desire. Back and forth the bull tossed his great palmated antlers, branching to fourteen points and embracing seven feet within the tips. His small eyes burned with a vicious and bitter light, while he roared with fury at sight of Buck.

From the bull's side, just forward of the flank, protruded a feathered arrow-end, which accounted for his savageness. Guided by that instinct which came from the old hunting days of the primordial world, Buck proceeded to cut the bull out from the herd. It was no slight task. He would bark and dance about in front of the bull, just out of reach of the great antlers and of the terrible splay hoofs which could have stamped his life out with a single blow. Unable to turn his back on the fanged danger and go on, the bull would be driven into paroxysms of rage. At such moments he charged Buck, who retreated craftily, luring him on by a simulated inability to escape. But when he was thus separated from his fellows, two or three of the younger bulls would charge back upon Buck and enable the wounded bull to rejoin the herd.

There is a patience of the wild—dogged, tireless, persistent as life itself—that holds motionless for endless hours the spider in its web, the snake in its coils, the panther in its ambuscade; this patience belongs peculiarly to life when it hunts its living food; and it belonged to Buck as he clung to the flank of the herd, retarding its march, irritating the young bulls, worrying the cows with their half-grown calves, and driving the wounded bull mad with helpless rage. For half a day this continued. Buck multiplied himself, attacking from all sides, enveloping the herd in a whirlwind of menace, cutting out his victim as fast as it could rejoin its mates, wearing out the patience of creatures preyed upon, which is a lesser patience than that of creatures preying.

As the day wore along and the sun dropped to its bed in the northwest (the darkness had come back and the fall nights were six hours long), the young bulls retraced their steps more and more reluctantly to the aid of their beset leader. The down-coming winter was harrying them on to the lower levels, and it seemed they could never shake off this tireless creature that held them back. Besides, it was not the life of the herd, or of the young bulls, that was threatened. The life of only one member was demanded, which was a remoter interest than their lives, and in the end they were content to pay the toll.

As twilight fell the old bull stood with lowered head, watching his mates—the cows he had known, the calves he had fathered, the bulls he had mastered—as they shambled on at a rapid pace through the fading light. He could not follow, for before his nose leaped the merciless fanged terror that would not let him go. Three hundredweight more than half a ton he weighed; he had lived a long, strong life, full of fight and struggle, and at the end he faced death at the teeth of a creature whose head did not reach beyond his great knuckled knees.

From then on, night and day, Buck never left his prey, never gave it a moment's rest, never permitted it to browse the leaves of trees or the shoots of young birch and willow. Nor did he give the wounded bull opportunity to slake his burning thirst in the slender trickling streams they crossed. Often, in desperation, he burst into long stretches of flight. At such times Buck did not attempt to stay him, but loped easily at his heels, satisfied with the way the game was played, lying down when the moose stood still, attacking him fiercely when he strove to eat or drink.

The great head drooped more and more under its tree of horns, and the shambling trot grew weak and weaker. He took to standing for long periods, with nose to the ground and dejected ears dropped limply; and Buck found more time in which to get water for himself and in which to rest. At such moments, panting with red lolling tongue and with eyes fixed upon the big bull, it appeared to Buck that a change was coming over the face of things. He could feel a new stir in the land. As the moose were coming into the land, other kinds of life were coming in. Forest and stream and air seemed palpitant with their presence. The news of it was borne in upon him, not by sight, or sound, or smell, but by some other and subtler sense. He heard nothing, saw nothing, yet knew that the land was somehow different; that through it strange things were afoot and ranging; and he resolved to investigate after he had finished the business in hand.

At last, at the end of the fourth day, he pulled the great moose down. For a day and a night he remained by the kill, eating and sleeping, turn and turn about. Then, rested, refreshed and strong, he turned his face toward camp and John Thornton. He broke into the long easy lope, and went on, hour after hour, never at loss for the tangled way, heading straight home through strange country with a certitude of direction that put man and his magnetic needle to shame.

As he held on he became more and more conscious of the new stir in the land. There was life abroad in it different from the life which had been there throughout the summer. No longer was this fact borne in upon him in some subtle, mysterious way. The birds talked of it, the squirrels chattered about it, the very breeze whispered of it. Several times he stopped and drew in the fresh morning air in great sniffs, reading a message which made him leap on with greater speed. He was oppressed with a sense of calamity happening, if it were not calamity already happened; and as he crossed the last watershed and dropped down into the valley toward camp, he proceeded with greater caution.

Three miles away he came upon a fresh trail that sent his neck hair rippling and bristling, It led straight toward camp and John Thornton. Buck hurried on, swiftly and stealthily, every nerve straining and tense, alert to the multitudinous details which told a story—all but the end. His nose gave him a varying description of the passage of the life on the heels of which he was travelling. He remarked the pregnant silence of the forest. The bird life had flitted. The squirrels were in hiding. One only he saw,—a sleek gray fellow, flattened against a gray dead limb so that he seemed a part of it, a woody excrescence upon the wood itself.

As Buck slid along with the obscureness of a gliding shadow, his nose was jerked suddenly to the side as though a positive force had gripped and pulled it. He followed the new scent into a thicket and found Nig. He was lying on his side, dead where he had dragged himself, an arrow protruding, head and feathers, from either side of his body.

A hundred yards farther on, Buck came upon one of the sled-dogs Thornton had bought in Dawson. This dog was thrashing about in a death-struggle, directly on the trail, and Buck passed around him without stopping. From the camp came the faint sound of many voices, rising and falling in a sing-song chant. Bellying forward to the edge of the clearing, he found Hans, lying on his face, feathered with arrows like a porcupine. At the same instant Buck peered out where the spruce-bough lodge had been and saw what made his hair leap straight up on his neck and shoulders. A gust of overpowering rage swept over him. He did not know that he growled, but he growled aloud with a terrible ferocity. For the last time in his life he allowed passion to usurp cunning and reason, and it was because of his great love for John Thornton that he lost his head.

The Yeehats were dancing about the wreckage of the spruce-bough lodge when they heard a fearful roaring and saw rushing upon them an animal the like of which they had never seen before. It was Buck, a live hurricane of fury, hurling himself upon them in a frenzy to destroy. He sprang at the foremost man (it was the chief of the Yeehats), ripping the throat wide open till the rent jugular spouted a fountain of blood. He did not pause to worry the victim, but ripped in passing, with the next bound tearing wide the throat of a second man. There was no withstanding him. He plunged about in their very midst, tearing, rending, destroying, in constant and terrific motion which defied the arrows they discharged at him. In fact, so inconceivably rapid were his movements, and so closely were the Indians tangled together, that they shot one another with the arrows; and one young hunter, hurling a spear at Buck in mid air, drove it through the chest of another hunter with such force that the point broke through the skin of the back and stood out beyond. Then a panic seized the Yeehats, and they fled in terror to the woods, proclaiming as they fled the advent of the Evil Spirit.

And truly Buck was the Fiend incarnate, raging at their heels and dragging them down like deer as they raced through the trees. It was a fateful day for the Yeehats. They scattered far and wide over the country, and it was not till a week later that the last of the survivors gathered together in a lower valley and counted their losses. As for Buck, wearying of the pursuit, he returned to the desolated camp. He found Pete where he had been killed in his blankets in the first moment of surprise. Thornton's desperate struggle was fresh-written on the earth, and Buck scented every detail of it down to the edge of a deep pool. By the edge, head and fore feet in the water, lay Skeet, faithful to the last. The pool itself, muddy and discolored from the sluice boxes, effectually hid what it contained, and it contained John Thornton; for Buck followed his trace into the water, from which no trace led away.

All day Buck brooded by the pool or roamed restlessly about the camp. Death, as a cessation of movement, as a passing out and away from the lives of the living, he knew, and he knew John Thornton was dead. It left a great void in him, somewhat akin to hunger, but a void which ached and ached, and which food could not fill, At times, when he paused to contemplate the carcasses of the Yeehats, he forgot the pain of it; and at such times he was aware of a great pride in himself,—a pride greater than any he had yet experienced. He had killed man, the noblest game of all, and he had killed in the face of the law of club and fang. He sniffed the bodies curiously. They had died so easily. It was harder to kill a husky dog than them. They were no match at all, were it not for their arrows and spears and clubs. Thenceforward he would be unafraid of them except when they bore in their hands their arrows, spears, and clubs.

Night came on, and a full moon rose high over the trees into the sky, lighting the land till it lay bathed in ghostly day. And with the coming of the night, brooding and mourning by the pool, Buck became alive to a stirring of the new life in the forest other than that which the Yeehats had made, He stood up, listening and scenting. From far away drifted a faint, sharp yelp, followed by a chorus of similar sharp yelps. As the moments passed the yelps grew closer and louder. Again Buck knew them as things heard in that other world which persisted in his memory. He walked to the centre of the open space and listened. It was the call, the many-noted call, sounding more luringly and compellingly than ever before. And as never before, he was ready to obey. John Thornton was dead. The last tie was broken. Man and the claims of man no longer bound him.

Hunting their living meat, as the Yeehats were hunting it, on the flanks of the migrating moose, the wolf pack had at last crossed over from the land of streams and timber and invaded Buck's valley. Into the clearing where the moonlight streamed, they poured in a silvery flood; and in the centre of the clearing stood Buck, motionless as a statue, waiting their coming. They were awed, so still and large he stood, and a moment's pause fell, till the boldest one leaped straight for him. Like a flash Buck struck, breaking the neck. Then he stood, without movement, as before, the stricken wolf rolling in agony behind him. Three others tried it in sharp succession; and one after the other they drew back, streaming blood from slashed throats or shoulders.

This was sufficient to fling the whole pack forward, pell-mell, crowded together, blocked and confused by its eagerness to pull down the prey. Buck's marvellous quickness and agility stood him in good stead. Pivoting on his hind legs, and snapping and gashing, he was everywhere at once, presenting a front which was apparently unbroken so swiftly did he whirl and guard from side to side. But to prevent them from getting behind him, he was forced back, down past the pool and into the creek bed, till he brought up against a high gravel bank. He worked along to a right angle in the bank which the men had made in the course of mining, and in this angle he came to bay, protected on three sides and with nothing to do but face the front.

And so well did he face it, that at the end of half an hour the wolves drew back discomfited. The tongues of all were out and lolling, the white fangs showing cruelly white in the moonlight. Some were lying down with heads raised and ears pricked forward; others stood on their feet, watching him; and still others were lapping water from the pool. One wolf, long and lean and gray, advanced cautiously, in a friendly manner, and Buck recognized the wild brother with whom he had run for a night and a day. He was whining softly, and, as Buck whined, they touched noses.

Then an old wolf, gaunt and battle-scarred, came forward. Buck writhed his lips into the preliminary of a snarl, but sniffed noses with him, Whereupon the old wolf sat down, pointed nose at the moon, and broke out the long wolf howl. The others sat down and howled. And now the call came to Buck in unmistakable accents. He, too, sat down and howled. This over, he came out of his angle and the pack crowded around him, sniffing in half-friendly, half-savage manner. The leaders lifted the yelp of the pack and sprang away into the woods. The wolves swung in behind, yelping in chorus. And Buck ran with them, side by side with the wild brother, yelping as he ran.

AND HERE MAY WELL END THE STORY OF BUCK. THE YEARS WERE NOT MANY when the Yeehats noted a change in the breed of timber wolves; for some were seen with splashes of brown on head and muzzle, and with a rift of white centring down the chest. But more remarkable than this, the Yeehats tell of a Ghost Dog that runs at the head of the pack. They are afraid of this Ghost Dog, for it has cunning greater than they, stealing from their camps in fierce winters, robbing their traps, slaying their dogs, and defying their bravest hunters.

Nay, the tale grows worse. Hunters there are who fail to return to the camp, and hunters there have been whom their tribesmen found with throats slashed cruelly open and with wolf prints about them in the snow greater than the prints of any wolf. Each fall, when the Yeehats follow the movement of the moose, there is a certain valley which they never enter. And women there are who become sad when the word goes over the fire of how the Evil Spirit came to select that valley for an abiding-place.

In the summers there is one visitor, however, to that valley, of which the Yeehats do not know. It is a great, gloriously coated wolf, like, and yet unlike, all other wolves. He crosses alone from the smiling timber land and comes down into an open space among the trees. Here a yellow stream flows from rotted moose-hide sacks and sinks into the ground, with long grasses growing through it and vegetable mould overrunning it and hiding its yellow from the sun; and here he muses for a time, howling once, long and mournfully, ere he departs.

But he is not always alone. When the long winter nights come on and the wolves follow their meat into the lower valleys, he may be seen running at the head of the pack through the pale moonlight or glimmering borealis, leaping gigantic above his fellows, his great throat a-bellow as he sings a song of the younger world, which is the song of the pack.

The End

Interview With Author Kyle Owens

Author of the Vegas Chantly Series, Red Onion Mountain, & Others

ADV: You currently have two Vegas Chantly novels out, and many of our readers know about your ever-dedicated sleuth and protagonist, many don't. Can you briefly explain the premise of your Vegas Chantly mysteries?

KO: Vegas Chantly is a comedy mystery novel series in which the main character, Vegas Chantly, is in her early twenties trying to make ends meet as best she can as a private investigator. Joining her, or perhaps it would be better to say interfering with her on all her cases is her mother, Eleanor. You can look at it as The Gilmore Girls meet The Rockford Files.

ADV: We particularly love that we acquire a good visual of each scene as the plot progresses, and the dynamic between Vegas and her mother is a humorous sort of tension that really, really works. How did the idea that this would make a great book series come about?

KO: I came up with the name Vegas Chantly while mowing the yard. I had thought she would be my version of a female James Bond. However, she evolved into a private investigator and the mother was just supposed to be in the opening scene of the first novel, "Checkmate a Killer," but she had other plans. She is so fun to write for that she wouldn't be silenced.

ADV: Shifting away from Vegas now, another novel from you very recently launched titled, *Red Onion Mountain*. Fill us in on what this is about.

KO: *Red Onion Mountain* is about a boy named Price Mullins growing up in the Appalachian Mountains in 1941. His fifth-grade teacher told him that he showed a great talent for writing and encouraged him to keep a journal about all the going ons in his life as a writing exercise. So, he began writing about his best friend, Billy, his mother and his three sissies, about the day he went fishing and caught a snake, the day he found a baseball and about a goat named Courage. You know, just everyday boy things. It's kind of my version of Huckleberry Finn and Tom Sawyer.

ADV: When Kyle Owens isn't writing, what can he be found doing?

KO: I work for a land surveying company, and I mow lawns.

ADV: Any hints about what we can expect from you in the future?

KO: I'm currently writing book 3 of the Vegas Chantly series, *Haunted Hollow* about a haunted house. I also draw the comic strip "Pop and Fries the Awesome Guys!" for **Adventure** magazine. I have written a two-hour TV pilot for Vegas based upon the first novel, *Checkmate a Killer*. I'm now working on a humor comic book entitled "Uh-Oh!"

I've written several TV pilots (both live action and animated), a horror novel and several short stories all of which I'm trying to find a home for.

Because humankind fails to learn from past lessons, we find that many circumstances from yesteryear are repeating themselves yet again. The commentaries that follow here and in future issues were originally published by *The Mohave Valley Daily News between 1993 & 2013*--and in many ways they apply to today.
We are grateful to republish these commentaries written by Darryle Purcell in full and unedited. His own brand of humor and style can deliver insight, provoke thought, and even boil blood.

Pet psychics may have uses

Feb. 14, 1997

I JUST FINISHED READING AN INTERESTING ASSOCIATED PRESS FEATURE OUT OF the Peoples' Republic of Berkeley, California. The story is about pet psychics.

One woman claims to be able to talk to animals through her telepathic powers. She solves animal problems either on the phone, or for a few extra bucks, through house calls.

"While I'm on the phone with the person, I form a picture of the animal in my mind," the psychic claims. "Then I begin communicating with the animal by exchanging sounds, feelings and pictures."

The story describes one visit the psychic made to settle the squabbles of a dog, a cat and a rabbit that live together. She closed her eyes and, while holding each animal tightly, spoke for them. The channel discussion apparently solved their furry little problems.

Another pet psychic from Kansas pines for the acceptance of California. "In California people don't laugh at you when you tell them you're an animal psychic."

Well, I can't speak for a whole state, but I am from California. And I laugh at a whole lot of things going on in that land of fruits and nuts.

Anyone crazy enough to hold a cat up to a phone so some Ace Ventura wannabe can "read its mind" and solve its psychosis is either a candidate for the West Hollywood City Council or the Shady Rest Funny Farm.

In case you haven't figured it out, I'm not really a New-Wave kind of guy. I believe that if there were real psychics they would be doing productive things like averting disasters and making killings at the track, not guessing at how long John John Kennedy's marriage will last, predicting what Michael Jackson will impregnate next and holding psychiatric sessions with Bunny Foo Foo.

Even our own newspaper astrologer Jeane Dixon is questionable. For one thing, she died last month. We have her predictions through March, which we are running in the *Daily News*. But how good can they be? If she had really been a psychic, wouldn't she have put a note in her column last month saying, "Please forward all my mail to my syndicate editor after Tuesday as I will no long be alive"?

If so-called pet psychics were really able to communicate with animals, wouldn't they be conversing on a more basic level than solving disagreements between dogs, cats and rabbits? After all, most pets' needs are really basic: food, shelter, a place to relieve themselves, a pat on the head once in a while, a few disgusting things they do for their own pleasure and a little social intermingling with their own species. I have a feeling that any self-respecting cat wouldn't discuss his/her private life with some nosy California fruitcake anyway. And while we're at it, I believe it's illegal in several states to allow a dog, a cat and a rabbit to live together.

Of course the story does come out of Berkeley, the only town in California that makes Santa Monica seem like right-wing militia country.

But perhaps I'm wrong. (I'd like to say I'm the first to admit when I'm wrong, but there are usually quite a few other folks who beat me to the punch.) Maybe these pet psychics aren't nuts or larcenous fakes. Perhaps they really have a God-given ability to "walk and talk and squawk with the animals." If that is so, they could be put to better use than playing Frasier Crane to neurotic collies. They could be used to direct Benji movies; several could periodically swim along the California coast and persuade sharks to leave the surfers alone; some could legally assist military K9 dogs in species harassment litigation; perhaps some could help foul-mouthed parrots clean up their language; and one Republican pet psychic could help Whitewater investigator Kenneth Starr interrogate Socks.

THE HOLLOW HORROR

K.R. MOORE

Light faded around the young man Vaut, as he regained consciousness and fell onto the dirt below. Laid out across what seemed like a barren desert.

Clueless as to where he had ended up and why, he simply checked his wrist for the device that had blown him there.

The wristwatch-like contraption that had once said:

Planet: Earth
Population: 8,038,950,104
Had suddenly switched to:
Planet: Unregistered
Year: 8036

The population status was the least helpful as it was obscured by a swirl of colorful static. No doubt the sign of a nasty system glitch.

Being glad his red astronaut-inspired suit allowed for breathable conditions wherever or whenever he warped to, the time traveler sighed and kicked himself for overloading on the system's radiation before attempting to jump back home.

Carefully, he traversed the new land, searching for anything that could give him a clue about where he ended up. That was when he spotted them.

Buildings. And not simple alien architecture as he had seen before. They were skyscrapers composed of bricks and metal, as if he had never even left the 21st century.

Confused and distraught, Vaut searched around for more clues. None of the buildings had a door but they did oddly enough have windows along with high-up power lines at the very top.

Above the lines, he saw misty clouds of strange varying colors amidst something that made his heart race even more. The Earth's moon, but there was something drastically different.

It was in half. Both pieces donned something of a massive cleave.

Vaut slowly grew increasingly unnerved and checked around for more oddities. He banged upon the device repeatedly before coming across a forest or at least what used to be one. For all the vegetation was white as ash and chipped like brittle candy the moment Vaut tried to pluck some of the leaves.

The investigation was going nowhere and more than ever, Vaut hoped his device would recharge and give him a ticket off the wasteland before he went mad.

He checked again and saw much to the sorrow then relief that while he still wasn't able to make another jump through time, the population glitch had been auto-debugged over time.

Population: 1

Vaut raised an eyebrow and looked around the wasteland, doubting that there could only be a single person on the planet. The device does not count the one wearing it so the questions just kept flooding in.

Vaut scoured the land more, checking deeper into his device to find the planet's current time of 12:30 pm. Another anomaly as the moon pieces were clearly on display and the sky couldn't have been darker. Vaut would make out the constellations if he had the time.

He was so caught up in his debacle about the time that he hadn't even noticed the steep hill he stepped too far over and tumbled into the dirt yet again.

He jumped up angry again but alarmed to find more buildings, all very familiar yet oddly high with power lines at the top.

What really caught his eye were the vehicles in the area as well. Not only the first of its kind but also seen there but yet again, oddly reminiscent of Earth from the 21st century.

Vaut grinned and traced along the side to open the door. Only to find that there was none. Losing his patience, Vaut opted to punch the window only for his suit to warn him of critical damage as he discovered far too late that the inside of the car was not what it seemed. An interior completely composed of a dark matter substance, condensed and blacker than the void of space itself.

Vaut pulled back and hurried behind a fragile tree for cover, taking note of the alarm blaring in his suit. That was when he saw the trail of blood leading back to him and checked his hand. As soon as Vaut's suit made contact with the black blob, it sucked in part of his glove and with it, a fair bit of his flesh all in less than the blink of an eye.

No longer curious, Vaut went into full safety mode. He was prepared to do anything to keep himself alive and planned to run deep into the forest from hopefully anything else that could hurt him.

However, as soon as he set his foot down, the ground began to shake. Vaut was amazed at the sudden feeling of life emanating from the dead planet before terror set in. The quakes were massive, forceful, and nonstop with the ground itself jutting up. It was almost as if something was punching the crust from within the planet itself.

While running in horror, another jut of the ground resulted in Vaut being launched into the sky. As he gathered his bearings, he saw the power lines in more detail. They were far bulkier than he believed with a pattern of holes as well.

Soon, the awful truth of where he had landed began to set in. The lines above him weren't power cables, but chains. Shackles that he could see for a brief second, extended far past the planet's atmosphere and into the moon pieces which themselves were chained together with massive chunks of metal in between.

Vaut tried to calm his mind of the implications when his head came slamming down into the hood of another car, tearing open the roof a bit. In a second, he had rolled onto the ground and away from the void within. However, that second was more than enough for the substance inside to rip the helmet and air supply off his face along with a bit of hair and skin.

Bloodied and gasping for air, Vaut lay limp as his purple and orange bangs covered his face while blood began to travel down his face and seep into his suit.

The air was terribly thin. Even on the surface, it was hard to think, but that second experience with the car confirmed his fears. What ripped his flesh off inside the car, was an indefinitely condensed black hole.

He limped away from the deadly district, not sure how the former residents of the planet managed to achieve something so against the laws of science even to him, the time traveler. But it wasn't the end of his theory.

The chains along the planet and moon with all the buildings being at least skyscraper level topped off with the bisected satellite's scrape marks looking like something more specific.

Claw marks.

His ears then split at the pain of a hypersonic roar sending him to the ground.

The ground housing exactly where it came from. It clicked right then and there for the battered Vaut. This planet that reminded him of Earth so badly, was no longer a planet.

It was a prison.

Vaut seized as the fear took him over. A race of dark thoughts about an unimaginable force existing sometime, somewhere in the universe that would need an entire planet to encase it in. He then looked back at the device on his wrist again with realization and read it out loud shrilly.

"Population... one?"

The ground cracked, sending up dust and sand to consume the area. Vaut fell to his knees, unable to see and certainly no longer able to breathe as red light radiated from below, being the only source on the planet.

Vaut had no way of escape and closed his eyes, bracing for the end. He hadn't realized until it was too late that it was the pooling of his blood on the ground that awakened the celestial beast. He dug his own grave with the shovel of foolish curiosity, and now the beast was coming to finish burying.

As he made peace with his short life, a new light shined in the corner of his eyes. The bright blue of his wristwatch that was displayed only when the charge was full. He looked around as his vision slowly lost color to realize that the light emitted from the ground must've been radioactive.

Wasting no time, he brought his hand up to the home button and was instantly zapped back to his own time. Just narrowly vanishing as a plume of concentrated ash and radiation blasted where he once stood, followed by a celestial monster roaring in rage.

As Vaut was carried through the ray of light, his mind only sped up the flow of questions, including whether that planet would truly be Earth one day. After a time, he did something that he had heard of in history books but hadn't tried himself until just that moment.

He prayed.

Thanking every higher power he could think of for his escape and begging that whatever planetary titan that may have been, it wouldn't occur until long after his time in the universe was over.

The End

Orchard Corset

OrchardCorset.com
Ph. 1-866-456-7411

★★★★★ 04/23/19

Customer service and sizing experts

Customer service and sizing experts are very helpful and responsive. Feeling great about my order!
koma876omen

★★★★★ 04/25/19

Very comfortable

Fits like a glove and is super comfortable. Highly recommend for daily use.
Dayna L.

★★★★★ 04/24/19

Gorgeous!

I knew I had to get this one when I saw the teaser picture for it. It's even more gorgeous in person. Fits well even though I have...
Read More
Amy H.

Corsets to suit your purpose:
waist training, weddings, costumes,
back pain relief, or just for fun.

-Sizing Experts Available 7 Days a Week
-Only Steel-Boned Corsets, Never Plastic
-Interest Free Pay Over Time Option!
-Rewards program
-Men's Corsets too

SODUKO ANSWERS

6	2	1	9	4	5	7	3	8
4	3	9	8	7	2	5	6	1
7	8	5	6	1	3	2	4	9
3	9	4	1	5	7	6	8	2
8	7	2	3	6	9	4	1	5
5	1	6	2	8	4	3	9	7
9	6	3	7	2	8	1	5	4
1	5	7	4	9	6	8	2	3
2	4	8	5	3	1	9	7	6

Look forward to beginning your Spring in 2024 with reading adventures in *ADVENTURES* Issue 11!